THE BISHOP'S MAN

LINDEN MACINTYRE is the co-host of *the fifth estate* and the winner of nine Gemini Awards for broadcast journalism. He is the author of the bestselling novel *The Long Stretch*, nominated for a CBA Libris Award. His most recent book, a boyhood memoir called *Causeway: A Passage from Innocence*, won both the Edna Staebler Award for creative Non-Fiction and the Evelyn Richardson Prize for Non-Fiction.

The Bishop's Man

A Novel

Linden MacIntyre

JONATHAN CAPE
LONDON

Published by Jonathan Cape

2 4 6 8 10 9 7 5 3 1

Copyright © Linden MacIntyre 2010

Linden MacIntyre has asserted his right under the Copyright, Designs
and Patents Act 1988 to be identified as the author of this work

First published in Great Britain in 2010 by
Jonathan Cape
Random House, 20 Vauxhall Bridge Road,
London SW1V 2SA

www.rbooks.co.uk

Addresses for companies within The Random House Group Limited can be
found at: www.randomhouse.co.uk/offices.htm

The Random House Group Limited Reg. No. 954009

A CIP catalogue record for this book is available from the British Library

ISBN 9780224089722

The Random House Group Limited makes every effort to ensure that the
papers used in its books are made from trees that have been legally sourced from
well-managed and credibly certified forests. Our paper procurement policy
can be found at: www.randomhouse.co.uk/paper.htm

Printed and bound in Great Britain by
CPI Mackays, Chatham, Kent ME5 8TD

To Carol

BOOK ONE

† † †

Oh ye sons of men,
how long will ye turn
my glory into shame?
PSALMS

The night before things started to become unstuck, I actually spent a good hour taking stock of my general situation and concluded that, all things considered, I was in pretty good shape. I was approaching the age of fifty, a psychological threshold only slightly less daunting than death, and found myself not much changed from forty or even thirty. If anything, I was healthier. The last decade of the century, and of the millennium, was shaping up to be less stressful than the eighth—which had been defined by certain events in Central America—and the ninth, burdened as it was by scandals here at home.

I was a priest in a time that is not especially convivial toward the clergy. I had, nevertheless, achieved what I believed to be a sustainable spirituality and an ability to elaborate upon it with minimal cant and hypocrisy. I had even, and this is no small achievement, come to terms with a certain sordid obscurity about my family origins in a place where people celebrate the most tedious details of their personal ancestry.

I am the son of a bastard father. My mother was a foreigner, felled long before her time by disappointment and tuberculosis.

I was, in the most literal sense, a child of war. I've calculated that my conception occurred just days before my father's unit embarked from England for the hostile shores of Italy, on October 23, 1943. There is among his papers a cryptic reference to a summary trial and fine (five days' pay) for being AWOL on the night of October 17. I was born in London, England, July 15, 1944.

Isolation? I had, though perhaps imperfectly, mastered celibacy, the institutional denial of the most human of transactions. I was and am, to a degree, excluded from my peer group, my brothers in the priesthood, for complex reasons that will soon become apparent. But at the time I thought that I'd discovered an important universal truth: that isolation, willingly embraced, becomes the gift of solitude; that discipline ennobles flesh.

In that evanescent moment of tranquility, I was feeling okay. I see it as another life, the man I was, a stranger now.

I'd spent the weekend in Cape Breton, in the parish of Port Hood, filling in for Mullins, who had gone away with his charismatics or for golf. Escape of some kind. Mullins likes to pace himself. I'd planned to extend my visit by a day, to spend that Monday reading, meditating. The village of Port Hood is a pretty place and restful. I grew up in the area, but my personal connections there were limited. I could pretend to be a stranger, a pose I find congenial.

Mullins and the good Sisters up the road had given the glebe a comfortable tidiness. Anyone could feel at home there, as in a well-maintained motel. It has a remarkable view of the gulf and a small fishing harbour, just along the coast, called Murphy's Pond. It was a pleasant change from the incessant noise and movement at the university an hour or so away, where, normally, my job was dean of students. In truth it was, as my late father used to say in a rare ironic moment, not so much a job as a position. Others did most of the real work. I was, in fact, in a kind of pastoral limbo, recovering, ostensibly, from several years of hard, unsavoury employment.

The phone aroused me on that Monday morning in Port Hood and launched the narrative that I must now, with some reluctance, share.

"The bishop needs to see you."

"What does he want now?" I asked.

"He didn't say. He said to come this evening. To the palace."

I know now that I was stalling when I drove to Little Harbour, which is another, smaller fishing port just off a secondary road on the southern edge of the parish.

The harbour seemed to be deserted. Among the vivid particulars of that October morning in 1993 I remember a blue heron, knee-deep, transfixed by something in the quiet, oil-still water. Then I heard a throbbing diesel engine and at that moment observed a tall radio antenna mounted upon what might have been a crucifix. It was moving slowly above the crest of a low ridge in the near distance. The transient cross and the gentle rumble seemed unrelated until a boat suddenly appeared around the jagged end of a breakwater. It was a fishing vessel, about forty feet long, bristling with aerials and with a broad workspace behind the cab. The name, the *Lady Hawthorne*, might have been an omen, or maybe I just think that now, in the clarity of hindsight.

The boy standing on the bow was about eighteen years old. A rope dangled casually from a large left hand. He wore the uniform of the shore—jeans, a discoloured sweater unravelled at the elbows, knee-high rubber boots. He had a thick mop of unfashionably long hair obscuring his brow and neck. His face was tanned. He stared straight ahead but then turned and nodded, a moment of distracted curiosity as the boat slipped down the long throat of the harbour, stem turning a clean, whispering furrow.

It was about eight o'clock. The blood-red sun hovering behind me lifted a flimsy mist and held it just above the surface of the water. I felt the first stirring of a breeze. Something about the boat, perhaps its name, and the posture of that boy caused me to defer my anxieties for the moment. It was so rare to see someone that age stationary, sombre. I was more accustomed to a rowdy adolescent enthusiasm. This young man, I realized, was exceptional only because of time and place. Maybe any one of them in those circumstances would have been the same. Quiet. But he caught my attention nevertheless and linked the moment to tender places in the memory. Doomed boys and men: in retrospect they all have that stillness.

The man at the controls was probably my age, tall and heavy-set. They were, to my mind, almost reckless then, rushing through the narrow passage, past a nestling line of sister boats. But just before the wharf there was a roar of reverse acceleration and the *Lady Hawthorne* seemed to pivot in a tight circle then drift gently into a space between two others, bow pointing seaward. The boy stepped casually ashore with the rope. The older man was already at the stern, gathering another line into a coil, which he tossed up onto the land.

The two fishermen were winching some large plastic boxes onto the dock as I was walking back to my car. Father and son, I assumed. They didn't seem to notice me.

I was almost at the car when the older man spoke. "Wicked morning, eh, Father."

I turned.

"I never forget a face," he said. "Father MacAskill, isn't it?"

"Yes," I said.

He walked toward me then, holding out a large hand. He seemed a bit unsteady. The boy was back on board the boat and out of sight.

"Dan MacKay," he said. "I think I heard you're from up around the strait."

"Yes. And you?"

"I'm a shore road MacKay."

His hair, the colour of sand, was streaked with wisps of grey. A name stirred in the memory.

"Danny Ban," I said. "They used to call you Danny Ban, I think."

He blushed. "Years ago. I'd hate to think of what you heard. Danny Bad was more like it, probably."

I laughed.

"But I don't live here now. I'm up in Hawthorne. Been there for years. Built my own place after the young fella came along."

"Hawthorne," I said. "I noticed . . . the name on your boat."

"You know the place?"

"I've heard of it. But I've never been there."

"You should drop in sometime. Visit the house."

"Maybe I will."

The boy was walking toward their truck, ignoring us.

"The name is on the mailbox at the lane," his father said. "MacKay. We're the only ones up there."

"Thanks."

He turned then and walked toward the truck, where the boy was already waiting at the wheel. The engine roared impatiently to life. I wondered again about the unsteadiness in his pace. From being on the boat, I thought. Sea legs.

He'd hardly closed the truck door when they were off, rear wheels spinning in the gravel. The truck stopped briefly where the wharf road meets the pavement. You could tell by the angled heads that they were talking. Using their secret language, the dialect of intimacy. Single words and obscure phrases conveying volumes.

"I'm a shore road MacKay," he'd said. A brief biography and, for those who know the place, a genealogy, all you need to know summed up in a single phrase. Once, I might have felt a little envious. But somewhere along the way identity has ceased to matter, where I'm from, inconsequential. I have become the cloth. That's enough for anyone to know.

"Come by any time," he'd said. "For a visit."

And that's how things begin. Needs dressed up as hospitality.

There was a rusty freighter in the canal that technically sustains our status as an island. The swing bridge at the end of the mile-long causeway was open, the road lined with cars and trucks impatient for their mainland destinations. I welcomed the delay. The bishop always has a reason when he calls; he always has a "special" job.

I've often tried to remember how it started, how I became his . . . what? What am I? I suppose it's all a matter of perspective. I'll put it this way: for other priests, I'm not a welcome presence on the doorstep.

The first summons by the bishop had seemed innocuous enough. The particulars are almost lost now, obscured by far more troubling memories, but I remember what he said: "I've asked you to come here because you have a good head on your shoulders."

He wanted me to handle a delicate matter. That was how he would describe them all. Matters that were delicate. Issues that required a good head and a steady hand. It was probably the late seventies. I'd only just returned from my two years in Honduras.

"After what you've been through down south," he said, "you'll probably consider this kind of Mickey Mouse. But things are getting out of hand here. Dear old John the Twenty-third, God rest his soul . . . he had no idea what he was getting us all into."

I remember listening carefully, trying to anticipate where he was heading.

He sighed deeply. "There's a young priest . . . You probably know him."

I probably did, at one time.

I'd prefer not to name the place specifically. Just imagine one of many threadbare little communities clinging to the hundreds of bays and coves that once had integrity by virtue of their isolation. The priest in question and his young housekeeper had become a source of local gossip. I do remember that she had a pretty face with warm, frightened eyes and a full mouth that trembled when I asked her if Father was in. But mostly I remember the culprit's attitude. It was his smugness, his unspoken sense of superiority. It was his obvious certainty that he'd transcended the lies and postures that had trapped the rest of us, we lesser priests, in our barren inhumanity. I've heard and seen it all many times since then.

I said: "Your housekeeper seems to be putting on weight." I smiled, coldly, I hoped.

He laughed. "I already know why you're here. Let's not beat around the bush."

"You go first," I said, sipping at my tea.

He told me that "in all sincerity" the situation made him a better person. He actually believed it. I confess I felt like hitting him. I think I arranged a period of reflection in Toronto and he was gone in a few weeks. I persuaded her to lie low for a while. Life is full of temporary absences, I told her. It was that simple. But it was only the beginning, a sad rehearsal for the challenging assignments yet to come.

I was rattled by the time I reached the campus. It's difficult to say for sure why. The reference to Hawthorne? The boy on the boat? Given what I now know, it could have been either, but it was, in part, almost certainly the summons from the bishop. The bishop only calls when there's a problem.

"You know about the bishop?" Rita reminded me.

"Yes."

"And you have an appointment at three this afternoon. An incident on the weekend."

"Incident? What kind of incident?"

"Campus police found a fellow on the roof of the chapel. They think that you should handle it." She smiled, sympathetically, I thought.

I guess by then a part of me accepted that I'd become a specialist in discipline. Technically it's part of the dean's job, and I was officially a dean. In truth I had neither the academic nor the occupational background for such a post. Just the temperament and, by default, the practical experience. I was a clergyman posted to a small, nominally Catholic university because my bishop didn't really know where else to put me. At the peak of my usefulness I was attached to the diocesan chancery, but I soon became too controversial even for that busy place. Toxic, I suppose, is not too strong a word. My colleagues know about my history, my experience rooting out perversions, disciplining other priests, and sometimes students, when the cases are particularly sensitive. The Exorcist they've called me. Behind my back, of course.

A student on the chapel roof?

"He had a handsaw."

"A saw?"

"Go figure."

The bishop was expecting me at seven. I decided to walk. The town was quiet. On Monday nights the students usually stay in because they're broke or hungover or both. Bored waiters stood outside the silent pub, the smoke from their cigarettes curling like fog around them in the still October air.

"Winter's not far off," I remark, walking by.

Once, the reply would have been swift and respectful. Yes, Father. Hand raised quickly to the cap. You can feel the snow in the air already. Good evening to yourself, Father. Now they stare. They're just suspicious. Burly boys in baseball caps, arms folded. We are a fallen species. Strange men in black, stunted by the burden of our secrets. I smile. What if they knew the whole story?

I try to remember all the times I've made that walk through town to see my bishop. Past the looming cathedral, the bowling alley, the pub. Past what was, in my student days, a restaurant called the Brigadoon. We had rules back then. Lights out at eleven. Up and out in time for Mass at seven. No alcohol or women in the rooms. Virtue was the essence of the status quo. Virtue was the norm, they taught us.

Times have changed.

I fumble for the rosary in the pocket of my overcoat. The mindless recitation always helps subdue anxiety.

The first sorrowful mystery. The agony in the garden. The smooth, small beads are soothing on the fingertips.

The bishop's palace is set back from Main Street, among dark chestnut trees. I don't know why they call it the palace. It's just a house, large to be sure, and elegant. The designation "palace" probably had more to do with the authority of the old man inside than the architecture.

He met me at the door. I anticipated the welcoming aromas of cooking, but the place seemed clean and empty, vaguely like the cathedral on St. Ninian Street.

"I forgot," he said. "Herself had the day off. I'm hopeless in the kitchen. You didn't eat, did you?"

"No."

"Well, I'm starved. You order up a pizza. It'll be on me. You'd have a dram?"

"I would," I said, "if you coaxed me."

"Help yourself. I'm on the phone. There's a takeout menu on my desk."

He disappeared again and I headed for the sideboard in his study, where the whiskies were lined up in crystal decanters. I poured a drink. Picked up the phone, heard someone talking far away, quickly opened up another line and dialed the local take-out. Then sat down to wait. Our Saviour, hanging on the large crucifix above the desk, was staring down at me. He seemed to be saying: You again? What now? I wish I knew. I could hear the bishop's voice faintly in another room. He was speaking loudly. But then I heard what seemed to be a laugh.

I'm sure he wasn't that informal for everybody. I had special status because of my unusual history. My adult life, I suppose, could be measured in the spaces between my visits to that little office. How many years since I first sat there, a student, earnest in the throes of my vocation, oozing piety and purpose? I can see him now, sitting serenely beneath that crucifix.

"I think I want to be a priest," I told him, heart pounding.

He listened quietly, but in the manner of one who already knew far more than I was telling him. He was smiling, but the eyes were not encouraging. "Why would you want to be a priest?"

I wasn't ready for the question. I assumed the Church was like any wartime army, always looking for recruits.

"I might need time to think before I answer," I said carefully.

"Good. Take all the time you need. The answer is important. It could one day save your soul."

He never asked again, which is just as well, for even now I'm not sure what I'd say.

My eyes drifted back to the crucifix. The Saviour's face exhibits a kind of weariness that I can easily relate to. When all is said and done, I thought, I don't really have the stomach for this anymore. Disciplining wayward priests and drunken students.

The door opened suddenly. I want to say he "swept" into the room. You could imagine the swish of vestments, medieval dust rising around sandals. He was wearing running shoes, cords and a cardigan. His silver hair was disorderly. He went straight to the sideboard and poured himself a stiff drink. The bishop grew up in a place called Malignant Cove and clearly loves the reaction this disclosure always gets. You laugh as though you haven't heard it a hundred times before.

"You were in Port Hood for the weekend."

"Yes," I said. "Mullins called out of the blue."

He was pouring generously. "Coincidentally, I was just on the phone about a matter indirectly concerning Port Hood. And you."

I was trying to imagine what it was.

"You remember Father Bell . . . the notorious Brendan Bell?"

"Yes," I said warily, thinking to myself, So that's what this is all about. Brendan Bell. What now?

"One of your former clients," he said.

"I remember."

Bell was supposed to be the last of them—"the last station on our *via dolorosa*," was how he phrased it. The bishop actually promised. This should be the last of it, he'd said. Maybe that's why I recall that particular encounter with such clarity.

The first time I met him, Bell was sitting exactly where I was sitting at that moment. It was in the winter, 1990. He made quite an impression, an Anglo-Irish Newfoundlander, a little shorter than I am, but most people are. Dark brown hair pulled back tightly into a tiny knob-like ponytail, a brilliant smile that seemed genuine, and nothing whatsoever in his manner that might reveal the miserable circumstances that sent him to us. But I soon found out that he was in a spot of trouble. The bishop of St. John's was asking for a tiny favour.

I suggested Mullins in Port Hood.

"You'll like Port Hood," I said. "But they won't put up with any bullshit there."

Bell smiled at me and nodded. "I hear you loud and clear."

"You probably knew he was in Toronto," the bishop said, now sniffing at his drink.

"That's where he was heading after Port Hood," I said.

"Your Brendan has applied for laicization. That was Toronto on the line just now. Wondering if we'd put a word in. He wants to be fast-tracked."

"What's his rush?" I asked.

"He says he's in love."

"In love with what?"

"He says he's getting married."

"Married? Brendan?"

The bishop nodded, a tight smile causing the corners of his mouth to twitch.

"Marrying a woman?" I said, incredulous.

"That's what they do, though you never know, up there in Toronto."

"So what will you do?" I asked.

"I said I'd help. Brendan married—good for the optics, don't you think?"

The pizza arrived and we moved to the kitchen. The bishop was carrying our glasses and a fresh bottle of Balvenie. He arranged two places at the table, tore sheets from a roll of paper towel.

"You've been ordained, what, now? Twenty-five years, I think." He was speaking with his mouth full.

"Approximately."

"Are you planning anything . . . some little do to mark the special anniversary?"

"No."

"I suppose," he said, chewing thoughtfully, "you have no family to speak of. I suppose it would be different if you were in a parish."

"Perhaps."

"You must sometimes wonder why you've never had a parish of your own."

I shrugged. "You've told me more than once. I think you used to call it my 'asymmetrical' family history."

"You were a curate once."

"Assistant."

"Well, never mind that. I sent you down to Central America. In 1975, wasn't it?"

"Yes."

"Those were the days, when I had manpower to spare." He shook his head and studied me for a moment.

"But it wasn't exactly a 'manpower' decision, was it?" I thought he'd ignore the comment.

"You went through a hard patch, true enough," he said. "But it defined your special gifts. I'm loath to quote Nietzsche . . . but . . . you know what I mean. You're a strong man. A survivor. I always knew that."

I nodded uncomfortably.

"I consider that period a little . . . hiccup . . . in an otherwise exemplary priesthood." He sipped the drink, reflecting, I assumed, upon my exemplary service. "Ministry takes many forms. Tegucigalpa revealed yours. The Lord's methods aren't always obvious to us mortals."

"I suppose," I said, attempting a wry smile.

I had three drinks in and more than half the pizza was already gone when he got around to what I was really there for. He said he wanted me, after all these years, to take over a parish. A little place. Nothing too strenuous.

"Me?"

"Time to settle down," he said. "I figure you're ready for some new challenges. What would you think of Creignish?"

"Creignish," I repeated.

"Yes," he replied.

"I can't see it. I wouldn't have a clue what to do there. And I'm perfectly happy at the university."

But I knew his mind was made up. He had that sorrowful look he sometimes gets when exercising God's authority.

"Having priests semi-employed at the university became a luxury we can't afford a long, long time ago. There's no shortage of lay professors and administrators. Look around you."

"But the Catholic character of the university? People from all over send their kids here for what they expect to be a Catholic education."

"We're more concerned about the Catholic character of the countryside, the solid places like Port Hood and Creignish. Malignant Cove."

I knew I was supposed to laugh. "But—"

He raised an apostolic hand for silence, then stood and paced the room. "Look," he said finally. "I regard you as a clone of myself. So I'm going to be frank." He took the bottle, splashed both our glasses. "I thought certain . . . matters . . . were all behind us. But there have been developments."

"Developments?"

"Nothing to concern yourself about just yet. But next year could be tough. Big time."

Instantly, half a dozen names and faces flashed before my eyes.

"Not Brendan Bell?"

"No, no, no," he said impatiently. "That's old history. We seem to be entering phase two now. The lawyers are getting into the act. I'd like to get you out of the line of fire."

"What line of fire?"

"I just want you out of the way. You never know what lawyers might come up with. I think Creignish is perfect. Off the beaten track."

We sat in silence for a full minute, the old house creaking around us.

"You're going to have to tell me who it is," I said. "Which one they're talking about."

He reached for my glass, which was still half full. "Let me freshen that."

"Look, I'd appreciate just a clue . . . just to know how worried I should be."

"It's none of them and all of them. You can relax."

The face and tone were unconvincing. We sat and stared at each other.

Finally he said, "You've been mentioned."

"I've been mentioned."

"You know how it is these days. Everything a conspiracy. Cover-up. You, me. Now we seem to be the bad guys. Whatever happened to trust and respect, never mind the faith?"

"Mentioned by?"

"The damned insinuating lawyers."

"What are they insinuating?"

"It's only speculation about how we handled certain matters. They keep going on about something called 'vicarious liability.' Did you ever hear the like of it?" He tilted his head back, staring at the ceiling, lips puckered. "Vicarious my foot." Then he sighed and sipped his drink. "You've turned out to be my rock. It was as if providence revealed your strengths to me exactly when I needed you. But now it's time for you to get lost in parish work and pray that this thing blows over without bankrupting us."

"But Creignish?"

"You'll have no trouble settling in. You're from around there. They'll know the kind of man you really are, no matter what they might or might not hear."

I stared at him. I thought: He's dreaming. But argument was futile.

"For how long?"

"As long as necessary."

At the door, when I was leaving, his mood became enthusiastic. I was going to love parish work, he said. "Especially Creignish. Good old-fashioned people there. You'll do a bang-up job. You're going to be a real priest for a change. Anybody comes looking for you, that's what they're going to find. God's shepherd, tending the flock."

"When do you want me to go?" I asked.

"The sooner the better."

"I'll go in the spring," I said.

He looked dubious.

"Unless, of course, the bailiff is on the way already."

He didn't react to my irony, just said, "Suit yourself . . . but keep your head down in the meantime." Before he shut the door, he said, "I heard about the kid on the roof of the chapel the other night. What are they doing about him?"

I shrugged and waited.

"They say he had a saw or something, that he was heading for the cross . . ."

"I'm giving him a break," I said.

"Good. You know who his father is."

And he shut the door.

† † †

Walking home on that cold October night, I was barely conscious of the town, the small clusters of subdued youngsters
straggling along the street. A fine drizzle filtered through the
low-beam headlights of a passing pickup truck. A fluorescent
light flickered in an office and another window filled with darkness. I felt disoriented. It was his mood. The heartiness was false.
Something large has rattled him. He's sending me away again.
Where did this begin?

And then it is 1968 again and I am on this street, walking full
of purpose in the opposite direction, toward the railway station,
with a suitcase and a briefcase, the sum of all my secular posses-
sions. Walking tall, bound for a place that I now dare not name
for fear of stirring best-forgotten trauma. It is June, an evening
sweet with early lilac and the hum of hopeful voices talking
politics. June '68, a renaissance of sorts, at least for me. I was
reborn, a priest.

Oh, yes. He told me that time too that I was going to love the
place, the place I dare not mention now, in middle age. And by
the way, he said, you'll be with an old pal of ours.

"Surely you remember Dr. Roddie . . . your old philosophy
guru. He'll be there with you. He said he'll keep an eye on you.
The two of you can spend the long winter evenings reading the
Summa to each other."

"Father Roddie?"

"I knew that you'd be pleased. He's taking a little sabbatical.
Teaching college students burned him out. He could have gone
anywhere . . . I offered Rome. But he insisted on helping out in
a parish for a while. Isn't that just typical?"

The street was almost empty. The drizzle warmed below my
eyes, ran like tears beside my nose. Father Roddie. I'd almost

forgotten him. A dormant apprehension glowed within me, then, just as swiftly, dimmed. It can't be Father Roddie this time. He'd be nearly eighty now. I laughed aloud.

"Father Roddie. Wherever did you get to?"

A student shuffled by, stopped and turned. "Excuse me?" he said.

I hurried on.

The campus was quiet but for the throb of music from the residences. I was near the chapel, so I turned toward the stone steps leading up to its double doors. They were unlocked but yielded with reluctance. I dipped my fingers in the holy water then slid into a pew near the back. The gloom flickered near the altar. Somewhere in the basement auditorium someone was practising scales on a clarinet. A tuneless wail of notes gave substance to the shadows around me until I felt that I was wrapped in a suffocating shroud, lost in the endless carnage of days since I first embarked upon this journey into ambiguity. It's ironic when I think of it: the beauty of the priesthood used to be the promise of its certainties.

The clarinet faltered. A music student struggling with a hard passage from *Rhapsody in Blue.* The wind rose outside, tapping at a window.

Tap tap tap.

"Hello . . . are you in there?"

Tap tap tap.

"Father Roddie?"

The door is ajar. I hear a sound. Someone moving.

Just walk right in, he'd said. The hearing isn't what it used to be.

I walked right in.

An old priest's sanctuary, drape darkened, sound muffled by reams of books, ancient tomes promising the wisdom of the ages.

"Father Roddie?"

He's at his desk, expression calm and cold. "And what can I do for you."

Not a question. A comment.

"I had a question . . ."

"What about?"

And then I see his visitor, the boy, stricken. Pale with guilt.

I think I must have slept there in the chapel for a while. It was late when I returned to my room. Then I remembered: Creignish. I had a mental picture of the place, the side of a low mountain of the same name, a few miles from where I grew up. Oh, well.

My eye moved to a bookshelf, stopped at a black book spine. *John Macquarrie / Existentialism.* I removed it from the shelf, turned to the neat handwriting on the title page: *Tragedy and limitation are part of what it means to be human . . .* Then: *Welcome back from your sabbatical. Found this in Boston. Perhaps our paths will cross ere long. RM.*

And then the scrawled signature: *Roddie MacVicar. December,* 1977.

I closed the book, and then my eyes. The images were overwhelming.

"I don't care what you think you saw."

The bishop's neck is pulsing, a purple swelling throbbing at the centre of his forehead, outraged roseola nose aglow.

"I know what I saw."

"You think you know."

"I know."

"Our eyes play tricks."

"I know."

"We know nothing. We believe. We have faith. It is our only source of hope. But that isn't the point. You had no goddamned business spying."

Spying? I just stare.

"I sent you there to help them out, not to snoop."

I turn away from his outrage. Study the crucifix above his desk.

"You're talking about a saint," he says, quiet now, the rage replaced by injury. "A saint. A prince among men. I know him well. I've known him since we were students. You should aspire someday to be his equal."

The bishop, finally calmed, declared that it was my "asymmetrical upbringing," my "dysfunctional home life" that was at the root of my deficiencies. It caused me to see the worst in everyone, he said, and to be too inclined to read things in then jump to wrong conclusions. I don't understand the family dynamic, and until I do, I'll never be a parish priest. A parish is the ideal family, he said.

"What are you trying to tell me?"

He waved an impatient hand. "Let's not get analytical. Let's just say you need some special on-the-job experience. Which is why we're thinking of sending you away for a while."

We?

"We're thinking of somewhere in the Third World, where things are simple and straightforward. A good place for you to experience the richness of family and parish life and the undiluted faith of the common people."

The Third World?

"We happen to have an arrangement with the archdiocese of Tegucigalpa . . ."

"When?"

"They're expecting you next week."

I poured a whisky, sipped it straight. It was Tegucigalpa then, Creignish now. In a way it's easier this time, I thought. Nothing in my life, since then or yet unlived, could ever be like Tegucigalpa. And this time I'll have months to make the mental adjustments. And who knows? Things change. By spring we could all be different people.

I surveyed my tiny room. And if I go, I won't have much to pack. Mostly books. Some photographs. A frugal wardrobe. One of the advantages of my calling: we travel light.

The sun was slow in '94. The drift ice from the Gulf of St. Lawrence stayed late, blocking the advance of spring somewhere near Montreal. The wind still cold, the hills around me tawny, splotches of dark evergreens brooding.

Crossing the causeway, I felt a sudden need for a toilet and I remembered there was a washroom at the information bureau they installed on the island side of the strait many years ago, just after they finished the link to the mainland. But the place was locked up, awaiting summer and the strangers for whom it and the toilets functioned. I walked around the end of the building and emptied myself there, huddling close to a stone chimney to escape the attention of passing cars and the southeasterly wind.

Across the strait the rain was blackening the stone on the carved flank of the cape where they had gouged out enough rock for the crossing forty years before. The mauve strait waters flashed silver highlights in the wind. The air was sharp with the smell of sulphur and a salt fish tang. Great plumes of steam fleeing before the chill wind slanted over the pulp mill that has transformed the place.

At the base of the cape there is now a large pier, and on that day a huge Canada Steamship Lines bulk carrier was tied up there, loading stone. I'm told the rock from the cape makes excellent pavement, that people haul the stone from the cape away for roads in distant places. I once believed it would make the road that would bring all those places here. Or pave the way for me to leave forever.

1975. november 9. left miami about 3 on taca flight 801. one stop, at san pedro sula. lush countryside, mountains, plantations green as golf courses. banana groves with gushing irrigation pipes and smoke from small fires rising . . . they call it the third world. but it is like a garden. and it smells like home. smoke and decay. almost familiar.

A sudden gust of wind dashed my face with a cold, salty spray. I turned toward the car. The causeway forks in three directions at the top: town to the right, Creignish a hard left, and, a few miles up the middle, a non-place called the Long Stretch, where I grew up. A country road, basically. The old home is still there. It is my only connection, apart from memory. *Almost* the only connection: there is a neighbour, John Gillis, with whom I share a troubled history. The fact that he was briefly married to my sister is only part of it.

My sister's name is Effie and she's all I have by way of family. Effie and her daughter, whose name is Cassandra and who has, in the blur of time, evolved into a young woman. I don't think I'd recognize her anymore. They live in Toronto.

At the first clear view of Creignish I stopped and studied the stern old church in the distance, with its modest dome and crucifix grimly overlooking the flashing bay and the distant mainland. You'd hardly notice Creignish before you'd passed it. Some houses strung along the lap of a low mountain with an old church and glebe about halfway up its rocky flank. The parish is called Stella Maris. Star of the Sea.

The eye is drawn to the broad expanse of St. Georges Bay, which sprawls before you, narrowing as it approaches the Canso

Strait to the south, reaching toward invisible Prince Edward Island to the northwest. The dark outlines of Antigonish County define the mainland shore.

Creignish. *Creig* means "rock." It also means Peter. Upon this rock, said Jesus, I will build my church. And Peter's church stood there, rocklike, on the stony banks of Creignish, a visible symbol of authority and permanence, like the Mother Church herself. Impervious to death and time and the winds of history.

I realized I'd parked at the end of someone's driveway. On a low knoll at the top of the lane there was an old house that had grown shabby since the last time I noticed it, many years before. I struggled to remember a name, something MacIsaac. And I realized that I once knew most of the people around here. Now they and I are strangers, set apart by the sacrament that I embraced in 1968.

The old glebe house stood to the right of the church, at the end of a steep driveway. A tidy cemetery on the left wrapped around a hill with a large crucifix on its crown. The porch door was sticky and I had to use my shoulder to force it open. Inside there was a damp, familiar smell of decay and turpentine. The scent of history. The odours of my childhood. The Third World reek. Woodsmoke and kerosene. DDT. Boiled tea and old clothing. Rot.

The door to the kitchen was unlocked and it swung wide to reveal a sterile interior. White walls. A tile floor of alternating white and black squares. A silver Saviour hung on a black cross above a doorway to the interior of the house. A pantry door, nibbled at the corners by mice. An unturned calendar, January 1991. More than three years old. I tore it down.

I stood still there in the chilly kitchen for what seemed like a long time, trying to warm the moment by thinking of the place as home, but there was no comfort in the memory. I felt the presence of all the solitary men who stood like this before my time, staring into a lonely future. Probably kneeling to acknowledge acceptance of their fate.

I knelt.

Jesus. I didn't ask for this, but help me make the most of it.

I sought the worn wooden prayer beads in my jacket pocket.

tegucigalpa's airport is dingy, full of sullen men with guns. weary inspectors deferring to my collar. alfonso was waiting. had a little paper sign with something like my name in heavy ink. FR. MACKASGAL.

I peer into the gloom of what will be my study. The other peril, I tell myself, is silence. I was so accustomed to the sounds of other people's lives around me at the university. The old priests coughing and shuffling in nearby rooms, awaiting their eternal rewards. Squealing, slamming doors. Students rampaging in and out. Incessant booming stereos. Traffic passing endlessly on West Street. No more of that. Silence now. I must consider this a welcome change. Learn to work with silence. The silence can become a passageway to better places.

Up a creaky stairway. This must be the bishop's room, I thought as I peered into a large dark space. Every glebe house has a special guest room for the bishop. There was a faint smell of clammy wallpaper. I could see the dim shape of a bed and a dresser with a large water jug and wash basin. I could feel the dampness of disuse. I walked toward a slash of light and pulled back drapes, exposed a window. There were clumps of dead flies between the panes of glass. The sun was beginning to press weakly against the filmy sky. Small fishing boats dotted the choppy grey sea. Inside the room, the anemic light revealed the face of a sallow Jesus on the wall. On another wall, the Blessed

Virgin, a hand raised in salutation, a child with a dead man's face in the crook of her left arm.

I lit a candle on the bedside table, hoping to defeat the smell of loneliness. Opened a sticky drawer. More dead flies.

A smaller bedroom along the hall. Bathroom. A second large bedroom. Closet door ajar, metal coat hangers entangled. A faded *Blue Boy* print on one wall and another crucifix above the naked bed.

Back downstairs, in the study, I found a large safe, pointlessly locked; the combination was taped to the outside of the door. It was full of ledgers. Records of births and baptisms, marriages and deaths. Parish finances. And photographs of old men in black suits and liturgical vestments.

You had no goddamned business spying . . .

I study a stern, anonymous face above the Roman collar. Pious, slightly arrogant. He is wearing a hat even though he's obviously indoors. Concealing baldness? A hint of hidden vanity? Was he one of those whose secret weakness undermined the Rock as nothing had before?

Maybe they were classmates, he and Father Roddie. They'd have known each other. Old men, presumed exempted from temptations of the flesh.

I closed the safe.

I don't belong here.

But this is the priesthood. This is what you're for.

But that's not why I'm here.

There was a radio on the desk. I switched it on. The house filled up with mournful country music. I unpacked the few photographs that I'd brought from my rooms at the university. One I've carried with me everywhere. There are two men in uniform, one of them my father, and a third in work clothes with a hunting rifle in his hand, and a dead deer draped on the fender of a truck. There's an inscription on the back: *October '41. Home from Debert.* Three men, decades younger than I am now, faces still defined by innocence and curiosity, yet to be rewritten by experience. My father's name was Angus. These were his closest friends, Sandy Gillis, in his army uniform, and Sandy's brother Jack, holding up the deer's head, a knowing expression on its lifeless face. Effie gave it to me. It had once belonged to John. He didn't want it when they finally broke up their marriage. The rifle in Jack's hand was the one his brother Sandy used in 1963.

That photo, in a way, is my biography: three men who shaped what has become my life, created what became my family. My sister Effie, briefly married to Sandy's only offspring, John Gillis. And Sextus Gillis, the son of Jack, closer to me than a brother once, smitten briefly, like his cousin, by my sister.

In another photo, Effie is a child, red hair wild and unruly. And there is a more recent, formal portrait, Dr. Effie MacAskill Gillis, or Faye, or *Oighrig nic Ill-Iosa* as she sometimes styles herself now that she's a scholar. The sharp-tongued history professor, with a rare smile for a stranger's camera.

And then there is the photograph from Puerto Castilla. Three ordinary people on a holiday. The younger me, tall and leaner of jaw, longer of hair. Jacinta in the middle, shorter, arms outstretched to catch our shoulders, hauling us together. Dark Alfonso on her left, me on the right. We are smiling.

In one of seven boxes filled with books I find my diaries.

1975. nov. 26. harsh dreams and the humidity and crowing roosters drive me out of bed early. dawns are pink and misty here. people emerge like shadows from the darkness with their packages and their children. trinkets, fruit and vegetables to sell, families trudging toward the glow of day. there is an old

woman who cooks on a bucketful of burning charcoal. through
doorways i see women bending over open hearths and the tor-
tillas. everybody friendly to the new priest. and dogs barking at
the roosters. the old woman at the smouldering bucket calls me
padre pelirrojo.

I closed the journal, then placed it and the others on top of an
empty bookcase. There were a dozen journals. Careful, coded
records of my years of ministry. The record of my sordid service
for our Holy and Eternal Mother, a source of self-recrimination
but also of security. At the university I'd leave them prominently
displayed. Reminders of who I am and whom I work for. At the
university, my visitors would eye them nervously. They'd mean
nothing here, except to me.

I arranged the journals carefully by year. Then I set the photographs on the mantel above a blocked fireplace. They are as
alien as I am, I told myself. Strangers here. Strangers from the
dead past. Chilled, I found a thermostat, turned the dial and
heard the distant rumble of a furnace.

In the house where I grew up, I have another photograph
from just before that first assignment, in Honduras. I haven't set
eyes on it in years, though I remember it in detail—the dreamy
expression, the piety of innocence. One day it suddenly became
too much. A reminder of all the contradictions. I shoved it in a
drawer. I couldn't find it now even if I wanted to.

My sister Effie was the only one to notice it was gone. It was
during one of her rare visits home.

"What have you done with that lovely picture, your ordination portrait?"

"I put it somewhere," I said.

"I still have mine," she said. "It's in my office in Toronto.
Everybody comments."

It was the innocence that bothered me, I think. Maturity has stripped away my palliative optimism.

they call me pelirrojo. padre pelirrojo. father red, because of my red hair. they should be careful calling anybody red around this place, alfonso says. back home in salvador they called me red. which is why i'm here. jacinta seems concerned. she has unusual green eyes.

The day's weak light was failing fast as night approached. I might feel warmer in the church, I thought.

It was dim there and a kind of peace fell over me. Shadows absorbed boundaries, enlarging the possible, making the hollow, vaulted places more vast than I remembered. Surfaces and corners softened. Shadows from a solitary vigil light flickered. I noticed I was not alone. Among the wavering shadows a dark, motionless form, someone crouched in prayer before the banks of votive candles to the right of the altar. I stayed in the back. The prim kerchief told me it was a woman. I sat still, touched by her devotion.

There used to be a rail between the people and the altar. A little fence. Women were not allowed inside the fence except to change the linen, scrub the floors. I remember women with their hair covered, working silently, efficiently, to minimize their time in the forbidden spaces. And I remember Sundays, people kneeling outside the sanctuary, elbows on the starched cloth of the altar rail, faces buried in dry, knobby hands. People lined up to receive the Blessed Sacrament, eyes intense with devotion and hope. Cape Breton, Honduras—the features blur in my memory. People shaped by hardship and faith into a common character.

There was a flare of light at the front. The dear woman was lighting candles. Thanksgiving? Anxiety? Light now flickered in a red receptacle, casting rosy shadows. The glow of faith and hope.

A shadow rose. I heard the clink of a coin. Another light flared briefly. Another candle. Another movement as she made the sign of the cross.

She must be old, I thought. Lighting candles, praying for some small reprieve.

The church creaked as a cold wind rose outside. A suffocating silence drifted down from dark recesses in the hidden ceiling as the cold currents of air wafted over me. The woman hurried by, head down, arms wrapped across her chest as if cradling a child. She didn't see me. The glass front door whispered shut behind her.

Back in the glebe, I found a loaf of fresh homemade bread and a bag of tea biscuits on the kitchen table. And a note.

"If we'd known you were coming, we'd have baked a cake . . ."

They'd drawn little music notes around the words. I vaguely recalled an old song. Ethel Merman singing "how'dya do, how'dya do, how'dya doooo."

"This loaf of bread will have to doooo."

It was signed Bob O.

Bobby O'Brian showed up later to apologize in person for the lack of preparation, the shabby glebe. The women were beside themselves, he said. New priest coming and the beds not even made. I assured him everything was fine. He said that he'd been president of the parish council, but since there hadn't been a resident priest for a couple of years the council had lapsed. Just in suspension, though. A lack of manpower. But ready to go again now that I'd arrived. Just say the word. His wife made the bread by way of contrition for the state of the glebe house. One of the priorities of the place was a new house for the priest.

I told him again, the place was fine.

"Did you try it yet? The bread?"

"Yes," I lied. "It's fabulous."

"I'll tell the wife. She makes the best bread in the county."

I smiled.

Bobby was middle-aged, prematurely balding and on the heavy side. It was great to have a priest again, he declared. To see a light in the window of the old place.

"Kind of hard to take, not having a priest. We were sure they were going to shut us down for good, after so many years. Would you believe we were the only church in the area once, years and years ago? St. James we were back then."

I nodded and smiled and said I knew that.

He said, "Of course you do. I'm forgetting, you grew up in this neck of the woods. I did a little homework. Back of Port Hastings, you grew up. Out the Long Stretch."

"Not too much homework, I hope."

I forced myself to smile again.

"The wrath to come . . ." Those bleak words of absolution say it all, now that I think of it. The grim warning in the burial prayers. I think it was at a funeral in 1970 that the innocence first began to wash away under a pounding rain. I remember a stormy day, the pungent incense fumes blowing back in my face, censer clinking on its chains, rivulets of water creeping out around the edges of the artificial turf that hides the muddy evidence of our mortality.

Poor Jack Gillis. His death was as unremarkable as his life. He was visiting my father late one night and dropped dead.

His only son was glassy-eyed. "What the fuck was that all about?" Sextus said, gesturing angrily toward the casket. "Is that it?"

Jack's sudden departure had caught him off guard. Jack was relatively young. There was so much left unsaid, undone; death should have meaning, not this feeling of betrayal, of something interrupted. Sextus repeated all the common phrases of confusion after unexpected loss, but later, calmed by liquor, he became more analytical. He spoke of how his father, travelling for work, was mostly absent from his life; how their occasional coexistence always suffered from anticipated separation. It was how most people grew up here, in this godforsaken place, scrabbling for survival.

"You don't have to explain," I assured him.

In the end he admitted his real anxiety: a father's death reveals the awful tragedy of deferred conciliation. "I'm not talking about reconciliation," he said fiercely. "I'm talking about the basics. I'm talking about what you, yourself, know all too well."

I just listened. It's my job, I told myself. I nodded, gripped his shoulder reassuringly. "You'll be okay." This I knew for sure.

Sextus bounced back quickly, as he has always done. It's never long before he finds some sleazy analgesic. That was how I saw it then. How easily our lowest needs take over and redirect the heart away from grief. I see them still, Sextus on one side of Jack's open grave, my sister and her husband John, standing close but somehow disconnected, on the other side, John's face a mask of pain. He loved his uncle Jack. Or maybe he could already feel the other bond, could see the future coming.

I hear the awful words again: "I am seized with fear and trembling, until the trial shall be at hand, the wrath to come."

"That day, a day of wrath, of wasting, and of misery, a great day, and exceeding bitter. When Thou shalt come to judge the world by fire."

My priestly words linger in the flap of wind. I observe my sister's stealthy glance, the ghostly smile.

"I am desperately unhappy," she has told me.

"I blessed your marriage," I'd replied. "You will find the strength. You and John, together."

She laughed.

"Eternal rest grant unto him, O Lord." And in the pouring rain, the mourners murmured the response: "And let perpetual light shine upon him."

Perhaps John was still unconscious of the mute transaction happening between his cousin and his wife. Truthfully, I see it only now, knowing what unfolded afterwards, the monstrous betrayal she later justified by calling it compassion.

"Sextus needed me," she said. "My husband didn't."

After Mass on my first Sunday, I had lunch in the hall with the Catholic Women's League. Some of them I recognized from high school, self-conscious girls transformed by time into plump and pious matrons. I wondered if they remembered me as I remembered them. They wanted to know if I'd support them in a campaign to revive the daily rosary in the home. Why not, I thought. We need it now more than ever before, they said, and I nodded.

We used to say the rosary for peace, I said. Maybe we could focus on the Balkans or the Middle East. The Holy Land especially. They seemed uncomfortable with that, and proposed the integrity of the family and the sanctity of life instead. We should pray for strength against the forces that are bent on destroying traditional structures in the home. And life itself. That's where all the problems start. Crime and wars included.

More tradition, more religion, more tribalism—just the cure for Yugoslavia, I thought.

"You'll have to help me here," I sighed, raising helpless hands. "I don't have much experience in a parish."

"Oh, we'll look after you," said one, vaguely flirtatious.

The others laughed like the girls they used to be.

I realized the flirt looked vaguely familiar, but I couldn't remember a name. Then she was serious again.

"The family that prays together, stays together. We have to get back to that idea, and then all the other problems will take care of themselves."

She said her name was Pat. Some distant image stirred. We were somewhere unremembered, and she and Sextus were together. A night-blue sky over the black glitter of the sea. I struggled to remember, eventually gave up and promised to mention the rosary from the altar sometime soon.

On their way out, I overheard their whispering, talking about me.

"Well, he's different," said one.

The others murmured in assent.

Sextus showed up unannounced on a Sunday afternoon in May. He said he was home from Toronto for an extended visit. I had trouble hiding my surprise and I suspected there was something wrong because he hugged me. Walked straight in, arms wide, and grabbed me.

"You look fabulous," he declared. "Maybe there's something to this celibacy racket after all. I should try it." He was fidgety, couldn't stop moving, checking out the meagre contents of my dreary room. "Bless me, Father, for I have sinned . . . It's been at least ten years since my last visit . . ."

He was smiling then, one knee slightly bent, head slightly tilted. He said it was amazing how nothing seems to have changed in the old 'hood. He was staying out at the old Gillis place, the Long Stretch. Temporarily.

"The old place."

"Yep," he said. "Me and John, two old *bodags*, making tea for one another."

I guess my face revealed my skepticism.

"I know what you're thinking," he said. "Effie said I should check the place for firearms before venturing in. But John and I put all that crap behind us long ago."

Eventually he said that he'd had a small health scare. "Some medical issues," was how he put it. He was standing in front of my bookcase and plucked a volume.

I ventured: "So it's been ten years since you've been home?"

"More like eleven," he said absently. "Macquarrie, eh? Funny name for an existentialist. I thought they were all French or German." He sat, flipped open the cover. "Nineteen seventy-seven. That was just after you got back from . . . that place. Who was RM?"

"Old priest. Former philosophy prof."

"Existentialism, eh?"

"One of my interests," I said.

"Mine too, lately."

"I didn't realize."

He sighed. "One day a Paki doctor sticks his finger up your ass and you just know by his face. This is bad, speaking existentially."

There was a long silence.

"So that was the health scare," I said, to break it.

"I'm okay. It was a false alarm."

"Thank God."

"I did," he said. "It's shocking, just how quick the faith comes back."

Before he left, he stood for a while before the mantel, studying the photo of my sister.

"Just look at her."

I couldn't read the tone.

"Believe it or not, she was a major help when I was . . . pretty down there, for a while."

"I'm glad to hear that," I said.

Then he picked up my photograph from Puerto Castilla. "Who's he?" he said, pointing at Alfonso.

"A guy I knew," I said.

"And the babe?"

"Another friend."

Then it was the picture of our fathers and his uncle Sandy. "I think this used to be in the old place," he said.

"Effie got it from John when they split up. She gave it to me."

"Did you know that Uncle Sandy used to have a picture of Gracie Fields, from the same time, just before they went overseas? I wonder where that one got to? It was autographed. It's probably worth something now. On the back of it she wrote: *Wish me luck as you wave me goodbye.* Then her name. Scrawled, but you could make it out, clear as anything."

"I didn't know."

"I always wondered where he got that. There was a man, eh, Uncle Sandy. It wouldn't surprise me if he took a run at old Gracie. You remember how he was?"

"Oh, yes."

"And look at himself, my old man. Poor old Jack." He shook his head. "They didn't have a clue. But then again . . ."

"I didn't know that you were coming home."

"I meant to call," he said, and smiled. "You know the way it is, how time goes."

"I know."

Now that I'm in middle age, the nights are always difficult, I find. I toss my body into various positions, awaiting sleep, but I just grow more alert. When I do sleep, my dreams persuade me that I'm still awake. I tell myself perhaps I need pills. Sextus said he took medication for a while for sleeplessness. Said it's very common at our age. Especially in times of stress. And of course the stress increases with the weight of years. But he won't take medication anymore and has started smoking pot instead. Said he can get it for me, any time. It's everywhere in town. Better for you in the long run, he said.

I smoked pot once. Alfonso had it. Where he got it, I have no idea. I remember laughing a lot, an innocent hysteria. Lying here alone, swathed in the damp silence of the old house, I think of Alfonso as frequently as I think of Jack and Sandy Gillis and my father. What goes through our heads when suddenly we have to face the inevitable? Death imposed, or death chosen? Occasionally the questions drive me out of bed, to get up and get out to try to shake the feeling of despair. At the end of life, I wonder, how much comfort, really, is belief? Did it help them?

Sometimes I'll shuffle to the bathroom, study the face in the mirror, now baggy-eyed, skin sere and thin. Soon throat and chin will become one continuum of sagging flesh. The ravages of half a century expose themselves at night. Time, the vampire, sucks away the juice of youth while we're asleep. I can imagine the women from our earnest little meetings, and see them in such solitary moments. In their mirrors. In their husbands' eyes. The night and time are harder on the women.

The women named me Pelirrojo.

The red hair now has a dusty look to it, fading like everything else. Bulging flab below the rib cage. And it gets worse from here on. After fifty.

dec. 16. alfonso nagging me again today about my spanish, or lack of it. says i'm useless here without it. the only word you've learned, he said, is pelirrojo. i'm going to hand you over to jacinta. gracias, i said. worse things could happen to me.

† † †

The doctor once told me: Don't just lie there. Get up. Do something. And on many nights that summer I would follow his advice, leave the house for the damp, cool air outside, the fragrance of the mountain. The sea would whisper as I made my way through darkness to the silent church to kneel before the bank of candles. And I would think of Jacinta, wondering where she was. And pray to Alfonso, remembering his fate. Wondering what, if anything, went through his mind.

> *jacinta works at the hospital. she is a specialist in malnutrition and works with children. pretty in a modest way. very dark hair accentuates the green of the eyes. the kids are something else. sorrowful, silent, dark, empty faces, gap-toothed, snot-encrusted noses. thin hair the colour of clay. scab-encrusted scalps. ribs sticking through tissue-flimsy skin. you wonder how they get like that. jacinta will teach me to speak spanish . . . fluently, alfonso said.*

Jacinta. My secret garden, the place where understanding blooms.

{ 3 }

Early in July, Effie called to say that she'd be coming home for a visit. I was briefly tempted to comment on this odd coincidence, she and Sextus, after such long absences, returning. She claimed the purpose of her mission was to celebrate my special birthday. My turning fifty.

"This I've gotta see," she said.

I laughed and said that age is just a number, a convenience for administrators, bureaucrats and bookkeepers.

"Then we'll celebrate your health, wealth and common sense."

I offered her the bishop's room, but she told me she'd be staying at the old place. Home. "If that's okay."

"It isn't really very comfortable," I said. "Still pretty primitive."

"I plan to do something about that."

So I told her where the key was. Under a stone on the doorstep.

"I know what you're thinking," she said.

"You haven't even seen the place for years. I haven't done much since."

She ignored me. "The place seemed solid then, no sign of damage. Nothing that a little TLC won't fix."

"Go crazy," I said.

She'd been back once before that, briefly in 1987, her first repatriation since the cruel abandonment of John, the unseemly flight with Sextus after his father's death seventeen years earlier. She didn't explain her long absence or the unexpected end of it, just said she wanted to visit the old place on the Long Stretch. Our old home.

"Do you really—"

"Will you come with me?"

It was the last thing I desired. "Of course," I said.

The tension grew as we neared the old place that time in 1987. She sat silent, arms crossed. I stole glances at her face, but it was closed. And then we were there, stopped on the roadside, studying the low-slung structure that had once been our home.

"It looks good," she said. "The vinyl siding makes it almost new. When did you do that?"

"A few years back. Just after Honduras. I considered shingles, but—"

"I'm glad you didn't," she said. "I like the siding . . . It makes it . . . I don't know."

"Like plastic?"

She shrugged and frowned.

Outside the car, she hesitated. "Home. This was home." She sighed deeply.

She stood back as I unlocked the door. She was chewing on her lower lip, arms still folded.

"Maybe it's too much to absorb all at once. Why don't we wait?" I said.

She shook her head. "This just feels really weird."

She remained standing there beside the car for a paralyzing minute longer. Then she started walking, slowly, thoughtfully.

Immediately inside the door, she drifted away from me, face drawn. I let her go, imagining her thoughts. Then I could hear her careful footsteps and knew she was wandering in the direction of her childhood bedroom, high, hard heels rapping slowly across the bare floorboards. Then there was silence. I sat at our old kitchen table, watching.

"It's a strange thing," she said, "to not remember a mother. It's like a big hole in your life."

"Maybe it's just as well," I said. "You'd mostly remember sickness and sorrow."

"Maybe. But I think it's always best to have a memory . . . of something. Good or bad."

"Perhaps."

She was standing in the doorway to the tiny bedroom. "I remember it being bigger," she said, walking into the empty space. She stopped and turned. "You got rid of my bed."

"The mattress springs were rusted out. And it was an odd size. You couldn't replace the old mattress. So I sent it to the dump."

She was smiling at me. "You don't have to explain."

"I thought maybe . . ."

"No." She paused by the window for a moment, then stood in the corner farthest from where her bed used to be. "He'd be here. I can still see the cigarette glowing."

"Let's go."

"It's okay. It's years since I even thought of it."

I studied her closely. My sister. So detached from our history, and yet consumed by it. To distract her I asked, "Do you remember anything about our mother?"

"She's always been a ghost."

"And our father?"

She laughed. "I remember the day we moved here. I must have been, what? Four or five?"

In memory I hear the sudden rattle of the train all around us. The air is acrid from the locomotive smoking outside and the men smoking inside. Our father is leaning toward the window, looking out, his body fluid, moving gently with the swaying car.

There's a sleepy rhythm to the click and clank of iron rolling over steel. From time to time I hear an urgent howl from somewhere ahead of us. The train screaming danger at the empty countryside, the sullen trees. And I am aware again of the expanding distance from the heap of earth we left behind in the field of tall white stones, and that we four, now, are only three.

A truck rattled by outside. I glanced toward the window. It was John Gillis.

"Was that who I think it was?" she asked.

"Will you go to see him while you're home?"

"I don't think so." She studied my face, looking for judgment or reassurance. "I can feel Daddy in the room," she said at last. "You were never afraid of him, were you?"

"The old man? No. I disliked him. I judged him. Then over time I got past it . . . But you don't hate him anymore, do you?"

She smiled.

This time it was John who told me she'd arrived. He called on a Wednesday morning. "There was a light on in the old place last night. I was wondering."

"Effie must be home," I said. "She told me she was coming."

"Ah. And how is old Effie? Or didn't she change it to Faye after she went away?"

"She's back to being Effie."

"That's good. The Faye was kind of fake. I thought, anyway."

"You should drop in. Say hello."

"I might."

Mid-morning on my birthday, which fell that Friday, the phone rang. I was standing at the picture window, studying the vast, flat bay, interpreting the ripples on its dark blue surface, trying to anticipate the weather.

"Happy birthday," Effie said. "I'll be expecting you at seven."

"Expecting me where?"

"Out home. Where did you think?"

"Where are you calling from?"

"I'm at John's. I dropped by to invite them. John and Sextus. I thought I should remind you."

"I think I'll pass," I said.

"Remember. Seven sharp."

The phone went dead.

Maybe to get it over with, I went early. The old house reeked of cleaning fluids, gentrified by burning wax. Candles flickered and the blinds were drawn to exclude the setting sun, or perhaps to prevent disclosure of what she was doing to the house.

"You'll have a glass of wine, or maybe something stronger."

"Something stronger," I replied.

She poured a stiff Scotch. "A little toast to us. Before the others come."

"Right. The others."

"Don't worry about it," she said, and kissed me lightly on the cheek.

John arrived first. He's younger than I am and his body has an adolescent slimness, but I noted that his hair has gone almost white. Apparently he jogs a lot for fitness and for sanity. He caught Effie's hand, bent his head toward hers. Their cheeks touched. Her eyes were tightly closed.

Then Sextus barged into the room, singing a flat "Happy Birthday," and knocked me off balance with a bear hug. This is becoming a habit, I thought, this hugging. He had a bottle of wine in each hand and I heard them clank dangerously behind me. He released me, then placed them on the cupboard with a flourish. He shook Effie's hand with mock formality, bowing slightly. She dipped, face faintly pink. Then he took her in his arms, started a slow waltz around the kitchen, singing loudly: *"Can I have this . . . dunce . . . for the rest of my life . . ."*

John stared, eyebrows raised, mouth-corners twitching, struggling to seem amused.

"I see you've had a head start," Effie said.

She broiled steaks, assembled a simple salad, and as we ate, we rode the currents of wine back through time to places that were safe. John, who drank only water, was mostly quiet.

Once, he asked abruptly: "Is this the same old table?"

Effie said: "The very one."

"If it could talk," he said. And grunted.

After that we all went quiet for a while, each drawn back to memories best not compared. I think there was music somewhere, instrumental music with haunting undertones. Irish, I think.

Then Sextus broke the silence. "You didn't tell them, did you?" He was speaking to John.

"Tell them what?" he asked.

"My news. I'm staying around, for a while at least. Moving into an apartment in town. John is devastated." He pointed a finger at his cousin and laughed.

After a few more glasses of wine, I returned to the Scotch. Effie at some point proposed a toast. "So here we are," she said. "Here's to the birthday boy. And the best years still to come. Here's to fifty. They say it's the new forty."

We drank.

"And to all my boys," she continued, smiling toward her two ex-husbands, raising her wineglass daintily. She too was a little drunk by then. They both sat with slightly foolish expressions on their faces.

And I remember blurting to Sextus later on, "You don't find any of this strange?"

"Of course it's strange," he said softly, leaning close. "It's twisted. So fucking what?"

I nodded, grasping the simple logic the way that only alcohol makes possible.

"Hey," he said, "twisted is the new normal." Then he laughed and grabbed me in a headlock. My drink splashed my lap.

I struggled. "Don't do that," I said, the anger like a jolt.

"No matter what," he said, releasing me, "we're family, for God's sake."

And I felt the unwelcome surge of cheap reassurance.

The rest of the birthday is blank.

But I know that the kitchen was tidy and filled with a pale blue light when I came to on the lounge. It took a moment to remember where I was and then it was as if the old man was there again. A shadow hovering near that door on the far side of the kitchen, where her bedroom used to be.

I found shoes. Carried them into the blaring morning light.

Outside, the air was cool and moist and loud with early birds. Somewhere in the distance, the resolute sound of a large truck, tires ringing on the cold asphalt.

Backing out of the yard, I realized there were still two vehicles parked there. Effie's rental and the red half-ton that Sextus drives.

August arrives on chilly mornings but softens in the afternoons. On a sunny Sunday, just after lunch, relaxing on the veranda with a Bloody Mary, I was reviewing the words of my morning homily with some satisfaction. A parish, I'd discovered, is a platform. Article Four, *Presbyterorum ordanis:* " . . . apply the perennial truth of the gospel to the concrete circumstances of life."

Pat approached me after Mass and clasped my hand a bit longer, I thought, than she should have. Pat is divorced. People talk. But I didn't really mind the warmth, the graceful touch of a woman's fingers.

"I couldn't agree more," she said.

I saw sincerity in her eyes and it touched off something close to pleasure. I even asked myself: Dare I believe that I'm beginning to feel more positive? Maybe that's what happens in your fifties.

That morning, working from parables about graven images, I was able to make some points about community. How in the absence of community we become strangers to each other, part of the universal alienation (without using that exact phrase). Alienated from ourselves, we seek to find our identities in what I called the Super Strangers, the phony personalities and fashions of commerce and celebrity. The false idols of the modern world. I took shots at Michael Jackson and Michael Jordan and a lot of other Michaels. The archangels of sleaze, I said, spreading a low, universal vulgarity. Where else would I have been able to do that and be listened to seriously? Certainly not at the university.

"It's not fit," Pat said. "The commercial propaganda mixed in with all the other garbage on TV."

The previous Sunday my sermon had been a thinly disguised lecture about garbage along the roadside. Disorder in the countryside reveals disorder in the soul, I'd said. Perennial truth and concrete circumstances. My mission statement.

I'm told that Father Chisholm at St. Joseph's often talks of justice. But when I think about justice, I think of Alfonso. Justice for Aguilares, he would say, smiling self-consciously. That was his true vocation and, it turned out, his fate. Justice. It has been a hollow word to me ever since. Father Roddie would say that this has always been my problem, this emotional reaction to a word, part of a banal self-righteousness. Alfonso said it better: words in the absence of action are meaningless. Someday, I'll dare to say that somewhere.

Summer was beginning to wane, but on that early August Sunday afternoon the sky was a sharp mineral blue and the vast water absorbed it and the sunshine bounced back restlessly.

Pat lives with a teenaged daughter and her widowed mother. She actually asked me out once. A "Platonic" invitation, she called it and I wondered if she really knew its meaning.

"Momma is a big help," she said. "But having her in the house kind of limits my social life, if you get my drift. So I go to Parents Without Partners in town, mostly for companionship. I wish you'd come sometime. You can be my date." And then she laughed.

"Why not," I said.

"I'm being bad. But really . . . I'd like to take you there to meet our group some night. Maybe you'll get some ideas for starting something here."

"Are there all that many singles?"

"You'd be surprised. Tons of singles. Even married people, living like singles . . . if you know what I mean."

I noted that my glass had, somehow, emptied. I felt the buzz. Lunch had been a few sandwiches left over from a social function in the hall the night before. An entire Sunday afternoon could melt away just staring at the glittering water. In the distance I could see a small boat approaching from the north, slowly passing the spear tip of land that gives Long Point its name.

Maybe another Bloody Mary.

On the way back from the kitchen with my second drink, I picked up the binoculars a former occupant had left behind. Some past pastor. Some past pastor's spyglasses. Try saying that after a *third* Bloody Mary. I have a way with words, I'd discovered since I became a regular homilist. The ideas rise up out of nowhere with startling fecundity and the words just follow, like the wake behind a boat. The key, I thought, standing there peering through the binoculars toward where I thought the boat should be, is to keep your lingo simple. Talk the way your congregation talks.

It was a typical Northumberland fishing boat, raked gracefully from high stem to transom, with the distinctively expansive workspace aft of the cab. Truthfully, I didn't know a Northumberland from a kayak at the time. It's something I've learned since. There was a froth of water churning at the stern, a graceful wake opening behind her like a bridal train. I could count five people, two men sitting on the washboards, three women who seemed to be in lawn chairs. The men had dark bottles in their hands. Silent mouths moving. Women, heads tossed back in silent laughter, hair fluttering. Men in golf shirts with brown arms. Brown woman shoulders. Long woman throats. I felt an unexpected pang. I could enjoy that, I thought. The boat. The water. There's something pristine out there, where life originated if Darwin is to be believed. Something like envy swelled within.

Intimacy.

It's a word Sextus used all the time. It's what you look for at a certain point in life, he'd say. Intimacy. We strive for it because we need it.

Down on the tennis court beside the hall, someone was batting a ball against the chain-link fence, chasing it, whacking it again. I directed the binoculars toward the sound. A woman wearing tiny shorts, scampering after the tennis ball. Alone.

I smiled. Tiny shorts on tennis courts. And a softball diamond. A new parish hall. Somebody accomplished something here.

Which of my predecessors was it? The place had come a long way since the fifties and Father Donald Rankin. What does it take to mobilize people?

That was Alfonso's dream. Mobilize the people, for that's where the true power lies.

What about the Holy Spirit?

Yes. But where do you think the Holy Spirit lives? In the hearts of the poor, she lives.

Not many poor here in Creignish anymore, I thought. Relatively speaking. Not like in Honduras. Not even like in my father's time. So many men had to go away back then, like poor Jack Gillis, always in pursuit of wages, leaving sons at home to cultivate anxieties. My father home, anaesthetized by booze.

The woman with the tennis racket runs like a deer, I thought, white teeth flashing like the froth behind the distant boat, chasing the ball with long, smooth strides. I wondered: is she married? Images resurfaced, I felt the gentle movement in my chest. It's why the poets focused on the heart.

I raised the glasses to the bay again, located the silent fishing boat, wondered where they could be going. Men and women fused in their silent intimacies, going nowhere in particular. The causeway from the mainland blocks the strait. Getting through by boat is complicated by the canal, the swing bridge. They're nuisances, these boats, when you have to wait in the long line of traffic while they pass. But I could see why people fall in love with them.

Now a man and a woman were standing near the stern, his arm over her shoulder, her face impressed upon his neck.

Once, there were boats and a wharf at the village, before there was a causeway and a bridge. Ocean-going vessels sailed by silent and unhindered, heading toward the bowels of North America. And there were open fishing boats with no instruments of any kind, engines that sat in the centre and made a *bang-bang* kind of sound when running. In the fall, larger boats that looked like schooners came from Prince Edward Island loaded with bags of potatoes and buckets of salt herring. During lobster fishing a large motorboat came round. Men lived on it. I remembered the wharf smells of decayed fish and creosote, burlap and the dank smell of old sweat. And liquor. And the sounds of the men talking on the lobster buyers' boat.

And a man asking me if I was Angus MacAskill's.

And I said yes.

Come on down, he said. Meet some people who were with your daddy in the war.

There were men sitting around a small table in the forward cabin staring at me darkly.

This here's Angus MacAskill's.

They just continued staring and the look said they knew something I didn't know. There was a bottle of black liquor in the middle of the table.

One picked up the bottle and held it out. How about a little snort for the young fella?

He seemed to mean it. I declined politely.

If he's anything like his old man, he'd suck rum out of a cow's arse.

Somebody behind me laughed. Then they all laughed.

The man and woman on the boat were now embracing.

On the last Sunday of Effie's holiday at home that summer, I thought I'd surprise her with a visit. She was at the kitchen counter fiddling with a new coffee maker. Sextus was standing behind her, arms around her waist, face buried in her neck.

"I didn't hear your car," she said impatiently, patting her hair. Her face was scarlet.

"I didn't mean to startle you."

"I've made some coffee. How do you take it?"

"Milk, no sugar."

Of course, I thought: she's sleeping with him again. I smiled.

"What?" she said aggressively. Off balance.

"Nothing."

"I bet."

Sextus refilled his coffee cup.

"And how is the new apartment?" I asked.

"Perfect," he said. "You must come by. I'm still in the process of moving in."

"So I see."

Pat talks a lot about neediness. The importance of companionship.

"Companionship?"

"It's something you can only understand if you've been through the loss of it," she said. "I envy priests in that regard, your freedom from emotional entanglement."

The hollow rubber whack of a tennis ball. There is something sad about playing tennis with a fence. Her bare brown legs blurred as she dashed in pursuit of the fugitive ball, full white blouse-front wobbling. I put the glasses down.

This is not a good idea, standing here drinking Bloody Marys, secretly watching wobbling blouses, people going about their intimacies on boats.

Was it really only yesterday that John called to tell me that my sister was gone again? It didn't surprise me. She's always had an aversion to farewells.

"I didn't notice any lights last night. I wasn't keeping an eye on her or anything. It was just something I noticed."

"You don't have to explain."

"I admire her guts, staying there. The place is full of memories. Not all good."

"I think she had . . . companionship . . . some of the time."

"Even so."

"I hear you," I said.

"One of these days . . . one of these days we should compare notes."

"We definitely should."

I noticed the solitary tennis player was walking toward a car. The boat was near a small point just south of where I stood.

I stretched in the sudden chill . . . the afternoon descending toward the evening? Or could it be the onset of irrelevance? I've heard it's what most people fear, turning fifty. But how can a priest become irrelevant? The needs are never-ending. Every face before me, staring back from the pews, every one is an opaque window on a bottomless pit of anxiety. I represent their hope. How can I feel excluded? I'm sure that even Bobby O. has problems, if I dared to ask. Maybe it was up to me. Maybe I should just invade their unintended privacy. Maybe they're waiting for some evidence of my concern for them . . . waiting for me to make the first move.

One last look through the binoculars. The boat was almost gone around the point, the man and woman at the stern now standing apart, facing each other, hands joined as if exchanging vows. The memory of another boat resurfaced, a father and his son. And I remembered what he'd said: You should drop in sometime. Visit.

I'd said I might. Sometime.

{ 4 }

It might not be such a bad life, I thought as I drove, head buzzing as the vodka metabolized. People mine their childhood experience to understand the existential outcomes. Sorrow, poverty, disaster. Our personal history on the Long Stretch could have been an exculpatory treasure trove if that's what we were looking for, a wealth of excuses for all our adult failures. But we seem, somehow, to have survived. Effie even came away with character and curiosity intact, and she has become a scholar of ancient Celtic cultures. I suspect her mission was to somehow dignify our shattered heritage. My mission wasn't quite as clear. But that didn't seem to matter anymore. I became . . . the cloth.

I laughed silently.

It's all in how we look at things. On a sunny day the clouds don't matter even if the experts say they do.

I sensed in Bobby O. someone I should really get to know if I had any realistic hope of being useful in this place. He is untypical in his optimistic generosity. He says we can worry about tomorrow when *and if* tomorrow comes. There should be a dozen like him. He's like the culture in the yogurt, the source of a larger life. A few like Bobby O. and you have community. Through him, perhaps, I could continue what my predecessors started. Obviously someone had had a secret for mobilizing people, for making them care about the parish in a time of secular distractions. What did they expect from me? Was I to be a catalyst? Or is the clergy's role more passive now: a symbolic conduit to a better place . . . some reassurance that the here and now is only a beginning?

There was a working parish council again, women engaged in the good fight for family, both living and unborn. Serious talk of a parish bulletin, which would be my responsibility. Editor and censor. I told them up front that I had almost no parish experience other than a spell in Honduras, which didn't really count. I didn't tell them why it didn't count and I didn't mention my first pastoral assignment, where my priesthood started and almost ended. I told them that in many ways I was a novice.

"Clearly not a nun . . . but you get my drift."

They giggled.

Nothing in the seminary or since had prepared me for what I now faced every day. Relating an opaque theology to contemporary circumstances. Seeking guidance in the ruminations of great medieval minds, now rendered unintelligible except in transparently manipulative parables, the old promises and threats designed to sway the superstitious, now empty. I thought of Pat and laughed aloud. I thought of Sextus and my sister. There was nothing in my experience, personal or pastoral, to help me deal with these realities.

But it didn't seem to matter. It seemed to be sufficient that I was here. It hurts, they've told me, when a place loses a school, a post office, identity. Losing the church would be the last straw. I agreed with everything. The church is the guardian of life itself, a lonely sentinel. I didn't tell them what I really thought: how the spire has been supplanted by the satellite dish. I dared not tell them what I think about the right to life.

They wouldn't listen anyway.

† † †

I realized that I was driving northward, aimlessly. Maybe I could drop in unannounced and share an hour with Mullins in Port Hood. No intransigent anxieties in Mullins, nothing that can't be handled in the time it takes to pound a small pock-marked ball into a slightly larger hole eighteen times on a sunny afternoon. I could visit Mullins. Catch up on the gossip. Mullins helped with one of my successes. Brendan Bell. The fugitive from Newfoundland. I could have sent him anywhere, but Mullins seemed to like him. God, if he had known why Bell was there, prissy Mullins would have had a fit.

Mullins—someone said at a recent priests' retreat—Mullins wouldn't know hot pants from sweatpants!

Big haw-haw-haws.

Then Brendan went away as planned, no harm done, married by now I'm sure. His new disguise.

Married.

Christ.

The image returns. Pathetic Parents Without Partners clutching at each other in the slow dancing, trying to recover whatever thing the missing partner stole. Wounded people limping toward a momentary refuge in a bed. Probably only reminding one another of the fragile joy they thought was permanent in that distant moment when they were all swaying and sweating and singing "Could I have this dance for the rest of my life?"

Pat actually tried to persuade me to join them on the floor.

"No way." I laughed, appalled.

Whoops. What was this? A sign I'd never noticed before marked a turnoff. Hawthorne Road, a narrow gravelled side road, vanished at a curve. I slowed and turned, a supernatural influence directing me. Or booze. But still I felt like an intruder.

Drop by any time, he said. Danny Ban whom they used to call Danny Bad. Perhaps it was time to visit Hawthorne. Find out why.

I ask my father: Where is Hawthorne?
  He just stares.
  Is it far?
  It's far, he says.
  How far?
  Who was talking about Hawthorne?
  Nobody.
  Good. I don't want to hear any more about effing
Hawthorne. Okay?
  Okay.

I entered the lane with the mailbox marked MacKay fully intending to back out again, turn and retreat back down the gravel road. Then before me was a large split-level house with two cars and a half-ton in front. A dog roared. A door opened. I waved from where I sat then drove forward. There were small fields on either side of the lane, their corners invaded by stumpy spruce trees. Probably vast meadows once upon a time, now shrunken by the creeping forest.

And I suddenly remembered, vividly, the heap of fresh earth, dead flowers scattered. Now there was just Effie and me and our father standing on the side of a narrow road that skirted a shabby section of the city. The vast chaotic steel mill belched smoke and ash and a fine red dust.

"This is where she'll always be," he said. "Remember, when you're bigger. You'll always know you'll find her near the smoke."

Effie was clutching a shabby doll, her expression sombre.

"And over there," he said, pointing, "that'll be your grandma."

"Who was she?"

"I don't know."

"Was she from here?"

"No."

"Where, then?"

"Hawthorne."

"Where's that?"

"It doesn't matter."

The house was relatively modern. Beyond it, a barn leaned perilously, a stout beam propped against one wall to prevent complete collapse. What appeared to be the hull of a new boat rose optimistically nearby, swaddled in tarpaulin.

Danny Ban descended from a high deck at the front of the house. He was moving carefully, one hand gripping the railing. The wary dog stayed close to him.

"The MS is an awful friggin' nuisance," he announced.

"You have MS?" I said, surprised.

"Yeeeees," he said impatiently. "But there isn't a damn thing we can do about it except take it cool. Live quiet. A big change for me." And he laughed. "Glad you came by."

"My first time. Actually, there might have been a family connection here."

"Oh?"

"My grandmother."

"And what would her name have been?"

"To tell you the truth, I'm not sure."

"I see." He looked away for a while. Then, to break the unexpected silence, he said, "Come on. Let me show you something." And he led me toward the new boat.

He bought the fibreglass hull on the mainland, he said. He and the boy were building the cab, finishing the interior themselves.

"Gonna be like a yacht. Nothing but the best of wood and fittings. Nothing wrong with a little comfort while you work."

Inside the house I met his wife, Jessie. "I know you from church," she said. "You've filled in once or twice for Father Mullins."

"I was telling her how I met you at the harbour that morning," Danny said.

"I guess you're into boats," said Jessie.

"Not really," I said, and laughed.

They'd met in Toronto, where he worked during the sixties. She'd been a secretary. He took hard jobs in warehouses, pick and shovel on construction sites, digging ditches. Thought he'd moved up in the world when he landed work at the Glidden paint factory. Slavery instead. But then he got into the iron-workers' union and started making decent money. Worked on the TD Centre. The CN Tower. A natural-born rigger, they all said. He was fearless in high places. But when he heard there was an old fellow selling out his fishing gear back east, boat and licences, he decided to come home. Bought everything from old Gillis in Hawthorne. His ticket back.

Everything was tickety-boo for more than twenty years. The young fellow's arrival was the icing on the cake. Then, just as things seemed perfect, they turned sour. "Isn't that always the way?" he said.

Jessie left us with our tea and biscuits while he was explaining his illness to me, how he'd felt a sudden loss of energy a few years earlier but regarded it as aging until one morning he woke up and couldn't see.

"Stone blind," he said. "I nearly had a shit hemorrhage, pardon my French. It was in Halifax they gave me the news. It was kind of a relief. The blindness was temporary. The MS was permanent, but it couldn't be as bad as being blind. At least, that's what I thought . . . at the time." He fell silent then, sipping at his tea.

There was a heavy footstep on a stairway leading from the lower part of the house, then the boy loomed. He seemed taller, heavier.

"There you are," his father said. "Pour yourself a cup."

The boy had a ball cap in his hand. "I think I'll go out," he said.

"Okay," his father said. I thought the tone was guarded. "This here's Danny. Danny *Beag*. Meet Father MacAskill."

"Call me Duncan," I said. "It's been a long time since you've been *'beag*.'"

"*Beag* means 'small,'" his father said.

"I know," I said.

"Of course you do," said Danny Ban. "I keep forgetting you're a local yokel."

The boy was anything but small. He shook my hand silently, a coolness in his expression. Interested, but guarded.

"Father is in Creignish," said his father.

"I think I heard your name somewhere before," the boy said. "Weren't you at the university?"

"I was."

"You knew Brendan Bell, I think."

I could feel the rush of colour to my face. "Slightly," I said.

"I'm pretty sure he mentioned you. He was here for a while. I think your name came up. MacAskill. You don't hear it very often. He knew you somehow."

"It's possible."

His face was impossible to read. He turned then, toward his father. "I might be late."

I remember asking, almost robotically: "So, how well did you know Brendan?"

The boy just shrugged and looked away. "Everybody knew Father Brendan."

Then he was gone. I think that I forgot to say goodbye when he was leaving. I had a hard time concentrating because of that other, invisible presence in the room. Brendan Bell. I heard the roar of the truck as it raced away.

The visit withered after that. Outside, groping for a safe place to engage, I asked his father, "When do you expect to get this new boat in the water?"

"We'll get her in before the fall. We'll put a drive on soon. Want to do some tests, make sure she floats even and everything is working proper. Don't want any surprises in the spring."

"And what did you do with the boat I saw you in, when we met that morning on the shore? The *Lady Hawthorne*."

It was a formality, but it sparked a new enthusiasm. "She's for sale," he replied. "Down at the harbour. Great little boat for somebody."

And I may have said something like, I always wanted a boat, since I was a kid hanging around the shore.

And he said: "Really?"

I tried to retreat from his obvious enthusiasm, but he was already remarking how so many old fishing boats are being cleaned up and converted for recreation, and if I was interested he'd be only too happy to make a special arrangement.

Embarrassed, I went into full withdrawal. "Good Lord, I wouldn't know the first thing about a boat, one end from the other."

"You'd be surprised how simple they are," Danny Ban said. "Nothing like a good old wooden boat."

† † †

Brendan was the last of them. That was the bishop's promise, and he kept it. One last small assignment. An easy one, compared to so many of the others. A special favour to the bishop of St. John's. Take this fellow off their hands for a little while, find some useful work for him to do, someplace where he'll stay out of sight and out of trouble.

Port Hood was my idea.

The bishop cautioned: "The fewer people in the know, the less the risk of slip-ups. Just make it look like a favour to Father Mullins and his parish. Charismatic renewal has added to his workload—this will take the pressure off. In any event, Bell is low risk. Seems there was only the one lapse, some drunken groping. At least, that's all they know about. Compared to some of the others over there, Bell is pretty small potatoes, otherwise he'd be in the clink where he belongs. Mostly it's a drinking problem. That's the problem with them all, I'm sure."

"Father Mullins isn't exactly a teetotaller. But he has a low tolerance for excess. In anything. Except for sanctity. And golf, of course."

The bishop grinned his crooked, boyish smile. "Port Hood is a brilliant idea. Mullins makes the perfect nanny."

We both laughed at the image.

And there wasn't a ripple all the time that he was there. I visited. I monitored the situation scrupulously. I admit I had an anxious moment when I heard that Bell had started up a youth group. I hinted to Mullins: "Brendan had a drinking problem in Newfoundland. Let's hope he's being responsible around the young people."

"I'm on the lookout," Mullins promised. "But I don't think there's a thing to worry about. I've never seen him with more than a glass or two of wine at a meal. And the kids just love him. He has a marvellous way about him."

And that was it, not a hint of misbehaviour.

Driving back to Creignish that evening, I re-examined young MacKay's demeanour in my mind. Did I see insinuation in those hazel eyes?

Maybe I was more unnerved by the expression on his father's face when I didn't know the name of my grandmother. It had been a moment of unintended revelation on my part. Not to know your grandma? Around here, most around my age will rattle off four or five generations at the slightest hint of interest. The *sloinneadh* it's called. Part of the dying heritage and, to my mind, no huge loss.

There was a light on in the glebe house when I got home. I had connected a lamp to a timer after Bobby O. said they like to see a sign of life there, like the sanctuary light above the altar. But I did it mostly for myself. Something about darkened houses brings back unwelcome memories.

"You knew Brendan Bell," the boy had said.

Too well, I'd felt like replying. And realized I didn't have to. Those searching eyes could read my mind.

The bay is flat, endless pewter beneath the rising moon. Hypnotic. I'd acquired the bishop's liking for Balvenie. I justified the cost by keeping my consumption low. Sitting in the living room, the amber puddle in the crystal glass, the mind revives the flavour of harsh dark rum in coffee cups.

Maybe it was the rum. Something that induced disclosure. Other than the bishop, Alfonso was the only one who knew why I was in Tegucigalpa. He listened like a child, puzzled, non-judgmental.

This old priest . . . was with a boy?

Yes.

And you are sure of what you saw?

I laughed. The bishop had asked the same question. But he was challenging: How do you know what you saw? You admit the room was dark. What are you? A cat?

I had asked myself that same question, more than once. How could I be sure? I didn't want it to be true. Father Roddie. Dr. Roddie. My mentor, my guru, the giant intellect who took me seriously. But there was no room for doubt. When I met the boy hurrying toward the door, the truth was written on his face.

So that's why you are here. In exile from the truth.

Yes.

I remember Alfonso's bitter laugh.

And you? I asked.

He waved a hand dismissively and reached for the rum bottle.

Same thing, in a funny kind of way, he said. I was trying to do something for innocent people who are getting screwed.

I sip the Balvenie, fighting the sorrow that always rises when I think of him, which lately seems more frequently.

It was a Friday night, late August I recall, soon after my visit to Hawthorne, when somebody knocked on my door. It was young Danny MacKay, wearing a blazer. I could smell the shaving lotion.

I asked him to come in.

"Dad was saying you were thinking about the boat."

I laughed. "That's an overstatement." I offered him a beer. He waved it off.

"I was in the area," he said. "Thought I'd just drop in. The old man was mentioning the boat."

He smiled. He had his mother's eyes, dark and hooded, eyes that belonged to someone twice his age.

"You've got a nice spot here," he said.

"It's all right. A bit too much space for one. It was built at a time when you'd have housekeepers and a lot more visitors than now."

"I like old houses. This is like what I want for myself some-day." He was looking around, studying detail. "The old fella. Dad. He was saying you seemed interested in the old boat . . . and since I was in the area . . ."

"Ah, well," I said, feeling a sudden panic. "I think it would be a bit of a stretch. What do you think?"

"Whatever you think yourself. But if you decided . . . we could work something out." He was already moving away, his nervousness palpable.

"I wouldn't know the first thing about a boat," I said.

"Piece of cake. I could show you."

"I'll let you know," I said, and promptly shoved the notion from my mind.

Driving by Little Harbour one chill October evening, I noted that the *Lady Hawthorne* was still sitting there in the grim light that lingers after the sun has gone. There were already boats on the land, propped upright on empty oil barrels and blocks of timber, blind-eyed, broad-shouldered, hibernating creatures.

There was something irresistible about those silent boats on that evening in October. I still don't know what it was. Maybe it was the memory of that Sunday afternoon in August, the quality of life I saw unfolding on a boat.

That night I telephoned.

I tell myself it was a whim. A few thousand dollars for a hobby. Danny told me that the engine alone was worth about ten thousand. He just wanted to get it off his hands and, at the same time, he was happy that somebody would get some pleasure from it. It would be fun, he said, for himself and the young fellow to help an amateur learn to drive a boat.

"You said it wasn't difficult," I said.

"Nah, it's just a matter of getting used to a couple of things."

"Like what?"

"Nothing complicated. There's no brakes and you're steering from behind. It's like a wheelbarrow."

I told myself it would be like rediscovering the place. The bay was a new world, a potential sanctuary.

"It might be good for the young fellow to get to know you," Danny said.

Don't be so sure, I thought.

I said I'd be happy to pay whatever he asked for. A boat is worth whatever you think you need, he said. Four thousand was plenty. The business took ten minutes.

The next day was sunny and warm. I stood on the wharf studying my acquisition, fondling the ignition key in my jacket pocket. I've been around boats all my life, but now I noticed details I'd never seen before. Ropes tied specifically, the relationship to other boats around her. The sheer bulk. How does it start? How do you get it out of there? More important, how do you get it back inside so limited a space? How do you make the damn thing stop if there are no brakes?

Young Danny was beside me. "Would you like to take her out?"

"Not today," I said quickly. "I have to get back to the house. I have somebody coming."

It wasn't a lie. The young woman on the phone had said she'd like an appointment and I asked if she could come that night. I recognized the name but couldn't put a face to it.

"Any time you feel up to it," Danny said. "But it'll have to be soon. We're getting into another storm season."

"I can hardly wait," I said. And suddenly I believed it.

At home, I made a toasted cheese sandwich and a cup of tea. Opened a can of spaghetti. The supper-hour news was on TV. The world had moved on to new horrors. Bosnia. Rwanda. Palestine, always Palestine. Never anything about the South these days. No more Nicaragua, Guatemala or El Salvador. Never anything about Honduras anymore. The Yanks lost interest, it seems, when the Cold War thawed. All the ugly little proxy wars down there no longer mattered and mysteriously ended. It was just as well. Too many painful memories. Alfonso and his tragic justice mission. And Jacinta. Where was she now? In the months after

I'd returned, I was addicted to the news, anything that might have information on the liberation struggles that had cost my friends so much. And then . . . the news became unbearable too close to home. Boston. Newfoundland. Too many dirty secrets bubbling below the surface, threatening to ooze out into the glare of media exposure. Too many Brendan Bells.

I muted the TV and called Sextus. "You aren't going to believe what I did today."

But he was only mildly surprised. "This makes sense. You and a boat."

I laughed. "I never had anything to do with a boat in my life."

"Oh, I remember when we were kids, you were always around the wharf. Anyway, you need something like that. An escape. If it can't be some old woman, maybe an old boat will do the trick. At least the boat won't talk the ear offa you."

There was a shy knock at seven-thirty. When I opened the door, I recognized immediately a young woman I'd seen in the church each Sunday since I'd arrived. Unusually pious for her age, I'd thought. Her name was Sally. A MacIsaac. She said I knew her father and I agreed, although I didn't. I still have trouble keeping the names and faces straight.

"You're originally from around here, aren't you?"

"Yes and no," I said.

She laughed. "How can it be both?"

"It isn't the same place now. The place I'm from is gone. Buried under all the new stuff."

She seemed satisfied by that.

"So what brings you out on a cold night?" I asked.

She passed a slim hand through her hair and looked away. "I have a boyfriend. He's not from the parish. He wants to get married someday."

"Okay. When did you have in mind?"

"Oh. Not for a couple of years," she said.

"Okay. So . . . is your . . . boyfriend a Catholic?"

"Oh, yes."

"Well then," I said, "I can't imagine any big impediment. You know they insist these days on some premarital instruction. I don't know why. What would I know about marriage?"

We both laughed.

"And anyway, a lot can happen in a couple of years."

"Sure. That's why I wanted to talk now." She was sipping at a cup of tea, fidgeting a bit. I asked her if she wanted more. "No, no," she said, then stared at me for what seemed like a long time.

My face was probably showing the confusion that I felt.

"There's no doubt in my mind," she said, and smiled.

"Okay," I said, waiting.

"But sometimes I'm not sure what he's really thinking . . . or that I know him well enough for . . . for a life."

"How long have you known him?"

"Oh. Forever. All through school. But he's changed in the last couple of years. People say I'm making a mistake."

"What people?"

"My folks. My girlfriends."

"I see."

"I thought maybe I could get some advice from you. I heard what your job was at the university. Dean or something. Maybe you know guys better than I do."

"Everybody changes during their teens," I said.

"I never had another boyfriend, so I can only go by him."

She seemed embarrassed then, and I knew she was sorry she'd come.

"Maybe I'm just making too much of it."

"Look, any time you want to talk, I'm always here. Even if it's just to have a cup of tea. Bring him with you sometime."

"Yes," she said, standing. "They say something happened to him. Some bad experience. It affected him."

"What kind of experience?"

"I don't know. But I thought . . . maybe he'd talk to somebody like you. Somebody he could trust."

"He'd have to make that call."

"Yes."

"I don't suppose I know this fellow?" I said.

"Actually, you do. I think you bought a boat from him today. From his dad, at least."

For a week I'd drive down to the shore and just stare, until I grew conscious of people watching me. Eventually I started the motor, but the thought of untying the ropes and abandoning the land filled me with terror. So I just stood there gunning the diesel engine in ecstasy and fear. There were usually two or three men standing on the far side, watching silently, hands in pockets.

"One of these days," I said as I was leaving.

"For sure," they replied. "No rush." They were smiling.

After about ten days, young Danny called and asked about the boat and I told him I thought everything was fine. Engine seemed to be running well. Everything as it should be.

"You should really take her out for a run," he said. "Charge up the battery. And before you put her away, maybe change the oil. I'll show you how."

"Put her away?"

"For the winter."

"Right."

"Actually, Dad was saying I should give you a few tips on driving her."

"That would probably be wise."

"What are you doing tomorrow?"

I was up early and the day was warm. I took my coffee outside and stood at the top of the driveway looking out over the bay, which was black and seamless for as far as I could see. I noticed a car near the tennis court and walked down.

The woman was in her mid-thirties, trim and I suppose pretty. Honey-brown hair, searching grey eyes, a spray of fading freckles. She was wearing flimsy wind pants and a dark V-neck sweater over a white shirt, and she was bouncing a tennis ball lightly. When she spotted me standing by the tall chain-link fence, she called out a greeting and walked toward me. That's when I remembered her from August. White blouse, playing tennis with the fence.

"I think I've been stood up," she said. "I was expecting some-body. Do you want a game?"

I laughed. "I wouldn't know how."

"It's simple. I hit the ball toward you and you hit it back. If I hit it more often than you do, I win."

She looked familiar. Something about the eyes, but I was sure we'd never met.

"I'm Duncan MacAskill," I said.

"Father MacAskill," she said.

"Call me Duncan."

"In that case, call me Stella."

I laughed. Stella. Stella Maris.

"I know," she said, looking up toward the church. "It's an old joke. Distant cousin of Roger, the old baseball player."

"Stella what, then?"

"Stella Fortune."

I smiled.

"It's a long story," she said, rolling her eyes. And I thought, My God! And went silent for a while.

Finally: "I haven't seen you—"

"No," she said quickly. "The Stella is as close as I get to identifying with the Church lately. The gender thing, I guess. I don't feel . . . welcome."

"That's too bad."

"I'm sure you hear that all the time."

"But you live here."

"Yes," she replied. "Up the mountain road. The new place. I'm surprised you didn't know."

"Should I have known?"

"My tennis partner is a friend of yours, I think. Sextus Gillis."

"Okay."

"We knew each other years ago, in Toronto. Then we met again, in town, at a social for the divorced and separated. The walking wounded."

"He goes to those?"

"We both did. Once. We're both . . . single. At least, he said he was." She laughed.

"I'm fairly sure of that," I said, although I wasn't.

There was another long silence as we looked each other over. The fence between us gave me comfort. I realized that I was out of words and wanted to leave but didn't want to seem abrupt.

"What do people normally call you?" she asked.

"Father. But I'm trying to break that habit."

Her face was full of questions, but she said, "Okay, then. Duncan."

"I'm sure I'll see you around."

"If you're ever up the mountain, drop in for tea."

"I will."

"I'm always there in the evenings and on weekends."

She smiled then, and I could feel the awkwardness that always sends blood rushing into my face.

"By the way," she said, "I think you know my sister."

"Oh?"

"Jessie MacKay, in Hawthorne. Married to Danny. I hear you bought their old boat."

I smiled. "No secrets here, I guess."

"You better believe it."

As I walked up the hill, I heard her car engine starting.

jan. 24. it looks like i'm going to have to stop the spanish lessons. or get another teacher. something in alfonso's manner. i think he suspects something or he's jealous. i'm not sure how to handle it. and, god forgive me, part of me enjoys his speculations.

Young Danny was waiting at the harbour, the engine already running. He released the ropes and shoved us away from the floating dock.

"Okay," he said. "Put her in forward."

I hesitated, shoved the wrong lever. The engine roared, but there was no movement. I imagined crowds at dockside, smirking.

Then he was beside me, hauled the throttle back and shoved the gearshift ahead. The boat moved gently forward. I tried to steer, but she balked momentarily, as if aware of a stranger at the controls. Then she grudgingly swung her bow . . . too far. And we were heading toward the side of someone's large, expensive boat. He gently reached past me again and corrected the wheel then stepped back, arms folded. I was sweating as we moved slowly along the line of docked boats toward what seemed to be an impossibly narrow channel out of the harbour.

"You're doing great," he said.

Once outside, I shoved the throttle forward again and my heart accelerated with the diesel. The boat surged.

"Excellent," he said. Then turned and walked toward the stern and just sat there, looking around.

We sailed toward an island that seemed to be about five miles out. "Henry Island," he called out, pointing. The roar in the cab was deafening. The boat was determined not to follow a straight line, and when she'd veer away from the wind she'd pitch violently against the frothing waves. After about half an hour I turned back. The ride became smoother. Danny took the wheel and I went outside, then climbed toward the bow, clinging to a rail above the cab.

I was startled by the near silence there. The wind was icy and my teeth were chattering. Perhaps to reduce my exposure to the chill I lay flat, head over the side, watching the rush of water. Sluicing, foamy furrows fell away cleanly from the flared bow, the sea opening behind like a ploughed field. I thought I heard a strange, sad murmur, a voice I hadn't heard for years. What are you saying to me?

Approaching the mouth of the harbour, Danny opened a window and shouted up, asking if I wanted to take her in. I shook my head. I'd hardly got her out; I couldn't imagine manoeuvring my way back in and docking. He managed to do everything at once without hurrying. Turned and tucked the boat smoothly alongside the dock, stepped ashore and secured both lines, then turned off the engine. I just watched.

Ashore, my ears were ringing, my face was on fire. I was chilled to the bone, but I just wanted to laugh.

Just before he left, I said, "So you knew Brendan Bell."

He shrugged. "Sort of. Everybody sort of knew him. Where did he eventually end up?"

"I heard that he's in Toronto. I think he's left the priesthood."

We stared at each other for a while. Then he said, "That doesn't surprise me. I always thought he was more cut out for a place like that." He was smiling and it disarmed me.

"Were you in the youth club?"

He nodded.

"So what was your impression of Father Brendan?" I asked.

He shrugged, looked away briefly, then asked me, "What was *your* impression?"

"I hardly knew him. Met him once in Antigonish. A couple of times here, when I'd drop in on Father Mullins."

"Mullins," he said dismissively.

I decided to make a small investment. "Well, Mullins can be a bit of a *calleach*. Do you know what that is?"

He laughed. "An old woman. I suppose so, though for my money he's a bit of an asshole, Mullins."

I felt the sudden heat in my face. "Let's say I didn't hear you say that," I said.

"Let's say I don't give a shit if you did or not."

I had looked away, but I could tell from the tone that he was staring at me still. So I faced him, locked on his eyes, fashioned a chilly smile. This, after all, was my specialty. "Maybe you'll elaborate. Maybe you'll tell me what your problem is . . . with Mullins."

The fire in his eyes flickered then died. And he looked down, cleared his throat and spit. "I shouldn't have said that. I don't really have a problem with Mullins. It probably isn't about Mullins."

"Is it anything you want to talk about?"

"No," he said, too quickly.

"If it isn't about Mullins, who?"

"It doesn't matter," he said, moving away.

"Is it about Brendan Bell?" I asked.

"Who?"

"Brendan Bell."

"Nah," he said, focused on his foot, which was scuffing a rut in the dirt. "Look, I better mosey. I got things to do, and you probably do too."

"Yes."

"We'll go out again before we put her away for the winter, eh?"

"I hope so."

"Look," he said, "I . . ."

But he turned suddenly and walked away.

I sat in the car for a long time before leaving. What is it that attracts the Bells? Priests of old were father figures. What happened?

Bell once told me with confidence: "People will see whatever they need a priest to be. Father, saviour, coach, ombudsman, shrink. Lover, even. Now that people don't really need priests, they don't see us at all."

"You're saying we're obsolete," I said.

"More like invisible."

"So why did you become a priest?"

He shrugged. "Limited career options. Infantile piety. Need to please. Who knows?"

"Or invisibility?"

I thought the jibe would bring him down.

"That too," he said, and smiled.

I wanted to say: I knew a man who became a priest to save the world. His world, at least. His people. A man who thought the priesthood was an agency of justice. I wanted to say it and the moment felt right. But it would have meant devaluing a precious memory. And it would have invited intimacy.

"What about you?" Bell asked.

"I don't know," I said finally.

"I hear you," he said.

"What will you do after this?"

He gave it some thought, then shrugged. I remember we were sitting at Mullins's kitchen table at the time. "Maybe I'll just stay here. I'm getting attached to the people. It feels a lot like home."

And he grinned.

We went out once more that fall, on a grim, grey day. Danny Ban came with us. This time I eased away from the dock and out through the mouth of the harbour without any appearance of uncertainty and without any help. Outside, she pitched and bucked in the quick, choppy waves. And I remembered Alfonso's advice, on horseback for the first time in Honduras. Ride with her, he said. You ride with the horse, not on top of her. Become part of her motion. It was true for the boat too.

I opened the throttle and looked around. Young Danny and his father were standing back near the stern, smiling.

The wind was bitter and the plunging bow sent shivers of freezing water over the cab. The two Dannys moved forward to stand out of the wind and sudden showers, looking back over the stern. Danny Ban was huddled deep into his coat, trembling.

I swung in a large loop and headed back. "It's too cold," I called.

"Cold?" Danny Ban shouted. "You call this cold?"

I let young Danny take the boat back in, and as he tied up, his father asked, "What do you plan to call her?"

"Call who?"

"The boat. He's putting the old name on the new one. Can't have two named the *Lady Hawthorne*. You can call this one anything you want now. After somebody special, maybe. Like your mother." He rubbed his chin, thinking.

Walking by us, young Danny said, "You could always call her *Sinbad*, after the sailor fellow in the fairy story."

"What?"

"You could make it *Sin*, comma, *Bad*." He'd stopped and was smiling slightly.

"That's hilarious," his father said sourly as the boy turned away, now cackling at his own joke. Then, to me: "Give yourself lots of time to think about it. It's an important thing, the name of your boat."

"*Jacinta*," I said, remembering the voice.

"The *Jacinta*? What would that be?"

"Just something that popped into my head. It's Spanish, for a flower."

"Spanish, eh?"

"I worked in Central America for a while. Learned some Spanish."

"Yes. I heard some priests from here did that."

"I think I'll call her the *Jacinta*."

"That'd be different," he said. "The *Jacinta*."

I could feel my face growing warm from speaking the name out loud.

"That's often how the best ideas come," he said. "Just pop into your head like that. Yes, the *Jacinta*. That's a good one." And after a silence: "How are you liking it up there in Creignish, anyway, Father? Must be a change after the university."

"Yes, a big change," I said, still savouring the name I now could safely speak.

"All those young people over at the university. Must be a big change, by yourself in Creignish."

"It was time for a change."

"Look," he said quietly, "you didn't get a chance to talk to the young fella?"

"Not really. He isn't much for talking."

"That's different too. Used to talk the ear offa you. His little joke, before, about naming the boat? *Sinbad?* That's the way he always was. Dizzy jokes and pranks."

"They all change. It's part of growing up."

"Nah. It's more than that. For one thing, you can't get him to darken the door of a church anymore. Christ, he used to be more faithful than I was. Serving on the altar almost every Sunday. Mullins needed somebody, short notice, for a wedding or a funeral, he'd be there like a shot. And when that young Newfoundlander was around . . . Brendan something . . . he was down there all the time."

"Is that so," I said.

"Then—poof—he just quit. Maybe if you talked to him."

"It'll be up to him," I said.

"I know. I know." Then he laughed and, with a large paw on my shoulder, said: "Maybe you'll put a word in for all of us, next time you're talking to the Almighty."

I said I would.

His son called, "Hurry up," and waved.

I shouted up to where he was standing, beside the truck: "I can hardly wait for next summer."

He shouted back: "There'll be lots of summers."

It's one of those memories I cling to now, to rebut those who say it was only a matter of time. He told me himself and I can still hear him: *There'll be lots of summers.* And he was smiling when he said it. He wouldn't have lied. Not to a priest.

{ 6 }

A southeast gale near the end of October stripped the mountain of its colour. Then it was November. The autumn days filled with rain that flattened fields and turned them into mud. The rain washed the hillside clean and now it lay bare, waiting for the snow. Leaves of chocolate and scarlet and lime plastered and clumped in the driveway and on the concrete doorstep of the church. This time of year the country turns to business. Pleasures finished, all the tourists gone. From the altar I asked for suggestions, parish activities that might get people involved. Half the population seems to be on a pension of some kind. Old-age benefits. Early retirement from the mill. People with time to kill, Sextus likes to say, before time kills them.

But there was hardly any response to my request for ideas. Someone mentioned bingo. I declined.

"Maybe we could start something here . . . for the divorced and separated Catholics," Pat suggested.

"If you think we need it."

"Actually," she said, "most people prefer to go to town."

"Things takes time," Bobby O'Brian told me.

Danny called on a Sunday afternoon. "I don't like to bother you, but I think we might need some advice."

"Okay."

"I might be out of line. We really don't know each other all that well . . . You can tell me, straight up, if—"

"What's up?" I asked.

"The young fellow. He's in a bit of trouble."

"Really?"

"I think he went on a twister last night. Was a hockey game at the arena and I guess they celebrated a bit too much afterwards. Went on a rampage with the half-ton truck. Did a fair bit of damage."

"Is he all right?"

He laughed. "Oh, yeah. But his mother is pretty upset. We were wondering if you might put in a word for him."

"A word? With whom?"

"Father Mullins."

Mullins?

Young Danny had driven his truck onto the lawn of the parish church in Port Hood. Spun up the sod, knocked over the sign for the Sunday Mass schedule, and was in the process of destroying the turf in front of the glebe when his wheels sank into the mud. Mullins caught him in the act. Sitting there spinning his wheels insanely. Nearly burned the clutch out of the truck, according to his father.

Mullins was unforgiving, and he had already called the RCMP. He was planning to turn the incident into a big deal.

"You don't know the lad as well as I do," Mullins said wearily when I called. "He's turning into a real nuisance. Maybe a stretch of probation would be good for him. I wouldn't want him in jail or anything. But maybe he needs a bit of time to cool his heels. Frankly, I think the big problem is booze. Maybe even drugs."

I listened carefully, agreeing that there should be consequences. But I thought maybe the stain of a police record might be a bit extreme for property damage.

"Property damage," Mullins huffed. "We're talking parish property here. The church, for God's sake."

I noted the astringent tone. Remembered the word the boy used: *asshole*.

"Well. It's only a lawn."

"The lawn this time. But what next? Next thing you know, they'll be tearing up the tabernacle. You hear about things like that. The vandalism."

I promised then to speak to Danny, maybe persuade him to pay for the damage. Make restitution.

Mullins wasn't impressed, but said he'd think about it and that he'd hold off on the charges for a few days.

"He isn't a bad kid," I said. "I dealt with lots like him at the university."

"You've got a lot to learn," said Mullins. "These aren't university kids. These are the leftovers."

I didn't notice her in the back of the church that Sunday until just before the end, when I was announcing that I wanted the teenagers in the parish to come to the hall for a short meeting the following Wednesday night. I wanted to find out what their interests were. Whether, together, we could cook up some activities that might engage them. Anything but bingo.

We made eye contact and she smiled slightly. When I was standing at the door shaking hands, she approached and I said that I was surprised to see her there and she said she came out of curiosity. Plus she wanted to express her appreciation for what I'd done to help the family. I suppose my face showed some confusion.

"Young Danny," she said. "What you did there was a big help. He isn't really like that. It was out of character."

Then I remembered that she was his aunt. His mother's sister. Stella.

I laughed and said something about everybody being connected to the MacKays, and she replied, "Well, you're from around here, you know how it is. Everybody is more or less related."

"I understand."

"Good luck with the young people. But it's going to be an uphill battle. Unless you can afford a bunch of video machines."

"It can't be that bad."

"Social life revolves around school. The school is in town. That's their community now. This is just where they sleep and eat."

"I want to change that," I said.

"Maybe you shouldn't rule out bingo."

The eyes were twinkling.

"Let me know if I can help," she said.

I watched her walk away, and there was an unselfconscious grace in the way she moved. Getting into her car, she turned, smiled awkwardly and gave a little wave.

Feb. 2. last night jacinta told me she struggles to remind herself that i'm a priest. she was laughing when she said it. i don't know what to think.

Wednesday night I waited in the hall. The coffee pot was gurgling. I'd said eight o'clock, but nobody came. At five past eight I heard a car outside crunching the gravel, but after a minute of silence I heard it drive away. Nothing has changed, I thought, remembering how nobody wants to be first. Nobody wants to seem eager.

By eight-thirty I could smell the coffee burning.

In Honduras they'd come just to listen to the stories of what was happening around them. Looking for hope in the news

Alfonso brought. Ferment in Nicaragua. Rural reform in El Salvador, where he was from. Christian communities, led by the lay people, taking over the work of the priests. Priests taking over the lay responsibility to fight repression, taking on the powerful. Priests in politics. Ordinary people and their priests, finally standing up to the elites, the handful of wealthy families that seemed to own everything. People risking life and limb for justice. Exodus 3, Alfonso kept reminding them. It's all there.

And the Lord said I have surely seen the affliction of my people which are in Egypt, and have heard their cry by reason of their taskmasters . . . I know their sorrows.

Stand up to the Pharaohs, he'd say, and they'd nod carefully. The Lord understands our sorrows. The Lord is on our side. Knowing that the Lord stands with us, everything becomes possible.

Maybe that's the problem, I thought. This place lacks danger. This place is spoiled by comfort and complacency.

At nine I turned off the coffee pot and the lights and left.

Bobby O'Brian told me that I shouldn't lose any sleep about it. That they started losing their young people right after they lost their school. You can't tell them apart from the town kids anymore. Whatever community means in their minds is anybody's guess.

"So I'm told," I said.

The message on my answering machine was from Danny Ban.

"The young fellow has something for you," he said.

They were sitting at the kitchen table. The boy was sullen, staring at his large, rough hands, a shock of hair partly concealing his eyes.

"Get it out," said Danny Ban.

The boy reached into a shirt pocket without lifting his gaze from the table and dropped a cheque in front of me.

I picked it up. "Twelve hundred. Well . . ."

"We got an estimate," said Danny Ban. "That's what it came to."

"You'll give it to Mullins," young Danny said.

"Father Mullins," said his father.

The boy gave a half laugh.

"I think you should give it to him yourself."

He looked at me then, and I realized that what I'd taken for defiance was actually despair. "I'd rather not. I don't want to face him."

"It can't be all that bad," I said. "It'll be good for both of you."

"I don't like him," he said.

His mother looked shocked. "Danny."

I laughed. "You don't have to like him. You just have to hand him a cheque and say you're sorry."

"Sorry?"

"Well, that's what people say after . . . a mistake."

He was shaking his head. "I'm not saying I'm sorry."

"Stubborn," his father said. "Too g.d. proud for his own good."

"Whatever," I said. "What if I go with you?"

He looked at me in surprise and I realized that, no matter how big, he was still a boy.

"What do you think?"

"I can handle it myself," he said.

"Okay."

"But my truck is still in the garage. If you could drive me, it would be a help."

"Sure."

"So when?"

"How about right now?"

He looked at me with dismay on his face.

†††

Driving, we talked about boats and how, by then, most were on the shore, waiting for the winter. And whether there would be a lot of snow this year, and the outlook for fishing in the spring. He was slouched against the passenger door, looking straight ahead, trying to avoid engagement, but I kept talking.

"There's a lot of pessimistic speculation about the fishery."

He laughed bitterly. "Tell me about it!"

"What do you think?" I coaxed.

"They're trying to kill the place," he said finally. "The DFO . . . fisheries officers, supposed to be on our side, trying to close the small wharves. Shutting down the fishery for the small boats. Setting everything up for the big draggers and the big-money people. And the Americans and Germans buying up the land and driving up prices and taxes so a local fella doesn't have a chance. If it wasn't for the old man having a boat and a few licences, I'd be long gone. I'll probably get his house someday. Otherwise . . ."

"You make it sound kind of bleak."

"It is bleak." And after a long silence he proclaimed: "Maybe it's time for a revolution."

Mullins was ungracious. He took the cheque and started to deliver a little homily about personal responsibility, but I gave him a look and he stopped.

"It wasn't about the money," he said, folding the cheque. "I just wanted you to be aware. Okay? We must take responsibility for our choices. I hope you've learned something."

Danny nodded.

†††

"I'm glad that's over with," he said as we drove away.

Driving up the Hawthorne Road, I told him I knew something about the stress of youth. And that he should consider me to be someone he could talk to frankly.

"That would be hard to believe," he said, opening the car door to leave. He was smiling.

"What would be so hard to believe?"

"You and stress. Growing up."

I just laughed.

"I always heard how things were simpler then," he said.

"We had our stresses too," I said, knowing just how lame I sounded.

"I suppose you did." He was staring at me with new interest. "People figure growing up out here in Hawthorne . . . it's all . . . *bonach* and buttermilk."

I wanted to say: I grew up in a place like this. I think I even understand what you're trying to say about Hawthorne. But this wasn't about me.

"A good way of putting it," I said. "The days of *bonach* and buttermilk are long gone."

"Right. Ma and Dad used to live in Toronto and they say they moved back here because it's supposed to be a safe place to bring up kids."

"You don't agree?"

"There are no safe places anymore. If there ever were." He was outside the car then, but he turned and said he was curious about something. "If you don't mind me asking, is it true that you were the guy who put the run on all those queer priests a few years ago?"

"Why would you ask that?"

"I was just curious. I've been following it. What's starting to come out over in Newfoundland and down in the States. Somebody was saying you had something to do with it here."

I looked away, the old tired sadness washing through me. "It isn't something that I can really talk about," I said finally.

"I suppose not. I admire you, though. If it had been me in your place, I'd have been tempted to do a lot worse."

BOOK TWO

††††

Depart from me, all ye workers
of iniquity;
for the Lord hath heard the voice
of my weeping.
PSALMS

Bobby O'Brian reminded me on a Sunday early in December that people would expect a special effort for the Christmas season. A nativity scene. Lights. The whole nine yards. In case I'd forgotten, having spent the recent years at the university, where others worried about such mundane things.

"They still take Christmas serious around here," he said.

The challenge perked me up.

Bobby and his wife were expecting their son home for the holidays. He was in his senior year at university, Bobby said proudly. I vaguely remembered a quiet loner named O'Brian wandering around the campus, or hanging by himself on pub nights when I'd stroll through the melee just to calm things down. Then: Maybe he'll be coming to see you, Bobby warned. Maybe a little heart-to-heart about things. He's trying to decide what to do after this.

"Send him along," I said. "That's what I'm here for."

December 15 the weather forecast, as usual, was imprecise. Only five centimetres, they predicted. Starting around noon. Coming back from town, I saw the first beads of moisture on the windshield. The leaden sky hung low over the breathless bay. The wind whispered as I was carrying the groceries and booze and newspapers from the car to the house, sending a sudden chill deep into my bones. Brace yourself, it said.

Dropping the bags in the kitchen, I glanced at the telephone answering machine and with a surprising twinge of anxiety noted that nobody had called while I was gone. I should be grateful, I told myself. But I couldn't get rid of an odd empty feeling, looking at that unblinking light.

By mid-afternoon, the hill above the house was disappearing behind hurtling waves of snow. A storm gives purpose to my idleness, I thought. Or justifies the lack of purpose. Maybe I should be thinking about a club for retired people. The place is full of pensioners, ever since the mill started cutting down the workforce by handing out redundancy packages. Too many able-bodied people with nothing to do but talk, or think of mischief. I can relate to that. Forget about the youngsters.

Stella, who works with troubled youngsters in the school system, concurred. She'd been showing up at Mass just frequently enough to make some informed observations about what she called the "demographics" of the Sunday mornings here. "Your core constituency is middle-aged or older," she told me. "So work with that."

According to the grapevine, people liked my homilies, which were short and down-to-earth, but were saying that I was remote and unsociable. Other priests would barge into their kitchens, looking for lunch or entertainment shamelessly. Their way of keeping in touch with the flock, she said. Nuisances, in my opinion, but she assured me people love the spontaneity of the unexpected visit. They mean it when they say just drop in. Gone are the days when the arrival of the priest meant trouble—sickness, death, marital distress, demands for money. I should get out more.

"You must know how to play cards," she said. "Auction forty-five, cribbage. If not, I'll teach you. I'm a killer at crib."

Stella, since I'd become involved with her relatives in Hawthorne, had become a regular drop-in at the glebe house.

"People don't seem to need much from a priest," I offered once.

"You'd be surprised." There was mischief in the way she raised her left eyebrow.

I distracted her by asking if she'd seen her nephew Danny lately, and the smile vanished. "That's a whole other story."

I waited for elaboration.

All she said was: "By the way . . . don't make any plans for Christmas Day . . . after everything."

"What's up?"

"Just keep it open."

The darkness thickened outside. Large, ragged snowflakes swirled just beyond the window, streaking tracers flashing past the street light at the end of the driveway. An invisible snow-plough roared past. The electricity failed in the middle of the early evening news.

Sextus had warned me about the winter. It's the one big test, he said. I reminded him that I'd spent more winters here than he had, but he pointed out that a winter living alone in an old house would introduce me to a kind of isolation that would challenge whatever survival assets I thought I had. Maybe even my faith. I assumed he was joking. "You're going to have to get yourself a girlfriend," he said, laughing. "You wouldn't be the first." He assured me that I wouldn't notice the loneliness until probably mid-February. That night with the storm hammering the house, the feeling of vulnerability was overwhelming. And it was only the middle of December.

Is this what drives priests crazy? Is there a link between deviance and isolation? How many deviant ministers do we ever hear about among the Protestants? Effie and Sextus attribute everything to celibacy. Alfonso would have disagreed.

Loneliness, he'd say, is the natural fear of extinction. It's that simple. We are liberated from loneliness by the Resurrection, not by procreation or society. Deviance is a loss of faith.

I remember saying to him: Try explaining that like you really believe it.

He stared at me, half smiling. And you don't, he said. It was not a question.

Today I'd ask him: What of idleness? What about the toxic mixture of idleness and isolation? Is this where deviance begins?

Mullins pretended to be surprised when I told him I was having trouble keeping busy. "Any time you're feeling bored, come on down," he said. "There's lots to do here." His best year was when Brendan Bell was there. "Took the load off in a dozen little ways. Reduced the grind. Be my guest," he said. "Better still, be my curate."

"Did anybody tell you Brendan's out?" I asked. "He's left. Up and got married."

"Doesn't surprise me a bit. Too much of a social animal for this racket, our Brendan Bell."

The truth of the matter, he declared, is that there really isn't much to do anymore unless you work hard to make yourself useful. Especially in a place like Creignish, where there's no school or hospital or jail. No critical mass of misery. So you have to get out among them. Figure out their needs. Boredom is a luxury. "Though I'm not surprised you'd find it quiet there," he said, "considering all the drama you've been involved in."

The lashing snow obliterates the memory of kinder weather. Will there ever be another summer? I tried to picture the *Jacinta*, now high and dry, propped up proudly among her sisters, prow thrust against the harsh north winds. It is a relief to imagine her perched there on the shore, out of the fickle, racing sea. A boat is like a mistress, I imagine. Unpredictable in her moods and physical needs. You never know when she's going to hit you with some new demand for attention or legitimacy. Not that I know much about mistresses. Or women in any capacity. Or boats.

But the name is perfect. *Jacinta*.

feb. 8. fifth sunday after the epiphany. fr. a. talking this evening about growing up. three brothers and four sisters. very poor, working a small piece of land for subsistence. puts my own growing up in perspective. but i want to know more about her. she's a mystery, he says. comes from the mountains in el salvador. he thinks she might have once been married back in their own country. el salvador, the saviour.

I was developing a grudging respect for old Mullins. The isolation didn't bother him. He could see that, maybe, I had too much on my mind. Maybe, he thought, I'm one of those poor fellows who thinks too much. Wallows in regrets. He told me straight out: You have to understand the feelings of a lot of people in the deanery. Those were difficult times for all of us. There are a lot of conflicted feelings about the way things were handled. But I shouldn't take small quibbles personally, about my mysterious connections with the bishop, my mysterious involvement in certain . . . shall we say, disappearances. "You know what they used to call you?" he said.

"Yes," I replied.

He laughed, shaking his head. "You know what I mean, then. But don't worry. It'll all work to your advantage some fine day. Monsignor MacAskill? Nice ring to it, don't you think?"

But what would Mullins have thought if he knew what happened to me just that morning? Walking through the mall, fighting the tide of seasonal hysteria, I noticed a young woman approaching through the mob of shoppers. Our eyes met only briefly. But I knew her right away. She flushed suddenly and looked away and walked quickly by. She had a child by the hand. He was staring back at me as she tugged him onward. I realized I was caught in a kind of paralysis. Just standing there. I walked on, flushed and shaky, no longer sure why I was there. I happened to be near the liquor store, so I went in.

The liquor store clerk seemed to know me, and there was something familiar about his face, too. The name eluded me.

"You grew up out on the Long Stretch, didn't you?"

"Yes, I did."

"I knew the Gillises there. You aren't related to them?"

"No. They were neighbours."

"It's a pretty common name around here, Gillis. One of them just moved home from away."

"Sextus."

"You know him?"

"Yes."

"Quite the cat, that Sextus."

"I suppose."

The woman and the child were waiting as I left, the bag of liquor clinking in my hand.

She had her arms folded tightly across her chest. Her eyes were wide and dry, but her lips were contracted in a small, tight pucker, presumably to keep the lower lip from trembling. Head cocked to one side.

She is no longer pretty, I thought, her features eroded by the life that has happened to her since—what year was it?—just after Honduras. Was it '77 or '78? And then I remembered the priest's name and that I'd never known hers, even then. Life is full of temporary absences, I think I told her.

"When I realized that he wasn't going to come back from where you sent him, I knew I had to give the baby up," she said. "I thought you'd want to know that."

I stared at the little boy.

"That's my sister's," she said. "He's only five." And then: "Did you really think . . . ? For God's sake, my baby would be almost sixteen now." She was staring at me, some of the wildness gone.

"I'm sorry. Time goes by so—"

"That's pathetic," she said.

And then she just turned and walked away, the small boy trotting after her.

Remembered prayers hum in my head in times like these, times of troubled idleness. The absence of external stimulation leaves a vacuum to be filled by memory and imagination. We hear the inner voices when there is no sound but consciousness. I always try to drown them out with prayer. Old remembered formulas, words fused by repetition into rhythmic stanzas, a kind of poetry if nothing else.

The troubled mind drifts like snow, rearranging banks of memory.

What would our father think if he could see the old place now? The kitchen is a sunny yellow. There are oriental carpets on the floor. Effie's old bedroom, just off the kitchen, is now an office. There is a rustic harvest table and a chair. A filing cabinet. Her books and manuscripts, brought in boxes from the city, were piled helter-skelter when she was there last summer.

One day I asked her: What about the ghosts? What about the memories?

"You know as well as I do," she replied with that inquiring smile that lights her face.

"I admire your strength," I said.

"We get strength from resistance. You must know that. Fighting to survive makes us invincible. If, of course, we manage to survive." She touched my cheek. "What's the matter? You look as though you're going to cry."

"Get away with you," I said. "Me cry?"

Wind and frost and moisture on the windows form exquisite patterns like lace, etched crystal ferns with human facial details. The rising storm batters the hypnotic silence, loosening the fragments of a lifetime.

I remember that the bishop's call in 1980 was unexpected. He wanted a meeting, at the palace. It was to discuss an urgent matter of some delicacy. Another pregnant housekeeper, I assumed. Or some fool wanting to get married. There's something unstable about my generation of priests. Maybe it was the liberating notions of John XXIII, the mighty humanist. He opened the doors to the romantics, to people with misty concepts of theology, infused with adolescent impulses about love. My seminary class was crawling with them. Mystical flower children with mixed-up notions about charity and holiness, confusing carnal impulses with altruism. Destined for disaster. You could smell it, but you couldn't do a thing about it. They're the ones who started packing up and leaving in the seventies. Marrying and breeding like the good Catholics they are.

But I knew right away when I arrived at the palace that it was more serious than that. You could see it in the old man's face.

After he told me, I insisted that I had no stomach for what he was talking about or what he wanted me to do. Surely he could remember why he banished me to the Third World.

"God damn it, you weren't banished anywhere," he said, face flushed. "I want you to get off that kick once and for all." He looked away, suddenly self-conscious about swearing.

I just sat and waited. Point made.

The priest in question was a former classmate at Holy Heart. The bishop told me I was the one man he had with the guts to handle this.

"Guts?" I said.

"It's one of the things you can be sure you have. Guts, balls. Call it what you want to."

I'd never heard him speak like this.

"You've got what it takes," he said, jabbing my stomach with his forefinger. "I can spot a strong man a mile away."

"Plus I've got the practical experience. Isn't that what this is all about?"

"I don't know what you're referring to." He seemed to mean it.

"Surely you remember—"

"This is different."

"How—"

"You were wrong that time. Dead, dead wrong. Let's move on. This is an entirely different situation."

"What's different?"

"Some layman has complained. Someone's trying to make trouble."

"Okay," I said wearily. "What is it I'm supposed to do?"

"First, you'll have to get the family onside. Convince them that we're taking it seriously and that appropriate measures will follow. That's mainly what they need to know. That we're going to take decisive action."

"What kind of action?"

"We'll figure that out as we go along. It isn't something for which we have a protocol. And, please God, this isn't something we'll ever have to face again."

I remember asking myself: Does he really believe that? Does he really think that I was wrong?

Canon law is clear, the bishop said. "Keep your eye on the ball."

You have to think of them as strangers, he said before I left his place that night. They'll use anything. Collegiality. The brotherhood of the cloth. Just remember, they're damaged and they're desperate, but you have your job to do.

It must have been the expression in his eyes that reminded me of Calero, the policeman in Honduras. A former soldier, talking about assassination with impressive authority. Smiling softly, but with a terrifying intensity in the eyes. Never hesitate, Calero said. Never make eye contact, like I'm doing now. Say nothing. Walk up quickly. Do it. Drop your weapon. Walk away. You have to close your heart and seal it off from the deed. His eyes were glittering. This will be helpful to know in many situations. Getting rid of a bad employee or a troublesome girlfriend or eliminating a dangerous enemy. Same thing. He smiled.

And I remembered how Alfonso left the room, saying nothing.

"What's wrong with him?" Calero asked.

I shrugged.

He laughed. "It isn't really killing. It's just rescheduling. We all die someday."

The bishop said: "Don't hesitate to use the trappings of authority. Wear everything—black suit, stock and collar. The chasuble if necessary. Hang the crucifix around your neck. Of course, I'm joking. But draw attention to the institution. And don't forget: it's the integrity of the institution that's at stake. Something larger and more important than all or any of us."

One look at the man who met me at the door on that first awkward visit to the family in question instantly convinced me that the bishop's cautions were correct. He was large through the shoulders, big-bellied, a heavy-equipment operator according to the file. Obviously hostile. Anticipating an encounter with another potential pervert, maybe. But in the actual presence of the cloth the lines on his weather-beaten face soon softened and rearranged themselves in a mask of pain and confusion.

"Come in," he said.

The boy was in the living room with his mother, who was smoking a cigarette, her face a mask of contempt.

"When did it happen?" I asked.

His father answered. "It was about five years ago. When he was serving on the altar. We never suspected anything at the time. It only came out recently. At school, with the guidance counsellor."

"How old were you?" I asked the boy directly.

"He was only eleven friggin' years old," the mother said.

"You probably know the guy," the father said. "He'd be about your age."

"Would you be comfortable telling me what happened?" I asked gently, ignoring the parents.

The boy shrugged, blushed slightly.

"Go ahead," the father said, lighting a cigarette.

"He came on to me," the boy said. "We were just sitting there talking about something. Close together like. Then he started talking about sex things. Telling me I shouldn't feel bad about getting . . . you know. And that even priests get them sometimes. And he took my hand to show me and I never thought anything of it. He was a priest, right? Then the first thing I knew he was—"

I could feel a liquid substance stirring in my gut.

The father interrupted. "I always knew there was something funny about that one. The way he always had young fellas around the glebe. Giving them stuff. Lending them the car even. Now I hear he even let them drink."

"Just beer," the boy said.

"He'd offer them liquor," the father said.

"Can you tell me how far this went?" I asked. "He took your hand."

"I'd rather not," the boy said, looking nervously at his father.

"I got him to write it down." The father handed me a thick envelope. "This thing went on for quite a while. It's all here."

"That's good," I said. "I'll read it. We can talk again. In the meantime—"

"He wanted to go to the cops," the father said. "But I put a stop to that. Figured there wouldn't be much point. Cops going after a priest? Not likely, eh. Figured the bishop would be best to handle this."

"You did the right thing," I said.

"I want that bastard in jail," the boy blurted, eyes suddenly full of tears.

"You shut your mouth," his father said quickly. "He's still a priest."

I sat for a long moment, head down, hands clasped before my face. Fighting the embarrassment and nausea. The room was silent. Help me here, I was thinking. Help me find the words and the wisdom to navigate through this. Then I felt the anger swelling within me, imagining the fool who exposed himself and all of us to this potentially lethal awkwardness. And an unexpected wave of resentment directed at the whining adolescent in front of me, dredging up this garbage to deflect God knew what crisis in his own miserable life.

"In the name of the Father, the Son and the Holy Spirit," I said, crossing myself.

Father, mother and son instantly lowered their faces and clasped hands in front of themselves.

"Lord, comfort us in this time of pain and sorrow. And grant us the wisdom to conduct ourselves in a spirit of healing and justice."

We sat like that for a full half minute. I stood then, clutching the damning envelope, and approached the boy, reached out and shook his hand. "I'll read this. It was wise to put it in writing. But you should know that I am in no doubt, no doubt at all, about the truth of what you're telling me. I believe you. The bishop will know of this. Corrective measures will be taken. There really isn't anything the police can contribute at this point, but if that changes, I promise you we will spare no effort to ensure that something like this never happens again."

"I wasn't the only one," the boy said.

"Never mind," said his father. "Father just told us that he's going to deal with it."

"God bless you all," I said, with a brief gesture of benediction.

At the door, the man confided that the boy was going through some difficult times. Doing badly in school. They recently found some pills in his coat pocket. Painkillers, it turned out. Stolen from his grandma, who has brain cancer. They'd always been an open family, talking things through. Figured they'd deal with this head-on. That's when the stories about the priest surfaced.

"I believe him," the father said. "But I think it's all a part of something bigger."

I agreed.

"They're right," I later told the bishop. "I think something major happened."

"I was always leery of that fellow," the bishop said. "Always organizing 'youth' activities away from the parish. Big in sports. What do you think they'll do?"

"I don't think they'll do anything. What about the letter?"

"I'll take care of it. And what about buddy? What should we do about him?"

"You tell me."

"We'll get rid of him," he said.

"How?"

"I'll think of something. You've done your thing for now."

"For now?"

"Best if it's you who breaks the news to him. You're a contemporary, I believe?"

Walking back to campus through the silent town, I was asking myself: How could I not have known? We were in the seminary together. I'd seen him a dozen times since ordination. Was I blind? Or did the priesthood change him? The bishop said he was glad that I was shocked. A good sign, he called it.

I should have asked him: why was it a good thing to be shocked this time? The last time I was shocked, he sent *me* away. And then I remembered what I told the family, about justice. Something about healing and justice.

You debased the word, I told myself. What kind of priest have you become?

"So what's new at church?" my father asked.

A flat question, not mocking. He was holding a cup of tea before his face, elbow on the table. It was when he'd move the cup to his lips I'd see the trembling.

"I talked with Father after Mass."

"Go 'way with you. Not about me, I hope." When he laughed, tea dribbled from the corner of his mouth.

"About after I graduate, next year."

"Ah, yes. You really think you'll graduate?"

"Where in Scotland was my mother from?" I asked, and his face clouded over.

"Who wants to know?"

"I need to know. I need her baptism certificate. And I need to know where you were born and baptized. And when. Plus your parents' names."

He looked away. "So why would the priest be interested in the family tree?" he said, staring out.

"I need to know."

He shrugged. "I got a bible upstairs. They gave it to your mother. When she left home over in the old country. I'll look for it. I think there's a page of names."

"Really?"

"As for me . . ." He laughed. "Well. That might take a bit more work."

"You said you were brought up. Adopted."

He looked at me sharply, as if about to speak. Then looked away. Sipped shakily from the cup, put it down. Began to roll a cigarette.

"So where were you born?" I persisted.

He sighed. "Out back," he said after a long pause.

"Out back where?"

"It doesn't matter."

"What if it does?"

"Why would it?"

"I think I want to be a priest."

"A what?"

"They need to know. There must be records for adoptions."

He laughed. "Records o' what? She gave me up. I never saw her again. I couldn't tell you what she looked like. They used to say, 'He never had a mother. His aunt had him.' Comical, eh? That's what I put up with."

"But—"

"You just tell whoever wants to know it's none of their g.d. business."

"You told me once your mother came from some place called Hawthorne."

"I told you that?" I expected anger, but the eyes were sad.

I just stared.

He stood up, looked away, then headed for the door. Just before he closed it, he turned and said: "You'll never be a priest."

I just stared.

"They don't let sons of bastards in the priesthood."

I asked Alfonso: Why did you become a priest?

Because I'm a coward, he said.

He could see the confusion in my face.

The priesthood was my disguise, he said. My life insurance.

But unfortunately, I had this urge to do something.

What was the alternative?

He laughed.

An AK-47 maybe?

The bishop's words came back: *They're desperate men. They'll use anything.* The policeman in Honduras made it clear: it should be swift and clean. And that was how I did it. I remember how his face lit up when he saw me standing on the doorstep. His old classmate from Holy Heart. I didn't smile. Once inside, I didn't hesitate.

"You're in a lot of trouble."

He wept. The sobs rose in spasms. "It will kill my mother," he said. "All she wanted from her life was to see one of us ordained. I was the youngest of seven. I was her last chance. They slaved and sacrificed to get me through. And now?"

I struggled to keep the Honduran policeman in the forefront of my mind. Don't ever let him engage. Desperation endows great strength to the doomed.

"We were in the sem together—"

I cut him off. "Your mother doesn't have to know. The point is, nobody must know."

"She'll know."

"You should have thought of that years ago. Act like a man for once."

The look was incredulous. Like a man?

"God forgive you," he said.

Forgive *me?*

The bishop was smiling when I reported back. "He can relax about his poor old mother," he said. "We've loaned him to Boston. I figure with the wops and the Irish down there, he'll keep his nose clean if he knows what's good for him."

I remember an unexpected feeling of achievement.

"We have to be careful," the bishop said, draping a collegial arm across my shoulders. "We can't get hung up on the homo part of it. The natural revulsion." He grimaced to emphasize his point. "You have to control your imagination. You have to set your prejudice aside. It has nothing to do with being queer. It'd be the same if they were chasing women. This is about the violation of a sacred vow. It is an act of personal rebellion that challenges the very foundations of the Church by jeopardizing the faith of ordinary people. Scandal, Duncan. This is about scandal. The Holy Mother Church being scandalized by little men. Weak little misfits. We have to root them out. Word of this garbage gets around . . . who knows what the impact might be. You know yourself how you were affected by what you only *thought* you saw. Imagine someone who's been through it for real."

For real?

I laughed. It was a reflexive expression of surprise. He waited for my mood to pass.

The room seemed suddenly small and airless.

"You don't look well," he said.

"I'm fine," I said.

Alfonso told me that he was the first in the family to get beyond grade five.

So was I, I said.

People were amazed, he said. Did I tell you that my father was a half-breed? They all thought that I'd amount to nothing? A half Indian . . . descended from the Pipil.

The what?

The Pipil . . . an ancient community.

A man of the Pipil, I said.

He looked away and sighed. Very original, he said.

Contrite, I said, I can believe it. Nobody thought I'd amount to anything, the way we were. My father was . . . illegitimate. A drunk. They didn't want me, because of him.

He took my hand in his. We're brothers, he said. Really.

They never really wanted either one of us.

"A vocation," Father said, "would be a blessing for the parish. The last one was before my time. Father MacFarlane, I think."

I listened carefully.

"So when you see the bishop, emphasize your own determination. The purity of the call you've heard. Voices even."

I nodded.

"You've heard voices?"

I shook my head.

"It happens sometimes. All the saints heard voices. It's a sure sign of sanctity."

Yes.

"So when you see His Excellency, you'll have to gloss over certain . . . blank spots in the family. On your father's side."

"Yes, Father."

"Emphasize your dedication to the larger family. To your true and Holy Mother Church."

"Yes."

"I'm clear, then?"

"You are."

I told the bishop: "The records were lost in a fire. You understand the way it was. Old wooden churches burning down. It happened all the time in the old days."

Sunshine streamed through the window, wreathed him in a beatific halo. God in Heaven was amused. You could almost hear celestial whispers, but they were saying: Look who wants to be a priest! Listen to him!

His Excellency was nodding. It was our third meeting. He said he was surprised to see me back.

"A fire," he said. "I suppose there is a record of that . . . fire?"

I ignored the question. "In winter, people would bank the stoves the night before a Mass. Something would overheat. Chimneys would catch fire." I shrugged.

He sighed. "It was awful," he murmured. "The destruction, due mostly to carelessness."

I thought: He's buying it.

"Documents for half the older people in the diocese are gone," I said. "I suppose that we could get an affidavit."

"An affidavit, eh? You should go into canon law," he said, half mocking. I took it as encouragement.

I can still see him sitting there, below that glowering crucifix, hands folded on his stomach. Smiling thoughtfully.

He shook himself, as if struggling against boredom. "We normally need some kind of documentation. To prove at least that you're a Catholic. Baptized. Confirmed. It's also nice to know something about the quality of family life. I'm not sure if an affidavit will do the trick. You know what I think of affidavits."

"No."

"One guy lies, the other swears to it."

"You have my baptismal records. My mother died. You have her death certificate. The rest you'll have to take . . . on faith."

He smiled, picked up a document and studied it. "TB," he said, shaking his head. "Awful, the carnage that it caused around here. Like in the Third World, it was. No different."

"She was from Scotland. An island in the Hebrides. I've written to a parish there. But it'll take a while. Anyway, I've heard everybody there is Catholic. Where she came from. I'd like to start next fall."

He didn't seem to be listening. "But you don't know anything about your father's people?"

"Like I said, the records have been lost."

"And he doesn't know?"

"He has shell shock," I said. "Something from the war."

"He met your mother overseas."

"Yes. In England. I was born there, actually."

"Your dad," he said at last. "He was in the CBH?"

I nodded. Yes. The Cape Breton Highlanders.

"Served in Italy?"

"And northwest Europe. Holland."

"Never able to work since the war."

I nodded.

"I was in the North Novies, but I was young. It was near the end. I missed all the action. Never got any closer than Camp Borden. Always regretted that. Missed the biggest event of my age." He sighed. "So you haven't got a clue where your father's folks were from."

"I've heard about a place called Hawthorne. In Port Hood parish."

"MacAskill isn't a very common name around here for a Catholic. That's why I have to ask. There could be . . . impediments. You understand?"

"Of course. You can't just take anyone who comes along."

"Truer words were never spoken," he said.

It was at the end of the fourth visit that he told me: "I'm going to give you the benefit of the doubt. We'll consider your father's genealogy a small . . . lacuna, shall we say. A little blip."

He pronounced it "bleep," the way my father did. And I was suddenly startled by the resemblance between them.

"You won't regret it," I promised.

In the morning, I was wakened by the sound of a machine in the driveway. The storm had ended, probably late at night judging from the snowdrifts in the fields. Through the window I could see Bobby on his tractor, bucket down, biting large holes in the smooth drifts that blocked the road. Moving methodically, attacking the deep white barrier that had briefly offered an excuse for my isolation.

{ 8 }

Christmas takes over the memory temporarily. And memory makes every Christmas bittersweet. Each of the senses stores identical impressions year after year. We hear the same sounds, see the same colours, inhale the same fragrances. The language of Christmas is unchanging, full of false celebration and hysterical goodwill. Personally, I'd rather be in the Third World for Christmas.

"The Third World!" Stella was laughing at me.

She'd telephoned two days earlier. Christmas was going to be in Hawthorne, at Danny's. He wanted us all to come. Including Sextus. They knew each other from their younger days, working in Toronto. He needs the support of friends, I thought. He's struggling with his illness. He's feeling his mortality.

I told Stella that I was expecting my sister home for the holidays.

"Well, bring her too," she said. "I'd love to meet her. Sextus has told me all about her."

I doubt it, I thought. But only said: "I'll let you know."

"I'll get a room ready," I told Effie after she announced her plan.

"Don't go to any bother," she said. "I think I'll stay in town."

I didn't pursue it. I knew what she meant.

"What about Cassie?" I asked. Effie's daughter, my niece.

"She's planning her own holiday. She and some journalist

friends are going to Mexico, I think. Christmas in the heat. I couldn't picture it myself. But that's her choice. So, rather than spend the holiday alone, I just decided. Spur of the moment."

"You'll rent a car, I suppose."

"No. Sextus will meet me at the airport."

Stella said she'd pick me up at five. They were planning dinner for early evening. Her car was warm and softly scented. I thought, Her bedroom probably smells like this. Music murmured from a disc in the car stereo. Something classical, but with a Christmas theme. The darkness thickened as we drove. Soft pools of red and white and green light made a confection of the snow in front of blazing houses. On this unusual day, I thought, we can believe that all is harmony and warmth within those inscrutable dwellings, even if our knowledge tells us otherwise. Beyond Long Point, a fat moon glittered on the swelling bay.

We drove in silence, concentrating on the road, but once, I stole a glance and she was smiling slightly.

Driving up the Hawthorne Road, she said: "I always thought I was a shore person. But there's something special here. The place is named after the American writer, you know."

"I didn't know that."

She was nodding.

"I thought it was the tree," I said. "They say the crown of thorns on Jesus' head came from the hawthorn tree."

"I wouldn't be surprised. The tree of thorns."

And then we were at Danny's.

Sextus was already there, and Effie. He seemed to be the designated bartender and poured a stiff drink, handed it to me. He was casting a salacious eye at Stella.

"You know her, I believe," I said. "From tennis."

"Stella? Oh, yes. The wonderful, impenetrable Stella."

"What do you mean by that?"

"A lady full of mysteries. If you can get around that, you're a better man than I am. She's got a wicked backhand."

He winked. I laughed dismissively.

Waiting for dinner, Danny and Sextus entertained the room with outrageous tales of misbehaviour during their younger days away from here. I watched young Danny for reactions to the exaggerated anecdotes. His face was flushed, smiling in tolerant affection. The look, I thought, of one with stories of his own.

"So you're the new priest in Creignish," said a middle-aged man who was sitting beside me.

"I am," I said, trying to remember a name. William something, I recalled. Stella's cousin who lived with her aunt. He was tall, about my height, with a large stomach, a florid face and watery eyes that suggested a history of heavy drinking.

"Willie Beaton," he said, extending his hand.

I grasped it briefly.

"I get a kick out of the stories they'll be telling," he said, nodding toward Danny Ban. "Quite the performers those two were, if you believe the half of it. Danny Bad, they called him, for good reason."

I just smiled.

"I guess we could all tell a few stories, eh, Father," he said with an insinuating grin.

The room was suddenly too warm.

There was a dreary sameness to the scenes. The rooms all seemed to smell and look alike. Potpourri or carpet cleaner, or both. Pastel colours. Sturdy furniture, probably bought from one of the pay-when-you-feel-like-it merchants shouting out of their oversized TV sets. Swedish wood stoves. Rooms overheated.

Long silences. At first I was confused by the tension, which I finally attributed to embarrassment on the part of what we were calling the victims.

In spite of how much I've learned since then, I still wonder about that word. *Victim.* What does it really represent? Uncertainty? Guilt? Victims of whom? The predator? Their weaker selves? What complex web of circumstances does that prophylactic word conceal?

"That isn't your job," the bishop said. "Circumstances? They're for cops and lawyers. We have to settle these things before that crowd gets involved."

"What if they want money?"

"We'll deal with that if it arises."

"The wife had a doctor's appointment," the man said, handing me a mug of coffee. "She's been on medication since this shit came up."

He sat opposite me, a low table between us. There was a large art book beside a red glass ashtray. You remember the obscure details. They buffer all the odious realities. He was a businessman, the jeans he was wearing looked stiff and new, yet-unwashed. My formal suit, my collar, meant nothing to him now. The circumstances made us equals.

"The boy is in school. I thought we should talk this over man to man."

"Yes. But I should meet him."

"You will. He'll be home in an hour or so. How was the drive down?"

It was a two-hour drive, but it took me three. By then I'd developed an aversion to these trips. I had stopped at a little restaurant and lingered over tea for as long as I could endure the glances and the stares drawn by my black suit, my Roman collar.

"This is hard to talk about," the man said. "But let's cut to the chase. I want that man out of here toot sweet. I don't care where he goes. But I want him out of here. Preferably out of the Church entirely."

"I understand," I said.

"If he was anything but an effing priest, I'd shoot him, if you'll pardon my language." The contempt in his expression was all-inclusive. "I'm gonna tell you right up, straight, and I don't want you to take this personally. But just looking at you sitting there gives me a problem. That's what he's done. That's what he's done to me, for God's sake. I don't even want to think about the young fellow and how he feels." He waved a futile hand in my direction then looked away. "The collar . . . Christ, I was an altar boy myself. That collar meant something. It carried more authority than a badge. Now? I could just . . . rip it off of you."

"If it would help, I'll—"

"No, no. Christ. Don't do that. I'm sorry."

It was by then a familiar story. Devout family. Boys on the altar. Excursions. No suspicions of anything. Then a personality change. The boy seems withdrawn, uncommunicative, showing signs of rebellion. They think it's growing pains at first. Then they find pot or pills and it explains everything for a while. They read how excessive use of cannabis makes them moody, causes school performance to suffer. There is a confrontation. Eventually, the tearful, heart-stopping allegation.

"I imagine it's like getting shot," the father said. "My dad was in the war. Got hit in France, a few days after D-Day. Said you don't feel a thing at first. The pain comes later, gradually."

I said I understood.

"Thank Christ he isn't around for this," he sighed. "Dad was from the old school."

I sipped my coffee, waiting. They have to get it out.

"The thing that gets me is that I used to hear about this kind of stuff and I'd always minimize it. Isolated situation, I'd say. A bad apple in every barrel. Or you'd hear about a case that went on for years. I'd ask myself: How can someone be a victim for years . . . repeatedly? Over and over again. Why don't they stop it? They must, in some way, be complicit. That's what you're thinking. You forget they're only kids, dealing with the ultimate in moral authority." He seemed to pause, to pull back from the brink of bitterness. He shook his head. "Then it happens to yourself. Right in your own family."

"You weren't exactly wrong when you thought it was a matter of 'isolated incidents.' I have to assure you that this—"

"Whoa," he interrupted. His face flushed as he raised a cautionary hand. "We're both grown-ups. Let's not bullshit each other. I've been following what's going on. In Newfoundland. Down in the States. What the Indians are saying about those schools."

He got up then and took my mug to the coffee pot and refilled it. The angry spasm seemed to pass.

"He's such a good boy," he said, shaking his head slowly. "From the day he was born, you just knew that this was one of the special kids. Sweet-natured. Smart. Spiritual in a way you don't see often in little boys."

I could sense the returning outrage.

He lit a cigarette, tapping off the ashes even before they formed. "This was the last thing I expected. You're ready for the little fender-benders and the mood swings and the booze and the pot. I mean, it isn't so long since I was young myself. And we went through it all before, with his older brother. I thought *he* was haywire. I mean the booze thing. Even dope. But nothing like this."

Tactical opportunity. "And where is he now?"

"Who?"

"Your older boy."

"He's at St. Mary's. Maybe you heard of him. On the football team."

"Ah," I said, smiling, insinuating that I knew of him.

"We were going to send this one to St. FX. That's where you are, isn't it?"

I tried to read his face for insinuation, but failed. "Didn't you play football yourself . . . I seem to remember . . . ?"

"Hockey. You have a good memory. I actually tried out for Winnipeg. When the old WHA was going. Got homesick, though. I'm impressed anybody remembers. How's the coffee?"

"Fine," I said.

A healing silence descended for a moment. I presumed his mind was briefly back in Winnipeg.

Eventually I said: "I'd like to hear as much as you care to tell me. And I want you to understand that this is just for the record. We are in no doubt about the truth of what you've already told us. I want you to understand that. Our only concern is the well-being of your son. And of course . . . and this is why I want to talk to him . . . any other possible . . . victims. We have to know the extent of this . . . situation."

I knew that the anger was in check for the moment but that I would have to deal with it again when the time was right. When the tears were ready. Anger is safest when there are tears close by to extinguish it.

"Okay," he said, and breathed deeply. "Jesus, this is hard."

"Let's just pray for a moment. Privately, if you wish. Let's ask for guidance here. And justice. In the end, that's what we want."

He nodded fervently, lowered his head and clasped his hands before his face. In less than a minute he was sobbing.

† † †

When we sat down to Christmas dinner, they asked me to say grace, and after I finished I noticed the William person still smiling at me. The eyes, at least in my imagination now, were full of secret information.

Stella was seated across from me. She winked.

The old lady beside me was William's mother, the aunt. Peggy.

"I imagine you're happy to see the end of Christmas," she said, nudging me. "I always feel sorry for the poor priests at Christmastime."

I smiled. "It isn't as busy as it used to be."

"I suppose not," she said, turning to her plate.

Later, the old lady, Peggy Beaton, nudged me again, leaned close and said: "I suppose you have the Gaelic too."

"The what?" I said, confused.

"Your sister has beautiful Gaelic," she said, nodding toward Effie.

"Oh, yes. No. I'm afraid most of mine is gone. Like everything else." I tried to laugh.

She clucked her tongue in disapproval. "It's like the faith. All watered down now. Or gone altogether. The times we live in, I suppose."

She sighed.

I was shocked by the boy's youth. Or maybe he just looked younger than his years, standing there dwarfed by his father, who brought him into the room, large arm draped over his shoulders.

"This here is Father MacAskill," he said. "The bishop sent him. We've been having a good chat. He wanted to meet you."

The boy was timid. His handshake tentative and soft. "Hello, Father," he said quietly.

The discussion was delicately phrased. The first incident happened during a visit to Halifax for a hockey playoff two years earlier. They stayed in a hotel. Father Al came to his room late. Checking, he said. To make sure the boys were all accounted for. Wouldn't want to lose one of you, he said, joking. Father would make you laugh. But he wouldn't leave. You look miserable, he said. I think you need a hug. It all seemed so normal.

How wrong he was.

And why didn't he speak up sooner?

He had no answer. Just shrugged and looked at his father.

We worked together to sedate the worst of it with clinical evasions. Bum. Penis. Anus. The boy knew those words but didn't know the proper words for the acts in question, so he eventually stumbled and fell silent.

And when he started to sniff, his father lost control.

"God damn it," he cried, bringing his fist down suddenly on the small table in front of me.

"Please, Dad," the boy pleaded.

After dinner, Effie whispered: "I see you and Aunt Peggy hit it off."

"Aunt Peggy?"

"Their aunt, Peggy. I was talking to her."

"Oh, yes. You made a big impression."

"We might even be related," she said brightly. "I had her do her *sloinneadh*. There were some familiar names."

"I wouldn't know," I said. "When did you become an expert on the family tree?"

"Stop it. You're as curious as I am."

"About what?"

"The Gillis connection. Peggy was a Gillis, originally. She thinks our grandma might have been a Gillis."

"I only know of one Gillis connection that seems to matter to you," I said playfully.

She gave me a look of disdain then walked away, arms folded.

Sextus noticed the tension. His eyes said *Whaaat?*

And then insinuating William was standing there with a cup of tea trembling in his hand. He was staring at Effie as she went. "A beautiful lady, your sister is, if you don't mind me saying so."

"Yes, I suppose she is."

"I was listening to herself and Mamma talking *gaidhlig*. It was lovely to hear the two of them."

"You obviously have it yourself," I said.

"Ah, well. *Beagan droch ghaidhlig*, as they used to say. Then of course, they'd say there's no such thing as 'bad Gaelic.' Right?"

"That's what they'd say."

"Your sister says we might be related, in a roundabout way."

"Did she now?"

"She didn't say exactly how. Through your grandmother, I think."

"They say everybody around here is more or less related," I said, and he nodded.

There was a sudden commotion in the kitchen. Loud greetings. And a gush of cheer and chilly air. Then Sextus entered the room to inform us that a fiddler had arrived, one of the new crop of local young musicians making reputations far afield. There was still a childish innocence about him, a warmth that started in the eyes and enriched a toothy smile. Beside him was Danny's girlfriend, Sally. The fiddler, she told me, was her brother, Archie. After introducing us, she walked away in search of Danny.

"I heard about you," said Archie. "I don't get to church as often as I should. I'm on the road a lot. But they say you're giving the place a new lease on life."

I laughed and shrugged. I then noticed his friend, who appeared to be a little older. He told me his name was Donald.

"Donald O'Brian," he said. "You know my father, Bob. In Creignish."

There was something familiar about the adolescent rasp in the voice. From the confessional, perhaps.

"I remember you from campus, but you probably don't remember me," he said. "I live downtown."

I said I remembered him. "Your father is the backbone of the parish," I said.

He smiled broadly. "The old man should have been a priest. Of course . . . where would that leave me?"

We laughed. Where indeed!

And soon Sextus was handing out drinks again and young O'Brian was sitting stiffly at an old upright piano in the living room. The fiddler was on a wooden kitchen chair beside him and the music became a living thing that danced among us.

Afterwards, the old lady, Peggy, asked her son to sing a song. "Come on, Willie. *Gabh oran*. Chust one."

Willie looked sheepish and declined, but Peggy insisted and the room went quiet.

"I'll just sing one, then," he said eventually.

I realized I understood the words. Age reopens forgotten places in the memory, I thought. Then I caught young Danny MacKay staring at me. His posture struck me as aggressive, one elbow propped on his knee, hand cupping the side of his face, the other hand clasping his thigh.

"What did you think of the song?" I asked him afterwards.

He made a derisive gesture.

Then the singer was squatting beside his mother, talking quietly. And she began to struggle to her feet.

Stella moved quickly. "You aren't leaving," she said with exaggerated disapproval.

"It's late," Aunt Peggy said. "And it's starting to snow again. Willie is getting anxious."

"But it isn't late at all," said Stella. "And you're only up the road and it's only a little flurry anyway. I can see the moon."

"No, no," William insisted, already guiding the old lady out of the room, tension in his face.

Near Danny's chair, old Peggy stopped and he stood and gave her a quick, gentle embrace. William stood back, watching silently.

When they were gone, Sextus remarked, "There goes one strong argument against temperance."

I asked what he meant.

"Some other time," he said. "You know his claim to fame?"

"No."

"He's never been across the causeway." He tilted his head, arched his eyebrows in mute disapproval.

"So, how well do you know Stella?" I asked.

"Not nearly well enough. I met her when she first landed in Toronto. You should have seen her then."

She stepped briefly into the kitchen, smiled, went out again.

"Ohhhh, yes," he said. "Then I saw her at a singles thing in town."

"I didn't realize that you were that hard up. Cruising singles functions."

He looked at me with a slight trace of hostility. "By the way, Effie and I are thinking of leaving soon. What about yourself? Maybe you want to wait. Obviously you have your own ride." He nodded in Stella's direction.

"I'll get my coat," I said.

† † †

We held back briefly near the door while Willie and his mother got their coats and boots on. On the way out, the old lady paused, took my hand in hers.

"Be sure to come and visit. I was talking to your sister, Effie. She says maybe we're related. And she said you've got lots of *Gaidhlig* . . ."

I laughed and winked. "We'll see."

I felt a sudden weariness. After months of inactivity, the days before Christmas had become endless hours crouched in the confessional, tedious visits to the housebound. Mass Christmas Eve. Mass at midnight. Two masses that morning. I was aware of a great weight. Anxiety and weariness. Or maybe a yearning.

Stella seemed to read my mind. "You really have to go?"

"I really do."

"Some date you are," she said, and poked my ribs playfully.

The wine, I thought. It's the wine that makes her eyes go green like that.

Then young Danny was in front of me, a drink in his hand. "Can I get you something, Father?"

"No. I'm thinking of sneaking away."

"Hey, it's just getting started."

His warmth seemed genuine now, and it occurred to me that this might be his essence, the basis of his friendship with his father.

"I did something the other day," he said. "I didn't want to bother you. But there was an old tarp in the barn and I used it to cover the back of your boat. Keep the snow out. Snow is bad for the old wooden boats. I didn't think you'd mind."

"No. Thanks," I said.

There seemed to be a struggle behind the slightly amused

expression on his face, something he wanted to say but couldn't find the words for.

"You're kind of different," he said at last, encouraged by his drink. "Not the kind of priest I'm used to."

"That's probably a good thing," I said, perhaps too quickly.

"I'm used to Mullins," he said, and laughed.

"Mullins isn't so bad," I said carefully.

"I suppose. Given half a chance he'd be all right." And he fell silent again, looking at the contents of his glass. "But I don't think a fellow would be able to talk to Mullins . . . about things. You know what I mean?"

I waited for more.

"I tried once. To talk to him. It was a big mistake."

"That's too bad," I murmured.

"You, now. I figure a fellow could talk to yourself about anything. Right?"

"I hope so."

"Maybe one of these days."

"The door is always open," I said.

"Okay, then," he said, suddenly awkward in his manner and movements.

I nodded in the direction of the two musicians, who were chatting quietly, the music finished for the moment. "You'd know those guys pretty well, I suppose."

He just stared. Then he stood up. "I'm kind of old-fashioned. They're a bit too modern for me."

The smile was gone.

"Charity," the bishop said. "I'm wearing holes in the knees of my trousers praying for charity. It's something I've always been short on. I don't mind admitting it. Intellectually, I know things work out. They go away. They'll think things through. Thank the

Almighty for a second chance. Then they'll come back to us, prepared to serve . . . often better priests for the encounter with their weaknesses. Better able to understand the weaknesses of others. Remember Augustine.

"But it's in here," he said, pointing toward his bony chest. "It's in here I have the problem. I have a hard time getting past the dirty details. I have a hard time not judging."

"Maybe," I said carefully, "the judgment is legitimate. Condemnation might be called for. If I had my way, we'd hunker down, hold our noses and let the proper authorities handle them."

The reaction was instantaneous. "The proper . . . *authorities?* You think the cops and the prosecutors are the proper authorities? Have you seen what's been going on in other places? The feeding frenzy . . . all the enemies of Catholicism dropping their phony ecumenical masks, thrilling at the discomfort of the Mother Church. Lay people using every opportunity to play up their own anticlerical agendas at our expense, blathering about celibacy, for God's sake. As if celibacy is at the root of all perversions. You've got to get that thinking out of your head, boy. It's an ugly world out there. We have to handle this ourselves. Keep the enemy out of it."

"I don't disagree. But we can't forget about . . . the . . . other parties. The youngsters."

"Go ahead and say the word," he mocked. "'Victim'? Is that what you're trying to say?"

"Call them what you will. I'm seeing damage there."

He waved a hand dismissively. "They'll get over it. They're young. If it wasn't this, it would be something else. The dope. The cars. The promiscuity. Life is damaging, but never forget the healing power of the Sacraments. The Sacraments mitigate the damage. We can't let a bunch of misfits and complainers undermine the Sacraments."

And I'll admit it now. It made sense to me back then.

† † †

Outside, the night was brightened by the pristine snow, a looming moon and flinty stars. The air was sharp and clear but tinged, I noted, by the spicy tang of marijuana. Effie and Sextus were in the car, waiting, engine running.

I stood for a moment, patting my pockets as if searching for keys. Instinctive subterfuge. Then I looked around.

"You're leaving, Father," said the fiddle player. You could see the glow of the cigarette in his hand.

"I am," I said.

Archie was relaxed, but Donald O'Brian actually looked frightened, hanging back in the shadows.

I considered neutralizing the moment with a disarming acknowledgement of the smoke, but decided against it. Too soon for such familiarity, I thought.

I walked toward the car, snow crunching beneath my feet.

Too modern, Danny had said.

I smiled.

The drive home left me edgy. Sitting alone in the back of the car, I was conscious of a feeling not unlike a childish disappointment. Perhaps, I thought, it's my basic puritanism. People think that I'm straitlaced. Hard line, Effie said.

feb. 20. tonight i touched her face. i couldn't help it. i just placed my palm along her jawbone. her cheek is soft and warm. but i could tell it bothered her. she removed the hand, but held it briefly. and, god forgive me, i'm not sorry.

I knew there was no possibility of sleep. So I poured a strong drink. *A Christmas Carol* was playing on TV, and I realized that

I'd never really watched it all before, so I settled back to see it through. He understood it, I thought. Old Dickens. His insight into Christmas, the unity of past, present and future, the possibility of liberation through generosity.

As Alfonso said repeatedly: the Holy Spirit dwells in all of us, rich and poor alike.

The Ghost of Christmas Past was reminding Scrooge of forgotten happiness when the telephone revived me. It was Effie.

"Just checking in," she said. "I hope I didn't wake you."

"No, no. Is everything okay?"

"Sure. I just felt a little guilty. I was sharp with you before. Then watching you go into that dark house all alone. I should be staying with you."

"Come on. I thrive on solitude."

"Sure. That's what I used to think."

There was a long silence. I could hear slow music in the background.

"Did anybody talk to John today?" I asked.

"We tried to call this morning. To see what he was up to. There was no answer."

"Oh?"

"Sextus thinks there's a lady somewhere. And I hope so. You're both alone too much. It isn't good for you."

I ignored the loaded comment. And we just sat there, at our opposite ends of the ephemeral connection, wondering where to go next.

Finally, she said for the thousandth time that she wished the Church would wise up and allow people like me to find partners, that nobody should be expected to live in emotional isolation without becoming damaged.

"I don't think I'm all that damaged . . . yet," I said.

"If you don't mind me saying so, I couldn't help thinking how . . . natural it seemed, you and Stella arriving there together."

And, unexpectedly, I wanted to hear more. How did we look, arriving there together? Friends? A couple? A scandal in the making?

"Stella? You always were a bit romantic."

"Any time you want to talk."

"We should get some sleep."

"Okay. I just felt like checking in."

"Thanks," I said. "Good night."

feb. 28. i write this in the spirit of penance and humiliation. away from her i can't seem to concentrate on anything else.

{ 9 }

As I recall it now, those gloomy days just after Christmas 1994 revealed the sinister outlines of returning doubt. Eventually there's only so much reassurance to be had from Paul to the Corinthians: "He that is without a wife is solicitous for the things that belong to the Lord, how he may please God." Right. He was saying that if we are undistracted by the needs of women and children, we will be free to spend all our time in homage to the Almighty. And thereby we become a higher form of life. But then the flushed, boozy face of single Willie-what's-his-name from Hawthorne came back to me. How much of his time has he spent pleasing God? From what I've learned, single men like him have been in the forefront of inventing a thousand twisted ways to please themselves. Even single men who have sworn fidelity to our Holy Mother, our apostolic institution. Preying on the vulnerable young is only part of it.

The struggle never ceases . . . the battle between faith and reason.

"Have you never, yourself . . . ever . . . strayed?"

The question was delivered with the confidence of the damned. The man had nothing left to lose. In fact I had liberated him from a pathetic, corrosive, delusional sense of personal security. Before I showed up, he'd actually convinced himself that he'd escaped detection. I put a stop to that. The boy is talking, I told him, and I believe him. This isn't about he-says-you-say. This is about damage control.

His face revealed everything I had to know. He was down, now, to essential instinct. Accuse the accuser, one of their best tactics.

"I'd put money on it. You have your own skeletons," he said.

"That's neither here nor there."

Weak, weak answer. I know it. Pathetic, in a way. But in such circumstances one must not fall into their traps. They want to lure you to a place where there are no certainties and where there are no rules, where struggles are won by nimble creativity.

"You tell me," he persists. "And never mind the weasel evasions. You tell me with a straight face that you never, not even once, felt the heat of temptation. Man, woman, child, beast . . . something, somewhere, must have stirred the most natural impulse in *your* frigid being."

"The point," I replied, "is that we have made a conscious choice."

"Aw, come on," he said, waving an impatient hand.

I bulldozed onward. We were told up front. Explicitly. Choose between the desires of the world and the life of sacrifice and service. Nobody said it would be easy. In fact, we were told it would be hard. You stepped forward . . . accepted the order . . .

"But they didn't tell us how hard," he said.

I tried to read his expression for awareness of the double meaning. He had the eyes of a poker player. I decided to ignore the remark.

"Anyway," I said, "the big issue here isn't canon law. We're talking about the Criminal Code. You could be in a worse spot than you are, standing here in front of me. Just be thankful I'm not a lawyer or a cop. Worse still . . . if his father ever got hold of you. You should be bloody grateful."

He laughed, slapped his forehead theatrically. "Oh, oh. Now I get it. This is a situation that could normally be fixed by a thrashing or, say, a couple of years in Kingston Pen. And you . . . out of your innate compassion are going to spare me that. You're just going to make me disappear. Like a magician. Poof. Oh. Thanks a lot."

I think he realized that he'd gone too far, strayed into the self-pity that always dissolves the integrity of logic.

I just stared at him, letting it all sink in.

"Okay," he said finally. "Let's be real. It isn't like I'm gay or anything. It isn't like I'm queer . . . like this is going to be a long-term problem."

"What the hell has gay got to do with anything?"

"Oh. Mr. Progressive, all of a sudden. Mr. Political Correctness. Come on. It was a stupid mistake. I'm sorry."

"It was a lot of stupid mistakes."

"Gimme a break, for God's sake . . . He was looking for something. I happened to be a bystander. I was going through a bad time, mentally. Who's the victim here?"

"He's a kid, for Christ's sake," I blurted. "He was little more than a child when you first went after him. You exploited him."

"Exploited him? I exploited him? Do you realize how it started? I gave him a hug. So it went from there. But it was consensual. You saw him. He's a man, for the love of God—never mind his age. It started with a hug. I give lots of people hugs when I think they need them. People growing up like I did, not getting the warmth and love they need at home. So it went from there to a hand job. Not everybody is as lucky as you obviously were. Growing up secure . . . being nurtured. Being hugged. Full of moral certainties."

"Fuck you," I said before I had time to recover my control.

He turned his face away, but not before I saw the smile.

† † †

From my living room I can see down the hill, just below the road, to the new hall somebody built to replace the old barn-like wooden structure where we acted out our childish fantasies so long ago, channelling deep yearning and desire into the discipline of dance. Not the simulated copulation that passes for dancing now. The fiddle music drew the passions out and the physical energy of the jigs and reels frightened off the devils. Dancing was for fun.

"Have you ever . . . yourself . . . ever strayed?"

The answer echoes through the memory. I feel the trembling again.

Sextus came to me and said: "See those two girls over there? I've already lined them up."

"So what am I supposed to do?"

"Do? You do what Mother Nature tells you."

Inside the car, her shoulder pressing tightly into my armpit, I felt a bizarre kind of weakness bordering on nausea. I remember thinking, This is supposed to be exciting.

Sextus said, "Expect me to be gone at least an hour. The rest is up to you."

He winked. On the car radio Presley was singing a new song, "Treat Me Like a Fool," as if he didn't mean it.

The girl with Sextus was clutching a blanket like a child and smiling at me. And then they were gone along the shore.

And what if the bastard was right? Celibacy is the problem. Celibacy is unnatural and causes unnatural behaviour. The New Testament is terrifically unhelpful. A few vague references that can be used to argue either way. One of the "clients" actually tried to argue with me. I recall he hauled a book out, as if he'd been expecting my visit: "Reproduction is a primary function, an inalienable right . . . not to be extinguished by any vow." He seemed so certain: trying to extinguish primal needs can lead to mental illness, deviant behaviour at the very least.

I had no reply. Just a folder with his plane ticket, the introduction to the chancellor in Toronto. Directions to a place called Braecrest. Maybe I couldn't reply because part of me agreed with him.

This, I realized, is dangerous.

When we were alone, she leaned close to me, a small, serious face tilted upward, and said, "I hear you're going into the priesthood."

I felt the heat on my cheeks. She smelled of perfume and Juicy Fruit.

"I don't know," I replied, shocked by my false ambivalence. "Where did you hear that?"

She just looked away, distracted by the night, the soft sound of water washing stone, a rattling of gravel.

"What do you want to do?" I asked, meaning with her life.

"Why don't you just kiss me," she said.

I stared at her, thinking, That should be okay. No danger there. And I leaned toward her.

Her name was Barbara.

It all seemed so spontaneous, predetermined as if by some primitive code. The kissing, where to put a hand. Accelerated breathing. Restless, rustling movements, bodies nestling into primal configurations as if programmed by a higher power.

"Barbara," I whispered.

"Hmmmmm," she said.

This is natural, I thought. How everything begins. All life. How the species has endured all the challenges of human history.

It is only right that I should know this from experience. We suppress it at our peril.

But then I heard a gasp that was almost like a sob. And a cool breeze moved between us like a barrier. Then she was sitting up and staring through the car window. I thought she looked confused. The August night was pale blue.

"Did you hear something?" she asked.

"I don't think so," I lied.

She fell silent again, listening. "I guess you're mad at me," she said eventually.

"No, no, no," I replied.

"Everybody thinks . . . automatically . . . that I . . ."

"I don't," I said.

"Yes you do. I know what everybody says about me. That's why you brought us here. What do you think they're doing out there?" She was studying me miserably. "I wish you really were a priest."

"Do you? Really?"

"I could trust you then. I could, at least, talk to you."

The sorrow comes in waves, the way the restless shoreline sighs and rustles long after the passage of a distant vessel. I turn to the bookcase and the old diaries, the silent guardians of my secrets. I take one down. Open to a random page.

april 22. afterwards, she cried and cried and cried. but when i tried to comfort her she told me she was happy. the tears are happiness, she said . . .

There was a knock at the door and Bobby O'Brian called from the kitchen. I went out to meet him. He was standing there with his son, Donald. He handed me a package.

"Fruitcake," he said. "The wife sent it over. The old-fashioned kind, with brandy. Hardly anybody makes it like she does anymore. I think you've met the young fellow here. Donald."

We shook hands again anyway. He was smiling. The nervousness I'd noticed the last time I'd seen him was gone.

"I was wondering," Bobby said, "if you had a few minutes to spare. Something we wanted to discuss with you. Something we need from you."

I told them to follow me to the den.

"You do the talking," Bobby said to his son, who cleared his throat and thrust his hands deep into his pockets.

"I've been doing a lot of thinking," he said. "How I want to spend my life. What I want to do, long term. And I'm pretty convinced . . . that I want to become a priest. To try, anyway."

I was struggling not to seem surprised. I was more accustomed to watching them go, or encouraging them to leave before they became a liability to all of us.

"When did you decide this?"

"It's something I've always had in the back of my mind."

"He's always been different from other kids," Bobby said proudly. "I never encouraged him one way or another. You always dream of something like this, but you know from experience that it isn't something you can influence."

"I'm sure you've thought it through," I said to Donald.

"I have," he said fervently.

"But you must have questions."

"Hundreds. Maybe we can talk again. One on one."

"We can have all the talks you want," I promised.

He needed a letter of introduction for the bishop. I said I'd write one and we all shook hands again.

After they were gone, I sat for a long time staring out over the frozen fields. The dull, chalky day was fading. This time of year you can see the murky darkness rising like sediment, dirtying the daylight. What will I tell this Donald O'Brian? How much will I disclose about the isolation? The struggle against idle speculation, or worse? The pain of personal impotence? The sterility of moral power in the age of secular celebrity? Struggles I didn't know about before becoming a priest, or only in some abstract way that I was able to belittle and defer. Living alone but without privacy. The burden of trust without intimacy. Watching the endless nights rising from the scattered ashes of innumerable solitary days. Struggling with fantasies about the ordinary.

How much should he know of this, or we of him and all his secret challenges?

I poured a drink.

And I remembered Father Roddie, the philosopher, and his words the week before my ordination: Nobody is perfect, not in this life; but we have to show, by example, how to manage imperfections.

But Father Roddie didn't reveal to me the secret weapon for the management of imperfection. I had to learn that for myself. I had to learn about hypocrisy alone.

New Year's Eve, Stella called. Wanted to know my plans for the evening. I laughed. No plans. Tomorrow is Sunday. A workday.

"If you have nothing better to do, you can drop by for a drink," she said.

I said I'd think about it.

New Year's Eve. The end of 1994. After the evening Mass I decided to walk over to Stella's. I considered crossing through the field behind the church but was daunted by the likelihood of snowdrifts. So I took the longer way, along the highway then up the mountain road for about a kilometre. Years ago, in another country, I walked like this, still innocent of the perils that lie in the perceptions of others, walking toward the warmth of hospitality unconscious of any potential for danger there.

She was watching television. She had a glass of wine beside her, but there was also a bottle of Scotch on the cupboard. I poured, irritated finally by the nervousness that always grips me in moments like this. Envying people like Sextus, with all his certainties. I made the drink stronger than I normally would have.

"I expected a party," I said, and immediately regretted it.

"Cheers," she said, raising her glass. "We're it. I hope that doesn't make you nervous."

She was wearing jeans and a bulky turtleneck and her feet were bare. The occasion of sin? We watched the television in silence. During a commercial break she explained that she'd long ago concluded that she hated New Year's parties and all the false cheerfulness.

I agreed.

The program started again.

The tension diminished with my drink.

We spent the evening like that, sitting in big chairs sipping drinks, laughing occasionally at the television. Venturing briefly into large speculations, backing away from areas of potential disagreement. There's a warmth in her house, I thought. A living warmth, partly from the way she's arranged it. The furniture. The light. Rugs. Soft and full.

Could it really be like this? I mustn't spoil it.

"I like your place," I said.

"Thanks."

"There's talk of a new glebe."

"I heard. What do you think?"

"It doesn't matter to me. I probably won't be here long enough to appreciate a new place."

"What do you mean by that?" she said quickly. And I felt oddly thrilled by the anxiety in her voice.

"You know the way it is. Like the army. You keep getting transferred."

"Not necessarily. We expect commitment."

"Since when did the priest's commitment matter to you?" I said playfully.

"Touché," she said, raising her wineglass.

At midnight we toasted the year ahead and for a moment I considered taking her in my arms. In a brotherly way, of course. But I thought better of it. Fear of misunderstanding. It can start with something as simple as a hug.

"Here's to '95 and all it brings."

"All kinds of joy," she said. "I have a good feeling about '95."

Before I left, I mentioned that I'd had a visit from the O'Brians. Bob and Donald.

"Ah," she said. "They went to talk to you."

"Yes. Obviously you know why."

There was a long, deliberate silence as she studied the last of her drink. "Maybe a nightcap?" She smiled.

"I'm okay."

She sighed. "Donald told me, Christmas night, that he was hoping to talk to you. He was nervous."

"Nervous!" I laughed. "I can't imagine why."

"Because you caught him smoking a joint," she said.

"Does he actually think, after all my years at the university, that I'm shocked by the smell of grass?"

"Of course, you realize there's something else," she said.

"Oh? What might that be?"

She studied me for a moment then focused on the wineglass again, tipped it, swirled the contents thoughtfully. "He's probably gay."

I laughed. "What gives you that impression?"

She flushed. "Just a feeling that I get."

"Ah, well. We all have our little challenges."

I can see her still: the way she cocked her head to one side, skeptically, then looked away from me and smiled as if to some invisible third person in the room.

It was time to leave, but I lingered at the door.

"I'm glad you came over," she said. "I enjoyed it . . . the nicest New Year's Eve for years."

"Yes," I said. "For years."

And wanted to say more. But caught her hand briefly then let go, turned away and left.

There was a message on my answering machine. Effie and Sextus. Wishing me the best. Also asking if I'd heard from John.

Sitting alone in my darkened living room, staring out over the black bay with my second large whisky in my hand, I realized that, one day, I'd have to tell them everything. Probably for my own good.

april 29. after mass this morning, a man was asking questions about alfonso. pleasant fellow. well dressed. see him at mass regularly. he attends every day. speaks very good english. says he was once the local representative for coca-cola. talking about how much he admires alfonso, for his homilies on justice. calero, the name. he says he became a police officer. because of the way the country is heading.

In January it becomes impossible to defer the reality of winter and her casual betrayals. You feel that summer and her pretty sister, autumn, have gone perhaps forever. There is that sense of personal abandonment. That's when we turn inward, and hope to find some comfort there.

That was my message January 1, 1995. I thought it was an appropriate reflection on the meaning of Christ's birth and the eternal hope He brought with His arrival among us. The extraordinary promise that gets us through the dark days until the enlightenment of Pentecost and the rebirth of spring. And the promise that one day we will know a summer without end. Et cetera.

Afterwards, young Donald O'Brian told me it was awesome.

Four days into the New Year, Sextus called to tell me that when Effie went back to Toronto after her Christmas break, he was tempted to go with her. "Now I'm sorry I didn't. Got used to having her around. The place isn't the same without her. I can't imagine how you manage there, all alone. It isn't good for any of us. You, me, buddy out at the old place." Then, after a pause: "Speaking of which . . . if you get a chance, maybe you should look in on John. I think he's fallen off the wagon."

There was a polite knock at the door before I had a chance to react. It was young O'Brian. I told Sextus I'd have to call him back.

"I'll be heading back tomorrow," Donald said. "To Antigonish . . . I was wondering . . ."

"Ah, yes. Your timing is spot-on."

I had in fact just written his letter to the bishop. Two brief paragraphs. He was a member of the parish, baptized and confirmed, impeccable academic and moral history, strong family, father active in parish affairs, etc.

I invited him in and asked him to sit.

"When you get back, just call the office. He's expecting you."

"Ah."

He looked surprised.

"When I was in the army," the bishop said, "the people who had it worst were a couple of oddballs who hung around together all the time. Eventually everybody knew about them. You'd never see them doing anything, but you just knew. You could smell the chemistry."

I was, at this point, just listening.

"Funny about that, how you can tell. Some people can spot a misfit a mile away. I always figure there's no harm in them. But you can understand how some people get turned off, hostile even. Those two poor fellows, in the army . . . they had to put up with a lot." He was swirling his drink, suddenly distracted by the disappearing ice cubes in the glass. "A strange, strange place to find them. The army." He chuckled. "Of course, the war was on."

"What about the priesthood? Did you ever expect to run into it in the priesthood?"

"Ahhhhh. I don't like to think about it. It is, statistically, inevitable, I guess. And I suppose, theoretically, it doesn't matter, does it? We're all more or less eunuchs here anyway."

You couldn't tell if he was joking.

"Why are we talking about this, anyway?" He was momentarily confused.

"We were talking about O'Brian. But I'm not sure that I see the connection . . . with those guys in the army."

"Yes. O'Brian. I've seen him," the bishop said. "Playing the piano. Don't you think he seems a bit . . . effeminate? A little light in the loafers, don't you think? Not that it means anything."

"I wouldn't try to read anything into it."

"He's got talent, right enough. Full of music. We could use more of that."

"His father is the heart and soul of the parish."

"That's good. What is it he needs?"

Donald said, "I might as well admit, I'm kind of nervous about all this."

"I wouldn't be too concerned," I said. "There's no crime in changing your mind sometime down the road."

He didn't answer.

"Maybe you told me this, but when did you first get serious about a vocation?"

"It's been in the back of my mind for years. Tell me something. You've been a priest—what, now?"

"Going on twenty-seven years."

"You've seen all kinds of priests. Have you ever seen one that came even close to . . . the ideal?"

"Yes. Just one."

He was waiting, I suppose, for me to elaborate. When I didn't, he said: "That's good. You're lucky."

may 1. alfonso is away. tonight jacinta came to visit for spanish conversation. she didn't realize we were alone. i asked her if she'd stay. i don't know what came over me. she was shocked. i am a childish fool.

† † †

John was sitting at his kitchen table wearing a heavy jacket, staring straight ahead. His face was pale, unshaven, deeply lined, eyes sunk in shadows. He'd aged since the last time I saw him, at the birthday party. He turned his head slowly, seemed to focus. I was standing in the doorway.

"He-hey," he said. The smile was warm. "I was just thinking of having a little shot." There was a package of cigarettes open on the table. "Maybe you'd care to join me."

The careful enunciation and the exaggerated gestures told me he'd already had a shot and more. I just stood there.

"Well, are you going to come in or not?"

"People are worrying," I said.

He stared at me for a moment, then laughed. "Fuckin' A."

I removed my coat. "I'm going to make a pot of tea."

"Be my guest. Or host. Whatever." And he reached for the bottle in the middle of the table. The hand was trembling. Then he farted, long and loud. "Sorry."

"Don't mention it."

"That was the closest the old man could get to humour," he said.

"How long has this been going on?"

"He'd let one rip, then say, 'Better out than your eyeball.' Or, 'Speak again, oh toothless one.'"

"John. How long has this been going on?" I repeated.

The place was fetid, sink full of dirty bowls. He'd obviously been existing on cereal and toast and Scotch.

"Come on," he said. "It's Christmas."

"Christmas was two weeks ago."

"Is that a fact, now." He raised his glass: "Here's to the girls from Toronto . . . they say that they're hard to get onto . . ."

I reached for his hand to take away the glass, but he moved it quickly.

"Don't," he said. And for an instant it was his father sitting there, Sandy Gillis, dark and dangerous.

I turned to the stove to let the moment pass.

"So," John said eventually. "I hear herself was around for Christmas. Faye from Toronto."

"She hasn't been Faye for a long time. And yes. She stayed in town this time."

"I suppose," he said, puffing on a cigarette, "it would take a lot to open the old place this time of year."

"That's not so great for the jogging," I said, nodding toward the smoke.

He laughed, dabbed an ash onto a saucer. "Where do you think that Faye business came from?"

"Just a phase. She was young. Looking for a new identity."

"She's had her share of phases," he said, burping loudly.

"It seems to bother you. Him back in her life. Her coming and going here."

"That? Fuck, no. I'm a perfectly modern man."

The kettle whistled. I walked toward the stove.

"I never thought I'd live to see her back in that old house," he said.

"Where do you keep the tea?"

He waved toward a cupboard door. "She told me things, back when we were . . . young. It was pretty upsetting." He suppressed another belch. "I've done stuff I'm not very proud of. Because of things she told me. Not that I'm blaming her for anything."

"I know what you mean. We all—"

"No you don't. Nobody around here knows dick."

I poured a cup of tea, set it down in front of him. He stared at it as if wondering what it was.

"I'll get over this," he said. "In my own time." Talking to himself, as if I'd gone already. "Wicked how we screw each other up."

Then he dabbed his cigarette in the cup of tea.

{ 11 }

Young Danny MacKay was going downhill, according to reports from Stella.

"You have to talk to him," she said. "His parents are beside themselves. And stress is just about the worst thing possible for his father's MS."

"What's the problem?"

"Mood swings. Acting out. Sudden outbursts of verbal violence, even at home. Rumours of brawls in town."

"Sounds like growing pains."

"They *really* want you to have a talk with him."

"It isn't *really* my place. He's in Mullins's parish."

"Mullins," she scoffed. "Mullins is one of the reasons the Church has become irrelevant to the people who need it most."

"Come on now," I said.

She'd arrive evenings, unannounced, with food. Stay to chat over a drink. And when the chill and the silence that seemed to be essential features of the old glebe got to me, I'd instinctively head to her warm and welcoming house.

"People are probably gossiping," she said once with an easy smile. "You should throw them off by visiting other people too."

"You think that would do it?"

"It wouldn't hurt to try."

The grey eyes were unblinking and I could tell that she was waiting for me to advance the cautious conversation. I smiled.

She looked away. "Poor Danny. Then there's the relationship with Sally. I worry about her and her expectations. Some people lack the capacity for the kind of commitment Sally needs. That's something you can only learn from shared experience. Something we generally learn when it's too late. After failure."

"Was he from here or . . . there? Your failure."

"From there," she said without a pause. "I don't know if you understand that . . . about commitment . . ."

"Indeed I do. Indeed I do." Finally I asked: "Who was he? Your . . . failure."

"Him? Nobody special. A navy guy. I met him in Halifax. He persuaded me to move to Toronto. It's an old story. We saw what we wanted to see. Didn't see the obvious, until it was too late."

I waited, but there was nothing more, it seemed, worth saying. Then she laughed nervously.

"But I feel safe with you," she said.

They showed up unannounced. If Danny was going downhill, you'd never know by looking at him. He seemed poised and confident. Sally was apologetic. They were having a disagreement, Danny explained, and because they both saw me as an approachable type of older person, he said they should just come straight over. He didn't think I'd mind.

"It's kind of like we're half related anyway," he said jovially. "You owning my old boat and all. It's like you're married to my ex, in one of those . . . amicable arrangements you get nowadays. I can come by any time I want . . . to see the kids."

He was laughing now and I suspected he'd been drinking, or was high. I told them to come in. I was pleased to see them, no matter what.

"That's the sort of stuff we were talking about," he said. "Life over the long haul. I figured the way it was heading, we were going to need a referee."

"Oh, come on," Sally said. "Let's not be bothering poor Father. He's got more important things to worry about."

I told them I was boiling water for some tea. They both expressed an interest.

The mood had changed, though, by the time I returned from the kitchen. He was seated by the window with his coat on, staring out over the bay, chewing gently on some gum. She was studying the photos on the mantel. She took down the one from Puerto Castilla.

"Was that you?" she asked.

"Yes. A long time ago."

"And friends of yours?"

"Yes. Another time, another world."

"Oh. Where was it?"

"Honduras. Back in the seventies."

"I didn't know. That must have been amazing."

I shrugged.

"And do you stay in touch?"

"No. I lost track of . . . her." I noticed that my hand was shaking when I pointed, but she seemed entranced by our youthfulness.

"And him?" She was staring at Alfonso. "He's cute. Where did he get to?"

"Well," I said, clearing my throat. "It's kind of a sad story. About him. He passed away."

"My God," she said. "And him so young."

With that, I took the photo from her hand, returned it to the mantel. "He taught me some important lessons. About how to live. One of them is to take full advantage of every moment. Know what you're after. Keep your eye on the ball."

Pure bullshit, I knew, but a way to bring the focus back to them. She was listening intently. Even he, still staring out the window, seemed to be engaged. Unexpected news of death has that effect. Captures attention, if only for a moment. He was slouched deep in the chair, hands thrust into the coat pockets.

"Excuse me while I get the tea," I said.

"So, where were we," I asked, setting down the tray, "before we got sidetracked into ancient history?"

"I don't know," she said. "Coming here was his idea."

He cleared his throat, took his hands out of his pockets. "Not entirely true. Why don't you tell him what we were talking about before you dragged the Church into it?"

There was a heavy silence. You could see the sudden look of betrayal in her eyes.

He stood, walked to the tray, picked up a mug of tea. "You see, I know lots of couples our age who got married and after a year or so all you ever hear is how miserable they are. How they feel trapped . . ."

"That has nothing to do with us . . . and I'm sure Father knows all about it already."

"Maybe so, maybe no," he said. "All I know is that I see what happens to people when they get married and settle down too soon, before they really know what they want—"

"That's just a cop-out," she said. Then she looked at me directly: "What he's really saying is that we should just . . . live together, without getting married."

"Just temporarily," he said. "I'm not talking about civil or whatever it is. I'm just talking about easing into this thing . . . gradually."

"He's talking about shacking up," she said with a sorrowful smile. "Call it what you want. It's shacking up."

"Well," he said, "we wouldn't be the first, now, would we?"

Then they were both staring at me.

"Marriage is all about commitment," I said, searching for originality. When in doubt, ask a question.

"But I'm not sure I understand the problem. You're both so young. Both living at home . . . close enough to see a lot of each other. Any time you want, I gather. If you're in doubt about the big commitment . . . why not . . ." And I allowed a chuckle to finish the thought.

They looked at me blankly.

"Why not just leave things as they are? The status quo isn't exactly . . . hardship, is it?"

They were silent.

"And in any case . . . I thought you two were thinking long-term anyway. That there were no immediate plans for the big step." I shrugged and waited.

Finally she spoke: "Are you going to tell him or am I?"

He was back in the chair, buried in his silence. "There's nothing final," he said at last.

"He wants to go away," she said wearily. "He wants to go out west. And he wants me to go with him. And I say we get married first."

"And I say it would be a recipe for disaster," he said.

"And I say I don't want to live in sin. I don't want to be like everybody else. I want—"

"—to be just like Mom and Dad," he finished mockingly.

"And what's so wrong with that?"

"When did you start thinking about leaving?" I asked.

He waved a hand dismissively.

"It's all he's talked about since Christmas," she said. "Going to Alberta."

I stared at him, waiting.

"You have to consider all the options," he said. "The more I think of it, this place is fu—this place is on the rocks."

"I've been after him to go back to school," she said.

"There's a laugh," he said.

"Maybe it's just idleness," I said. "The new boat is pretty well finished. Right?" He nodded. "Once fishing starts and you get back out there, you'll realize just how far away Alberta is . . . and what you'd lose."

"The new boat was a mistake," he said miserably. "I hear there's even talk of closing down the harbour. Moving everyone to somewhere else."

"Really? Moving where?"

"It's just talk so far. Pig Cove. Murphy's Pond. It doesn't really matter. I've been around long enough to know, when they start talking about something you don't want . . . get ready for it."

"I agree with him on one thing," she said. "If we both went away, it would be too expensive to have two places. We'd never get far enough ahead so we could come back here and start again. Or ever have our own home. We'd be trapped in some strange place."

"And you think staying here and you working at the Wal-Mart and me going broke in the fishery is going to get us launched?"

"I'd rather sell my body than work at Wal-Mart," she declared. Then laughed miserably.

"You can see why we needed a referee," he said.

"I'm afraid you need a wiser one than me," I said.

"Anyway," he said, standing suddenly, "why don't we all sleep on this? Nothing needs deciding right away."

I agreed wholeheartedly, relieved at this unexpected reprieve.

Sally looked broken but got up to follow him.

On their way out, Danny stopped at the mantel and studied the photograph. "So what happened to your friend?"

I shrugged. "It was complicated. Complicated times in a complicated place."

"I've read stuff about that," he said. "He looks like a student."

"He was a priest . . . a heck of a priest. A Jesuit."

"And her?"

"She was . . . I guess . . . a nurse, a dietitian. More like a doctor, under the circumstances."

"I guess there's a pretty interesting story behind that picture."

"Good night," I said.

This one wasn't a priest I knew very well, which made the prospect of my visit a little easier. He met me at the door of the glebe looking slightly dishevelled, showing signs of stress. I could smell alcohol, though it was still morning. Possibly from the night before.

"You know why I'm here," I said when we were seated in his study.

"I could probably guess." He lit a cigarette and toyed with the match, watching it burn until it was almost at his fingers. For a moment I was distracted by the proximity of flame to flesh. He shook the match then and dropped it in an empty glass, sighed and slouched. "I'm aware of gossip."

"I'm afraid it's more than gossip."

"I see."

"But I want to hear your version of events."

"Why bother. I'm sure you've made up your mind already."

So I just waited, which was what I'd learned to do. Somewhere in the distance a fire truck started up a frightening cacophony of sirens and blaring horns.

"You try to do your job proactively," he said, fiddling with the cigarette. "You get bored. You go out of your way to engage with the young people. That's the place to start, isn't it? Maybe get them interested in a little bit more than the crap they watch on TV. Try to involve them in the life of the parish. Help make citizens out of them." He shrugged. "I'm sorry I ever tried."

"You seem to be denying that there was anything improper in your relationships with . . ." I nodded toward the notebook in my hand, but I didn't open it.

"I suppose it's all written down there," he said, staring at the notebook. "All the freaking lies."

"There are five names, each with several specific allegations. I can go through them. But I'm not going to name names unless—"

"You don't have to. I know who they are and I know what they've been saying."

"Okay."

"How much do you know about the five accusers?"

"I know what they're alleging."

He laughed. *Is that all you know?*

"Help me out," I said.

"Do your homework. Look for the common denominator."

"The common denominator?"

"Drugs. A bunch of little potheads. But different from the normal run of bad boys, the boys like I was—from the wrong side of the tracks. Down by the coke ovens. The guys who curse and swear and drink. Those, in your little notebook, are a bunch of little goody-goodies, little fags from Boulderwood who get caught using dope and start to make up lies to cover their tracks. They're *trauma*tized. They make me want to puke. But enough of that. What are you here for?"

"You're denying what they've said?" I flipped open the notebook.

He laughed and shook his head. "How long have you been a priest?"

"What's that got to do with anything?" I replied.

"How come I don't know you?"

I shrugged.

"Of course, I've seen you around and heard all about you. But you're one of the few I don't know personally. Why do you think that is?"

"I think this is a little bit off topic."

"Maybe. But you know, there was a time when we were all more or less on the same team. Brothers, in a way. It had to be that way. We covered for one another. Somebody screwed up and the impulse was to protect the institution. Avoid scandal. We're all human. Some of us slip up. Oh, we've all known Father So-and-So, the piss tank. And the odd guy who's banging some parishioner's wife or swiping money from the missions to cover a little gambling problem. But you never heard of them, outside the sacristy."

"Where's this going?"

"Now it's dog eat dog," he said, lighting another cigarette. "Someone makes a little slip and it's 'call out the troops.' It gets in the papers and it's 'throw buddy to the wolves.' Throw him off the freaking raft to make them go away . . . Can't have them poking around our underwear drawers lest they get stuff on the rest of us. Right? Isn't that the way it is?"

Before I left, I told him the good news. That we'd persuaded the families to drop plans to lodge a formal complaint with the police. The case was closed.

He looked away, managing to hide any feelings of relief. I knew it was an act and struggled to resist grabbing him and pounding his arrogance into pulp. Suppressed memories of my father and Sandy Gillis flooded my mind. Just for a moment I asked myself, Why can't I be like one of them? A man for a change. The way I once, briefly, was. Smash him down. Rejoice over the sight and smell and taste of his blood.

"It's really of no consequence to me," he sighed. "I will say that, in spite of what you might think, I'm relieved that the diocese will be spared a lot of unnecessary scandal and expense. I figured, when this all first arose, that it was about money. A bit of blackmail. I, of course, would have told them where to go, and I hope you would have too."

I interrupted. "*You* will go to Halifax tomorrow, early. *You* will be on a flight to Toronto at nine a.m. *You* will be met at the airport there and taken to a place called Braecrest. It's a treatment centre. If nothing else, it's a chance for you to deal with the booze problem."

"And after that?"

"We'll see." I handed him the package from the travel agency.

He accepted it and stared at it for a moment. "This Braecrest," he said wearily. "Does it by any chance have a golf course?"

It was mid-afternoon when I left him, and the thought of driving back to the university depressed me. The steel plant was still in business then and the reddish plumes hanging above the stacks of the open-hearth furnaces were like a summons. And then I was driving past the Tar Pond, past the sprawling mall on Prince Street and through the shabby streets of Whitney Pier. And though I hadn't been there in many years, it wasn't hard to find. The headstones, darker now from the years of soot and ore dust and airborne acid, more difficult to read.

I knelt, not so much in reverence but to once again examine the fading letters.

CATHERINE MACASKILL
MAY 15, 1920–MAY 24, 1951
Sith do d'anam

"Peace to your soul."

I tried to imagine a face, but there was only darkness, the roar and the clang of the steel mill below me, a thunderous silence within.

Who are you? Who am I? Did he ever, in his moments of intimacy, tell you about himself, his childhood? Did he ever mention Hawthorne?

It was dark when I left. I could have spent the night at Holy Name or Holy Redeemer or St. Anthony Daniel. Any one of half a dozen parishes with their rambling, empty houses. But I knew what my unannounced arrival had come to mean. I knew what my fellow priests would think, seeing me at the door. I could imagine the fleeting look of fear, then wariness. And then the long evening of formality. Or perhaps, after a drink or two, lectures on the wickedness of lay people and the anticlericalism that was surfacing and victimizing all of us. How we should all be covering each other's backs, not making matters worse, feeding the flames of hysteria.

I checked into the Holiday Inn on King's Road. On the way I stopped at the George Street liquor store and bought a bottle of whisky. That night I sat in the darkened motel room watching television until the bottle was gone.

12

It was late April before I encountered young Danny MacKay again. I was at the harbour and they were there, he and his father. Their truck was backed up to the side of the wharf and they were unloading lobster traps. The wind was raw, but the glittering sun was beginning to convey some warmth again and they were working in shirt sleeves.

Young Danny seemed sullen and I attributed his mood to whoever or whatever had caused a conspicuous bruise on his cheekbone.

"We're back for another year," said Danny Ban. "The MS seems to be stalled. Remission, they're saying. For who knows how long?"

"And how are things with you, Danny?" I asked the boy.

"Good," he said, continuing to heft the traps from the truck to the wharf. "Things are going good."

"I haven't seen you around lately. You should drop in some-time you're in the area."

"Maybe," he said. And walked away.

His father and I watched him go in silence.

"He's all right," Danny Ban said eventually. "He turned into a good man in spite of everything."

I waited for elaboration, but there was none coming.

He seemed to be studying the horizon, looking for clues about the weather.

"A fella never knows," he said after a long pause. Then he excused himself and called out to the boy: "I'll be back in an hour."

Young Danny just waved a reply. Danny Ban slammed the truck door and drove away.

I stood for about fifteen minutes, leaning against the fender of my car, trying to ignore the chill. Finally the boy reappeared. He seemed surprised I was still there. He walked over, removing his work gloves slowly, studying the ground. Then he smiled.

"I was thinking afterwards. It must have seemed kind of foolish to you, that evening. Me dithering about something as ordinary as getting married. Making such a big deal of it."

"It's a big step. You're right to think it through."

"There's things you don't know. You aren't the only one with things that can't be talked about."

"Maybe I know more than you think I know."

"Oh, I wouldn't doubt that. But there's a couple of things you don't know. Okay?"

"You're the boss," I said.

He laughed. "I'd never figure you as a priest. When I saw you and Aunt Stella coming in together at Christmas, I would have pegged you for anything but."

"A priest is just another man."

"Some are," he said, then looked away quickly.

"I said before . . . any time you want to talk."

"That picture. You and your friends, the woman and the other priest, wherever it was. I couldn't get that picture out of my head afterwards."

I was at a sudden loss for words.

"There was something in that picture. In the faces. Something powerful there. I couldn't tell you what. But it hit me, just looking at it." He spit on the ground. "Don't ask me what I'm trying to say. But I was thinking afterwards . . . whatever it was I saw in that picture . . . that's what's missing here."

"I could tell you about the picture sometime."

"I'd like to hear the story. Everybody looked so happy in the picture. Maybe that's what I'm missing."

"We should try to get the most out of our happy moments. They never last."

"Right on," he said.

"Danny, if you can't talk to me . . . there must be somebody. Talk to Stella."

"I thought maybe going away would do the trick. I thought maybe getting out of here. A change. But Sally just thinks it's me trying to give her the bounce. Me trying to dump her. You imagine—*me* trying to get rid of *her*."

"I'm glad you didn't leave. It's going to work out."

He looked away again.

I took a deep breath. "You mentioned once . . . work I had to do for the diocese. Involving some priests causing problems. I couldn't talk about it. I still can't. But . . . Brendan Bell . . ."

"I gotta go," he said quickly, and strode off toward the boat.

After Mass on Sunday, Sally hurried by me with her head down as I stood by the door acknowledging my parishioners. I hadn't seen her since the visit.

"Hey there," I called out.

"Oh, hi," she said as if she hadn't noticed me.

"You've been a stranger."

"You know the way the winter is around here. You go out as little as possible."

"I saw your young man the other day. Down at the shore."

"Oh," she replied.

"How are things going there, if you don't mind my asking?"

"They aren't going at all."

I waited for more. It was difficult to read her expression.

"A person can only take so much," she said at last.

Effie arrived in early June. She said she'd be around for a few days of what she called fieldwork. She was writing a book. She wanted to visit the old lady we had met at Christmas. Old Peggy, in Hawthorne. It was mostly just an excuse to come home on someone else's dime, she said. She had a small research grant.

"To research what?" I asked.

"As if he has to ask."

"So where will you be staying?"

"Somewhere warm," she said, smiling. "But I do want to open up the old place and air it out. I brought new curtains. Do you mind?"

"Be my guest," I said.

She thought the kitchen stove was shot. Would I mind if she bought a new one?

"Why don't you come to Hawthorne with me?" she asked.

"I don't think so."

"Come on. She's an old lady. She'd love a visit."

"I can't."

"You can't? Or won't?"

"I'm busy," I said.

Perhaps it was the idleness. The images would come back spontaneously, at unexpected moments. And the self-doubt.

I had him by his throat, hard against the wall. I remember his glasses tilted almost sideways on his face, his thin grey hair all sprung, revealing pink scalp, mouth moving but no sound coming out. The boy was gone. And I was suddenly uncertain. Did I really see a boy? Where am I? Who is he? What am I doing?

Maybe the bishop was correct. What we think we see doesn't always represent reality. The eye is unreliable sometimes.

Once, long ago, I saw a flash of something pale. Perhaps, as Father Roddie told me later, they really were looking for a missing pen behind the desk. A special pen, he said. You could believe it. I wanted to believe it. He had that quality about him, the kind of credibility that comes with utter self-confidence. And he was generous, reviewing what he called my "irrational" response. It is from appearances that scandals hatch, he said. He thanked me and forgave me, even for laying hands on him.

"You've been spending too much time with the existentialists. They'll get you in trouble every time." His eyes were teasing.

"I didn't mean to . . . touch . . . you."

"I'm a country boy. I've been grabbed before, and worse." He laughed. "You have powerful hands, you know. I can only imagine if you had hit me. Whew."

You want it to be true. You find comfort in the eyes, reassurance from the heavy hand that he has laid upon your shoulder, the sombre voice that speaks of collegiality, of character. He has been a mentor. He has been an exemplar. He is what you, in your pious dreaming, wanted to become. Revered, respected by lay and ministry alike. A priest who is also a Man. And thus you are reassured, all too easily. You agree, eventually: some time away will be restorative. And your bishop was prescient: it was in Honduras that your mission first came into focus; you saw, among the poor, the human fate as our Redeemer saw it, etched in lines upon the faces. I could see my mission in their eyes, the hope I represented. The bishop said I'd see the living faith the way it used to be. And he was absolutely right.

But in the darkness of insomnia, when the undisciplined mind revives the furtive images that started everything, there is the one that dominates, and it is unambiguous: the boy's face, livid with disgust, and then transformed to terror when he sees what must be knowledge in my outrage. It is an image that will not go away.

Effie stopped by briefly on her way back to Toronto, her field trip finished. I knew she was troubled, and I knew why.

"How much of Daddy's story do you know?" she asked.

"It depends. I know that his father never had a chance to marry his mother and that he died somewhere. Perhaps in the First World War."

"The people out in Hawthorne treated Daddy's mother like a tramp when she came home pregnant and unmarried. You knew that?"

"It doesn't surprise me."

"They basically sent her away to avoid scandal. The place was well named. Hawthorne. Think of *The Scarlet Letter.* Our grandma was Hester Prynne." She laughed but didn't smile.

"What are we driving at here?" I asked uneasily.

"You know she gave him up. For years he didn't even know her name, for God's sake."

"Why does this stuff matter?"

"Because people matter, their stories matter."

"Getting too wrapped up in 'people' and their stories can be dangerous," I said.

"You bet your boots. But what else is there?"

The expression on her face invited argument. Come on, it said. Roll out your revelations, about eternity and resurrection, life in Paradise.

"So. When will you be home again?" I asked.

There was a knock at my door on a hot Tuesday morning in early July. Hardly anybody knocked by then; they'd usually just walk in, call me from the kitchen. Through the window of the study I could see a small green car parked near the church, a BMW. I went to the door full of curiosity, and it was Brendan Bell.

He was smiling broadly, wearing a T-shirt, shorts and sandals. His face was tight and tanned, his black hair swept back and held secure by a dose of gel. The little ponytail was gone. On his left hand was a shiny wedding ring.

My curiosity passed for a welcome and he came in.

"I was just going to make some coffee," I lied.

He was passing through, he said. His wife had gone out west to visit relatives. This was a chance for him to touch base back in Newfoundland. Going to loop around Cape Breton on the way through. Perhaps stop in Port Hood for a day or so to look up some old acquaintances. "I heard you were here. How is everybody?"

"As usual," I replied.

"Mullins, still the barrel of laughs?"

I laughed with him.

"Actually, old Mullins and I got along fine," he said. "Mercifully, he didn't know about my sordid history. I thank you for that."

And he asked about the MacKays. "The young fellow," he said. "Young Danny. Junior, the kids called him. I really liked him. He'd be around the hall when the young people would get together. They'd come for evenings and we'd play music or watch videos or just hang out. That was the highlight of my stay. I thought maybe I'd look some of them up."

I replied that they were all more or less still around. Not much has changed.

"Great," he said, and finished his coffee. "I'd heard on the grapevine that you were here doing a spell of parish work. How do you like it?"

"A big change from the university."

His eyes moved restlessly around my shabby kitchen. The small silences grew larger.

"You asked about Danny MacKay," I said at last. "I guess you got to know him pretty well."

"Obviously I knew him. He kind of stands out." His face seemed troubled.

"He's going through some difficulties. He has plans to get married. A lovely girl from here. But the prospect seems to have precipitated a kind of . . . crisis."

"That's a shame. I found him kind of . . . deep. Compared to the others. Marriage is a big deal."

And there was another silence.

"Marriage seems to suit you well," I said, smiling.

He nodded, studying the coffee mug, then turned his gaze toward the window. "My God," he said at last. "I was admiring the view from here. I'd say you've scored the perfect job."

I agreed.

"There's a part of me that envies you," he said, "that questions the whole decision to leave. I guess they were right in saying 'Once a priest, always a priest.'"

And he said that one day he'd love to have a longer chat about things. The mind races, seeking openings, and finds only barriers. He got up to leave and I followed him toward the door.

"Maybe I'll add a day to the trip," he mused. "Call in on the way back. Maybe you'd put me up for a night. There are things I could probably talk about now that I didn't really have the stomach to go into when I was here before. You know what I mean?"

"I think so," I said, relieved that the reckoning was postponed.

"Anyway. That's for another day."

But he stood there for a long silent moment.

How do we judge? Handsome face, sincerity in the eyes, a deep intelligence crafting sentences out of surprising perceptions and ideas and humour. All the outward signs of integrity. Yet these are also the gifts of the actor, the con artist, the survivor. I knew from my experience the cunning of damaged people. There's a palpable uneasiness about him, I thought as I walked beside him to his car. And for a moment I considered stopping him. Hell, let's have a drink. It's afternoon somewhere. Let's talk. And I'll tell you about Alfonso, who was the kind of priest we all should be. And about Jacinta and my own brush with human weakness. And about my campaign to purify our Holy Mother Church by burying your kind in what I hoped would be impotent obscurity. And, in return, you can do what none before have done. Explain.

The little car drove down the lane and turned north.

Alfonso and Jacinta are more startled than anything else when I find them in the kitchen. I've interrupted the weeping.

I'm sorry, I say.

She rushes out, brushing past me as she leaves. He and I face each other across the tiny room. Then he smiles. Puts a forefinger to his lips, shakes his head.

Shhh.

Sextus phoned on a Thursday morning. It was, already, a hot, still day. The bay was flat. "I thought you'd be on the water," he said gaily. "I'll be there in twenty minutes."

I sat out on the deck. The heat was intense. A car turned up the lane. It was Stella. She was wearing a denim smock with metal buttons up the front. The top and bottom buttons were undone.

"I'm on my way to the beach," she said. "You should come."

She was bare-legged, wearing sandals, hair tied back, a lock of hair uncaptured near her ear.

"I'd love to," I said. And meant it. She smiled at me.

I offered coffee. She declined. Said she'd stopped in on business.

"What kind of business?"

She wanted to book the hall for Saturday night a week later. A little celebration for young Donald O'Brian, to raise some money for his studies at the seminary in Scarborough. "Obviously, you'll have to be there," she said.

I said I'd make a note of it.

She was hardly gone when Sextus arrived with a cooler full of beer. The sun was high and heavy. It was near noon.

"Days like this a fella can get depressed about all the years he pissed away in Ontari-ari-ari-o," he declared, stretching, arms high above his head.

Below us, the dark expanse of water throbbed softly, a distant yacht moved slowly southward.

"Let's get out there," he said.

Young Danny MacKay was standing at the stern of the *Lady Hawthorne* with a large hose, sluicing the deck. His face seemed grim, but when he noticed us he smiled, turned off the water. Sextus handed him a beer.

"It'll be nice on the island just now," he said.

"I haven't learned yet how to manoeuvre in there," I said.

"A piece of cake," Danny said.

The *Jacinta* sliced cleanly through the still water and all reality slipped away. The vestments hanging in the sacristy, the empty confessional, the crumbling glebe, strangers' expectations, deep, impossible questions about purpose and potential. Danny and Sextus were standing aft, beers in hand, laughing at some shared observation.

In the corner of the cab window, a horsefly struggled in a cobweb. The spider sat at the edge of his trap, watching. What does it take to extinguish the instinct to survive? Despair? Finally, perhaps, a deep understanding of futility.

I looked back toward the stern. Sextus and Danny were talking seriously, the warm breeze ruffling their hair. Sextus noticed me and waved. I turned back to the cobweb just as the spider wrapped his body around the struggling fly. The struggle ceased.

Sextus stood beside me then. "Let me steer for a while."

I stepped aside.

A distant beach was crowded with sand-coloured bodies. Danny was staring toward them, arms folded. Stella is among them, I thought, the denim smock and sandals discarded. Danny seemed to be waiting for something.

"Everything okay?"

He shrugged and smiled. No complaints.

"You seem troubled," I said, and slapped his shoulder. "You're sure everything's okay?"

"Isn't everybody troubled? One way or another?"

"One way or another," I replied.

"I bet you've got your own troubles, eh, Father?"

I laughed. Turned my attention back toward the beach. "Do you swim?" I asked.

He shook his head.

We stood in silence for a while.

"I saw a friend of yours the other day," I said.

"Oh?"

"Brendan Bell."

"I heard he was around."

"He seems prosperous. Driving a BMW. You know he's changed jobs?"

"I heard something." He drank from the bottle, his face expressionless.

A creeping uneasiness intruded like a cloud.

"We're almost there," he said. Pointing toward the light that sits just off the island breakwater. You couldn't see an entrance.

"I've never had the nerve to go in there."

We returned to the wheel and he gave instructions. Heart pounding, I tucked between two small speedboats, vulnerable as eggshells.

A profound feeling of achievement put all the large questions to rest.

Another beer to celebrate?

What, I asked myself, am I worrying about? He's fine. Just going through the usual stress of young adulthood.

"There's a little church up there," he said, pointing. "Real peaceful. It's from back when the island was a real community. Nothing here now but summer people. Americans. They hate it when locals like us come out. Disturbs their fantasies. But the church is kinda special."

"There's hope for you yet," I said.

He laughed. "The whole place will be like this someday," he said.

"Like what?"

"Like Port Hood Island. A summer resort for people from away. A few of us locals hanging on by our fingernails. Workin' for the foreigners."

"Never," I said. "You'd never let it come to that."

He stared at me almost mockingly, but he said nothing more.

On the way back, I heard a startling clatter on the roof. Sextus told me later that Danny was dancing up there, a strange jig to the rhythm of his workboots. Very weird, Sextus thought.

"I think the kid is cracking up."

"He's fine," I said. "People should just leave him alone."

On the Saturday evening of O'Brian's celebration the bay was dark and still as the sun settled. Mass at seven was crowded, cars and half-tons lining the lane and the parking spaces around the hall. I walked down the hill toward the hall at a quarter to nine, respectably tardy. I was to give a little speech, a formal send-off, and present Donald with a cheque from the parish. The sound of music grew louder as I approached and the babble of voices rose. Stella had arranged a liquor licence. An amplified violin screamed from a tinny speaker. A group of men stood near the door smoking. Among them I noticed young Danny MacKay. As I walked by, I attempted eye contact, but he looked away.

Inside, Stella asked, "Did you see who's here?"

"Danny?"

"Yes. I think they're here together. It's a good sign." She nodded toward Sally, who was selling tickets for the bar.

I try to remember the details now, imagining there was an odd discordance in the tunes, a certain sinister expression on familiar faces.

The young fiddler named Archie was on the stage, his cheek and ear close to the instrument, as if straining to hear each note above the background babble of conversation and laughter, his right knee jerking up and down, his foot pounding heavily on the floor. The guest of honour, Donald O'Brian, was intently hammering the piano, his proud parents standing near the stage accepting homage from their neighbours. Stocky men in shirt sleeves stood with plastic glasses, faces red, brows beaded with perspiration, their beefy wives busy at a long food table. Danny Ban was among them, leaning on a cane, sweat staining his crisp white shirt.

I caught sight of his son again, Sally speaking close to his ear, but I couldn't see her expression. He stood, hands in pockets, face tilted downward, nodding. They will have handsome children, I thought, but the notion dissolved quickly in the anxiety that always grips me in crowds.

The music stopped. I called young Donald from the stage, walked him slowly toward the centre of the floor, a fraternal arm draped across his shoulders, and I made my short speech. They laughed at anecdotes about my time at the seminary. Stories about young men who pushed the boundaries of tradition and discipline while I surrendered blindly to orthodoxy. Something I advised young Donald to avoid. Don't make my mistakes. Have some fun. I made safe jokes and imagined that the laughter was, in part, surprise. Listen! He can make us laugh! I had planned to close with some thoughts about humility and ordination and the joys and struggles of priesthood, but decided to end my little talk with a toast to the new seminarian. Everybody cheered and I saw Stella coming toward me with two plastic glasses.

I accepted one, raised it among the others, realizing that she was still there beside me and that we probably looked a lot like the other couples except for my clothes, black suit, stock and collar. Man and woman standing together among other men and women.

Donald thanked me when I presented the envelope. He told them that he only hoped he could live up to their expectations and asked for their prayers to help him in the struggles ahead.

Amen, I thought.

And when he finished, he turned and nodded and I imagined that there was, in the momentary glance that passed between us, a transfer of knowledge and understanding, and maybe even trust.

I turned to find Archie, the young fiddle player, standing nearby, arms folded. I winked and he picked up the instrument by the neck and plucked at a string with his thumb, a signal for the celebration to resume.

Beyond that clear moment my memory is imprecise. It seems I was alone, leaning comfortably against a wall. The drink I held was almost superfluous because I realized that I was already high on the music and the weather and a surprising sense, perhaps for the first time, that I belonged there. That life, thanks to these good people, and maybe for the first time since Honduras, had a purpose. In that moment I composed, in my imagination, a brief note to the bishop, thanking him for this assignment.

I closed my eyes briefly and let the music wash past. Is this how it is supposed to be?

There was a pause in the music. Someone replaced Donald at the piano and he was walking in my general direction, smiling. Then he stopped to speak to Sally. Her eyes were animated. She was nodding. He held her hand and they began moving toward the centre of the floor, presumably to dance.

Suddenly Danny was standing there with them. In retrospect, I'm sure I was the only one conscious of the tension. Some deep defensive instinct flashed a warning and I moved toward them.

Danny's hand was gripping Donald's arm. He was smiling.

I heard " . . . another fucking faggot . . ."

"Danny," I said, perhaps more sharply than I intended, and caught him by the wrist.

I never saw the move. I only know there was an instant loss of light. A blackness full of tiny flashes filled my skull. No feeling.

Then I could see his face near mine, unnaturally flushed, eyes bulging. But there seemed to be a sinewed, hairy arm across his throat, and his hands were clutching at it. And then another face, and it was speaking silent words in Danny's ear. And I could have sworn that it was Sandy Gillis. I tried reaching out. Sandy? But then they were all gone again into a speckled darkness.

My father is speaking now: Go ahead. Take your best shot. See what kind of a man you are.

Sandy Gillis is studying the barn floor, silently.

Come on, my father says, emboldened by his silence. God damn you. Let's settle it right here.

And then he's on his knees, head hanging, blood dripping, Sandy Gillis standing over him, saying nothing, arms hanging by his side.

I never saw it happen, only heard the sickening whack.

Stella was kneeling beside me, a look of horror on her face. Danny Ban was holding his son from behind in a tight embrace, struggling in a knot of people stumbling toward the open door. Young Danny suddenly stopped resisting and they walked out together. Sally ran after them, carrying the cane.

Stella pressed a towel-wrapped ice pack against my forehead, just above and to the right of my eye, where the flesh had become thick and tender. Something, perhaps the ice, sent deep cold probes into my brain. I took the pack away. Stella's face was grey, with a slightly yellow tinge. I looked around, desperately scanning faces. Sandy Gillis? Did I see dead Sandy Gillis? Was I dreaming? Then I saw young O'Brian hovering nearby, his face pale.

"That was a bit extreme," he said, vainly attempting to smile, but I could feel the disapproval in his tone.

"Really?" I said.

"You people didn't have to get involved. It wasn't necessary. I could have handled it."

"What people?"

"You and that other fellow."

"What other fellow?"

"It was my problem . . . you didn't have to . . ."

"Maybe we can talk about this another time."

"Right," he said.

"I can only guess what that was about," Stella said.

The Gospel the next morning was the tale of the Pharisee and the publican who went to the temple to pray. The Pharisee thanks God for his virtue and his piety. The poor publican is too ashamed of himself to do anything but ask for mercy. It seemed to fit the moment.

It was a small crowd. Near the back, big Danny Ban and his son were standing conspicuously, arms folded, watching me intently. The boy looked miserable and angry, as big and broad as his father now, I noted with my one good eye.

I considered breaking the rules and skipping the homily altogether, but looking at them in the back I realized they were waiting to hear something remotely relevant. I stared at them for a while, conscious mostly of the throbbing in my temple. No words came, so I just walked back to the altar and resumed the function that came automatically, without reflection.

"I believe in one God . . ."

At the door after almost everyone was gone, Danny Ban approached me. "The young fella has something to say."

"Sure," I said.

Young Danny hung back, arms folded, studying the ground.

"How are you?" I asked.

"All right." His voice was hoarse. There was a conspicuous redness on his throat. Then he raised his gaze to confront my face. The pain in his was unmistakable.

The words rose in me. "Let's just put it behind us."

"I didn't mean for that," he said.

His father's voice was unexpectedly harsh. "We didn't come up here for you to say that. We came up here for you to say what you have to say."

"I'm sorry," he said softly.

"I'm sorry too," I said.

He seemed surprised.

"No, dammit," said his father. "You got nothing to feel sorry for. I told him he was lucky we live when we do. Not so long ago he'd probably be excommunicated by now. Or worse. The hand rotting off of him with gangrene."

"I wouldn't worry about that," I said.

There was a long silence.

"I understand," I said finally. "I understand, and I don't need apologies. But there's a young fellow who probably doesn't understand."

Young Danny was shaking his head. "No. I'm not going to."

"If you really want this thing closed off," I said, "I suggest you go over to O'Brians' place right now. That's where you have some tidying up to do."

"I can't."

I looked at his father, appealing.

"I don't know anything about that," he said, raising a hand and looking away. "Hittin' a priest is one thing. The other thing is between themselves."

Their expressions were identical. Eyes steady, mouths thin, firm lines.

"Then there's nothing left to talk about," I said.

13

I think of Mullins often. For priests like him and others I
could name, the Gospels are rich with insights to be
applied to the human condition. They even find logic in
the superstition. They can trace a clear path through all the
infantile promises of literal salvation and arrive at an objective
truth that they carry in their pockets like a smooth, warm stone.
What is it about them?

Why, really, did I become a priest? The answer smacks me in
the face: I needed an out. I needed an escape.

Early the next week a young Mountie came by and told me
that I should consider laying a charge of assault. "Young MacKay
is a menace to himself and others," he said. "Maybe he needs a
wake-up call." I figured the policeman was no more than a few
years older than Danny.

"I think he knows what he's done," I said. "He's going
through a phase. We all do." I smiled, doubting that the young
man before me had ever known but one long proper phase.

He spoke again, but I wasn't really listening to the words, just
the tone. The flat, learned politeness that isn't politeness at all,
just a sterile formality. I wanted to say: "You sound like a robot.
Did you learn to talk like that in Regina?" But didn't, realizing
that he was probably a decent enough boy. And that it's the tone
I hear from almost everyone.

I heard from Stella weeks later that O'Brian was talking about moving to Japan. About going there to teach English, deferring his plans for priesthood indefinitely. Get a little time and distance between himself and everything, was how she put it.

"It's probably just speculation," I said. "People love jumping to conclusions."

"He's changed. I tried to discuss it with him."

"And did he tell you he was going to Japan?"

"No. Not in so many words."

"I think he'll be a good priest someday."

"You really do?"

"Yes."

"Poor Danny. It wasn't all his fault."

"No, it wasn't."

She searched my face for evidence of knowledge, then she placed her soft hand on the back of mine. "Someday we should talk."

"I'd really like that," I said.

The boat became an escape for me, but not a particularly healthy one. The original purity of the experience faded and I realized it was becoming a deep seduction, a place to hide.

"Going to do a bit of jiggin', are you, Father," they'd say as I lifted my cooler down from the dock, careful to avoid the telltale clank of bottles in the rattle of the ice cubes.

"You know me," I'd say back. "The fish have their own technology. The 'fisherman-finder.' Soon as I show up, they're gone."

That's a good one, they'd laugh.

There was an American, a writer from the *New York Times*, who kept a boat near mine. We'd exchange mild pleasantries from time to time.

"I hear you spent some time in Central America," he said once.

"Ah, yes. You know the place?"

"Covered the trouble there in the eighties. Nicaragua. Salvador."

"I was in Honduras."

"Aha. Among the Contras," he said.

"That was after my time."

A blonde woman in shorts and a loose tank top lounged in a deck chair at the back of his boat, studying me with an expression that revealed the remnants of some earlier disclosure, perhaps that I was A Priest. Our eyes engaged and I smiled. She quickly looked away.

Late in August, I saw Danny on the far side of the harbour, his boat hauled up in the mobile cradle. He was working in the shade under it, painting the hull with a long-handled roller. I could hear music. Straining to listen, I recognized a song from my university days. "Desperado."

The boy really is old-fashioned, I thought.

I decided to go over, to talk. About the Eagles. Don Henley. Cash in some of the currency acquired from living for so long in close quarters with the young. Then I noticed that occasionally he'd reach down to pick up a beer bottle, raise it to his mouth then stand there, head back, as if to drain it all in one swallow.

The next day the boat seemed abandoned in the slipway, and after two days fishermen were grumbling on the wharf.

"Danny's gone to sea with Captain Morgan," one of them told me wryly.

After three days I noticed a crew around the boat one morning, half-tons hauled up close to it. Four men were finishing the painting. When the paint was dry, they relaunched and floated the boat across the harbour and tied it up behind mine.

"Has anyone heard anything lately?" I asked.

"Oooh, yes," the man said, snapping half hitches around a post.

"Where is he keeping himself these days?"

"He's around. Under the weather, though. That old Bacardi flu, he caught."

He quickly tied a knot and left.

Unannounced, young O'Brian came to see me. He stood at the door looking nervous. I asked him to come in for a cup of tea or a cold beer. We hadn't spoken since the incident at the hall.

"No, thanks," he said. "I have something for you." He handed me an envelope.

"What's this?"

"I have to give you back the money. It wouldn't be fair to keep it."

I feigned confusion.

"You can explain to them."

"Explain what?"

"I've changed my mind. I'm not ready. Not now, anyway. I'm going to take a year and just travel. Think things through. Maybe after that. But I can't. Not now."

I protested that he shouldn't take the incident at the hall so seriously. That I knew young Danny MacKay felt badly about it.

"Do you really think he's the only one who thinks like that?" Donald asked bitterly.

"It doesn't mean—"

"No?"

I could feel the sudden anger.

"Do you really think he's the only person around here with that attitude?" He was staring through me and I could hear his unuttered question: What do *you* think?

I said nothing.

"I feel sorry for Danny MacKay, actually," he said at last. "For whatever hang-ups made him do that. He just couldn't keep it to himself, the way the others do. That guy is heading for big trouble."

"Keep the money. Travel can be expensive."

"Thanks, but I expect you can find better things to do with it. I hear they want to replace the Glebe."

"I'd do anything to make you change your mind."

He stared at me. Then, after what seemed like a long silence, he turned and walked away.

{ 14 }

Then it was late September. The weather in summer can be unpredictable, but Septembers are, almost without exception, an unbroken flow of warm, still days drenched in sunshine. I had the engine uncovered, floorboards up. There was evidence of dry rot in the planks below the fuel tank. I wondered if the MacKays knew about it before they sold it to me.

Next one will be fibreglass, I thought. And then, in a spasm of distress, I realized the dry rot didn't matter. In a few years I'll be gone from here. There won't be a next one.

I opened my cooler and brought out the rum. The bottle was wet and cold and comforting. I found a plastic cup and twisted the cap from the bottle.

There was a violent, startling thump. It was Danny. He'd jumped down from the dock and was walking along the washboard in my direction. His face was unshaven. He was wearing a ball cap backwards. I felt a momentary panic, sitting there with the incriminating liquor bottle in my hand. I fought annoyance.

"I was just pouring a cocktail," I said. "I don't suppose you'd be interested?"

"I don't suppose the pope shits in the woods," he replied. "Or is it the bear does that?"

I smiled.

He walked past me and stood at the stern, studying his boat with his hands on his hips. "You didn't happen to notice who put my boat back in?" he asked.

The tone was hostile, so I lied. "No."

"They could have told me."

"I'm sure they tried to find you."

"I'm not that hard to find."

When he turned to face me, I realized he was still drunk.

"I'll take it straight," he said.

"Are you all right?"

"Never better." He turned away again and studied his boat, drink in hand. "I'm thinking of getting rid of her anyway. I've decided. I'm going to pack up and head for Calgary. That's where the future is. This fishin' is for idiots."

I said nothing.

"The government wants us all out of business. All the little guys. Turn the whole effing thing over to the big companies that can afford to bribe the politicians."

I just listened.

"There's a job for you. Speak up about that stuff. Raise a little hell. Stand up for the little guy, that's what you should be doing. The way the old priests were, before they all went hippy-dippy."

I shrugged.

He went into a long silence then and finally turned to me and asked, "How come you just let me get away with that?"

"With what?"

"You know. At the hall."

"What do you think?"

He lit a cigarette. "You should have hit me back. That's what you should have done. You should have poled me. That's what old Father Donald would have done . . . so I've been told. That's what I deserved. I wouldn't have stopped you." He stared at me, puffing on the cigarette. "Somebody was telling the old man you used to be pretty good with your hands yourself. Never took shit off nobody."

"We outgrow that stuff."

He laughed. "How about if I gave you a free shot. Right now. Just nail me."

I stared, speechless.

"Come on. Right here. I deserve it. It'll be my penance." He stuck his chin out.

And suddenly, before me, I see the jutting faces of my father and our neighbour, Sandy Gillis, men misled by war to the belief that violence is a path to righteousness. I understand their problem now, how they got that way, how pain and guilt invite more pain. And I might have said to Danny, then and there, what I never said to them: Don't you think that you've been hurt enough?

But I simply shook my head and turned away, silenced by uncertainty. We just sat there sipping our drinks, avoiding eye contact, listening to the soft wash of the tide slipping by.

"Did you ever think of going back to school?" I asked at last.

"All due respect, Father, you're jokin'."

"You're still young, Danny."

"That's half the problem right there. I was born too late for anything that matters."

"You're wrong."

"We'll catch you later," he said, setting his glass on the wash-board then bounding up over the side of the wharf.

I wanted to call him back. But by the time I'd climbed up onto the wharf, his truck was racing up the shore road. I see it now, and the amber light of the falling September sun turning fields to gold and setting fires in the windows of the silent houses where all the secrets are.

†††

"I have a feeling that you know more than you're prepared to tell me. Am I right or wrong?"

Stella was silent on the other end of the phone. Then she sighed. "This is something very deep. He needs some help, but he isn't ready for it yet."

"Can you tell me anything?"

"No."

I put the phone down and only remembered afterwards that I'd forgotten to say goodbye.

Sunday, October 8. It occurred to me that Bobby O'Brian was avoiding me. People consider me to be aloof; a word I'd never have thought of, but Sextus used it once when he was explaining the trouble with people like me. We hide behind this forbidding exterior, he said, and it fools most people. He had a hand on my lapel, fingering the heavy wool fabric.

"The cloth . . . the outward sign of your authority," he said. "Something cultivated by old black-robed priests to save them from accountability." Sextus uses the word *accountability* a lot. And *transparency*. Words, I assume, that people use more often in the larger places. But Bobby O. never seemed to notice my aloofness. Bobby O. is one of those people who always seemed comfortable with the priest.

"Bob," I called out as he marched, head down, toward his car.

He hesitated. He was clearly wondering if he could get away with pretending not to hear me. So I broke away from a little group of women near the door of the church and walked toward him.

"I haven't seen you for a while."

"Been pretty preoccupied. Union stuff. You know the way it gets."

I asked him if he was hearing from his son.

"Ah, yes," he replied reluctantly. "He's doing good. Got a teaching job in Korea. Think of that. Korea." He was trying to seem pleased.

There was a long pause then.

"I'll be honest with you," he said. "It was embarrassing. I just don't know any other way to put it. He kind of built up all those hopes, then . . . running away like that."

"It isn't running away. He just needs time. He was wise to go away, where he can think about it without feeling pressure."

"It wouldn't have been any different for him. You know what I'm talking about."

And then I understood the anguish in his face.

"Things like that don't matter when you're a priest. Right? You have help, the Lord's grace. Isn't that what they tell us? I always figured he'd be safer as a priest."

"He'll be fine."

"I gotta tell you, I worry about him. It's a dirty rotten world."

"Say hello for me. And if he ever wants to drop a line."

"I'll do that." Then he said, "I hear young MacKay isn't doing so good. I hear he's been on a bender for weeks now."

I nodded.

"I feel bad about that. He used to be a nice little fellow. I remember when they were both in the high school. They were buddies."

"It'll work out," I said, feeling embarrassed at the poverty of the comment.

"Ah, well. Young people, eh?"

He headed toward his car, and I felt a wave of sorrow from somewhere deep, a place I rarely dare to go.

† † †

Thursday, October 12. Young Danny was on the phone in the morning.

"I was just wondering . . . I'll probably haul the boat out next week. How about if I do yours at the same time?"

"That would be fine," I said.

"The weather is closing in . . . they're expecting some storms. Might as well put 'er away for the winter."

"Can I help?"

"I'll handle it. Call it a little act of contrition."

We both laughed.

"*Ego te absolvo,*" I said.

"What?"

"You're forgiven."

"Cool," he said. "I feel much better now."

Then it was the fifteenth. I clearly remember a high wind out of the northwest flinging cold rain against the hills and the houses, autumn leaves cascading from the tragic trees, congealing in rich coloured clumps on the road. After Mass that day, the people ran to their cars holding their parish bulletins over their bare heads. Rushing to their welcoming homes. I stood in the doorway of the church for a full five minutes, watching the storm racing over the bay, gathering up the whitecapped water, smashing it against the land. Something about my house made me want to linger in the creaking church, where there were still traces of living humanity. My house, a dead place compared to this and the living storm outside.

Then I saw the red half-ton turning up the lane. Sextus, I thought with surprise.

"Isn't it grand," he said, standing with the rain lashing his face. "I love this. I drove out to the old place, but the wind is blocked by all the trees. Then I thought of you here, and the view. I brought a jug of wine. Thought we'd have a little brunch."

"Why don't you step in here before you get soaked."

"I just love the smell of it. The smell of the fall, nature throwing off the summer things. What else rots so fragrantly?"

I suspected he'd already started drinking, the way he was waving his arms around.

"Come on to the house. I'll fry up some bacon and eggs. Put on a pot of coffee."

He opened the wine. I had my Sunday Bloody Mary and set about the kitchen while he pulled a chair back from the table and sat there watching me.

"I hear young O'Brian is in Korea or someplace like that," he said finally. "It's just as well."

"I suppose."

"Not that he wouldn't make a good priest. I just don't know why he'd want to put himself through all that."

"All what?"

"The constant suspicion. And of course, the tension inside himself."

"I don't know what you mean." I had my back to him.

"They seem to be wired different, gay people, as they call them now. You know what I mean? Sexually."

"How do you know he's gay?"

"Everybody knows," he said.

"Eggs over?"

"It isn't the . . . orientation that matters. God knows, I've got nothin' against gay people. It's the repression that isn't natural. When you've got it all bottled up inside, you never know how or when it's going to break out. It always does, eventually."

"You're talking nonsense."

"Nonsense? You really think so? Take a look at yourself, for example."

I faced him then, spatula in hand.

"You better watch that egg."

I turned back to the stove. There was a long silence between us.

"I think you and my sister have been spending too much time philosophizing," I said finally. When I turned back to him, his face was a mask.

I remembered my drink, half finished on the table. I strengthened it with a shot from the bottle. He just watched me.

"Maybe I should clear something up here," he said.

"Listen," I interrupted. "Your personal life is none of my business."

The phone rang loudly. I briefly considered ignoring it, continuing the moment, which somehow felt important. But I picked it up and it was Stella.

"Thank God you're there," she said, on the verge of hysteria.

"It's okay. I'm here. With Sextus."

"We have to go to Hawthorne. To Danny's."

"To Danny's?"

"Danny's dead," she said.

Then she was sobbing. She'd just heard. She had to dress. She said it would take her fifteen minutes. I put the phone down and stared at it for a while.

Sextus was at the stove, scooping the eggs and bacon onto a plate. "What was that about?"

"That was Stella. It's Danny MacKay. He's dead."

"Jesus Christ," said Sextus. Suddenly he was trembling. He put the plate down. "Danny. Dead?"

"She's coming over."

He slumped onto a chair. We just sat there. Elongated minutes passing. The storm seemed to increase its velocity. The old house creaked. My electric clock made soft sounds like stocking feet as the large second hand twitched.

"I've read that's the way it happens," Sextus said.

I didn't speak.

"The MS weakens everything. The whole system. You had to know Danny, when I first knew him. Up in Toronto. He was . . . the last thing you'd ever imagine was Danny . . . He was like a frigging . . . Viking."

I was barely hearing him.

"Where did you put that bottle?" he asked.

I rose, retrieved it from the counter. Found an empty glass. Put it in front of him. Poured into his and mine. Sat.

"I remember once, in this queer little tavern on Roncesvalles. A couple of Italian bricklayers took it in their heads to—"

"I've got a bad feeling," I said. "I don't think she was talking about Danny Ban."

A car door slammed outside.

Somebody noticed that his boat was adrift just outside the harbour, edging into the deeper water. Obviously tied up carelessly, the boat came loose because of all the wind. Young Danny had been on a bender for weeks now, anyway. Wouldn't have been too fussy about the ropes. Then somebody pointed out that the wind doesn't normally get into Little Harbour, it's so sheltered. And even if it did happen to batter its way through the trees and down over the hill, the wind and the tide would probably have pushed the boat further inshore, toward the highway bridge. Not out into the storm.

That's when Cameron, who was a coast guard auxiliary, figured they'd better go out and get it themselves rather than go looking for Danny. So Cameron and his boy untied their boat on the Sunday morning, just after Mass, and they went out still wearing their church clothes, grumbling a little bit about people losing control of themselves and turning into nuisances. After they got a gaff on and pulled the drifting boat alongside, the boy, Angus, went on board.

Angus was about the same age as Danny, and they were worried afterwards that he might not get over what he found.

The body was in the cab, jammed into the corner of a tiny galley. The place was a mess. The rifle was on the floor in an astonishing pool of blood, which by then was black.

A full-length .303, and his arms were barely long enough to reach the trigger. But still he managed to shoot himself through the heart. It was mercifully quick, they said.

There was a note. Just four words. "There Is No Future."

There would be theories, memory ransacked for the flimsiest of clues. It had to be related to the incident in the hall. He hit the priest. He was finished after that. And there was talk about his girlfriend, Sally. How, after that, she dropped him like a hot potato and he was never the same afterwards. Then they'd speak about a public meeting. Government bureaucrats came down to talk about the fishery and the future of Little Harbour. Danny lost it. Called the DFO guy an awful word in front of everybody. One lousy word, someone told me at the wake, is all it takes with that crowd of bastards. That was when Sally pulled the plug. Gave him the ultimatum. It was after that he hit the poor priest.

He went too far that time.

But others were saying it was the other way around, that he hadn't been himself for years. They said: Looking back, you could see it coming. And everyone would nod, because grief makes us tolerant of absurdity, at least temporarily.

Danny Ban was solid through it all. I saw him stiffen when Sextus tried to hug him, holding a protective forearm between them.

Aunt Peggy and her son Willie made a brief appearance at the wake. I watched as they lingered near where Danny Ban was standing. Danny walked away, leaving them to their privacy. The old lady was holding Willie's elbow tightly. Before they turned to leave, he reached down and gently brushed the dead boy's face. And when he turned, I could see what looked like fury in his eyes.

Peggy nodded briefly and tried to smile. Willie stared straight ahead, spoke to no one.

Danny Ban resumed his place beside the casket. He was tall and broad, no evidence of his illness. And his boy was once again a child. I saw him as if for the first time. The face of a movie star, dusty with cosmetics that he didn't need. Hair coiffed by strangers. The tension in his mother stilled the room, and her face was a mask of bitterness. I stood before her, forcing out the pieties, struggling through the violence of her stare.

"I know you mean well, Father," she said eventually.

Mullins tried to put a stop to all the speculation. During the funeral Mass he preached a homily of surprising insight about suicide. Firm and direct. That it was an act of despair so profound as to cripple the faculties of reason. And that, where there was no reason, there could be no culpability. Speculation about causes was nothing more than gossip, he said firmly.

I'd heard it all before, of course, but coming from Mullins it sounded new because it revealed something new about him.

Mullins said, "The dead cannot be blamed for death. We cannot judge." And then he judged. "I'm told he wrote 'There Is No Future.' Think of that," he exclaimed. "Think of where we have arrived as a society when those who shape the circumstances of our lives and our communities can leave our young, the very embodiment of our collective fate, in such a state. There is *no* future?"

The homily became political. Mullins denounced the businessmen and bureaucrats who had mismanaged and abused God's bounty, and the fishery in particular. He denounced the politicians who let them get away with it. And gradually, words and ideas merged and became a palatable theory. You could feel the comfort spread throughout the church. A kind of absolution for us all. This tragic death was a cry of protest, a solitary cry for help . . . for all of us.

The words were welcome, almost sufficient to block the angry whisper still ringing in my ears. The quiet, rasping words I had listened to the night before, on the other side of the cloth panel of the confessional.

"Can you spell me off?" Mullins had asked. "It's like Easter all over again. The lineup for confession is halfway down the church."

I would not have wanted Mullins to ever hear the voice that haunts me to this day, and always will.

"I'm not the one that needs the confession."

The silences were filled by heavy breathing.

"Maybe you better do some hard thinking about who needs the confession."

I felt a numbness in my throat.

"You find that priest, that Brenton Bell they sent down here. And you find out who sent him here, and why."

Brenton Bell?

"Get out," I said, the numbness gone at last. "Get to hell out of my confessional."

Mullins stopped his homily as if halfway through a thought and walked abruptly back toward the altar as we all rose to recite our Credo. Stella was in the second row of faces, just behind her sister. Our eyes met and locked for what seemed to be eternity. Finally, I had to look away.

For the grim recessional, Stella had requested an organ version of the Chopin funeral dirge, but Mullins vetoed it. Too dreary, he said. The requiem is about our belief in salvation. There is pain, naturally. But we celebrate the hope that was God's gift, the assurance that we'll all share in His Resurrection. Eventually.

Danny was to be cremated, so we were spared the morbid graveside rituals. The pallbearers delivered his casket to the waiting hearse. As it drove away, people stood in small groups in the parking lot, not sure where to go. The sky was dark, the wind rising. There was a sudden squall of rain, and it was cold and feathery with sleet. From inside the church I could hear a violinist playing the last phrases of Niel Gow's "Lament for the Death of His Second Wife," a tune so sad, I thought, that even nature weeps.

BOOK THREE

† † †

Ye have heard how I said unto you,
I go away, and come again unto you.
If ye loved me, ye would rejoice,
because I said, I go unto the Father:
for my Father is greater than I.
JOHN 14

{ 15 }

Viewing everything in hindsight, the next five months acquire their meaning through a series of banal events. March 25, 1996, was the day my life began assuming what I expect will be its final shape.

I recall mostly a pageant of weirdness, but the police cruiser that tailed me all the way from town should have been the tipoff that I was in a state of moral peril. It didn't, not right away, for I was, for lack of more profound analysis, somewhat drunk. It was my way of trying to evade a lot of complex issues, a lot of nagging challenges, deep ethical questions for which I should long ago have found some viable accommodation. Like: where is the defining line between sin and stupidity? By Troy, I was groping for any distraction from the reality of the car behind me, not to mention certain things that happened back in town.

Who on earth, I wondered, might have named this place Troy? And why? Some classical scholar? Somebody who came from another place called Troy? Isn't there a Troy in New York State? Or Michigan? Obviously there must be one in Turkey. Or maybe it's because there was a beach here once, before the causeway. And the Gaelic word for "beach" is *traigh*, which sounds a bit like Troy.

As I passed the little convenience store in Troy, the Mountie was well back, near the beginning of the straight stretch. Lost interest, obviously.

Lost innocence.

I remember years ago, on hot Sundays in July or August, how the dry trees would crackle, filling the Sabbath afternoon with the aroma of burned sap. John and his father would rescue us if Sandy happened to be in a decent mood, load Effie and me into the car with them and drive us to the beach in Troy. *Traigh* actually works better, the more I think of it. Effie would argue that everything sounds better in Gaelic. *Mo run geal dileas,* for example. "My faithful fair sweetheart." Try it: *Morune-gall jeelus.* It leaves a sweetness on the tongue.

The Mountie's car was gone and so the sweet face of the woman back in town returned, restored the tension of the moment. She seemed sad, standing there, arms folded over her chest, head atilt. But there was a faint smile. No hard feelings obvious. She has lost none of the sweetness of her younger years. It has, in fact, been much enriched by sadness. Sorrow and warmth equal sweetness. Innocence. Lost. What was I feeling then? Guilt? Contrition? What's the difference? Alfonso would say that true contrition needs an action of some kind; otherwise it's only guilt, a shallow sentiment.

Traigh. Why not? Try.

On Troy Beach, doomed Sandy Gillis would sit grinning in the broiling sun, a beer bottle balanced on a stone, scratching the snow-white skin above his elbows, or as far back on his shoulders as he could reach, revealing the damp hair matted in his armpits, as we floundered around in the water. The missing part of his head would be more conspicuous in the summer. The white, hollowed patch of skin looked like a burn scar after flesh melts and stretches and heals all puckered, but I know it was from a bullet in the war. *Whack.* Tore off a section of the skull. Altered the brain chemistry to darken the memory of what went just before. Nothing but shadows where the war had been until just before the end of his life. They say that what you don't know won't hurt you. What he didn't know probably saved him until the night my father decided to enlighten him, to throw the switch, expose the darkened part of memory, reveal their crime. Or was it only sin? Or just stupidity?

"What they do in wars isn't really murder," I suggested many years ago, the first time John and I could talk about our fathers' homicidal history.

"Doesn't it depend on circumstances?" John replied. "What about civilians? What about killing civilians?"

"You're right. It would depend on circumstances."

More recently, John informed me that, in his personal experience, suicides grow calm, even ecstatic once the dread diminishes. It's all about control, he said. And he described how, just before the end, his father's anger disappeared, replaced by an odd stillness that John later saw as resignation. It was the closest Sandy ever came to grace, the way John sees it now.

"It has an upside, suicide," John said, smiling faintly. "You shouldn't be surprised that the young guy from Hawthorne called about the boat just before he did away with himself. The boat would be his way of touching base, without raising an alarm. He was already gone by then . . . in his own head, at least. Time doesn't matter anymore by then. A blessing, in a way."

Perhaps. It's like morality. Depends on whom you ask.

What did Father Roddie say? Violent death is sometimes justifiable. Some situations . . . situational. He had a dark sense of humour.

Someone told me long ago that Troy Beach had been completely stripped of sand and gravel. They used it all for the causeway and the foundations of the industry the causeway brought. For every benefit there is a cost. There is a causeway. The causeway created a harbour. There are jobs and wages because of it. And leisure time, for sitting scratching in the sun. But there's hardly anywhere to sit anymore. That's the way it goes. Last summer local people were complaining about a powerful stink around here, like raw sewage, coming from somewhere nearby. Coming from the shore. Everybody suspicious of the industry that came after the causeway, that brought their prosperity, liberated them from anxiety. Wanting me to make a fuss. Get involved. Make a stink about the stink.

Maybe, I said.

Driving by the place we used to call Sleepy Hollow, I noted the water pipe sticking out of an embankment at the roadside, water pouring. I felt a sudden thirst, checked the rear-view mirror for the Mountie, still couldn't see him. For as long as I can remember, water has gushed out of that pipe without fail. People would drive miles during a dry summer with barrels and buckets. Late, after a wild night, you'd stop there. Drink, splash the face, breathe the moist, clean air, refreshed. It's still there, sparkling pure. At least for now. Sand and gravel gone, but we still have the water.

I inhale deeply, searching for the phantom sewage smell, indignation gnawing on the memory.

Driving up the hill by where an elderly couple once lived, a brother and sister called Jack and Annie Troy, I take another furtive glance behind. Their name was really MacDonald. Around here they name people after the places rather than vice versa. There's a whole family called the Miramachis, but they're actually MacDonalds too. Unrelated. Maybe the policeman stopped at the convenience store. Or the water pipe.

John Gillis, I've decided, looks exactly like his father, and I told him so the day he visited, shortly after Danny's death.

"It's possible," he said. "I can't remember exactly what the old man looked like then. But I'm about the age he was, the day he did it."

November 22, 1963.

"It was an anniversary we can never forget, eh? Thanks to Kennedy."

"Do you think you can ever forget something like that, no matter what the date?" I asked.

John was standing by the bookcase, studying the journals. "They look like diaries."

"We've hardly ever talked about it, have we?"

"Maybe once or twice. So, what have you got in here?" He was turning one of the journals, front to back.

"Basically just notes about meetings, decisions. Did you ever keep a journal?"

He laughed. "No. I guess not."

"Too bad. There are lessons worth remembering in our past."

"I imagine. I imagine there's some interesting lessons here."

"Help yourself," I said.

He put the journal down, turned away. "Got enough of my own past to keep me going, even if it isn't written down. Got no room for yours, unless it's mine as well. But it's been a while since that, eh? Quite a while since we were family."

I waited.

"A conscience is an awful curse," said John. "Guilt can turn into a disease if you're not careful. That's the trouble with diaries, at least if you're honest in them."

"Do you think that was what killed your father? Conscience? Finding out the details of what happened there, in Holland, just before the end of the war?"

"I suppose it was."

"So, since it was my father who provided the details . . . I guess . . ."

"I wouldn't worry about it." He seemed to hesitate. "It's pointless trying to rationalize what we can never know." Then he said: "You take that business in the hall. When that young MacKay fella took the swing at you, then did himself in. You could cause an awful lot of trouble for yourself connecting dots when you don't have to."

"So it was you. You were there."

"Who did you think it was?"

I didn't answer.

"I came late. Bobby O. invited me. We worked together at the mill for ages. I saw what happened. You did nothing to provoke it."

"It's complicated."

He shrugged. "You took an awful wallop."

"It was nothing."

"I was afraid for the young fellow . . . I tried to hold him. I was worried what would happen to him after you got up. I remember when we were young."

Before he left, he said: "My real reason for going to the hall that night was to apologize, sort of."

"For what?"

"Back there in the winter, when I was on the bender . . . I got pretty gross. Sorry about that."

"There was nothing—"

"I'm afraid I've got a streak of the old man in me." Then he headed for the door.

Before he closed it, I said, "Maybe we both do."

"I doubt that. I used to wonder . . . do they do something normal in the final seconds, like, say, the act of contrition. And if they did, would it change anything?"

I didn't even try to answer.

† † †

After Danny's funeral, I saw Stella by her car, head down. When I approached, I realized she was fumbling in her purse, trying to find her car keys. Her eyes were red, cheeks wet.

"Are you okay to drive?" I asked.

She nodded. "I'm okay."

"I could drive you home," I said. Her sorrow was infectious. "We can talk."

She just shook her head. "I'm going to stay with Jessie for a while."

I was passing MacMaster's when I realized the policeman was behind me again and now he was flashing his lights, indicating that I should pull over.

Only then did I feel the danger.

He leaned close to my open window. "How are you today, sir?"

I knew him from our previous encounters, but I didn't think he'd recognize me because I was wearing a leather jacket and ball cap. My disguise.

"Could you step out of the car for a minute, Father?"

"Is there something wrong?"

"Just step out of the car, please."

"What's this about?"

"Just step out, please," he said, and stood back, making room.

I shoved the door open abruptly, climbed out. Staggered slightly.

"Would you come with me, please?"

He walked toward his own car, opened the passenger side of the cruiser, with his hand on my elbow. I climbed in, fuming. The dashboard was cluttered with electronic paraphernalia. He got in on the driver's side. He sat there for a moment, thinking.

"I'm going to drive you home," he said finally.

"Was my driving *that* bad?"

"I didn't notice the driving. But you do seem to have had a lot to drink."

"You're making a mistake."

"Where were you coming from?"

"A visit," I said.

"I stopped you because there's something I wanted to talk to you about."

Driving away, leaving my car stranded by the roadside, I was wrestling with the absurdity of the moment. I've been taught that the power of the man in uniform is from a lesser place than mine. But now I was under his control. We turned up the glebe house lane. The church towered over us but suddenly seemed to be as impotent as I was.

"What was it you wanted to talk about?"

"Father," he said, "you should know . . . there is somebody asking questions about young MacKay."

"That's strange. Who?"

"A reporter."

"A reporter? Why would that be news? It was months ago."

"He seems to be suggesting that the MacKay thing was tied into . . . other matters." He was studying me for a reaction.

I shrugged. "I can't imagine what he's talking about."

He continued to study me for a while, measuring. "I thought we could talk about it, but obviously not today. Maybe someday soon, when you're feeling up to it."

"Any time at all."

"By the way," he said, "did you ever know a priest named Bell? Brendan Bell."

"I knew a Bell, but he isn't a priest. At least not anymore."

He stared, then said, "I hope you'll remember that I did you a favour today."

You ask that Bell. And you find out who sent him here, and why. Then you'll know.

"You didn't happen to get a name," I said.

"Name?"

"The reporter."

"I'm afraid I didn't write it down." Then he reached across and handed me his business card. *Cpl. L. Roberts.* "You can reach me any time. Night or day."

Through the eye of memory, I watch the cruiser drive down the hill, turn south and disappear. The spirit sags. Missed opportunity for an act of contrition, absolution?

Alfonso's voice returns: The true act of contrition has to be a deed, an action that somehow leads to change. I study the Mountie's business card for a moment.

The other voice says: Don't even think about it.

Memory is episodic, a harsh and unforgiving landscape. Danny Ban was at the shore. It was November, barely a month after the dreadful day. I was getting ready to haul my boat out of the water and put her away for the winter. The *Lady Hawthorne* was in her usual place, just behind me. Looking at her made me angry.

Why, I wonder? Why should I feel anger?

Then Danny Ban was above me, hands in pockets. "How are you today, Father?"

I scrambled up and stood before him, trying to read his face. "How are you making out, Danny?" I asked, placing a hand on his forearm.

"Ah, well," he said on the intake of breath. Then, exhaling: "A fella never knows one day to the next."

I just listened.

"I thought it was me with all the troubles. He was young, eh? Strong and healthy. You take for granted nothing bothers them that much when they're young and strong. I was too busy thinking about myself, I guess." He looked away from me, studying the boat. "The women are taking it hard. Jessie and Stella. But at least they have each other. I'm glad for that."

"If there's anything I can do . . ."

He just shook his head wearily, then stooped, retied a spring line from the boat. "I guess I'm going to have to take her home. If she was made of wood, I'd just strip her down and burn her. But there you go. It's the way things are now. Everything fibreglass and plastic. Even the car."

He managed to smile.

There was talk of renaming the harbour for Danny MacKay, to bring him, somehow, back to life. MacKay's Point. Mullins thought it was a good idea, it had a double-barrelled meaning. I agreed.

Mullins had it on good authority that government people wanted to dismantle the place and that Danny's death might make their plans a bit more difficult politically. Putting his name on the harbour would make them seem more callous if they shut it down. It would be like killing the boy all over again. Each Sunday, it seemed, Mullins attacked the politicians and the bureaucrats from the altar with greater zeal. They're out of touch, he'd say. Paternalistic. Like the greedy merchants of the old days. Making our decisions for us.

I envied him his cause and his courage. Alfonso would be proud of Mullins.

But then the bishop called me. What's going on down there? he wanted to know. Is Mullins getting nutty in his old age?

Talking politics? Renaming harbours? MacKay's Point, my rear end.

I told him not to worry. The community was rattled by a suicide. A young fisherman named MacKay. Mullins is probably worried because there are a lot around here like him. Overextended at the banks, and the outlook for the fishery pretty grim. Mullins is trying to give them a place to focus, other than on themselves. Trying to give them hope.

"Well, be that as it may. You try to find a way to tell him to tone it down," the bishop said. "People are getting riled up. Our job is to bring people together, not divide them."

What people? I wondered.

"I'll talk to him," I said.

"Good. How are things otherwise?"

"Maybe you and I should talk."

"Any time at all," he said. "But keep an eye on Mullins. I want this political nonsense to stop. We've got to keep our noses out of public matters. That way, perhaps, they'll keep their noses out of ours."

{ 16 }

Father Chisholm, the priest in town, phoned in late November. He was brisk. Heard about what happened to your young friend from Hawthorne. I've been praying for him. Terrible, the pressures on the young these days. And by the way, could I take the evening Mass in town the Sunday coming? Just this once. Sickness in the family. Have to go away for a few days. We should get together when I'm back. We can talk about despair.

Perhaps.

"But I can count on you this Sunday?"

"I'll mark it down," I said. "November twenty-sixth. The evening."

We used to call it the drunk's Mass, but such blunt irony is out of fashion now.

"You're a good man," he said.

I still call it the new church, though it's been there for at least twenty years. One of the signs of aging, I suppose. Past time compresses. For me the place will always have that look of newness, with the sunshine flooding from a skylight just above the altar, modern slit windows, floors banked so the pews rise in front of me and to the sides like in an auditorium. And the faces are mostly new. Even those that look familiar seem to be at least a generation down from my experience. I said my first Mass in this parish, in the old church, the old St. Joseph's. One of the many that have burned down. Filling in for Chisholm on November 26 was a challenge. But it was being useful.

Sandy Gillis's funeral was on the twenty-sixth, four days after he shot himself. It was a Friday, but they didn't find him till the Sunday. They found him sitting in a hole in the ground, an old, abandoned cellar in the woods, a place out back called Ceiteag's. It took us years to find out why he did it. I asked the crowd to pray for Sandy's soul. A personal intention, I told them. I could see some nodding heads.

During the recessional I remembered certain faces, understood the hands raised to shield the whispering. Old MacAskill's boy from out back. Remember him? Up the road from Sandy Gillis. He'd pray for him, all right. He'd know all about it.

And I remember my father, in his cups, celebrating after my first Mass, telling me with surprising calm: "When Sandy Gillis done himself in there . . . you know, it was really my fault. I did everything but pull the trigger."

By then I didn't want to know. But he kept it brief and sanitary.

"I told him something that we done. Overseas. He'd forgot . . ."

"And what was it you did?"

"Ah, well. There was this young girl."

I remember waiting. Braced for more.

"It was her. The girl. She shot poor Sandy. He never remembered a thing afterwards, until I told him."

And that was all.

I remember reassuring him with notions of contrition, reconciliation. He listened respectfully, nodding.

"I hear what you're saying," he said.

† † †

Once outside, the crowd dispersed quickly. The bitter wind, sweeping up the strait from Chedabucto Bay, whipped the edges of the vestments. Thank you. Thank you. Hurry them along to finish off their interrupted weekend.

"Have you heard anything from Father Chisholm, how are things at home?"

"Everything is fine. He'll be back in a day or so. If anything comes up before that, call me in Creignish."

And then a face with traces of the familiar in the folds of flesh. Something about the eyes.

"You probably don't remember me," he said.

I struggled, on the edge of recognition. Probably I don't, I wanted to say. The chill was in my marrow.

"We were in school together. The old Hastings school, years ago. Don Campbell."

Don Campbell?

"Donald A.," he finally admitted. "From Sugar Camp. Out the Long Stretch."

"Ohhhhkay," I said. Remembering, vaguely.

"I got to be Don, working away," he said, smiling back at me.

"You're at the mill now, I imagine," I said, gripping a substantial hand.

"No such luck. Working construction. Coming and going. Away a lot. Probably why I haven't seen you for a while. Following the jobs. Out west, up north. You haven't changed a bit yourself. I'd know you anywhere."

The face was full and red, maybe from the wind, but the eyes were watery from long experience.

"It's queer thinking of you as Father," he said, laughing lightly.

I laughed too.

"I well remember Sandy Gillis," he said. "And the way he went,

in '63. The old man and I were there when they found him.
At Ceiteag's."

I just nodded.

"An awful shame when it comes to that. I guess he never got
over the war."

I nodded, looked away.

"Some mess he made. I'll never forget it. I was just a young-
ster myself."

"You have a family, I suppose," I said.

"Just the wife home now. Two boys. Up the way, one in
Toronto, one in the States. Though I see more of them than the
poor wife these days, with all the travelling for work. You'll have to
come by. Have a drink and reminisce. The house next to the
little store on the old Sydney road. You'll know it."

"Someday I will," I said.

I watched him go. Now he's known as Don, for having been
away. And I was thinking about our growing up together in that
strange place out back, outside the magic circle of significance.
And how much we hide in platitudes.

Sextus wasn't expecting me but didn't seem unhappy I was there.

"I said Mass for Chisholm this evening, and since I was in the
neighbourhood . . ."

"Come in," he said.

His apartment was dimly lit. A near-silent television flickered
in a corner and a book lay open on a coffee table.

"It came back to me this evening. Saying Mass in town.
Thinking about your uncle Sandy . . . It was thirty-two years ago
today we buried him, wasn't it? I was thinking of him during
Mass. Got them to pray for his soul."

"That's wild. It completely slipped my mind. You'll have a
dileag, for the cold?"

"No, thanks. Have you been hearing from my sister?"

"Now and then. I think she's staying put this Christmas. I wonder how John is doing these days?"

"He's fine. He came to see me. He's been on the wagon since February."

"That was a bad one, last Christmas."

"I don't think we have to worry about this Christmas."

He sat then, arms folded. "We'll see."

I appraised the room. "Actually, this is about all I really need. A nice little apartment. I don't know why we have the glebe house anymore. A waste of heat and power."

He shrugged.

"I ran into Donald A. Campbell this evening after Mass. You remember him. We were talking about Sandy. He said to say hello."

"You're kidding."

"Calls himself Don now."

"When did he come home?"

"He didn't say. I hardly knew him. He mentioned he was one of the ones that found Sandy. He was with the search party."

"He'd have been pretty young."

"A little younger than we were at the time."

"Donald A.," he repeated, smiling at some private memory. "I don't suppose the wife was with him?"

"He was alone."

He laughed aloud then. "Probably just as well."

"Oh? Why?"

"Surely you remember Barbara."

17

Mullins told me to wait in the kitchen. He had somebody in the office. He wouldn't be long. Twenty
minutes later I was still there, fidgeting. The kitchen
told you just about everything you'd want to know about him.
Bright yellow walls and clean white cupboards, a Formica coun-
tertop devoid of any clutter. Sink empty, aluminum and chrome
blinding in the mid-afternoon sunshine. Dry dishcloth draped
primly over a glinting faucet. Faint odours of furniture polish.

I used to enjoy coming here. The neatness, the meditative
silences when Mullins was away. The place feels stifling to me
now.

It was close to three in the afternoon. The sharp December
sun slanted through a window facing northwest. Port Hood
Island sat abandoned, waiting for the snow, the homes of the
summer Americans silent and secure. Water in the foreground
danced, tossing foamy spittle into the sharp wind. A chilly view,
I thought, but inside the sun warmed the sanitary kitchen.

The house was silent. Whoever he had in the office was either
mute or speaking very softly. I could feel an irritated boredom
settling into my bones. Typical Mullins.

In the summer I'd escaped to the island on my boat a dozen
times at least. Tucked the *Jacinta* inside the U-shaped wharf, the
way young Danny showed me on that hot day in July. Meandered
up to the little church he'd pointed out. Real peaceful there, he

said. Obviously he knew. I'd sit in meditative silence with the ghosts of the solid, thrifty islanders of old moving quietly around me. The odd board squeaking in the floor and walls the only sound.

"Wait in the kitchen," he'd said, as if I were a salesman.

Have a quiet word with him, the bishop said.

I'd kill for a drink right now, I thought. Next thing I'll be carrying a flask. Smiled to myself. The acorn doesn't fall far from the tree. Ohhhh no.

There was a large black housefly staggering along the windowsill and it reassured me in a way. A small imperfection to humanize that sterile place. The window in the bishop's room is full of them. Where do they come from? Hundreds clustered in black, miserable clumps. Are they dead? Or hibernating? How did they get in there?

I stifled a yawn. I wondered if he keeps a bottle in the cupboard like I do. I could look. What harm in checking?

The fly was now stymied in a corner. No. He recovered. Started up the windowpane. I decided to give Mullins five more minutes and remembered: Bell sat here. For a year. Eating, drinking, bullshitting. Entertaining God knows whom or how. What is it about a guy like Bell that draws them to him? The guitar? Maybe if I was musical. No. He had charm *and* talent.

I find it suddenly funny. God plays tricks. God is a joker who equips His cripples with gifts they use to pervert His holy will. And they flourish. People like me, designated to correct the perversions, undo the damage, languish like the sleepwalking fly. We ordinary mortals share the destiny of insects.

I watched the fly for another moment, struggling. Now he was on his back, legs moving mechanically in the air, slowing down. Batteries running low.

I wondered where Bell was at this moment. Driving some-where in his BMW, hair slick with gel, and the new wife admir-ing him. I stood, stretched, eyed the cupboard door more closely. What do you think you're doing? Turning into a sneak drinker. Worse than Bell.

Ho-hum. I checked my watch for the umpteenth time. Time's up. I opened the kitchen door. There was a fairly new deck just outside, a place to sit and watch the summer sunsets. A view inferior to mine, I thought. I decided to leave discreetly. No sense disturbing them, old Mullins and his secret guest. I actually felt relief, admitted that I don't really have the stom-ach for this anymore. Carrying messages from the bishop. Little warnings.

The air was stinging after the overheated kitchen. I felt refreshed. But before I reached the car, I heard Mullins's voice. He was standing in the front doorway, arms folded over his chest. There was a woman with her back to me, making her farewell. And when she turned, I saw Jessie MacKay. She seemed surprised that I was there, a bit disoriented.

"Where do you think *you're* going," Mullins called out merrily.

He looked briefly at the kitchen clock. "I don't suppose a cock-tail would be out of order? How about yourself? You take a drink?"

"On occasion," I replied.

From the cupboard he plucked a forty of vodka. Of course—no danger of detection on the breath. On ice, I tell him. He splashed tonic into his. Vodka-tonic was something he discov-ered in Poland, he informed me, during the second visit of His Holiness JP2, in 1983. Have you ever been? No. I was working at the university in '83. A different kind of ministry, a bit less glamorous. But he wasn't listening.

"Poland's all different now, I understand. But then? Communist, but utterly inspiring. A bit of repression suits the soul, it seems." He chuckled briefly. "At Częstochowa, oh my God, Jasna Góra, the shrine of the Black Madonna. Hundreds upon hundreds of thousands turned out to hear the pontifical High Mass on a Sunday morning. In the rain."

"I can only imagine," I murmured, thinking, Old Mullins sounds positively aroused!

"I almost panicked in the mob. My feet kept slipping in the wet grass and mud. The crowd? You aren't going to believe this. The crowd was so packed . . . so tightly packed . . . people jammed so tight, that afterwards the buttons all fell off my coat. That's the God's truth." He excused himself to go to the basement in search of another bottle of tonic.

"Don't bother," I called out. "I can live without the mix."

"Good grief, no. It's no bother at all. You have to try this. You'll be hooked." I could hear him humming a tune from the basement stairway.

"How's the drink?" he asked, waiting for my judgment.

"I'll strengthen it if you don't mind. It's delicious, but don't you find the tonic . . . sweet?"

"Help yourself," he said, gesturing toward the liquor bottle. "It's actually a summer drink. But I wanted you to try it."

I poured a solid dollop.

"Poland was *unbelievable*," Mullins said. "The faith of those people. The crowds at Mass. The defiant demonstrations. The floral crosses in the public squares. Jaruzelski actually trembled when he met the Holy Father. Bent the knee. I saw it on TV from my hotel room. It was awesome."

"I read somewhere that it was the beginning of the end for all that, the Soviet bloc and all the rest."

"It was indeed. And I was there when it started, God be praised. How often does a simple fella from around here get to see the start of history? Or the end of it . . . however you want to look at it."

I sipped my drink.

"Have you ever met His Holiness?"

"Yes," I said. "I was in Toronto in '84. At Downsview. I slept out all night with the crowd to get close enough. Nearly perished from the cold and the dampness, but it was worth the pain. Met him after the big Mass."

"Did you know that I was on the altar for the concelebration at the Commons in Halifax?"

"Get away with you!"

"Highlight of my life. The charisma of the man just radiates. You can't help but be affected by it. Inspiring. The man could have been anything. Could have led his country, maybe saved it from the Communists in the first place. Who knows? He'd have been an amazing general. A Sikorski and then some. And on top of everything, he's an artist. Writing plays and poetry. A blessing in our time."

"You're up on your Poland," I said, smiling.

"Made a study before I went. Got hooked on the history."

"Here's to Poland," I said, raising my glass.

"Right on. And to all the poor Polacks and what they've been through. Just think of the survival of that little island of Catholicism over the centuries. Against the Turks. Nazis. Communists. You name it. How's the drink now?"

"Well. They always say you can't fly on one wing."

I stared out at the dying afternoon, suddenly depressed, a small, cruel anger stirring.

"Chopin was Polish, wasn't he?"

"Indeed he was. A national hero." His face was quizzical.

"They wanted Chopin at the funeral last month, but you vetoed him in favour of some fiddle player."

"Oh, that," he said, waving a dismissive hand. "Everything has its place."

I studied my drink. Amazing what it does for poise. "I almost forgot. I've been told to raise something . . . I was talking to the boss the other day. The bish."

He was waiting, head tilted to one side, half smiling.

"I guess you've put the devil among the tailors, with the business at Little Harbour."

"Oh, that," he said with another wave of the hand, relaxing. "So what are they saying?"

"Nothing to worry about. But the boss thinks maybe you should crank it down just a little . . . Don't get me wrong . . ."

"No problem," he said with a weak smile. "But why didn't he tell me himself?"

His discomfort was sobering. I could feel the familiar tingling in my shoulders and neck. My readiness. "Probably it would have been the courteous thing—"

"Freakin' right," he blurted, then stood and reached for the bottle. Poured for himself.

"But don't . . . don't read anything into it. I just happened to be talking to him on other matters. I guess he assumes we have a connection because . . ."

He was watching, face wary, waiting.

"Well, we're almost neighbours," I laughed. "And you know the way the mainlanders think. Everything on this side of the causeway . . . just like one parish."

His eyes said he was unconvinced.

"Then of course there was the business with Brendan Bell."

"Bell? What business with Bell?"

It took me a moment to recover. We had told him nothing about Bell. "Oh, just that . . ." I said, reaching for his bottle. Stalling. "Hope you don't mind . . ."

"Help yourself."

"Speaking of Bell, civilian life seems to be doing wonders for him."

"Really?" he said, honestly surprised. "You saw him lately?"

"This past summer. I had the impression he planned to call on you, but I guess he didn't."

"I haven't seen hide nor hair of him since . . . God . . . how long now? Well, I'm offended." He waved a hand, staring toward the window. His face was troubled. "I seem to get left out of everything."

I took a small sip. "Let me ask you something," I said carefully. "How did you find Brendan as a priest?"

"Clear hopeless. Lovely guy to have around . . . but a priest? I don't know what he was thinking. He was more cut out for . . . the media. Or show business."

"Did he ever talk about Newfoundland?"

"Oh, all the time. You know the way they are. I figured by the end of it I knew everybody he knew over there. I'm amazed he never dropped in. He plays a mean round of golf, Brendan does."

I studied him closely and saw only innocence. I saw the trust, remembered just how quickly it can vanish.

I stood to leave. The headache I'd been getting lately had returned, throbbing. Possibly the start of a hangover. "About the bishop," I said. "I wouldn't be too concerned."

"It's just that . . . and I'll be frank . . . I'm a little ticked that he'd get you involved. I know you two are close, but this is different."

Different, I thought. And I wanted to ask, Different from what?

"Just tell him I think I know what I'm doing. Okay? He doesn't have to worry."

"I think I understand."

"The place has been profoundly unsettled by that business with the MacKays."

I agreed.

"Maybe I should call him myself, his highness. I can explain. I won't bore you."

"Whatever you think. Definitely. Call him."

Turning toward the door and almost as an afterthought, I asked how Jessie MacKay was holding up.

"Ah. Poor Jessie," he said. And he stood still for a while, just shaking his head. "I suppose I wouldn't be telling stories out of school if I said why she was here."

"I'm curious."

"Her visit was, coincidentally, not unrelated to yours." He laughed, studying his hands. "Will you have one more before you leave?"

"I shouldn't, but why not."

"She, even more than you and his royal highness, wants to calm things down. Put everything behind us," he said as he poured. "She wants me to reconsider renaming the harbour. Thinks it's pushing things too far."

I nodded.

"I just realized that she's also anxious that I back off a bit with the criticisms of the powers that be." He laughed ruefully. "Never thought I'd see the day when I'd be too radical." He shook his head, enjoying the notion. "I'll shut up. But maybe you could play more of a role yourself, with the connections you have through the boat. You're almost one of them. That little harbour is important to you people."

At the door he caught my arm and held me for a moment, face dark with concern. "There are bad things going on. These are good people, but weak. We have to lend whatever political power we have, though God knows it doesn't add up to much anymore. But nevertheless."

I nodded.

The sun disappears quickly in December. The darkness leaps up around you suddenly as the afternoon subsides, jamming icy fingers into your flesh. In truth, I didn't want to go home. I didn't want to face my crumbling glebe. Passing the Port Hood liquor store, I turned in.

It was dark when I stopped at the Little Harbour wharf. The place felt odd, abandoned. The bait shed silent. Ropes clinking on a metal gibbet that, in spring and summer, winches crates of lobster from the boats below. There were no boats now. The dark tide swept outward purposefully, little eddies swirling near the piles. A gull shivered atop a pole, shifting from foot to foot. I reached into the back seat where I'd placed the bag from the liquor store, fished among the large bottles for the small flask of vodka. Mullins is on to something. But he can keep his tonic.

Across the harbour, high and dry and braced by empty oil drums and substantial blocks of lumber, the *Jacinta* presented a regal profile. Her flared bow picked up the pale glow of a high harbour light. The emotion I experienced was something close to love. "Jacinta," I said aloud, cracking the seal on the bottle.

He's right. I should get involved. Fight for this blessed little place. Real justice for a change, an act of contrition.

Next to the *Jacinta*, long-lined and, at least in my imagination, lonely, stood the new *Lady Hawthorne*. Danny Ban had planned to take her home. Illness or his failing spirits intervened. Time to haul the boats, the boy said. He promised to look after it. Three days later he was dead.

Now his mother wanted Mullins to back off. Stop blaming bureaucrats. How much did she know? How much did Stella know? I hadn't seen her since the funeral. She hadn't called. Dread was gathering in my gut.

The vodka was cold and acrid in the throat, but the stomach was quickly warmed, the dread deferred. At least Mullins didn't know a thing about Bell and therefore hadn't got an inkling about linkage. Not yet, anyway. Nobody knew. Just the bishop and me. And we didn't know anything for sure. This was where it became easy to think of death as a solution for things. What big loss if Bell snuffed it? Let's say that little BMW of his took a sudden slide on the QEW, under the wheels of a very large truck.

You ask that priest, that Brenton Bell they sent down here.

There had been subtle changes since Danny's death. Among the men from the shore, when I'd see them I'd feel a distance I hadn't noticed before October. But maybe it was coming from the shared consciousness of loss. Maybe that's why Stella never called. Danny Ban didn't know a thing. But his wife seemed to know something. I could see it in her eyes, outside Mullins's place. A quality of pain from some private knowledge that only made it worse. Maybe they all knew something I didn't know. Or maybe they all knew what I thought I knew.

Danny Ban wasn't doing well at all, according to Mullins. Another mouthful, to get me home. Or, I thought, maybe I should visit them. Maybe I should go to Hawthorne.

O my God, I'm heartily sorry for having offended Thee.

There was one light burning as I drove up the long lane. It was in the kitchen, as far as I could tell. Their dog was barking. He cringed toward the car when I opened my door, tail swept low, rear end wagging, nose exploring my thighs and crotch. An outdoor light came on.

Jessie met me just outside. She spoke in a whisper. "I'd just as soon if he didn't know I went to see Father today."

I nodded, suddenly comforted by complicity. "I understand," I said, although I didn't.

Danny was in the large living room watching television. An American program about policemen. He quickly killed the sound.

"You don't have to turn it off," I insisted.

"Ah, well," he said. "Just passing the time."

I told him I was just passing by. Saw the boats at the shore. Thought of him and wondered how he was managing.

"Good," he said. "The place is some quiet now, of course."

"Stella was here, I heard."

"She comes and goes, poor Stella. It's a bad time to be alone. She and the boy were pretty close."

I nodded. He has become smaller. He didn't stand when I entered the room.

"It's the little things that get to you," he said. "It takes longer to get used to the small changes." He sighed.

Jessie asked if she could get me something. Tea or something stronger. Something for the chill.

"You decide," I said.

Danny ordered. "Get us both a drink of rum."

We sat, waiting.

"No," he said with a large sigh. "I couldn't bring myself to haul his boat home. I think of her as his. Having to look out every day and see that thing sitting in the yard—that would be too much."

Over the rum, he talked about the city. He and Sextus and their crowd revelling in a brief spell of indestructibility. "You never spent much time in Toronto yourself?"

"Long visits," I replied. "I have the sense of it. Which is close enough for me."

"I hear it's changed a lot. But it was a great place back then. The best of everything. All the work you needed, never stuck for something to do. A great crowd from home. Always a dollar in the pocket and a fast car to get around in. All a fellow needed."

"I missed all that," I said, trying to smile.

"In the summer you'd go to High Park or down to the Beaches and pretend you were home. You could look at that big old lake and imagine it was the ocean. Wicked, eh? You'd think if a fellow missed home that much he'd just pack up and go. But something kept you."

"What brought you back?"

He laughed. "If it was up to herself, we'd never have left. Right, Jessie? Did you know we met up there? Never planned to come back at all. But I got in a little difficulty. Figured it would be best to come home for a while."

"He got in a fight at a Down-Home dance," Jessie said sardonically. "That was the difficulty. As if that was something new."

On the silent television screen three policemen were holding a squirming, shirtless man on the ground while a fourth struggled to attach a handcuff to a wrist.

"It was with a cop, actually," Danny said, distracted by the TV. "He was doing security at the dance and he seemed to have it in for me. Anyway. For all I knew, they were going to put me away for squaring off with a cop. It was around that time the fishing gear and licences became available."

His wife laughed, took my empty glass and left the room.

"The funniest thing was I started getting Christmas cards from that same cop a couple of years later. Kind of his way of saying, if they wanted to do something, they'd have had no problem finding me. Real friendly cards. Every year friendlier, like we really knew one another. Actually, one came the other day. Where did you put that, Jessie?"

"It's around somewhere," she called wearily from the kitchen.

"He was saying how Toronto has changed. How it's gettin' dangerous. No more good clean fights, like in the old days. Nothin' but guns and gangs anymore."

Then there was a long silence.

"Isn't going to be much Christmas around here this year," he said.

I nodded sympathetically.

"I think he got to be deputy chief, that cop did. Retired now, of course."

"That's a good story."

"It was me persuaded Jess to come home. Big mistake, looking back on it."

Jessie returned and put a fresh drink beside me.

"Not to say bad things wouldn't have happened there too. But it's like you expect bad things to happen among strangers. They kind of catch you by surprise when they happen at home. You know what I mean?"

I nodded.

"He could have become anything, you know. With a few of the kind of opportunities you get in other places. He could have been a priest, for all I know. He talked about it once."

I nodded. The comfort phrases normally would rise from instinct, but I couldn't utter a word. So we sat quietly for another minute.

"I don't think I mentioned this before," I said eventually. "Father Bell, or former Father Bell, I should say . . . Brendan was around last summer asking about everybody. I don't suppose you saw him?"

"No," said Jessie. "But he called after the funeral and all. Expressing sympathy. He seemed to feel real bad about what happened."

"Salt of the earth, that Father Bell was," Danny said. "Typical Newf. Never knew a Newfoundlander I didn't like. It never crossed my mind to ask him . . . maybe Danny tried to get in touch with him. That's the hardest thing of all. Thinking he was so sad . . . and he never tried to talk to anybody."

Jessie bowed her head and became silent. Wiped her face furtively.

"He never talked to you. Right?"

I shook my head. "I never really got the opening."

"Oh, I can well understand that feeling," Danny said.

But even if I had had the opening, what could I have said?

I remember Sandy Gillis on the doorstep. I think it was the last time I ever saw him. Mid-November, 1963. He seemed sober, which was unusual. He normally only came to our place drunk. To start fights with my father. Every time they talked about the war, they fought. Is the old man in? No, I said, even though he was asleep on the kitchen lounge. But Sandy seemed uncharacteristically subdued. Something about him changed. Fight gone. He seemed to be staring at my feet. Ah, well, he said, it isn't anything important. But he continued standing there, as if trying to think of things to say. I think he asked about my studies. I remember his eyes, disconnected, as if wired into a different time and place, or some new, fatal knowledge. And still, the words were unusual for their warmth. I was uneasy. It was the disconnection between the words and the eyes and everything I knew of him. He turned suddenly and stepped away. Paused briefly.

"You don't have to mention to the old fellow that I was here," he said. "It was nothing in particular."

And he was gone. I should have seen what was coming next. But the future has no substance until it turns the corner into history.

18

The bishop seemed concerned. I had two calls in a week. Not from the secretary or one of his flunkies, but from himself.

"And how is Creignish these days?" he'd ask, as if he didn't know. That was mid-December.

"Creignish is just grand," I said. "Winter is settling in, of course."

"You should plan on a getaway after Christmas. Skedaddle for a week. Someplace hot."

"I'll think about it."

"Good." He then paused, as if wondering how to get to the point of the call, so I decided to help him.

"I spoke to Mullins," I said. "I relayed the message."

"Ah, yes. Mullins. Good." Then he cleared his throat. "You didn't happen to hear from some reporter named MacLeod?"

The name was familiar. I hesitated. "About what?"

"The kid from Hawthorne. The suicide. You know the family, I think. MacKay. This MacLeod's been calling around."

I hadn't heard from a reporter named MacLeod. "Who did he call?"

"Mullins."

"Mullins?"

"He called Mullins, asking about Bell. Didn't know the first name. I'm afraid Mullins gave it to him. Then Mullins called me, all confused. Asking what's up with Bell. First I thought you must have filled him in."

"The reporter is whistling in the wind."

"Probably," he said. Then: "I don't think we have to worry about him. We were wise to keep Mullins out of the loop. I think I've dealt with this MacLeod before, years back. Over some of the other stuff. He'll go away."

"And how was Mullins?"

"I think he was more concerned about the protocol of me sending you to talk to him about his sermons on the shore than about Bell or some reporter asking strange questions. Knickers in a knot over that. I stroked him and he felt better. But you don't think Bell . . ."

"I don't think so."

"Even so, there's the optics. This would be our Mount Cashel if the media got wind of it."

"I don't think there's anything to it."

"Would you happen to know how to get a hold of Bell?"

"Maybe. To do what?"

"Tip him off. Tell him to keep his head down. Don't talk to any reporters."

In the morning, I called the chancery in Toronto, told them who I was and that I was trying to find a friend who used to work there. Brendan Bell.

There was a chuckle. "Ah, Brendan." She just happened to know that he spent his winters in the south. In the Caribbean, she thought. "You know he's married."

"Yes."

"He's done well for himself. Turned into quite the business-man."

"Oh?"

"Hotels, I think. Anyway, he gets to spend his winters in the tropics, lucky man."

"You wouldn't happen to have a way of reaching him?"

"Well, I have a cellphone number somewhere."

A place in the tropics. A BMW. Hotels. A wife. I remembered the look of him the previous summer, all tanned and athletic. Handsome, you could say. Full of self-confidence. They say the eyes reveal the state of the soul, and his eyes were clear as the blue sky that day.

For a few foggy moments I couldn't be sure if I was sleeping or awake. There was a phone call. Someone named MacLeod. It was 1988 or 1989. There was an older gentleman, the caller said, an older priest, a retired professor, now an assistant at the cathedral . . . living on the campus. There was a rumour. They call him Father Roddie.

I hadn't heard. And why call me?

"Someone said that if anybody knew about it, you would."

"Someone is trying to lead you astray," I said. I ran my fingers through my tangled hair. I could see his face, a window on his sanctity.

Keep the bishop out of it this time, I thought.

Father Roddie was a bit dishevelled when he greeted me at the door of his apartment, squinting in the dim light. The years had bestowed a reassuring aura of harmlessness. He was pot-bellied and grey. His face had assumed what seemed to be a permanent expression of piety and kindness.

"Come in, come in," he said. "I haven't seen you for years." We shook hands. "You still have the grip," he said with a laugh.

I smiled.

"I'd forgotten all that," he said. "The misunderstanding."

I nodded.

"And you dropped out of sight for a while, I do believe. The missions somewhere, wasn't it?"

"Honduras."

"Ah, yes. Lucky you. I always regretted missing the experience of the far-off lands." He sounded genuine. "Actually, I remember you more clearly from before all that. When you were just a student. Quite bright. You stood out. Great grasp of . . . large concepts. You were interested in the European phenomenologists, I think."

We were still standing in his doorway.

"It's like yesterday," he said. "You'd be coming to my place in Chisholm House for our little chats. You must remember? You'd be spouting Heidegger at me . . . just to get my goat."

And we both laughed then.

"What am I thinking?" he said. "Keeping you standing here like a stranger. Come in. Come in."

His room was austere, but the walls were jammed to the ceiling with books, newspapers and manuscripts strewn about, and half-read books lay open on every available surface. We made small talk for just a minute or two longer.

By then I had developed an instinct for guilt. You could feel it in the room even before it became obvious in the eyes.

After a lull in the conversation he said, "I think I know why you're here." He sighed and smiled. Removed his glasses, wiped them slowly with his sleeve.

"Oh?"

"No Heidegger today, I guess. Just as well. I'm a little rusty on my German. Would you have a drink of something?"

"No."

"I'm aware of some of your . . . shall we say extracurricular activities during the past few years."

"Activities?"

"Oh, come on. The Exorcist. You must have heard that one. The Purificator. No malice intended. You've done some great work. Hard, thankless work, performed with admirable discretion." He sat there smiling, confidence returning like the tide. "A one-man Inquisition. Remember how mad you'd get when I'd bring up Heidegger's Nazi affiliations?" He never stopped smiling. "By the way, does Alex know you're here?"

"Alex?"

"Bishop Alex. We were classmates, you know."

"I didn't know."

"We play bridge once a week. We're partners. Maybe that's how I know about your . . . work. Alex thinks you're the cat's pyjamas. Wouldn't be surprised to see you in his job one day."

"I didn't know he played bridge."

"I'd been planning to talk to him, actually. About certain malicious stories. You've obviously heard them. There's a reporter spreading them around. A fellow named MacLeod, I think. You're sure I can't offer you anything? I think you like Balvenie."

"No, thanks."

"Well, then. Let's just get it out in the open. I'm glad you're here. I've been putting it off. Confronting this thing."

Always watch the eyes.

They were blue and I swear they twinkled. He had bushy white eyebrows, broken blood vessels at the tip of the nose.

He acknowledged that he had a drinking problem. It started in Korea. Didn't I know that he'd served in the army? Just stupid drinking then. But after he came back, he'd hit the booze to escape the flashbacks and the depression that haunted him. The things he saw. The things he heard about. Did I know he was a chaplain with the PPCLI?

The what?

Princess Pat's . . . light infantry.

I nodded.

"War," he said. "An awful thing. But you know that already." He sighed. "I thought, being a priest, I'd be able to handle it. I was sure the faith would help put everything in perspective."

He'd been getting help, he said, for the drinking. The other stuff? It wasn't worthy of response. Some poor little retarded girl and a combination of misunderstanding and miscommunication. "That and a chalice full of malice." He smiled. "But I suspect you know the way it is."

"I don't know what you mean," I said.

"Well. Your own father. Surely you, of all people, would understand."

"He says he's your bridge partner."

I said it lightly, to avoid offence or pain.

The bishop looked like he was going to be sick. "I can't believe you just landed in on him like that. It must have been a terrible shock for him, that kind of an . . . ambush. Especially with the history you two have. That business in the seventies."

"I didn't want to bother you."

"But you're bothering me now."

"Yes. I've asked around. Credible people confirm it. Father Roddie isn't a well man. Hasn't been for decades. Even he admits he has a problem."

He sighed deeply. "You just won't let go of it, will you. What did Father Roddie ever do to you?"

"There's possibly more to it than we know. I've met with one of the accusers, by the way."

"You mean the retarded one?"

"You know about her?"

He waved a hand dismissively. He was sitting behind his

desk, eyes cast down, fiddling with paper clips. "At least it isn't an altar boy this time. At least it's a . . . female."

"These things aren't about sex," I said.

"Whatever." He sighed. "Okay. Leave this to me."

"That really isn't—"

"I'll handle it," he snapped, eyes burning. "Are you getting hard of hearing?"

"Fine," I said.

"Is that all?"

"Father Roddie made a strange reference to my father."

"He did? So what."

MacLeod remembered me. There was familiarity in the voice on the other end of the line. "How're ya doin', Father?"

He reminded me our paths had crossed before, when there were rumours about some elderly priest. Did I know Roddie MacVicar? Doc Roddie, he was called by some. The eminent philosopher. Aquinas expert. Suspected pervert.

"I had him as a prof," I said.

There was gossip years ago. My name came up, according to MacLeod, because it seems I was a parish assistant where something happened. There was even a story of a physical confrontation involving me and the old man. And that I got exiled over it, to somewhere in Central America.

"Absurd," I said.

"That would have been some story, eh? What I heard was . . . you, I guess, half throttled the old guy. I said at the time, 'If what I hear is true . . . more power to him.'"

"Somebody was pulling your leg."

"I'm sure. Wishful thinking on someone's part. But maybe if there had been more of that kind of old-fashioned reaction to things back then, we wouldn't be in the pickle we're looking at now."

"What," I asked, curiosity now in charge, "was the eventual outcome of your story back . . . when was it?"

"The seventies, I think. I dropped it. I remember calling the bishop at the time. He denied it flatly. In the end he persuaded me that the potential damage to an important institution like the Church was a strong argument for discretion."

"I suppose there's something to that."

"It was probably the right call . . . then. I'm glad we didn't get sucked into the hysteria, like in Newfoundland and Boston."

"That wouldn't have helped anybody."

"Precisely." There was a long pause before he asked: "So you probably don't remember the second time I called?"

"Can't say I do."

"The old boy got up to it again. Late eighties, I think."

"Sorry," I said.

He laughed. "You gotta hand it to the old bugger. He must have been near seventy that time. It was about some handicapped person. A girl."

"And what happened to that story?"

"The usual. Nobody talking. The old stone wall treatment. Anyway. That's history. We might have a new situation now."

He said Brendan Bell's name turned up while he was following the recent prosecutions of priests in Newfoundland. He noted a reference to our diocese, Antigonish. A priest with a sex-related conviction in Newfoundland had ended up in Nova Scotia. Interesting, he thought, that they'd send him here. Did I know anything about it?

"What was the name again?"

"Bell. Brendan. I'm told you might have been acquainted with him."

"The name sounds familiar. It rings a bell." We both laughed. "Have you asked the bishop?"

"I did. He claims this Bell guy is out now. Gone from the priesthood. Hasn't got a clue where he landed. I thought of you. Maybe you'd know."

"Me? You obviously think I've been mixed up in all the scandals."

"Well . . . I wouldn't mind talking about that sometime if you're comfortable with it."

"There's nothing to talk about."

"Okay, then. Bell. What do you know about Bell?"

"I remember his name and I think I heard he got married, as a matter of fact. He dropped out of sight a while back."

"Got married?"

"That was what I heard, I think, from someone at the arch-diocese in Toronto. They definitely said that Bell was getting married."

You could feel the deflation on the other end of the line. "That's kind of weird," he said finally.

"What is?"

"Father Bell, getting married."

"Not so weird anymore. More than half of my classmates from Holy Heart are happily married family men now."

"Yes. I suppose. There's that. But Bell? I wouldn't have thought he'd be the marrying kind."

There was a long pause.

"I'll be honest with you, Father," MacLeod said at last. "I got a tipoff. That this suicide in Little Harbour—I'm sure you heard of it, this young MacKay fellow from Hawthorne—I heard it might have had something to do with abuse. This Bell guy's name came up."

This is where you say nothing.

"Are you still there?"

"Yes," I sighed.

"I know what you're thinking. The witch hunt, eh? People looking for sexual abuse under every rock."

"You have your job to do."

"I know. It isn't something I particularly enjoy. I appreciate your understanding."

"The truth is all that matters. We have to find the truth."

"Thanks," he said.

"Give me your number. Just in case I remember something."

When he hung up, I called the bishop on his private line.

"MacLeod surfaced," I said.

"What did you tell him?"

"You don't have to worry."

"Don't be too sure of yourself," the bishop replied. "The scandals in Newfoundland and the States are making them bolder."

"He sounded reasonable. This MacLeod says he spoke to you before, about Father Roddie. Do you remember?"

"Vaguely."

"He seemed to know certain details that only you and I and . . . well . . . one other person knew."

"I wouldn't give it another thought."

{ 19 }

Christmas was grim. The end of miserable 1995. Around suppertime on Christmas Eve, I called Sextus but got no answer. Heard a dozen vague confessions. Tried to nap but couldn't. Called John. Got his answering machine. Checked in on choir practice. There are four people in the choir. Three women and Bob. Bob has a warm baritone. They make an okay sound. Had a few cocktails alone, waiting up for eleven o'clock when I'd go over. Carols at eleven-thirty. The silent, holy night was still, air sharp. You could hear the heavy breathing from the bay, a giant lung. Feeling the poetry of inebriation. They say drinking alone is a bad sign. But what if you're always alone? What if solitude is the norm?

Sextus would have said if you worry about drinking too much, you probably aren't. But I never brought it up with him because it didn't occur to me that I might be. What was it my father used to say? All things in moderation. *You can drink like a fish as long as you're moderate.*

I nearly fell asleep on the altar during the Christmas carols. Midnight Mass is a blur in my memory. Waking up Christmas morning, I couldn't remember the end of it. I recall standing at the foot of the altar just before the end, improvising a windy Christmas message. I cringe, remembering my seasonal enthusiasm. In the morning, when I dragged myself back for the ten o'clock Mass, I found the vestments strewn around the sacristy. A tumbler of wine got me through the next hour.

What would it be like, I wondered, not being alone?

People were brief, almost shy, at the door afterwards, and I was grateful. And I was grateful for the sharp, clean air, refreshing as a glass of water. Exhaustion, I told myself. I'm just tired. The pieties of Advent and the wearying traditions of the Nativity. Hours sitting in the confessional, waiting for the occasional penitent. Unexpected visitors with small gifts. Fussing with the church. Lights, trees, the Nativity scene. Then the masses. It seemed more frantic than usual because that Christmas fell on a Monday.

Effie didn't come home for the holiday. Did she really think of it as home?

I slept most of the afternoon on Christmas Day and woke up in the dark, feeling uneasy. Poured a drink. The phone rang and it was Stella. She seemed stuffed up.

"You've probably been wondering," she said. "I sort of dropped off the face of the earth."

"How are you now? You don't sound so hot."

"A little touch of the flu."

"Ah, that's too bad. How are Danny and Jessie? It must be difficult for them."

"They're getting by. I was supposed to go to Hawthorne to have dinner there, but I couldn't face it. The flu got me off the hook."

"The flu can dig in this time of year."

"I'll be okay. Feel free to come over. I don't think I'm infectious anymore. But I don't have a turkey. Is that okay?"

"Turkey is overrated," I said.

"Like a lot of other things."

I laughed.

I felt the irresistible urge for another drink. Thought better of it. Looking out the big window at the bay. So peaceful there. Tiny lights in the distance, on the mainland. Outside, the wind was stirring. You could hear it whispering. The bay moved, repositioning itself to listen. The wind was trying to say something. I strained to hear. She's still my friend, I thought.

christmas night, '76. the evening became a blur with surprising speed. there was rum and wine. many bottles of wine. i remember a long table. at least fourteen people, all talking simultaneously. jacinta beside me, flushed and merry. plates of food. golden chunks of chicken and thick crescents of crusted brown potato. large bowls of salad. my comprehension of the language improves with every drink. there are long disclosures about life in unimaginable places. the excitement of political turmoil all around. toasts to ernesto cardenal, obando y bravo, the dawn of hope in managua. someone cried out vinceremos, and the place went still as everybody stared awkwardly at alfonso's flushed face. jacinta murmured vinceremos and raised her glass. then the babble resumed, punctuated by explosions of laughter.

she squeezed my hand. vinceremos. we will triumph. life was suddenly a torrent in my veins.

Stella was pale and bundled for warmth. "Come in," she said. "I'm making toddies. You'll join me?"

"Sure." Pleasantly surprised.

A priest rarely gets to see a woman's naked face. Stella's, that night, revealed dark shadows below the eyes and the small crinkles time etches there. Her lips were dry, her skin sallow, hair captured and secured by a small elastic band, except for a fugitive lock that draped the brow, occasionally blocking an eye.

This, I thought, is what intimacy is like.

† † †

*after everyone was gone, jacinta started cleaning up. alfonso
told her: leave it for the morning; it will be easier then. you
should sleep here anyway. it's late.*

*you're sure? she said. it's christmas, what could happen? i really
should go home.*

*just to be on the safe side, he said. you know where the spare
room is.*

"Let's make a promise," Stella said. "Tonight we won't talk about
Danny. Is that okay?"

I nodded.

We talked about her work. She was a high school guidance
counsellor with degrees in psychology. We talked about marriage, betrayal, alienation. I remember listening intently, refill-
ing glasses, clinging to slippery details, trying to store them in
the memory. Determined not to forget. But failing—there were
so many glasses, so many cascading images. I remember her
paleness went away. Face flushed, eyes shone. Eyes wept.

And then Danny's name. "We agreed not to talk about it," she
said. "It's all too terrible."

I think I sobered momentarily, but there were soon more
tears. I held her briefly. But mostly I remember just sitting,
staring at the table, talking. She was listening intently. Voices
and confusion.

She interrupted me. "Stella," she said, now smiling. "I'm . . .
Stella." She enunciated her name carefully.

"What did I call you?"

"Jacinta."

† † †

i want to see where you sleep, she said.
  what about alfonso? i said.
  world war three wouldn't wake alfonso, she said.
  and, jokingly, i asked: how would you know?

I woke up on her chesterfield. My head was on a pillow and there was a quilt bunched on the floor. I sat up quickly. Fully clothed, thank God. The house was silent. No evidence in the kitchen of where we'd sat. Table clear. Cupboard tidy. Not a glass or dish or empty bottle in sight. The place smelled antiseptic, as if scrubbed by fairies overnight.

I realized that I was conscious of all this because the room was filled with a soft blue light. Through a kitchen window I could see the black spruces on the mountainside, the snow packed around them in a harsh contrast. And the roof of my telltale car parked in her driveway. The clock above the sink reported that it was seven-fifteen. A surge of panic drove me to my feet.

Driving down the mountain road, I saw three recognizable cars go by. Men heading for the mill, irritably alert. One pale face turned toward me as his car flashed by. The priest on the road at that hour? Somebody sick on the mountain. Maybe that's what they would think. The priest should always get the benefit of the doubt.

The sky was a dark blue then with large cold clouds racing, giving the towering church steeple the appearance of instability. The swift clouds would stop and the church would sway. I had to look away, head spinning. I imagined the soft darkness and the silence inside. The unwelcoming house waiting.

The echo of the church door closing lingered as I walked toward the front and knelt in the sanctuary. Candles flickered.

Silence returned, broken only by the occasional mysterious creak or snap. I had called her Jacinta. A wave of sorrow swept up out of nowhere and I lay flat, face down, arms spread. Jesus, what is happening? There was no reply. The red carpet gave off a sweet-spiced odour, some kind of powder the women sprinkle when they vacuum.

I prayed.

"Alfonso, you must speak to me."

But it is Jacinta who replies.

"Happiness grows from the unity of heart and soul . . ."

Her hand was dry and delicate and warm upon my brow.

"Are you happy?"

"I am," I said.

"I love you," she said.

"And I love you."

The hand was gentle, respectful. Squeezing my shoulder. The voice saying hello.

"I saw the car in front. The door was open and the dome light on. I was worried about your battery. Then I realized you were in here. I thought maybe there was something wrong. You're okay, Father?"

"Yes. I know it seems strange."

"You remember me?" he asked. "Archie the fiddler . . . Don't worry about it. I've known strange—I've been to New York City."

"I remember."

He was squatting beside me, staring intently at his hands, working at something with his fingers. "I hope you don't mind," he said, swiftly licking at a crooked little cigarette. "Actually . . . I hear there's lots of religions use this stuff in their liturgy."

I looked at his face and he was smiling broadly.

He struck a match on his thumbnail, inhaled a cloud of smoke. Held his breath. "I don't suppose . . ." he said, exhaling, holding it toward me.

"No," I said quickly.

"It isn't easy," he said.

"No, it isn't."

"That's what I was telling Donnie. Think twice before you jump into something like this." He waved the cigarette around, taking in the silent church, the emptiness.

"How is he? Have you heard?"

"Okay, I guess." He stood. "I'd better mosey. Some old one is going to walk in here any minute now to light a candle for some-body. I think she'd find this weird. Unless she's been to New York City. Which would be unlikely."

I struggled to my feet.

Stella called at noon to ask how I was feeling.

"Fine," I lied.

"I'm glad we talked . . . It explains a lot."

I wanted to ask: What did I tell you and what does it explain? But there was a sinewy hand grasping my throat, blocking the words.

Finally I said: "I think I'm losing my mind."

Or did I only think I said it?

I finally reached him on the day after Boxing Day.

"I was devastated," Bell said, sounding it. "Has anybody figured out why?"

The connection was noisy, but the voice was unmistakable. He seemed to be shouting.

"Everybody and nobody," I said. "Mullins says the fishery. He was in a lot of debt and the prospects here aren't great. He was even thinking of leaving for the West to look for work."

"My God. Is that true?"

"We have to talk."

He was shouting. "What? Talk?"

"Yes," I shouted back. "I want to talk to you. How well did you know him? You were going to try to get in touch with him last summer."

I thought we'd lost the connection, but I could still hear traffic roaring in the background. Car horns blaring. Someone spoke to him and he covered the phone for a moment.

"I'm back," he said.

"Where are you?"

"Oh," he said hesitantly. "Miami, actually. Combining business and a little holiday. As you can tell, I'm on a cellphone."

I cleared my throat. "When will you be back in Toronto?"

"Not for ages. I have a place in the Virgin Islands. I'm going there for a few months."

"Did you manage to talk to him last summer, when you were here?"

"Look," he said, "why don't I get right back to you on a real phone."

"When?"

"Right away. Give me your number. I'll be back at the condo in . . . forty-five minutes."

He never called, and when I tried again, his number had been discontinued.

Pat was explaining: "My oldest daughter and her husband are living in Halifax and they've just had a baby."

"Congratulations," I said. "Your first grandchild?"

"Third, actually," she said, crossing her legs and settling into a comfortable position. "I just wanted your opinion on something."

Behind her the day was dissolving into a dirty shade of brown.

"Can I get you something?"

"God, no, thanks. I can only stay a minute. They're calling her Epiphany."

"Well," I said, struggling to look serious. "That's original. For a name. A bit of a change from the Stephanies and the Natalies and the Ashleys."

"Isn't it a little blasphemous?" She was leaning forward anxiously. Her sweater had a revealing loose, scooped neck.

"No. But maybe the name will cause her a bit of grief when she's older. Kids can be cruel."

"Don't I know it."

"I have a friend, for example. They named him Sextus. And—"

"Sextus Gillis," she said brightly. "Of course. You two grew up together."

"When we were growing up, people would try to tease him about his name. They can make life miserable."

"You think," she said. "How little it takes. And where is Sextus now? Somebody mentioned he moved back. They saw him at one of the socials. I haven't seen him for years."

"He's back. He comes by now and then."

"A piece of the devil he was." She laughed, and I could see in the dying light that there was a flush on her cheeks. "My God. Sextus Gillis." Then she was smiling at me. "I don't think you remember. I've been wondering all along. You don't, really, do you? From when we were younger?"

"Well, there's been a lot of water under the bridge."

"I used to go out with Sextus a bit. We actually . . . double-dated. Me and him, you and a friend of mine. You must remember."

I guess you're mad at me.

"Ah, well," I said, confused. "Dating didn't play a very big part in my younger days."

"Come on. You're not trying to tell me you don't remember Barbara?"

"I'm not sure."

"Well, I suppose if you were anything like your friend, I shouldn't be surprised. That fellow had more girlfriends than . . . I don't know what."

"Actually, the name has a nice ring to it," I assured her. "Epiphany."

"The truth of the matter—why I'm really here—is that they'd like to baptize the baby here. What would you think?"

"That would be great."

"God love you," she said. "They'll be so happy." She was leaning forward again, a hand resting on my forearm.

I allowed a moment's silence and the swift, giddy pleasure of her presence to pass through.

She sat back then. "Wasn't that awful about the MacKay boy? Him so young. I don't suppose you know the family?"

"Actually, I do."

She sighed. "I guess there's no way to understand something like that. Suicide. Such a waste."

The gloom was deepening and I considered reaching for the reading lamp behind my chair, but I didn't.

Then she laughed loudly, standing abruptly and smoothing her skirt. "Sextus Gillis. You tell that *donus* to come and visit."

"I'll pass it on," I said.

"I suppose he's aged, like the rest of us."

"Actually, he's quite fit, in spite of everything."

"That would be him all over. He was always so . . . I don't know how to put it."

I watched the tail lights of her car turn into tiny specks and vanish.

† † †

Alfonso knows, I whisper.

How could he know anything? She is laughing. Unafraid.

I feel it in my bones. He knows.

And what if he does?

We're priests?

You're men.

I have to talk to him.

She shrugs. I turn away.

Hey, she says. I turn back. She stands on her toes and kisses my cheek. Don't forget me.

How could I?

Search your heart, she says. The conscience speaks through the heart.

What about my brain? I say.

The brain can get confused, she says, with too many voices babbling. The voices of old and angry men. Listen to your heart. My heart says we should take a holiday together.

A holiday? But where?

Puerto Castilla, she says. We'll live on the beach, like ordinary people.

What about Alfonso?

We'll take him with us.

20

The bishop seemed distant, distracted. He was sitting behind a desk in the chancery, which was unusual, sipping a coffee that I'd bought for him at the local Tim's. He seemed sour.

"I hate bloody January," he explained. "It feels like we've had six weeks of it so far and we still have two to go."

"You had a break," I said.

"Some break," he huffed. "A bishops' conference in Ottawa in January. Actually, this abuse crap was all over the agenda. Everybody's having a problem all of a sudden. I suppose it could be worse. We could be dealing with the Indians."

He's beginning to show his age, I thought sadly.

"What's happening with us?"

"Nothing new," I said. "I spoke to Bell briefly on a bad line . . . still waiting for him to call back. He was in Miami."

"Miami?"

"I'm sure he'll call in his own good time."

"Don't get your hopes up. What about yourself? You said you wanted to chat."

I told him I just wanted to touch base. I wasn't so sure that Creignish was working out the way I'd expected.

"That'll happen," he said. He had his hands laced in front of him on the desk and seemed to be unusually interested in his fingernails.

"The biggest problem with parish work," I said, "is that there doesn't seem to be enough to do most of the time. I'm beginning to think that the needs of the spirit diminish with affluence."

"Affluence?" He laughed. "Affluence in Creignish?"

"Between the mill and the pensions everybody seems to get nowadays . . . people seem comfortable. They don't really need me. Maybe if you were looking to cut back . . ."

He stood then, stretched and walked around from behind the desk. Sat in the empty chair beside me. Sighed. Told me parish work is organic, you end up doing what they want you to do, no matter how hard you try to get things going. They get resentful if you get too pushy. If you're doing nothing and they aren't complaining . . . be thankful. It means they need nothing. You can wear yourself out worrying about it, he said. Ministry is about other people's needs. I know you need to be engaged. But your needs are secondary now.

"At the end of the day, we're public servants."

I was nodding, as if reassured. I told him I'd attempted to target the youth. Get some kind of organization started for them.

He raised a hand, smiling, shaking his head.

"That was a brave idea. But your timing is bad. Keep your distance from the young ones for the time being. No point asking for trouble. Safest place to focus is the Right to Life crowd. Or the charismatics. I know they're active down there. Can't do any harm there. Everything is black and white for them. The priest is god."

He stood and stared out through a window. My mind raced with items from an agenda I'd been memorizing on the drive over. Now I felt confused. I thought: I don't know him anymore.

"Why don't we just cut to the chase here," he said suddenly. "I heard about the little fracas last summer. How you got caught in the crossfire . . . between a couple of young scrappers at a social function."

"You heard about that?"

"Happens to the best of us. You shouldn't worry about it."

"How did you hear about that?"

"Trust me," he said. "I hear everything."

I laughed.

"I get the impression that, in your own mind, there might be some connection between the fracas and that Hawthorne suicide. I gather he was one of the boys involved . . . am I right? And that young O'Brian."

I nodded.

"Where is he now, by the way?"

"Travelling."

"People will invent their own narratives. It's what they do for their own mental health. Especially around here. They figure things out to suit their needs."

"But in that case—"

He raised his hand. "You have to keep your perspective. I suspect the narrative could be a lot worse, from our point of view. Young fellow loses control, strikes a priest. Suffers irreversible remorse. Loses his mind. Bang. He's gone. There could be a worse scenario."

I studied the crucifix above the desk, struggled to stay silent.

He looked at his watch then brightened. "Well, look at this. It's noon." Would I like a *dileag?* A little nip to cheer me up. He was trying out a new malt. Highland Park. Had I ever heard of it? No.

We were on our second when he caught my hand. Was there anything else bothering me? Anything in particular? "A parish can be a lonely place," he said.

"Loneliness has never been a problem for me."

He smiled. "I want to tell you a little story. A little narrative about myself." He sipped and continued to grasp my hand.

"Some people will always misunderstand. Accidentally on purpose." He was looking off into the distance. "I was a young fellow at Sacred Heart and there was a cook . . . years and years ago. A lovely country girl from Boisdale. Full of the devil and full of the Gaelic. I was pretty fluent then myself. We were always making fun of the old fellows behind their backs. She was hilarious."

He was shaking his head now, smiling dreamily. "Once, they caught us laughing in the kitchen. She was leaning on me. That was all. We were holding each other up, the way you do when you're weak from laughing. There was nothing improper. Just laughing after some mimicry of hers. I think she might have had her hand on my shoulder."

He wiped at his eyes. "There was hell to pay. You can't believe the fuss they made. The bishop got involved. Old Bishop John R., God rest him."

I was watching his face closely. There was a strange movement in the pit of my stomach. His eyes were damp.

He stood abruptly and said, "I wasn't getting at anything in particular. But it's a good little story, eh?"

"Yes," I said.

"Fortunately, it had a happy ending."

"Oh?"

"She married somebody else."

"Somebody *else?*"

"Did I say 'somebody *else*'?"

I nodded.

"Well, well," he said, studying the floor.

At the door I asked: "And where did the cook finally end up?"

"Ah. The marriage didn't work out. The groom was a war vet. A bit damaged. Last anybody heard of him, he was in the Detroit area. She's still around, though. She raised a couple of fine kids, I hear." He was rubbing his chin. "I don't expect my priests to be saints. I expect them to be men. But strong men. Right? A priest who is not a strong man is a sad case."

"Right."

"We're never tested beyond our capabilities. If we fail, well, we have nobody to blame but ourselves."

He hugged me warmly, held me a couple of seconds longer before pushing me away. "I've never been much for hugging men. Hugging is mostly for foreigners and phonies. But you're like my own flesh and blood. We're family. Do you know what I'm saying?" For a moment I thought he was watering up again. But he laughed suddenly and punched my shoulder. "You're going to be all right."

Stella seemed to be surprised when I told her: I think the bishop is worried about us.

"I don't believe it," she said.

"It's the impression I got. Someone here is gossiping."

"Everyone here is gossiping. It's how they deal with boredom."

21

January storms out, February swaggers in full of bluster and hostility. People disappear into homes and cars, invisible behind frosted windows. Cars and trucks are clouded perpetually in mysterious vapours. Shapes move inside shapeless winter clothing. People become their boots and coats and hats. Communication reduced to recitation, age-old commentary on the weather. Wicked cold. Snow like in the old days. The wind. St. Georges Bay a vast white plain of drift ice from causeway to the horizon. Dark dots visible through binoculars. Seals floundering. Men on Sundays shooting them for sport.

The Sunday Mass crowd dwindled as the very old and the young found reasons to stay home. The bishop had suggested that I take a break, skedaddle. Maybe he was right, I thought. Maybe I should break away. They could go to Mass in town. That's where they were mostly going before my arrival, during the hiatus. Chisholm owes me. He could cover for me. Stella recommended the Florida Keys. Or maybe I'd like the Dominican Republic, where she knew of a condo I could have for free. Just a week, she said. It makes all the difference.

March break, she threatened. She was making plans to go.

"I might go with you," I replied. Joking.

"Why don't you," she said. Seriously.

Right.

† † †

Young Donald O'Brian was phoning home once a week from Korea. The trip was doing him a lot of good. Nothing like distance to give perspective, Bobby O. said wisely.

Young Donnie was figuring maybe Toronto when he finished up. Not sure what he'd do there, but we pray, Bobby said.

"He'll make a great priest," I said dutifully.

A Wednesday night late in February, I came home from a card game at the O'Brians' to find the glebe alight. There was a car parked in front and, beside it, the red truck that belonged to Sextus.

They were sitting in the living room, laughing, drinks in hand.

Pat looked up, a bit awkwardly but unabashed. "Look what I found on your doorstep."

"Obviously you forgot," Sextus said.

"Forgot what?" I said, trying to remember.

"That I was coming by for a visit."

"Sorry," I muttered.

"And who should I bump into . . ."

"I wanted to drop by to talk about a date for the baptism," Pat said. "Now they want to wait until the summer."

"Summer sounds just fine," I said.

"Let me get you a drink," Sextus said, rising quickly.

And at that I had to laugh.

This, I thought when they were gone, is how it should be. Friendships should fit comfortably, merging and disengaging and flowing independently and at the same time interdependent, part of an unconscious choreography.

Alfonso knew. He was smiling through my anguish. She told me herself, unasked, in Puerto Castilla, he said. Actually, you walked in when she was in the middle of telling me. She was upset. She doesn't know where this is going.

That makes two of us, I said. But don't worry. Don't turn it into a big deal.

But if you hurt her . . . I'll kill you.

He was still smiling, but the eyes were serious.

She's very, very vulnerable, he said. Did she tell you about the crazy husband?

Husband?

Estranged. But crazy as . . . what do you call it? A shithouse rat. In the FAES. The army, back home in Salvador. Anyway, it's between the two of you and God. Just be careful.

Can we talk some more?

Of course, he said. All you want.

But there was a knock on the door. And through the glass I could see two policemen waiting.

MacLeod called again in March.

"I don't know where to go with this," he said. "I thought I'd run it by you. Did you by any chance hear anything about a letter?"

"Letter? There was a brief suicide note with the body. Basically . . . just four words."

"Yes, I know about that. But I'm hearing that there was something else. Something more explicit."

I said I'd ask around.

His voice went cold. "Father. No disrespect intended. But I'm not going to be fobbed off this time."

"I hear you."

Stella's call was innocent enough. An invitation to share some leftovers. Perhaps a glass of wine. It had been weeks since I'd seen her. Not since the bishop.

She said she was avoiding hard liquor for Lent but that I was free to help myself. I declined. Solidarity, I said.

A glass of wine with the meal, then, she offered. Wine being food.

The night was sharp with frost. Through the fields the walk to her place takes twenty minutes. I needed exercise, I thought, setting out. And there was a secondary thought: leave the car at home, no point advertising.

Crystals crunched beneath my feet. My head was light with freshness. Before I crossed the pool of light in her driveway, I looked around. Guilty reflex.

There was a car on the mountain road, parked in darkness. Parked where I'd never seen a car before. I hesitated, felt a throbbing uneasiness. Perhaps I saw a movement inside the vehicle. A shadow within a shadow. Time seemed to stop, a strange heaviness suffocated thought. Then a sudden flare of light inside the car, a match held briefly to a cigarette, and then the pulsing glow. I started running toward it, propelled by an unexpected rage.

The car leapt forward. Ignition, power transmission, tire traction, gravel rattling: all one guilty, panicked reflex. I was at the end of the driveway when the car flashed by. I reached out, mindless, touched the metal of a door, hand bounced back. But I saw the profile.

William?

"You're dreaming," Stella said.

"Who else could it have been?"

She laughed gaily. "Half a dozen I could name. Silly old bachelors from around. They all have crushes on me. Totally benign. It couldn't have been Willie. Come on, now. Let me pour a glass of wine. Lighten up."

"I've been trying to avoid the demon," I said, somewhat reassured. "It's Lent, you know."

"The demon?" She laughed. "Isn't that a Protestant concept?"

I followed her to the living room. She sat on the sofa. I sat opposite her, in an easy chair.

I asked about Danny Ban.

"He's fine," she said. "You don't know Danny as well as I do."

"What about closure? I thought people in your line of work were big on the idea of closure."

"Now you're mocking me," she said, laughing.

"I'm serious," I said, and suddenly I was.

She was studying me as if I'd revealed a new part of myself, and the look encouraged me.

"I want to ask you about something," I said. "Did you know there was a reporter asking questions about Danny's death?"

"No."

"I had a call from him. He was asking about a letter Danny wrote . . . before he . . . before the day he died. Something that spelled things out. Explicitly, the reporter said."

"Explicitly."

I waited.

She smiled and patted the cushion beside her. "Sit here," she instructed, like a mother. I stood, crossed the floor and sat beside her. "Here's to the future," she said, touching our glasses. "Happier times."

"Happier times," I said, wondering.

She sipped, reflecting. "This letter? The one the reporter asked about?"

"Yes."

"It doesn't exist."

"It was supposedly—"

"It's a fantasy. Certain people have an aversion to the obvious. The truth sits there, plain as can be. Because it's obvious, they assume it's false. The real truth, for some strange reason, always has to be . . . obscure. Reporters are the worst when it comes to that."

I pulled back.

"You saw that movie a few years ago . . . the Oliver Stone movie about Kennedy?"

"No."

"I was still in Toronto. Everybody was going on about it. The big conspiracy."

I said I'd read something.

"All crap. I've read everything about Kennedy. I'm an expert." She set her glass down on the coffee table, then caught the front of my sweater and pulled me toward her. Her eyes were searching. "It's time to think about life."

I agreed.

"Dwelling on tragedy is a waste of life. An abuse of the good things we get from the Almighty or destiny or whatever. That's your field."

"You're probably right."

"No. You don't mean that," she said, smiling, giving my sweater a playful tug. "Don't put me off. I mean it. Love life. Experience it. We're only here for a short while. We'll be dead forever." Our faces were then just inches apart. "Forget about the losers and the misfits. All the Williams. Are you listening? Come on."

She stood and I stood with her, a sudden fear-touched ecstasy causing unsteadiness, but she was holding me then, arms tight around me, face pressed against my neck. "This is what life feels like," she murmured. "Life should feel warm and safe."

Then she looked into my eyes and smiled softly, and kissed me lightly on the lips.

"You can spend the night," she said.

"*Happiness grows from the unity of heart and soul.*"

"That's nice," she said softly.

"What?"

"What you just said."

"I'm sorry," I said, the electric ecstasy now replaced by a dull sorrow.

"Just stay the night. It doesn't have to be anything heavy. I just need . . ."

She didn't finish. I realized I was supposed to understand. But I didn't.

"I have to do a lot of thinking," I said.

"I'm not asking for ideas. I just want to watch you fall asleep again."

"Again?"

"I'm not suggesting anything improper, you know."

"I know. But just let me take things at my own pace. Please."

"Sure," she said. And smiled. And made it even worse.

When I was leaving, she held me at the door. "Your friend. Alfonso. You told me . . . how he died. Don't you remember? You told me at Christmas."

"Oh, yes."

"Did they ever find out for sure? Who killed him?"

Her face became blurry suddenly. I had difficulty breathing.

"Yes," I said.

I sat staring at the bay until it turned a dull silver colour in the morning light.

I woke suddenly to the relentless knocking, instantly alert to multiple circumstances. Through an open corner of a window, the cars were dense around the church. An empty bottle. A glass on its side near my foot, carpet still damp. Whisky reek.

Life. Death. Closure. Misfits. Willie.

Am I a misfit too?

Knocking on the kitchen door.

"Ye-ess."

Scrambling now.

The child's voice. Am I ready?

Ready for what? Shit. It's Sunday again.

"Yes. Yes. I'll be right there."

Sunday morning and I forgot again?

The first reading. Paul to the Corinthians. Hard to get through. About charity. Charity is patient, is kind; charity envieth not, dealeth not perversely, is not puffed up . . .

The words seem loaded with mockery. Could they hear the hypocrisy in my voice? Somewhere else in Corinthians Paul assures me that purity is power, the freedom "to attend upon the Lord without impediment." Fine for Paul, I thought. Paul the Pharisee, who saw the light and laid down the law for the rest of us. Thanks, Paul.

I could hear the sound of my own voice, empty of conviction, intoning the mandated reading for the day. When I was a child, I spoke as a child, I understood as a child. But when I became a man, I put away the things of a child.

Am I really a man?

And in the Gospel, Jesus restored sight to the blind man. I wonder if he ever cured a hangover.

God forgive me.

Chastened, I spun a spontaneous and mercifully short homily about spiritual blindness. How the Resurrection restored our sight so that we might know the truth. Only after we embrace the truth does our redemption become possible. Truth and redemption. Codependents.

I studied the captive faces before me, momentarily restored by a passing sense of purpose before the dread returned.

It's time to think about life, she said. And this is it.

Non sum dignus.

Where is Father Roddie now?

In the renewed wave of futility I almost forgot the words of the Credo.

I wouldn't have recognized MacLeod except for the smile. He approached as I exchanged greetings with the people afterwards, desperate to get home. Open a beer, scrounge some lunch. Go to bed.

"Father," he said. And I knew by the voice and the ingratiating smile exactly who it was.

The fair hair was thinning. The paunch much too far advanced for a man probably only in his early forties. He seemed casually friendly, but I immediately suspected a serious reason for this unannounced visit on a Sunday. I asked him to accompany me to the house.

"I'm going to be right upfront," he said when I'd set a mug of coffee in front of him at the kitchen table. "We've got a problem."

I think I just stared, waiting.

"There was another suicide."

22

I stood in the anemic light of the dying day.

I am the pastor of Stella Maris parish, Creignish, Nova Scotia.

The thought was comforting. Something about the clarity and the objectivity. This is who I am. No longer the rootless Purificator, named for the small linen cloth we use to wipe the chalice before and after Communion. What wit came up with that one? So many of these priests are clever, funny men. The freaks are so rare. But they're the only ones I really know. How have I managed to spend twenty-seven years in this ministry and know only the bad ones? Why have I never been part of the wider community of funny, clever and perhaps even holy men? What is it that draws me to the tragic and the flawed?

I sat as darkness overwhelmed the struggling light.

Another suicide? Actually, it was the first, MacLeod said. A year ago. In British Columbia.

"There are affidavits filed."

"Affidavits?"

"From people claiming that they were victims too. That poor fellow in B.C. was only part of a larger problem."

"And did they mention Bell?"

"Oh, no. Not Bell. This is something altogether different. I'm surprised you haven't heard about it. Considering how tight you are with the bishop."

I wanted to call Stella, just for the comfort of her voice, but I couldn't because I knew I wouldn't be able to keep quiet. And I could imagine how her face would freeze over as I collapsed under the weight of what I knew. And yet I also knew what I desperately needed.

"Well, if it wasn't Bell—"

"Do you remember old Father Roddie MacVicar? I think we talked about him—God, it must have been six or seven years ago. Fooling around with some handicapped person. You kind of put me off the trail. Don't get me wrong, I understand entirely."

The smile was an accusation.

"Have you spoken to the bishop?" I asked. "About this suicide in British Columbia?"

"I tried. He as much as told me where to get off. But this much I know . . . he knew all about it."

"You're telling me the bishop knew about this all along?"

"This one and a whole lot more. Obviously, he's pulling out all the stops to, forgive me for saying so . . . to cover it up."

Monday morning, March 25, I realized that I was out of everything. Milk. Bread. Liquor. The drive to town is ten miles. Sixteen kilometres. I will never get accustomed to metric measurements. I weigh 182 pounds. I am six feet two inches tall. It takes thirteen minutes to drive the ten-mile distance, taking into account the usual hang-up at the rotary and the convergence of roads and causeway, cars bumbling for access to Smitty's or the Esso station or the motels. Often a traffic jam when the bridge over the canal is open to allow the passage of a boat. Was it possible that I remembered a blacksmith's shop there somewhere a million years ago? And a little canteen where we hung around as teenagers. A hangout for the handful of young people in the village and stragglers from town, inspecting the local stock.

That was a big word then. *Stock.* Depersonalized, agricultural. Aroma of wieners cooking on some electrical gadget with prongs. Sweating Pepsi bottles. Heavy chromed cars with dangling air fresheners and cowboy music. Sounds and smells of anticipation. Hormones buzzing in the restless stock. A horn blows. A stampede. Slamming car doors, splatter of gravel, the shriek of rubber and the old lady who ran the canteen craning her neck in disapproving witness, checking who was going where with whom.

Innocence.

I missed that, whatever value it had. I was Angus MacAskill's boy from the Long Stretch. A skinny fella with red hair and a hair trigger. Into the books all the time. No money, no car. But respect. Oh, yes. Respect was the word. You had to watch him. A mean streak, meaner than his old man. Almost as mean as that Sandy Gillis, also from out there. But his sister. Now there! No parents to speak of. She has a different kind of streak. All wool and a yard wide. But don't let her brother catch you even looking at her. Don't let him catch you even thinking about her. Don't ever let him hear you saying anything negative about his sister or his old man. You'll be dead meat.

John and Sextus always thought it was hilarious that people were afraid of me.

Friendly smiles in the liquor store—or were they too familiar? Father this and Father that, as if I was in there every day. Somebody familiar up in the glass booth where the manager works, bent over paperwork. Looked up, nodded in my direction. A face from school. A name without meaning. Or could it have been that I *was* there every day by then?

There was a display of miniatures near the cash. The cashiers were talking about the weekend. The man in the glass booth was looking off into the distance, rubbing his chin. I picked a mini from the display, looked at it briefly, then slipped it into my jacket pocket.

Jesus Christ. What did you just do?

I broke into a sweat. I imagined that the man in the booth was watching. The store was silent, motionless and very hot.

I proceeded to the cash, paid for the bottle of Scotch in my hand. The miniature in my pocket felt like a stone.

As I walked toward the door, I was overwhelmed by a sexual excitement.

At Tim Horton's I ordered a sandwich and a large black coffee at the drive-through, then parked in a private place. A small cocktail before lunch? Why not. I emptied the mini into the coffee. The sandwich was also breakfast. The coffee shop was bustling with trade. The town's social hub. Retired people and the unemployed, banished from their homes by edgy wives or loneliness. I don't miss that. Home is my castle because I'm the only occupant. If this was England, I'd be a vicar. A better word. A vicar living in a vicarage. But the vicar always has a missus. A missus vicar. And if we had a son, he'd be . . . *Mac Vicar.* Very funny. I open the bottle that I paid for. Pour a bit more into the coffee to improve the flavour.

She said it: Live life.

The young man in B.C. drove his big, expensive four-by-four pickup truck into a grove of trees somewhere on the B.C. Lower Mainland and shot himself. What do they mean by the Lower Mainland? I've never been to B.C. I should go. A man should see his own country. Stella said take a holiday in the Dominican Republic. Maybe I should go instead to B.C.

The note he left blamed Father MacVicar.

"Everybody called him Father Rod," MacLeod explained. "Apparently an awesome philosopher in his time. A Platonist, whatever that might be. An internationally renowned expert on Aristotle."

Did I detect a smirk?

Did I have any idea where Father MacVicar might be now?

No, I replied truthfully. In B.C.?

I understand somewhere in Ontario.

And how would you know that?

It's in one of the affidavits.

The Scotch and the coffee were like sunshine in my veins. I stared around. There was a crystal glare glinting off the other windshields. The large window of the coffee shop was impenetrable. If I was an ordinary man, I could have just walked in and sat and talked with the familiar people. But I am not an ordinary man. I am alone.

Did you really steal something in the liquor store? The tingling in my lap returned. I laughed aloud.

And then my spirits sank. I should have gone to see Stella. Wise, compassionate Stella. Told her everything. But where would I have started? What did I tell her before, when I told her about Alfonso? Did I tell her who killed him? Do I really know who killed him?

Yes.

Oh, Stella. There was so much goodness there. I'd be damned if I corrupted it. What is it about women? Why do we feel the need to turn to women, and in doing so degrade them, bring them down to the level of our lowest needs? I never really knew a woman before Jacinta. Only my sister, and she was just a girl. She is still just a girl. I smiled, thinking about my sister.

And there was Barbara. I almost laughed at Sextus and his ludicrous insinuation that we did anything more than fumble around in the back seat of a car on a moon-washed night at the shore. Where was it? Troy Beach. Why do they call it Troy?

The memory is warm now. And if there had been more than fumbling, I wouldn't have this gentle recollection of our innocence. I understand that she was anything but innocent, but I can now remember our brief time together with a purer kind of pleasure. No regrets at all. The way things should be.

But then there is also purity in the memory of Jacinta. No guilt whatsoever. Even now, after all these years, a sense of joyous satisfaction. Could that ever be repeated?

Donald A. said he and Barbara lived next to the little store on the old Sydney Road. Now he's Don, from working away, a stranger. I wondered what she looked like after all the years.

Drop by. He said it.

It was a tidy brick house. Don had done well in the construction trades. Even in March, the shrubbery seemed trimmed and cared for. Burlap wrap on the smaller bushes. Yellowed grass flattened as it was everywhere. Mulch on flower beds. Why was I there?

Live life, Stella said.

"My God, will you look at who's here," said Barbara. She was smiling broadly.

"You recognize me," I said.

"The hair. I'd know that hair anywhere."

Pelirrojo, I thought, and smiled.

I was in my leather jacket and jeans, baseball cap in hand.

"Come in, come in," she said.

The interior was heavy with a scent that Stella calls potpourri. Or maybe carpet cleaner. There was a lot of carpet. We went straight to the living room. Large generic prints of wild animals and flowers on the walls, furniture that was either new or mostly unused. She instructed me to sit. A large Persian cat jumped from behind me, stretched and yawned, then sulked out of the room.

"It's a miracle you caught me home," she said. "I've been out all morning."

By the look of her she'd been out at a beauty parlour. I calculated that she was just over fifty, but she could have passed for someone ten years younger.

"I bumped into Don," I said, "after Mass a while ago. I was just passing and stopped by on an impulse. I . . . I don't suppose he's in?"

"No. He's on a construction job at the mill. A big maintenance shutdown. Works all hours."

Suddenly I felt a profound awkwardness that all but silenced me. Why had I come here? "I won't stay. I'll come back another time for a proper visit."

"No. Don't be foolish. Sit."

And so I did.

"I was just going to make myself something," she said. "Coffee. Or maybe you'd rather a drink? I think we have everything."

"Maybe. For old times' sake."

"Yeeess," she said enthusiastically. "My God. How long has it been?"

"It depends."

"This is embarrassing, but did we go out together for a while?"

"Once," I said, feeling the blush on my cheeks.

"Young and crazy," she laughed, and left the room.

This can't be so bad, I thought.

I didn't remember the colour of her eyes, a pale blue, or her hair, which had become a rich auburn over time and with the attention of beauticians. She has kept her shape, I thought. Breasts actually larger than I remembered. Do they grow in middle age?

When she returned with drinks, I said, "You've done well for yourself. You and Don. It's a lovely place you have here."

"We get by. It was hard for a long time, with him travelling and the kids young."

"Don said you had two boys, I think."

"Yes," she said brightly, then fetched two framed portraits from the mantelpiece. Sat beside me. "Donnie and Michael. Both working away."

She was close, our thighs and elbows in contact. The boys were handsome in a rugged way. One of them had his father's boyhood face, even the trace of mockery that was never far from the mouth.

A giddy shiver passed through me. The memory or her thigh. Maybe both.

"He told me what they did," I said. "One's in Toronto?"

"Donnie is at the Ontario Food Terminal, for one of the big companies. Mike's the creative type. Designing websites in Boston, whatever that means. Wants to be a writer, if you can imagine."

"Fine-looking boys."

"They take after their father," she said, then returned the photos. "And yourself? I think I heard you were away somewhere. In the missions, was it, for a while?" She returned to the large chair a mile away across the room. Her brow was creased.

"Two years," I said. "In Central America."

"That would have been different."

"It was."

A momentary silence, both thinking back.

"I think it was probably only once or twice we went out," she said. "I don't think it was very serious."

"I don't think so."

"The reason I remember is that they teased me a lot about you, after you went to the san."

"The where?"

"What did I say?"

"The san."

"Oh God," she said. "I'm sorry. Last week was the anniversary of my mother's death. She passed away in Kentville. Forty years ago exactly. At the sanatorium there. I meant the *sem*. My head, these days." She shook it, smiling privately.

"San, sem. I suppose when you think about it, there isn't much difference."

Her head rolled back as she laughed. Her throat was white and the skin became as smooth as if she were still a teenager. And the words came back: *I guess you're mad at me.*

She was studying my face, perhaps remembering too. "Your mother also . . . if I remember rightly."

"Yes. Point Edward. Or St. Rita's, actually. They took her there at the end. She's buried in Sydney. Whitney Pier, to be exact."

"I didn't realize we had so much in common."

I smiled.

"But I guess it wasn't so unusual then. There was a lot of it around in the fifties. Not like now."

"Yes," I said.

She took our glasses to the kitchen.

"The strangest thing just came back to me," I said after the third drink.

"What's that?" she asked, head cocked to one side. She had refreshed her lipstick in the kitchen.

"You seemed to know that I was thinking of becoming a priest, even though I wasn't absolutely certain at the time. Maybe you felt safer, being with me."

"Oh, no," she said, clapping her hand over her mouth and blushing. "I doubt that. I was awful back then. I can't imagine what you thought, me bringing that up. Trying to tempt you, I suppose."

"Well . . . I still remember it."

She was blushing and looked away—toward the photos on the mantel, I imagined. "I can't believe I brought that up."

I realized then that we were holding hands. When did that happen? When she'd brought the third drink, she sat beside me. And asked about when my mother died.

"I don't remember much about it," I said.

"Neither do I, mine. But I was only twelve."

She is fifty-two, I thought.

"I have vague images," I said. "Adults telling me she was happier dead and that I should pray to her."

There was true sadness in her face. "It would have been worse for you," she said. She shrugged and squeezed my hand.

"My mother died in 1951," I said.

There was music somewhere. There was another drink. The light was fading in the room. Now she was sitting with legs folded beneath her, studying the contents of her glass.

"After you went to the seminary," she said, slurring slightly and laughing, "you wouldn't believe what some of them were saying. The girls."

The gurrels.

"Try me."

"That we . . . No. I'm not going to say it. You'd die." She put her drink down and caught her face between her palms, blushing and shaking her head. Her laugh was childlike. "They were saying that we had . . . *gone all the way*, as we used to put it. Can you believe it?"

I laughed, surprised by my calmness.

"Somebody went spreading that around!"

"I can't imagine who."

"You must think I'm terrible, remembering something like that how many years later. God."

"It doesn't feel like so many years."

"No," she said seriously.

"The years have been good to you. You haven't changed."

She blushed again. "But I don't think we did . . . did we?"

"No. We didn't. I'd certainly remember."

She was moving around the room, tidying up, when I returned from the bathroom. They have this instinct for tidying up. What would that be like? Somebody in the house with a natural urge to pick up and to clean up? A soft voice murmuring on an unseen stereo. This is the kind of place real human beings live in. Music in the background. I should have a stereo.

"It seems that we have met before and laughed before . . ."

"You're back," she said. "I was wondering."

"I really should go."

". . . who knows where or when."

"No, stay," she said quickly, then smiled. "I mean, there's no rush."

The phone rang. She chatted into the telephone briefly, then, looking my way with a wink, said, "You won't believe who I've got for a visitor."

I studied the floor.

"No. Father Duncan. Remember Duncan MacAskill? Yesssss. He was looking for you. So we were just having a drink, reminiscing. Yes. I'll tell him . . . There," she said, putting the phone down. "That was Don. He's going to be late. *Again.*"

I relaxed. Everything is okay, I thought, amazed. There is no deception. My car in front is now explained. Whatever happens in here is now conventional. Totally above-board. There is full disclosure. She waltzed across the room with an imaginary partner. I noticed that she had taken her shoes off. She had slender ankles, long, delicate feet. Red toenails.

"I love this song," she said.

I stood. "It's been years since I danced," I said. My feet were suddenly too large for the room. I was moving them slowly, deliberately. I could only think of her bare feet and my heavy shoes.

I stopped, stood still. I should take my shoes off. She misread my hesitation. Then she was full against my chest, face snug below my jaw. Pressing herself closer against me. Her forehead was hot. And then we were kissing.

She stepped back and sighed, tilted her head. There is beauty there, I thought. She has mysteries that are dark and rich.

"That just happened spontaneously," she said. "I hope you didn't mind."

"On the contrary."

"It must get lonely," she said.

Suddenly I couldn't speak.

"I know about lonely too," she said. She was holding both my hands. Then she put her arms around my waist and pressed her face against my shoulder. Then looked up. "I don't know why they automatically assume letting priests get married will make them . . . happier. Marriage is a lot of work."

"I think I should go," I said, fighting sorrow and confusion.

She nodded. "I don't blame you. Some old woman putting the make on you."

"You're lovely," I said.

She shook her head.

"Yes, you are. It's true. This isn't about you."

"The years are unkind to women," she said.

"On the contrary."

"You don't have to be nice."

I shook my head firmly. I wanted to reassure her further, that I was leaving because of fear—my fear of the voice I knew would occupy my head thenceforth, the fear of what the voice would say if we proceeded one step further than this.

I drew her to me. Sheltered from her searching eyes, I whispered, "I suppose you're mad at me."

"God, no. Why would you think that? Promise to come back?"

"I promise."

"I'm in the book."

I meant it, too. It will not be like the last time, I thought. And suddenly the sorrow came with the memory of Jacinta.

Passing the church in town, I noticed the police car in my rearview mirror.

23

John didn't stay long after we retrieved my car from the roadside. He came immediately when I called. I offered him a drink, but he was still on the wagon, he said. "I don't have to tell you what I'm like when I'm on the sauce."

I said nothing.

"But it's your lucky day," he said. "The Breathalyzer's no laughing matter anymore. The papers don't hesitate to nail a fella, even priests. You see their names from time to time, even judges." He was standing near my book-case. "Maybe a fella really should be writing things down, but then again, if you're anything like me, you've got an awful memory."

I thought: Perhaps a blessing. "Thanks for coming over. I didn't know who to call."

"I owe you. For last year, putting up with . . . whatever . . ."

"No."

"I can be an arsehole sometimes."

"You weren't."

"Another reason for avoiding diaries. Best to let the past just disappear."

After John was gone, I noticed the Mountie's business card where I'd left it on my desk. I picked it up. *Cpl. L. Roberts.* For an instant I considered calling him, to ask him what he knew. I laughed at myself, tossed the card aside.

The Mountie and MacLeod got nothing wrong. I'm the one who got it wrong.

"I've been shafted," I said aloud, and the words made me feel a little better.

The situation was straightforward. Father Roddie went to Ontario for treatment. Red carpet treatment, by the sound of it. A place called Orangeville. It was funny, almost. Red carpet treatment in Orangeville. I see tall maple trees and red brick buildings with Red Ensign flags. Many churches. A place where the clergy still retained some of the respectability of long-gone days. Something stirred in the memory about controversy in Orangeville a few years back. Something about the ordination of gay people by the United Church.

I can see Father Rod nodding sympathetically with his U.C. pals, counselling moderation and compassion. Lead by example, he'd say, and they'd listen to his wise words because he looks and sounds exactly the way moderate Protestants want to imagine R.C. priests to be. Like kindly bachelor uncles.

Old bastards, I thought. I struggled to banish the image of Father Roddie and the bishop bent over their cards, discussing their strategy. No thought given to the wreckage-strewn pathway old Rod had trod before that point. Apparently the suicide victim in B.C. came from Nova Scotia—somebody from before the banishment to Orangeville who fled to the west coast to escape his demons. But the demons followed. They tend to do that.

Rod was versatile. Retarded girls and frightened boys.

Briefly, the gallery of miserable faces assembled in my mind once again. Wretched. Embarrassed or angry or defiant. But always wretched.

"You don't know the whole story," Brendan Bell said quietly when I first gave him directions to Port Hood. Cross the causeway, turn left. After turning left, keep straight. I winked. Keeping straight is key.

He stared, then shook his head slowly. Smiled sadly.

"I'm sure I don't know the whole story," I conceded.

He seemed to brighten. "But I know what you're thinking, and I agree. 'The whole story' isn't really relevant, is it? I messed up. I'm glad it's out. Now I can get on with things."

"What do you plan to do?"

"I'm going to put in my probation and use the time to make a plan."

"That's good," I said.

Except that, while on probation, he reoffended. I was now convinced that I'd been taken in again.

And I remembered the voice from Honduras: Faced with destruction, the doomed find superhuman power to manipulate your emotions. You have the absolute physical power in your hand. The gun. But it's nothing compared to the power of their desperation. The power of the primeval will to live. Never allow engagement; never listen. Just pull the trigger, then walk away.

And that was how I did it, repeatedly. No engagement. No opportunity for them to cloud reality with their extenuating circumstances. Their cruel mothers and remote fathers. Their drinking/drug/psychiatric problems. Their loneliness and isolation and self-doubt. Their deep, deep philosophical issues, crises of faith, etc. It all boiled down, I knew, to character deficiencies.

"I could actually see you in this job someday," the bishop had said after Bell was gone, echoing the sentiment expressed by Father Rod. Is that where Father Rod got the idea? From Alex? During one of their bridge games? Or was it the other way around?

I could hear them: The young fellow has gumption.

A big word in that generation. *Gumption*. A word my father used a lot.

And then Alex dispatched his friend Rod to Orangeville. Episcopal Monopoly. A game. Passing Go. Collecting $200. Landing on Boardwalk, intact. Do Not Go to Jail. The secrets buried.

Now what?

I will not make the same mistake. I will not succumb to that kind of weakness. I'll find Brendan Bell and I'll not hesitate before I pull the trigger.

Alfonso and the two policemen spoke quietly outside for what seemed to be a long time. When he returned, his face was stony. He walked past without seeing me.

I stopped him. What do they want? I asked.

He ignored me.

Is there something wrong?

I have to go with them. They want to talk to me. Someone has been killed. Back home. A friend of mine. A priest.

He put his jacket on and went out again, drove away with them. I thought I saw the one they called Calero in the car.

According to MacLeod, the word is out. Word of the suicide in B.C. got back here to people in a parish where Father Rod put in a month or two some years back. Nobody thought much at the time about his comings and his goings. He was a philosopher who moved around a lot during brief recesses from the pressures of the university. How long had the bishop known about him?

At least half a dozen people had joined forces, hired a lawyer and sworn affidavits, and they wanted Father Rod's blood. The cops were busy trying to follow his trail back through all the places he'd been. The bishop wasn't being overly helpful, but I knew that the whole miserable mess was going to come out in the end. Including Bell.

"It'll be your call," the bishop warned. "But you're going to have to decide where you stand if this blows up in our faces."

The bishop can worry about MacVicar and the others. But I must find Bell, I realized. I sent him there. He must atone for both of us.

We are drunk now. The rum bottle almost empty. Alfonso has ceased his weeping. He has finally been able to pronounce a name. An unfamiliar name, at least to me. Rutilio. Have I never told you of my friend? Rutilio Grande? There was a real priest! According to the police, Rutilio and two parishioners were on their way from El Paisnal to Aguilares . . . Did I tell you that I come from Aguilares? They were driving in a car. To say Mass. I kid you not.

Alfonso is always using expressions like I kid you not, learned when he studied for a year in California.

On their way to say Mass. They were intercepted by gunmen and murdered.

They killed a priest? On his way to Mass?

He stared at me blearily. Oh, Pelirrojo, he said. The killers were also from Aguilares. My own people killed Rutilio.

And then he wept again.

Thursday evening, I saw the back of Sextus's pickup truck poking out from behind the house where Pat lives with her mother and her daughter. For a moment I considered stopping. They're probably playing cards, he and Pat and the old lady. That's what I need, a good game of Auction. Get my mind off things. The old lady would be thrilled to see the priest. But I drove on by. Maybe I should talk to Stella, drag everything out into the open once and for all. It's in her line of work, isn't it? Listening to people? I turned up the mountain road but saw immediately that her house was dark. I thought briefly of Barbara. She's in the phone book. I went home instead.

{ 24 }

The bishop called on a Thursday in early April. I'd been stewing about going to see him, trying to think of a way to tell him that I knew everything without provoking a confrontation. We have so much history. He has become my father. The breach would be too painful, but I just want out of this. If there's a parish open farther away from here, I want to go. Send me back to Central America. Send me to Rwanda, for Christ's sake. Then he called. We should have a talk, he said. I struggled to sound normal. He said he'd prefer to do it face to face.

"We're going to have to come up with a strategy," he told me on the phone. "Things are getting a little out of hand."

"I hear," I said.

"What did you hear?"

He seemed surprised, and it irritated me. "I had a visit from MacLeod," I said. "He basically told me everything."

"He basically did, eh?" There was a long silence as he waited for me to explain. "You better come over here," he said at last.

"Okay."

"Come now," he said.

"It's nine o'clock at night—"

"I'll expect you in an hour," he said, and put the phone down.

† † †

He looked older and smaller, standing backlit in the doorway. I'd been struggling with my emotions all the way over, dialogue buzzing inside my head. My goal was simple: to walk away from this.

Even I was surprised by how quickly it all unravelled.

"I want to know everything that MacLeod told you," he said without looking at me.

I studied his face carefully, searching for a gentler way to confront him.

"You haven't been entirely honest with me," I said, shocked at the sound of my own assertion.

His face flushed. He tilted his head to one side, eyes narrowed.

"MacLeod told me about the suicide in British Columbia. And he told me about the affidavits. And he told me about . . . Orangeville."

He seemed relieved. "What's any of that got to do with me being honest with you?"

"You failed to tell me the whole story of Father Rod. You didn't tell me you were covering up for him—"

"You're out of line," he snapped.

Silence hung and grew colder.

"Let's get back to the issues," he finally said. "What we do now. What we say. I've had a plainclothes Mountie here from Halifax. That's bad."

"I'm sorry," I said.

"What do you mean you're sorry?"

"I have nothing to offer. I thought our job was to get these guys out of circulation. How many more Father Rods are there? I thought our priority was to work with the families and the victims to—"

"Don't use that word in this house," he shouted.

"What word?"

"'Victim.' Don't you dare use that word in front of me, do you hear me?"

He was standing over me and a bolt of terror paralyzed my voice.

"You're with us or against us," he said, his voice hard and flat. "Victim, for God's sake. Don't make me sick." And he sat down, suddenly breathless.

I watched him as he recovered his composure. And as he calmed down, I could feel the storm gathering inside my chest and the ache beginning in my head. *With us or against us?* My mouth was dry. I stood up.

When I started for the door, he said, "Where do you think you're going?"

"I'm leaving."

I think I sat in the car on Main Street for twenty minutes before I finally drove off. Perhaps there was a childish part of me that expected him to follow. To open the car door, slide in. Save me. Say: Hell, what are we doing out here? Come on back in . . . I'll pour a Balvenie and we'll talk this through. I know I have a bit of explaining to do.

And over the drink he'd apologize and he'd explain how in our line of work we don't make many close friends. You hang around with other priests but rarely find true friendship. Usually they're just colleagues, at best acquaintances. And so, when you find a real honest-to-God friendship, it can sometimes acquire a value that outweighs your better judgment. And how very rarely you discover someone who is more than a friend. A kindred spirit. Family. That was what Father Rod was. Like a brother. Did you ever have a friend like that?

And I would tell him. Once, I had a friend like that.

I looked in the direction of the palace just in time to see the last of the downstairs lights go out.

I drove away. The night was darker than usual. There was an old man hitchhiking on the shoulder of a bleak stretch of high-way called the Dagger Woods. I was at least a hundred yards past him when some impulse caused me to slow down and pull over. I started backing up, slowed, stopped, waited. No one came, and as the seconds became minutes a strange chill crept through me and I put the car in gear and sped away.

may 20, 1977. i'm worried about alfonso. he's been in a funk since the murder of his friend in march. now he tells me that since 1972 there have been eleven priests and a seminarian assassinated in his country. since february this year, ten priests have been exiled . . . just like he was. did I not know that he, alfonso, was in exile here? eight others have been expelled, five of them tortured beforehand. i was one of the lucky ones, he said. he says he must go home. i tell him he must be cracking up.

Approaching my lane, I saw a car drive slowly down from the house, pause, then turn north. I couldn't see it clearly enough to identify a driver but was surprised to notice lights on in the glebe as I turned up. Then I saw Sextus's red truck parked in front.

He was in my study. He had a book open in his hand.

"Interesting," he said, closing it. "Everyone should keep a journal."

I took it from him, studying his face.

"I was passing by. The door was open."

"How much of this did you read?"

"Nothing of importance," he said, as if wounded. "I picked it up just before you walked in."

"Who was that driving away?"

"Driving away? I didn't see anybody."

The night is full of phantoms, I thought.

"I'm going to have a drink," I said. "Are you interested?"

"No," he said, yawning. "I think I'll take off. Where were you?"

"You're sure you won't have a nightcap?"

"No. I have to teach tomorrow. Somebody should do a story about the teacher absenteeism in the schools around here. It's great for substitutes like me."

I watched him go and braced myself for the despair. And with the click of the door behind him, it started. By the time I heard the roar of his engine, I could barely move to the liquor cupboard.

The living room was full of weak daylight when I woke on the chesterfield. Making my way painfully to my bedroom, I noticed that the door to the bishop's room was ajar. When you live alone, you notice the small changes. A door that is usually closed speaks to you when it isn't. When I peered inside, I saw a small dark shape on the floor beside the bed. It was a wallet. I picked it up. It fell open and I saw Sextus's Ontario driver's licence.

When the phone rang at mid-morning, I assumed it was Sextus calling about the wallet, but it was the bishop. He was conciliatory. He wanted me to come over right away. We should sit down together with the lawyers, get their advice. He used "we" a lot and I knew it was deliberate. There were the Mounties and there was MacLeod. There was going to be publicity and we needed guidance.

"We need a strategy," he said. "Plus, you have an in with MacLeod."

Finally I said: "I'm not sure what I can contribute."

I knew he was having a difficult time suppressing his exasperation.

"Don't you worry about that," he said wearily. "Just get your-self over here. I'm going to tell them two this afternoon."

When he was gone, I looked at the clock. Not quite noon, I thought.

Ah, well. It's noon somewhere. Reached for the cupboard.

{ 25 }

Ishowered and dressed. I think it was just as I reached for the can of shaving lather that I decided: No power on earth or in heaven could persuade me to go to see the bishop. I'm finished.

Pat came by a little later, before I'd completely lost control. I heard the car outside and had time to conceal my glass. I was sitting in the living room, breviary on my lap, when I heard her in the kitchen.

"Hello," I called out. "Who is it?"

"Only me," she answered in her merry voice. "Just checking in."

Plans for the baptism, I thought as she entered the room and perched on the arm of an easy chair. I waited, but she just sat and seemed to be studying me.

"You look so tired," she said eventually. "How have you been sleeping?"

I dismissed the inquiry with a wave of my hand. "You get old. You always look tired."

"Old. You're far from old."

"You're a nice lady."

"I was just heading for town," she said, standing. "Wondered if there was anything you need."

I assured her that I didn't need anything she could find in town.

She laughed. "I'll go, then . . . Do you mind if I use the bathroom first?"

There's a small toilet off the kitchen, but I heard her footsteps on the stairs, then I heard her moving about above me. And then silence.

When she came down, she seemed distracted and I asked if everything was okay.

"Yes," she said. With a weak smile and a wave of the hand, she left, and it was only when she was gone that I understood.

The wallet, I told myself. She was looking for the wallet, and I almost laughed aloud.

When Stella arrived, my cheer was much improved. This time I didn't have a chance to hide the glass, so I asked if she'd join me. She declined.

"You've had an early start," she said.

"Oh, come on. What's wrong with a cocktail before dinner?" When I stood to reassure her, I staggered, and sat down again quickly, hoping she hadn't noticed. Finally I said, "You'll have to forgive me." And to my horror, I felt hot tears of self-pity. Fortunately, she was looking away at that particular moment.

Then she stood in front of my chair and leaned to rest her hands on the arms, staring directly into my eyes. "I'm really worried about you."

I remember reaching up clumsily, attempting to draw her down toward me. But she caught my wrists and freed herself.

"No," she said quietly. She bent, reached down beside my chair and took my glass, and was about to leave when I spoke sharply. Considerably louder than I'd intended.

"God damn it, put that back."

She turned, a shocked expression on her face.

"I'm not a child," I said. "I don't need a mother."

The words seemed to hang in the air.

"I don't need a mother," I repeated. The words had a grand liberating ring to them.

"Fine," she said, and handed me the glass.

I didn't realize she was gone until I heard the door close behind her.

Then Mullins was standing in the room.

"Jesus Christ," I said sharply. "What is this? Grand Central Station?"

I'll say this for Mullins: he's quick on the uptake. "I seem to have come at a bad moment," he said.

"No, no," I said, struggling out of the chair. "You've come at the perfect moment." I was in danger of falling. "What can I do you for?" And I started to laugh. One of my old man's favourite expressions: What can I do you for? "Come on. Let me get you a little drink."

He had his hand on my arm, attempting to steer me toward the chesterfield. "Here, I think you should sit over here and rest. Close your eyes for a minute. I'll wait."

I tried to shake him off but, fearing a complete collapse, sat heavily. "I don't know how this happened," I muttered.

"It's okay," he said soothingly.

"Where did you drop from?"

"Just passing by."

I wagged a finger, eyes closed. "Lying is a mortal sin," I said.

I'm not sure how long I slept. Maybe an hour. When I opened my eyes, Mullins was still there.

"Hey," he said. "He is risen. Alleluia."

The room was softly lit.

"Let me get you a cup of tea," he said, walking toward the kitchen. "I took the liberty."

I struggled to my feet and followed him. He was pouring.

"I have a prayer group tonight," he said. "I'm afraid I'll have to be off. You'll be okay?"

"I'm fine. You didn't have to bother."

"No bother at all," he said, handing me a steaming mug. "I'd really like to stay, but—"

"Really. You shouldn't—"

"By the way," he added, almost as an afterthought. "His Excellency over the way called while you were asleep. Seemed surprised that I was here. I acted as though we visit all the time. He said he was expecting you . . . over there." He paused for a moment, expectantly. "I told him that I'd just dropped by and that you were out. I don't consider that a lie. Do you?"

Not a bad fellow, that Mullins, I thought, watching him disappear down the lane.

I realize, in retrospect, that it was inevitable Sextus would show up. But I was still surprised when he did. I must have known that he wouldn't be able to pretend he hadn't lost his wallet in the bishop's room, and I can't imagine that, with his devious mind, he wouldn't have known that I'd have figured out what he'd been doing there. It was all so sordid, and probably, in a different time and place, funny in a farcical way.

When he finally arrived, I was at the kitchen table and I had the wallet opened up in front of me. Normally I'd have felt guilty, exploring someone's privacy. When we were boys, he always carried a condom in his wallet. A French safe, we called it. The one place nobody would ever look. He only stopped when the familiar outline of the thing became permanently imprinted on the leather.

Now, no condom in the wallet. I understand women now take the responsibility. So much for *Humanae Vitae*. There was ninety-five dollars in cash. Credit and debit cards. The driver's licence. A health card. All in little slots. I'd decided to explore deeper into the recesses. He'd obviously had it for years and it had softened and rounded to conform to his hip. I found old movie stubs, some tickets for the Toronto Transit Commission. A laundry receipt from 1989. And a small photograph of Cassie. His and Effie's daughter. My niece. How did the bishop describe us? Asymmetrical, I think. A gentler word than dysfunctional.

"What are you doing?" he asked. I noticed traces of a chill in his tone.

"Just browsing," I said.

"That's my wallet."

"So I see."

"Do you mind?" he said, picking it up and examining it quickly.

I had Cassie's photo in my hand.

"I have to say," he said, colour rising in his cheeks, "I feel a little bit . . . violated."

"Do you now," I said calmly.

I knew he was in transition from anxiety to indignation. Probably fretted all the way here about how he was going to broach the subject of the missing wallet, already informed by Pat that she didn't find it where it should have been, at the scene of the crime.

Our eyes were locked. We've known each other so long, I thought, the mental processes are probably identical.

"Okay, then," he said finally. "Let's not fuck around. You found it. You know what's going on. Give me the picture."

"Just out of curiosity," I said. "How many times?"

"What is this? Confession?"

"Maybe that would be appropriate."

"Okay," he replied, smiling. "Four times. What's my penance?"

"And, also just from curiosity, what was the charm of this place? Why didn't you use your own pad for the little tryst?"

"What's the difference? It was spontaneous and it happened here. Plus, the old lady keeps her on a short leash . . . She doesn't want to stray too far." He quickly snatched the photo from my hand and shoved it into a compartment of the wallet.

"She's a beautiful young woman," I said.

"Pat?"

"No. Cassie. John used to say she looks like a Gillis. But I see my sister in her face."

He was looking at me suspiciously.

"Have you talked to Effie lately?" I asked.

"What's this all about?" he said.

"I don't know. Call me old-fashioned."

"That's your whole problem."

"Really?"

"I could see it in your face, looking at Cassie's picture. The longing. That's the tragedy of your predicament."

"Interesting way of putting it. 'The tragedy of—'"

"You need a woman," he said, taking a bottle from the cupboard.

"You seem to have some spares," I said, but he ignored me. "Are you offering to share your inventory?"

He turned and smiled. "I guess we're even now."

"Oh?"

"Invading each other's privacy."

"I'm not sure I follow."

"This Jacinta. You never told me."

"You said you didn't—"

"Ah, well," he sighed. "I guess I lied."

"You really are a prick."

"And this Alfonso guy. How did you guys ever work out your

little thing over—how do you pronounce that name? Jacinta? Or *Ya-cintha*. Your little . . . ménage."

I just stared.

"You walked in before I got to the end of the story. You left me hanging. When can I read the rest?"

"Be my guest," I said. "You know where my journals are."

I walked out.

The church, I realized, is always warmer than the house. A waste of energy, I suppose, but necessary. Old buildings suffer when neglected, like old people. You have to keep them warm and busy. I've failed to keep the old place busy. Confessions from time to time. Sunday masses. A funeral now and then. Hardly ever a wedding or a baptism. The wind outside has a different sound now. Softer in its exploration of the corners and the windows. Soft hands pressing. Spring, I realize. It is spring again.

It was spring, May 29, 1977, to be exact. It was Pentecost Sunday. You could smell the freshness, the fragrance of hope. In the soft mornings the flower scents and the tart charcoal smoke mingled in the heavy mist when I'd creep through the silent house, getting the coffee ready for Alfonso and the others. But on this Sunday morning, May 29, he seemed to have risen before me. I know it was the twenty-ninth because, the evening before, he remarked that this day would be John F. Kennedy's birthday. If he had lived, he'd be turning sixty. Hard to imagine. Kennedy an old man. And we speculated briefly on a different kind of world. A world without Johnson, without Nixon. Maybe without Vietnam. I wouldn't be so sure of that, someone said. Kennedy was also an imperialist.

And now I could see a light from the tiny cubicle Alfonso calls his office. He didn't answer when I softly called a greeting.

I imagined that he did, but I now know differently. He was always quiet in the mornings. Alfonso was not a morning person. And when I brought the mug of coffee to where he was sitting, I realized that he had probably been there all night. He had his head down on the desk. It had become his common practice to stay up late, long into the small hours of the morning, reading, writing. Sleeping there was not uncommon, ever since March and the murder of his friend Rutilio. Always reading and writing. It was his way, he said, of finding truth in chaos.

I touched his shoulder gently. Hey, buddy, I whispered. Room service. He didn't move. And then, in the light of the reading lamp, I saw that the papers spread in front of him were black-ened from a viscous stream that began behind his ear, followed his jawline and his arm over the back of his pale, motionless hand, covering his documents then dripping over the edge of the desk, finally pooling on the floor around my feet.

I heard the sound of wind stirring, but it was not the wind. It was the church door, opening carefully, closing softly. I felt his presence behind me. Breathed deeply.

"I wasn't sure where you went," he said quietly.

A small sound then, some tiny creature scurrying, disturbed by our voices.

"It's peaceful here," he said. And then he was beside me. He was carrying a tumbler and it was almost full.

"Take a sip."

I did, and it was strong. Straight liquor.

"I really am a prick," he said. "Why didn't you just slug me?"

"I haven't slugged anyone for years. Plus, it doesn't help."

We were side by side, looking straight ahead toward the small, flickering lights beside the altar.

"True," he said. "There really isn't anything we can do."

"No."

"Just go with the flow, I guess."

We sat like that for a while, handing the glass back and forth.

"We're the spawn of the most screwed-up, violent, self-absorbed, navel-gazing century in human history."

"Hmmmmm."

"And buddy up there, hanging on the Cross," he said, nodding toward the front of the church. "He's done dick-all to mitigate it. He dropped the ball. Agree or disagree?"

"What's it doing out?" I asked. "Is it windy?"

"God, no. It's beautiful. It's almost spring."

A car drove past.

"Who was this Alfonso, then?" he asked. "He must have been some heavy guy. Politically."

"Ahhhh. Alfonso."

Who was Alfonso?

"Alfonso was . . . I don't know. Just a priest, I guess."

BOOK FOUR

††††

In the Lord put I my trust:
how say ye to my soul,
Flee as a bird to your mountain?
PSALMS

{ 26 }

And then it was June. The corrosive winter wind had stripped long flakes of paint from the hull of the *Jacinta*. A cab door had blown open. The VHF aerial veered crookedly, half off the roof. I made a list of the jobs I had to do. Charge battery. Change oil. Sand and repaint hull. Replace ropes. The clarity was a relief. Perhaps it would clear the way for larger questions and answers. The sound in the distance, a vehicle rounding the turn by MacDougall's, was a distraction. I stopped and watched. It was a truck.

I returned to the examination of my boat. A week of work, I figured, and she'd be ready for the water again.

The truck slowed, turned toward where I was parked. It was Danny Ban. He drove carefully over the rutted ground. Stopped and climbed out, a large hand gripping the door frame as he steadied himself. He approached carrying a cane, shook my hand wordlessly, examining my face.

"It's staying cold," he said.

"It is."

"June is always like that here. You can't trust the slut."

I smiled. I noticed a faint trace of alcohol on his breath. I'm more conscious of it now.

"How are you, anyway, Danny?"

"Ah, well," he said, studying the horizon. "Gettin' by." He turned away then, to study the *Jacinta*. "She's looking a little the worse for the hard winter we had."

I nodded.

He moved slowly between the boats, bending, examining, eyes narrowed. Reached into his pocket and removed a jack-knife, opened the blade and jabbed at the bottom of the hull in places. "She's in good shape, considering the shape she's in. A little soft here and there, like the rest of us." Stood straight and smiled. Then looked toward his son's boat. The *Lady Hawthorne*. "This one stood up okay. That's where the fibre-glass puts them ahead of the old ones. Snow gets in, but it doesn't bother them."

The face was sorrowful. "I suppose you heard. I sold her last month. Got a decent offer and figured what the hell. She's no good to me. Just another reminder. Got enough of those. I told the fella I'd prefer if somebody took her out of here altogether. Jackie Dan J. sold the *Lady Amy* and she went to Cheticamp. That's what I wanted. Somewhere far away from here. But buddy said he wants to stay here in Little Harbour. So I told him he was going to have to change the name and paint her a differ-ent colour. He agreed to that."

There was the sudden roar of a diesel reversing, a boat returning from the lobster banks, positioning itself below the winch at the loading dock. We stood and watched for a while.

"Cameron Angus D. is late today," he said.

"So who bought it?" I asked at last.

"Oh. I didn't tell you. That American who ties up behind yourself. Dave. He needs something for getting back and forth to his island. Wanted something bigger than the one he had so he can make her into a yacht eventually."

I laughed. The American.

Finally he said, "You were away for a while."

"Yes. A little rehabilitation."

† † †

Though it was near the start of spring, winter still ruled the darkness. Our feet crunched the crystal snow as Sextus and I shuffled beside his truck, thinking the words that failed to capture our regrets. He laid a hand on my forearm briefly, then opened the truck door and climbed in.

Under the cab light his face was pale. Looking straight ahead, he turned the key, and the sound and smell of the engine restored a welcome normalcy to the sinister night.

And it occurred to me, as he backed away, that I had seen that face before. The unusual concentration of the self-absorbed, the isolated. Despair, suddenly revealed. I watched as he drove away, tail lights fading.

"Be careful, my friend," I said to the darkness.

I could not have anticipated Alfonso. I didn't understand the history, the sociology, how people place themselves in the path of inevitable disaster, even if they don't want to. I didn't understand the politics. I didn't even understand the language properly. I was a stranger there. I am not a stranger here, but I am no less impotent.

There was no weapon to be found, only its effect. The fatal entry was behind his right ear. There was no note. Only afterwards did I realize that the message was embedded in the deed itself, a message from some other hidden source. *Beware*.

This I learned from Jacinta.

That desk, she said, is his Calvary. He died for all of us. Like his friend Rutilio. Crucified.

She was calm. Her anger now was everything, no longer obscured by her goodness. She gathered him up and went away to bury what was left of him in Aguilares, where he was born, where at least his memory will continue.

† † †

After Sextus left, I sat and watched for the promised sunrise, but I must have slept. His last words in the church: I wish you'd told me about it; it would have explained so much.

And I said, I don't think so.

When I woke, the room was full of light. I heard the quick, ringing roar of a passing pulp truck on the road below. I knew Stella was at work by then, but I rang her house anyway. Got the answering machine. Can you come by after work? I need a favour.

Then I called the bishop.

Danny seemed to sag with weariness as I explained briefly. Things were getting dodgy with the liquor, I told him. There's a facility in Ontario. I went there for forty days to dry out. Did a little thinking. It was a good break.

"You were tough," he said. "You just up and checked yourself in?"

"Actually, I talked it over with the bishop first."

"I'd never have suspected."

"No, no, no," I said, forcing a laugh. "It wasn't that far advanced. We just wanted to nip it in the bud before it got serious. It's something I have to watch. It's in the genes."

"Well, yes. We all have that."

"This is just between us, Danny."

"Oh, Jesus. You don't have to worry about me," he said.

"I know that."

"Forty days, eh? You can claim credit for two Lents, skip next year."

I laughed. "You never know. I might start skipping a lot of things."

He seemed to be chewing on the inside of his cheek. "Like . . . I wouldn't even want to think about that," he said, eyes fixed on mine. He turned and started toward his truck, then paused. "Why don't you come up sometime. To the house. I think it's time we had a talk. Man to man."

"Sure," I said, sudden anxiety rising. "Is there anything in particular?"

He ignored the question. "What did you call that . . . facility? In Ontario?"

"Braecrest."

Stella stood in the middle of the kitchen with her hands on her hips. Her face was a blank. "You obviously had company."

I just shrugged. I was standing in the doorway to the living room in the T-shirt and jeans I'd worn the day before. I could smell the rankness of my own body, sour internal gases and the alcoholic sweat. I could have cleaned up, my kitchen and myself. I considered doing so half a dozen times. But I was unable to rouse myself from the stupor that held me in my chair in a kind of paralysis all day. Maybe I wanted her to see my place like this. See me in my moral nakedness.

"Sextus came by," I said.

"That explains a lot."

"It got out of hand, obviously. I don't remember much after a certain point."

"Okay," she said, slipping out of her jacket.

"I didn't ask you to come here to do housework."

"Oh?" she said, arching her eyebrows.

"I need you to drive me over to Antigonish. I have to see the bishop."

"I see."

We just stood and stared at each other for a long time.

"First I think you should take a shower," she said. "I'll be back."

After she was gone, the bishop called. Bring a bag, he said. Plan on a few days away. Okay?

I sat for a long time on the stern of the *Jacinta* after Danny Ban had gone, legs dangling, chores forgotten. The water just over the dunes and beyond the waving marsh grass danced and flashed. Inviting. Its roughness concealing merriment, hard, glittering blue under the cloudless June sky. There was a sudden racket above my head, and when I looked into the sky I saw a heron flapping furiously high above, pursued by a screaming bald eagle. The lumbering heron, unaccustomed to speed, was well in front, but slowly I watched the gap between them close. There was no evasive action by the larger bird, just resolute, long-winged strokes, until the eagle was upon him. They locked in a brief, savage encounter that lasted only a few seconds. The heron fell, broken, fluttering slowly toward the shore. The eagle soared away in angry triumph.

I jumped from the boat and walked toward the water, eyes scanning the beach. He was nowhere to be found. I walked the shore for an hour, determined to find him. He had disappeared, as all broken creatures inevitably do.

Finally I just stood, facing the sea and the distant islands. The breeze was turning colder as the sun melted down, the foamy surf tumbling in the sand, inching closer to my feet. I asked myself: Did that really happen? Did I imagine that?

A party of gulls seemed to take up the search, swooping low along the beach, banking seaward then returning for repeated passes closer to the sand and stone.

† † †

Stella noticed the overnight bag and raised her eyebrows.

"The bishop told me to bring a bag. He implied I might be gone a few days."

"I see," she said.

"What do you see?"

"It'll all be for the best."

Driving up the long hill on the far side of the causeway, I asked, "What if I don't come back at all?"

"You'll come back."

"I've packed for more than a few days. I have a hunch."

"A hunch."

"I have some experience in these matters."

"What matters are you talking about?" she asked, squinting at the empty road.

"You'll know soon enough."

"Are you in some kind of trouble?"

"Yes."

"I won't ask what. As long as you know . . . I'll be here."

The bishop listened quietly, nodding, fiddling with a pencil as I spoke. Occasionally he made a note. Once he opened a desk drawer to study something. Then shut the drawer again. I was trying to get what I wanted without sending up too many warning balloons. Keep it in the realm of vagueness. It certainly wasn't overwork. But undoubtedly a lot of stress. Nothing I couldn't handle, he was sure.

"But maybe Creignish is the wrong place right now. A bit too close to home," I ventured. "Maybe I should really get out of the way. Go—"

"Maybe," he said. He seemed distracted.

"It occurred to me that a real change might be what I need. Something far away, like Latin America." I tried to smile.

"I do think you need a rest."

"A rest? I don't need a rest. I need an exit."

"I disagree." He was working at avoiding eye contact, distracted by the desk drawer. He kept opening it then easing it shut.

I decided to try a different tack. Was there anything new on the legal front?

"Don't worry about that," he said. "It's under control . . . more or less. Anyway, you're out of it now."

"I am?"

"I think that's half your problem. I loaded too much on you over the years. Let you get too involved in things I should have handled myself. I'm sorry about that." He didn't sound sorry. "Anyway. You've lost perspective and it's my fault."

I tried to speak, but he raised his hand.

"I'm not going to defend Roderick. He isn't perfect. But who is? Are you?" The blue eyes were glittering. "Am I?" he asked, then looked away. "But he isn't what you think. I know him as well as I know myself."

"I'm told there are affidavits," I said, braced for the backlash.

He sighed. "I've seen them. It's all fantasy. Not a concrete fact in the pile. Vague allegations. I saw something on TV the other night. False memory, or something like that. False memory syndrome. There's a lot of that around now. People accusing their fathers of all sorts of things. Teachers. Look at all that residential schools business. They're even after a bishop out west somewhere. People who can't defend themselves."

"There's the suicide . . ."

"Suicide. You of all people should understand that suicide is completely subjective. There's no shortage of reasons for suicide."

"But Father Roddie—"

"What I've decided," he said, clearing his throat and coughing slightly, "is that you need a spell of rest. Institutional rest.

Not like the last time. Honduras was another mistake. This time you need to be where things are controlled, where you don't have to think about anything . . . outside yourself."

"Wait a minute—"

He opened the drawer again and this time he drew out a large brown envelope. "You'll find it all in here. Plane tickets, brochures and a bit of cash for spending. You leave for Toronto tomorrow."

"Toronto . . ."

"You'll be picked up there. At the airport."

"Braecrest," I said.

"A good place. You'll get what you need there."

"I know all about Braecrest," I said bitterly.

But the meeting was over. I've heard people trying to describe their emotions upon being fired, or getting life-altering news from a spouse or a doctor. Now I know the feeling. Part fear, part confusion. But also relief. The locked gates of inevitability represent an inverse kind of liberation. Freedom from freedom. Suddenly my head was aching.

Braecrest.

"You're booked in for forty days," he said. "You'll be surprised how quickly it'll go by. Then we can talk about the other matters."

"Forty days. Forty days in the desert and then . . . crucifixion."

"Come on," he said, smiling at last. "You're overreacting." He stood. "I'll show you to your room."

"My room?"

"You'll spend the night here. I have a student coming in the morning. To drive you to the airport."

I shrugged. "I'd like to go home, actually," I said, overwhelmed by a feeling of loneliness.

"No," he said firmly. "It's begun. The rehab has begun."

"Someone brought me here," I said.

"Sure. He'll understand. I'll go out and tell him."

"No. I'll go."

"Suit yourself."

"Forty days?"

"Forty days."

Everything will seem different after a spell away, he promised. Then we'll see.

"By the way," he said, as if he'd just remembered, "MacLeod is planning to run his story. Any day now. I got that from the lawyers yesterday. I think it's written and ready to go. It's up to his bosses to get the nerve to print it. You haven't heard?"

I stared. So this is it.

"You'll be thankful to be away from it. One thing to be grateful for—I gather he isn't touching that Hawthorne suicide business. Apparently there's nothing about Bell at all. At least not now." He was studying me carefully. "We're obviously not going to just sit by and let it happen. But you'll be safe and sound when we counterattack."

And the truth dawned: he doesn't trust me.

"Does Braecrest have to know that I'm . . . a priest?" I asked.

He was taken aback. "You'll not be the first clergyman to pass through there. But I know what you mean."

"I'd like to keep a low profile."

"The institution will know. As far as the others are concerned, that'll be up to yourself."

"Good," I said.

"Morality resides in motivation. No point in advertising our problems. But . . . remember Peter in the garden."

I must have seemed confused.

"Denying the Saviour," he said. "Three times he did it, fulfilling the prophecy. 'And the cock crew . . .'" Then he laughed and whacked my back. "Go out and get rid of the poor fellow we've left sitting out there. Give him my apologies."

Stella seemed to be asleep. The car seat was pushed back and tilted. Her hands were loosely folded on her lap. Her face was turned in my direction, a trace of a smile around the mouth. A stray lock of hair fell across her brow. A hand moved automatically to brush it back. She wriggled her shoulders, pressing herself deeper into the seat. Life, I thought. Barbara. Jacinta. Stella. They all have that in common. Life hammering within them. The incessant call of life, drowning inhibitions.

I suddenly wanted to turn and walk away, never to be seen again.

The liquor store is open, I thought. It is next to a motel. The bus terminal is a short walk through town. I'll get through one more night with the help of the alcohol, then . . . tomorrow . . . start fresh. I will disappear. I will go south again. El Salvador is relatively peaceful now. Pick up where I left off. Become useful this time, because I am different now. Knowledge has overtaken faith.

I realized that she was watching me. She leaned across the front seat and unlocked the car door. I opened it.

She didn't seem surprised when I told her I was leaving for Ontario in the morning. I told her that I'd be gone for a while. She nodded.

Then she got out of the car and put her arms around my shoulders and buried her face in my neck. I could imagine the bishop watching from a window. But I didn't care.

Stella told me: "I wish you'd talk to Danny. We're worried about him."

"I saw him at the shore yesterday," I said. "I went down to check the boat. He showed up. He seemed okay to me."

She raised her eyebrows. "Maybe it's your effect on him. He's more comfortable with you. If you feel up to it, you should just drop by. I think he'd like that. He seems to be drinking a lot. You might be able to help. He talks about you. He seemed to go adrift when you were gone."

"Maybe I can talk to him now that I'm all rehabilitated myself," I said, trying to sound amused.

"I didn't mean that," she said with a trace of impatience, and turned away. "Only if you're feeling up to it . . . It was just an idea we had."

"We?"

"Jessie is awful worried about him."

He said it himself: It's time for a man-to-man talk. And I was ready for it. But the planned words and ideas all fled the moment I walked into his kitchen. I'd been avoiding people. I don't know why. I've heard recovery does that sometimes. Total withdrawal. From booze. From drugs. From other people.

"It never used to rain in June," Danny said. He was standing, staring out his kitchen window. "At least as I remember it.

June was always hot days . . . You'd be in school chomping at the bit to get outside. You'd already be in swimming every chance. Now look. It's damned near sleet out there."

"It's still *early* June," I said.

"I suppose."

The rain-streaked window distorted the bleak countryside. Wind thumped the house. An old clock clicked away the long seconds.

"The way I figure it," Danny said, lowering himself into his chair at the end of the kitchen table, "they have to be gone for at least as long as they were here before you can start forgetting them."

I was studying my empty teacup.

"It's like you're missing a tooth." I noticed that he pronounced it *thooth*, the way the old man did. "You've got a missing thooth and your tongue keeps going to the blank spot . . . as if one of these times the thooth is going to be back where it was. Do you know what I'm saying?"

I nodded.

"I expect it's going to be like that. Indefinitely. We had him here near twenty years. This house was basically for him. It's all about him, actually. I don't think the house will ever get used to it. The change. I figure it'll be years before we stop hearing him and feeling him . . . and waiting for him to walk in the door, or come galloping up out of the basement looking for food."

He stood again, walked slowly to the stove. Studied it for a moment. "The wife and I have actually been talking about selling the place. That's when we can talk about anything."

I cleared my throat. "I wouldn't make any hasty—"

"The big discovery was how little else we ever talked about, over the years . . . outside of himself. Now we don't dare talk about that. That's pretty well off limits. Which means it's kind of hard to find anything to talk about anymore . . . anything that matters to the both of us."

"You need time," I ventured.

"It's always harder for the mother," he said. He returned to the table then. "But what about yourself, Father? You didn't come all the way out here for a rehash of all that."

"Well . . ."

"Tell me all about your trip to Ontario. That whatever-it-was-called. Where you disappeared to."

"Braecrest."

At the Toronto airport there was a pale, fat seminarian holding up a sheet of paper with MAKASKEL in large crude letters. I assumed he meant me and walked over. He smiled.

"They told me to watch for red hair," he said.

I nodded. How much does he know?

"You're Father Duncan?"

"I am." The red priest, Pelirrojo.

"I'm Ron. I'm to drive you to Guelph. They said you could give me directions once we get there."

The directions were carefully typed on a sheet of paper in the brown envelope. There was a smaller white envelope that contained money. There was also a note.

There should be enough here to cover incidentals. You'll need to buy a few things. This should be enough for everything.

These are the directions to the place once you're off the 401. The driver won't necessarily know the way. And he won't know the purpose of your trip. God bless you. I will be praying for you. Before we know it you'll be back here, good as new.

Y'rs in Christ.
+AE.

Underneath the typed initials he scrawled his name. Alex.

Braecrest. Once the private home of a wealthy businessman. The main building was of imposing red brick and had a green copper roof. Cornices and pillars and darkened windows. Vast lawns and sculpted bushes, discreet flat-roofed modern buildings of pale brown brick tucked away among groves of budding maples, birch and poplar. Towering basswoods, ripe with rusty buds. A monastic ambience. Quiet men wandering, singly or in pairs. Dead silence, but for the sound of a single-cycle engine somewhere in the distance. Perhaps a leaf blower, clearing up the evidence of winter's ravages. I'm told I have to share a room. It's policy.

I said that I could live with it.

The physical discomfort didn't seem to last long. It was over by day four. The headaches and sweats, gone. No more grinding in the stomach. My clothing didn't hurt anymore. And for a few days that was enough to sustain a feeling of improvement, almost optimism. I only noticed the deeper hangover as the days went by.

That, I also got accustomed to.

Each morning I would wake predictably, as if roused, at 4:45, deep, deep anxiety creeping slowly through my confusion. The profound uneasiness someone labelled angst. Was it Heidegger or Sartre? How they've grappled for the proper word, all those thinkers. Anguish. Dread. Despair projected on the wall, spindly moving shadows, etchings from some outside light I never did identify. And the unfamiliar sound of another living presence nearby, the quiet breathing, just below the threshold of a snore. Jude, the meek and ever-considerate roommate, managing to suppress even the unconscious evidence of his existence.

Each morning at 6:25 he'd touch my shoulder.

"Time for the gym-nauseam," he'd say.

† † †

"The wife thinks I need something like that," Danny said. "A spell drying out. Not Ontario. Closer to home. She thinks the old monastery probably, over on the mainland. She brought it up a couple of times."

"It would have to be your decision."

"That's for sure. But the way I see it, there's a few things I have to sort out for myself before anything like that."

I just watched.

"There's the big 'why,'" he said. "Why why why why why. It's all I keep asking myself."

"Do you have any idea?" I asked carefully.

"I just know one thing for sure. I'm not buying that shit about them closing the harbour. There's more to it than that. Mullins can preach all he likes. But I know the kid. He wasn't going to go and do something like that over politics."

A gust of rain spattered the window with a sound like sand.

The gym at Braecrest was a busy, unpleasant place, animal sounds mingling with metallic clangs and bangs, human smells and chemical cleaners intermingled. The odours of institutionalized aggression, weary-looking men busy on stationary bicycles and treadmills and mats, exercising in slow motion. Jude and I would walk around the perimeter, swinging our arms by our sides and in circles, over our heads in stretches. We were about the same age.

"Just look at the poor t'ings," Jude said on our first morning. "You wonder what they t'ink they're accomplishing at this stage."

"So where are you from, Jude?"

"Originally . . . I'm from Newfoundland."

We'd walk around the perimeter of the gymnasium and finally out and through the lush green footpaths of the vast Braecrest estate, each alone within his privacy, to watch the sunrise.

How hard it is to recover any sense of why I was in Honduras or Creignish or Braecrest or anywhere else during this long journey away from where I started. My sacred vocation. My vows of service. A blur of sacramental encounters, in retrospect like one-night stands. Have I ever really paid attention to the mumbled evasions on the other side of the confessional screen? Have I ever really spoken my true feelings about the ignorant, intoxicated bliss of the marriage ritual? Or the phony, infantile expectations of the sacraments? Did I ever really care about the right to birth? And what about the rights thereafter? After we impose life on the unborn, then what? If we have a right to the beginning of a life, what about the middle and the end? And do we have a right to risk or, finally, reject the life we never asked for? To just lie down and wait . . . for . . . what?

Danny Ban said: "For a while it was just the anger. Going around just pissed off all the time. Not sad, if you can believe it. Just . . . pissed right off. Then it hit me, standing by his grave one day. It was Christmas. I went there bitter as cat shit. How could he do that? Taking the easy way out. Then I realized. No, boy. What you did took courage. What you did took guts. Whatever your reasons were."

I nodded.

"Of course, according to Mullins and the rest of you . . . if he wasn't crazy when he did it, he's probably in hell." The eyes were damp and his large hand suddenly grasped my sleeve. "But what if you're in hell already? What if your life turns into a little slice of hell? And it isn't of your own making? What are you supposed to do then, eh?"

I think it was at that moment all my words dried up.

"It was after that I could feel the sadness. I think it was better to be mad. You get over being mad, eventually. But this damned sadness just won't go away."

"So, what do you do for a living?" Jude asked during our first walk.

"A bit of this and a bit of that," I replied.

"I hear what you're saying," he said quietly. He stooped quickly and snatched at something on the ground, then he stood, turning a rusty object in his fingers. "This is a sign," he said, smiling.

"A sign of what?"

He handed me a small pin, and when I turned it over, it was a yellow happy face.

"Kitsch. Some smart person threw that away," I said, maliciously tossing it aside.

"Ah, no," he said softly, moving to retrieve it.

"You have a sister living in Toronto," the medical director said.

He was tall and young and pale, with black hair slicked back. The sign on his door said *Dr. Arrowsmith*. You wonder where a name like that comes from. Maker of arrows, I suppose. A medieval occupation.

"I've never known an Arrowsmith before," I said, to make conversation.

There was a trace of a smile at the corners of his mouth. He didn't lift his eyes from the page in front of him. "Are you close?"

"Next of kin. I guess you can't get much closer than that."

"Yes, I suppose." He turned the page. "There's a note here. You'd prefer not to be singled out as . . . clergy."

"If it isn't a problem."

He shrugged. "Any particular reason why?"

"Any particular reason why my profession should be conspicuous?"

"No. But I'd like to know if this means that you're in . . . some kind of transitional phase."

"I don't have an answer for you."

"You do realize you're sharing a room with another priest?"

"So I gathered."

"You don't have a problem with that? We could move you."

I shrugged. "It really doesn't matter."

"Good."

Danny sighed heavily, stood with difficulty.

"Got to take a slash," he said, then moved off slowly down the hall. But when he returned, I could smell the familiar fumes. Rum.

He isn't even trying to be deceptive, I thought. You can hide the ambiguous reek of vodka. But not rum.

He sighed again. "It's probably just the time of year. This is the first spring since I moved back here I haven't had traps in the water. Matter of fact . . . it's the first time in more than a hundred years one of us shore road MacKays don't have traps in the water. It's something when you think of it."

"Yes," I said.

"Some nights you wake up and it hits you," he said, staring at the table. "You feel some desperate, I can tell you. Like you dropped the ball somehow." He was shaking his head. "I suppose it's everything coming together. Himself gone. Me stuck in the house with this goddamned disease. Maybe if I could be busy. If I was able to get out there, fishing like before."

His dog came out of another room, paused by his knee for a moment, studied his face, then eased himself under the table and settled by our feet, curled up with his snout resting on a haunch.

"I can't explain what it feels like, out there on the water with the sun coming up. Then you realize, it's all over. I have to imagine it was something like that with the young fellow. All that talk about the future. A feeling of something being . . . destroyed. But that wouldn't have been enough. There was something else. Something he couldn't face. Not for another minute."

And then there was just the sound of the wind and the clock.

Even though it was only April, it felt like May at Braecrest. The air was damp and cool and rich with the fragrances of new growth. Spring birds chirruped cheerfully. Chickadees dee-dee-deed somewhere near but unseen. We'd stop at a look-off where they'd installed a rustic bench, cut out of logs. We'd sit.

"That's the escarpment," Jude said once, pointing to a high ridge cutting across our line of vision from the southeast.

"Is that so?"

"It's one of the defining topographical features of southern Ontario," he said softly, almost as though talking to himself. "Actually, it's one of the most interesting geological sites in the world."

"I've heard of it."

"Starts down near Niagara Falls and goes aaaaalll the way up to the end of the Bruce Peninsula."

"No kidding."

"Seven hundred and twenty-five klicks. Loaded with fossils. Hundreds of millions of years old. I taught high school geology in Ottawa."

"Well, well."

"The amazing thing is that there's a system of hiking trails all along it. I often wanted to take a month off and walk the whole darn thing. That would be awesome. Hiking and camping all the way."

"I don't suppose there's much stopping you," I said.

"True."

He fell silent then, obviously thinking about it.

"The wife thinks it has something to do with the girlfriend. That Sally. You knew she dropped him?"

"I figured."

He shook his head. "It goes to show how much the wife knows about the MacKay men."

"They were close, though," I said.

"Ohhhhhh, yes. They've been going around together since they were kids. First time I set eyes on her I couldn't believe it. Homely as a brush fence she was. Then she blossomed. Filled right out. Turned into one good-looking girl."

The dog stirred. Danny reached down and scratched between his ears.

"But it doesn't matter. There's nothing there to explain something like that. No way."

The wind and rain outside were getting louder. Or maybe it was the suffocating silence of the house whenever he stopped speaking.

"Of course, there was the thing in the hall in Creignish. But we talked about that. He was okay after that. Your reaction helped. Thank you for that. I understand there's still talk, but, by Jesus, I better not hear any of it."

"That had nothing to do with it."

"I shouldn't be bothering you with all this," Danny said after a long pause. "The doctor in town was saying I should be talking to a therapist."

I wanted to reach out, to reassure. But I couldn't even do that.

"What could a therapist do, anyway? You can't take the milk out of the tea, right?"

"You have to make up your own mind."

"Every time I think of going to one of them shrinks, I keep thinking of what the old man would say if he could see me. A good swift boot in the arse is all I need. That's what he'd say, and he wouldn't be far off the mark." He laughed. "I suppose you saw a few shrinks yourself, in that place . . . in Ontario."

The psychiatrist was a thin, athletic man, probably a decade younger than me. His name was Dr. Shaw, but he looked South Asian. He had my file in front of him. Look upon this as an opportunity, he was saying. A gift. Everybody should get an opportunity to take stock of things at some point, crisis or not. We all have our demons. I thought: He thinks he knows what I will know when I am finished here, and he believes that I will feel a certain awe and gratitude. This foresight makes it possible for him to overlook my sullen silence now.

"Your name," I said. "Isn't it Scottish?"

"I invented it. I used to be S–h–a–h. I'm in the business of reinventing people." He smiled.

"I want to make a couple of things clear," I said.

"Of course."

"I didn't come here by choice. And I have no idea what this place can do for me."

"That's perfectly understandable," he said. Then he stood. "Let me introduce you to your group. Just first names. No details necessary."

"Thank you."

There were half a dozen men of different ages and backgrounds, yet somehow similar. I wrapped my arms around my rib cage.

"This is Duncan," the group leader said. "He'll be with us for a while."

"HELLO, DUNCAN," they said in chorus.

I sat down. The shrink left quietly.

The leader asked if I would like to talk a bit about myself.

"Some other time," I said.

"I'm Scott and I'm an alcoholic," he announced, unasked.

There was a supportive murmur from the others.

"Make yourself at home," he said. "You're among friends."

They spoke about addiction as a common condition we all shared. A feature of some common culture we must try to come to terms with. Repeating with frequency that we are alcoholics, or addicts. I was reminded of how much I loathe the word "we" when used by strangers. It is coercion. But I sensed they got a certain feeling of comfort from the inclusiveness of "we." And in the constant assertions: I'm an alcoholic. I tried it once and there was a feeling of easy and unexpected progress. Like after you've said "Bless me, Father, for I have sinned. I confess to the almighty God and to you, Father." The false righteousness that comes after you've said "I'm sorry" even when you aren't.

The room was always too warm.

"What do you do for a living, Duncan?" somebody asked.

I was stumped for a moment. "Human resources," I said eventually.

Off to one side, Jude eyed me, eyebrows raised.

Danny went to the bathroom again, apologizing.

"It's worse at night," he said. "I'm up at least once an hour, wringing the mitt. That's what the old man used to call it when he'd be pissing over the side of the boat. 'I'm just wringin' out the ol' fishin' mitt.' For me it's the old prostrate. They say it swells up on you. I suppose that'll be next thing. Prostrate cancer."

"Prostate," I corrected.

"Prostrate sounds more accurate," he said.

He laughed and shuffled away.

† † †

One member of the group was obviously a journalist. I felt I'd seen him somewhere before, then realized it was probably on television. He would never stand when he talked. He'd lean back on the hard metal chair, ass forward, legs stretched out, arms folded, head cocked to one side. Journalism is fuelled by alcohol and other drugs plus vanity, he declared during one of the sessions. A lethal cocktail.

But he talked mostly about a harsh father, a prairie farmer. He spoke dramatically about the desperation of surviving on the land, and about feeling trapped and stunted, longing for the day he'd get away. But he never really arrived anywhere he felt he could belong. Calgary, Winnipeg, Ottawa. Always imagining that he'd find his purpose in some kind of critical mass of energy and talent when he arrived at the next, larger place. But he always remained the outsider. His voice trembled.

The room was silent as a grave.

Finally, he settled in Toronto and got drunk and stayed that way until certain vital organs started giving out.

"You know, it takes about five years to really fuck yourself up," he said. "That's when you start to get really self-destructive."

"I don't think it had much to do with his concerns about the future," I said carefully. "But if it wasn't about his fear that he might not be able to make a go of it here, what do you—"

"I've been over everything," Danny said, shaking his head. "Every possibility. Sometimes I think maybe there was no deep reason for it at all. That's the trouble with guns. It's so easy with a gun. If you're impulsive. It's just done without really thinking it through. And he was impulsive. I guess."

"Do you think he talked to anybody? . . . Confided in anybody?"

"I'm suspicious about his mother. It's like she knows more than she's letting on. But you can't get a peep out of her. I've quit trying."

"How close was he to Brendan? Father Bell?"

"Now that would have been somebody worth talking to. They might have talked. But nobody seems to know where Bell ended up. You wouldn't have any connections, now, would you?"

I shook my head. "No," I lied.

"I suppose you have a family?" Jude said.

"No," I laughed. "No kith, no kin."

"That's unusual. You being east coast and Catholic."

I couldn't suppress my surprise. "What makes you think that?"

"First there's your accent. And . . . you left your rosary out on the table this morning. I wasn't spying."

"Very observant," I said, relaxing.

We studied each other for a moment, recalibrating. I remembered thinking, He knows nothing at all about me. I never felt so free. Maybe I was wrong.

"Which of course would make you close to my own age," he said.

"Oh? How so?"

"The rosary," he said confidently. "You never see that anymore."

I study the endless mass of the escarpment for a while. "So, tell me about being a priest," I say at last. "What's that like nowadays?"

He laughed. "A pretty big subject, that one. Especially nowadays," he said with a smile.

"I'm only guessing," I said uneasily.

"That's okay. You've got me pegged. I'm a reverend father."

There was another long pause.

"It's actually one of the questions I hope to answer for myself while I'm here," he said. "All 'about being a priest.' Nowadays." Then, after another moment, he put a hand on my knee. "I'm going to play a little game. I don't want you to tell me anything about yourself. I'm going to guess your line of work. Don't worry. I won't pry. I'm just going to figure it out for myself. All right?"

The absurdity makes me smile. "Okay by me."

"Right now I'm leaning toward the military. Something in the military." He sits back then and folds his arms, smiling broadly. Pleased at the prospect of a relationship, even if it's about a game.

I stand. "Since you're a priest . . . I told you a lie before."

"Oh?"

"Actually, I have a sister."

He nods. "I have nobody. Only child. Both parents gone to their rewards."

There is a light fog that gives the escarpment the appearance of a medieval hillside village. I can imagine the shapes of parapets and battlements. Tall trees, sculpted by the moving mists to look like ghostly towers. I say to Jude that it must be more than a little awkward to be a priest from Newfoundland in a place like this at a time like this.

"How so?"

"The scandals and the like," I say.

He laughs then falls silent for a while. "Frankly, I was surprised that you'd agree to stay in the same room with me after you found out what I am."

"It doesn't bother me," I say through a sudden wave of irritation. I knew, from the first moment I heard that I'd be rooming with a priest—this was penance. I sigh, perhaps too obviously.

"Anyway," he says. "You don't have to worry. I'm not one of Them."

I looked at him. His eyes were squinting as he tried to pick out geological details in the distance. "So you're just a garden-variety drunk, like the rest of us."

"Not even that," he said. "Never took a drink in my life. Except out of a chalice. You didn't happen to bring binoculars with you? The birds here are something else."

"No," I said, remembering golden afternoons studying the boats and ships silently ploughing through a flickering sea.

"You're okay?" He studied my face. I must be careful around this one.

"Of course."

"No," he continued. "Nothing quite as straightforward as alcoholism or sexual deviance. I think they're related, don't you?"

"I wouldn't know."

"I've known some of the people involved," he sighed. "Actually, a good friend, down in Burin. A Father Foley. It's almost always something that's brought out by liquor. I'm not excusing it or suggesting it isn't in there even when there's no liquor around. But I think it's a simple case of reduced inhibition, loss of judgment and character weakness. A combination of the three."

"I wouldn't be so sure," I said.

"That's just my own observation."

"I knew a priest from Newfoundland once. Maybe you heard of him. Father Bell. Brendan Bell."

"Oh, dear. Young Brendan. Well, well, well. So you knew young Brendan Bell."

There was a subtle variance in the sound outside, a soft bass tone, not unlike the wind. The dog rose under the table. Trotted toward the door, hard nails clicking on the floor. Barked sharply. Danny leaned across the table, placed a discreet forefinger on the curtain.

"Here's Willie," he said. Then sat back. "Actually," he said, drawing a circle on the tablecloth with the large forefinger, "I never got around to telling you this. But I knew your old man. Angus was his name, wasn't it?"

I must have looked surprised.

"I thought of it that day we met you at the shore . . . back . . . I forget when it was. A couple of years ago. But yes. I knew old Angus. We worked on the boats together."

"The boats?"

"Before they were making paper here, they shipped the raw wood pulp out by boat. All over the world it went. You'd get a few days' work when there was a boat in. That's where I ran into him. He never had a car. So I'd give him a lift occasionally. And now and then we'd stop at the old tavern, Billy Joe's, and have a couple and talk."

I just stared.

"He was awful proud of yourself, that's for sure."

The dog barked twice more.

"Shuddup," Danny said sharply. "Go lie down."

The dog looked at him apologetically.

Danny leaned toward the window, moved the curtain again. "Oh. Looks like he's leaving. It must have been your car. He'd figure if you were here, Jessie'd be here too." He watched. "Yeah, he's gone. Willie's been on a little toot. Went up to Toronto last month. First time off the island. Hasn't been the same since he got back." He chuckled. "Jessie can't stand poor Willie. Jessie or the dog. They get right hostile when he shows up. Women and dogs think they know when a man doesn't like them. Claim to have an instinct. She says Willie doesn't like women or kids or dogs, and they all sense that right away."

"You hear that," I said.

"Instinct is great. But I wouldn't put too much stock in it."

"Actually, I saw Willie in Toronto. I was staying at my sister's after Braecrest and he was there."

"And how was he?"

"Seemed fine to me."

"Ah, well. He's been on the sauce since he got back."

"Jessie and Willie are first cousins, aren't they?"

"Yes. You know, back somewhere in the woodpile, you might be related to him yourself."

"Oh?"

"I just figured that out lately. Thinking back to your old man. Old Angus."

"When was it you worked with him?"

"It was shortly after I came home. Around '70. Not long before he died, actually. I heard about it afterward. Didn't he freeze to death?"

"Yes."

"An awful thing, that, but they say it isn't a bad way to go."

"I suppose," I said. "If we get to choose." And instantly regretted it.

He looked away for a while, studying a spot on the floor. Then he stood and stretched. "I guess your dad had a hard time in the war. He never talked much about it, but you could tell. You can usually tell, when they won't talk about it, that there's probably something to talk about."

"There was something. Some incident, late in the war. We never really talked about it either. When you're young, you aren't usually interested."

"Well, isn't that the way. The things I'd like to ask the old man now. When it's too late." He was shaking his head slowly. "Oops. There it goes again. The old bladder. Sorry about this. I'll be wearing frigging diapers before you know it." And he headed for the hallway, lurching slightly.

When he came back, he said, "I'd offer you a drink, but I imagine, after all the trouble you went to getting off of it, you wouldn't be interested."

I waved a hand dismissively. "My sister mentioned once that we might be related to Willie."

"Ah, yes. How did it go? Through the Gillises out here. There was a family. All died out now. Jessie's grandfather and Willie's mother were brother and sister. And I gather there was a close relative. A cousin, I believe, who went away young then kind of dropped out of the picture. Your dad said that might have been his mother. I gather he never knew his real mother and father."

"So I understand."

"Wouldn't that be something. All of us related."

I laughed.

"Poor Willie," he said. "There's no harm in Willie."

Jude was struggling inside his memory.

"I think we're a little bit related. Brendan and me. If I have it right, my grandfather's mother was a Bell. Anyway, we come from the same place. A little village round the bay. I'm sure you never heard of it. He was only a little fellow when I left."

"When did you last have contact?"

"Oh, I can't remember. It would have been around the time I left. But I was getting news all along, when my folks were still alive. It was the second-biggest thing that ever happened to the village. Him going off to be a priest. I, of course, was the first big deal." He sighed. "It's hard to explain what it used to be like when a young fellow from a place like that ended up in the priesthood. It was like you belonged to everybody."

"I can imagine."

"So it's bad news for everybody when it doesn't work out. Right? A huge disappointment."

"So Brendan didn't work out?"

"Well, you might have heard yourself. He left. Went into business. Did well for himself, but it wasn't the same thing."

"Did anybody ever figure out why he left?"

"I guess so. But it isn't something anybody would want to talk about. Not openly."

"I understand. You wouldn't by any chance know how to get in touch with Brendan?"

He looked at me in surprise.

"Some friends of mine," I said, staring off toward the flanks of the escarpment. "They were close. I think they'd like to know where he got to."

"I think I have a phone number somewhere. A Toronto number. It might be in my book. Somebody from home gave it to me . . . in case I was ever in Toronto."

We retreated back into our silences. Somewhere nearby someone laughed.

"That's encouraging," he said. "The sound of happiness."

"So, Jude, if you don't mind my asking—what brings you here?"

He sighed. "I'm a thief."

The word just sits there between us. *Thief.*

He's smiling. "And what about yourself? What brings you here?"

"That's a complicated question," I say.

"You don't strike me as one of the usual run of addicts."

"I'm not. But I'm curious about you. I've known a lot of priests."

He stared at me. "How do you react to a priest being a thief?"

"I'm assuming that you're speaking metaphorically," I said.

"No," he said cheerfully. "I'm a plain, unvarnished rip-off artist. Stole from the parish where I was an assistant. Knew how to fix the books so it wouldn't show. Then, of course, there was an audit."

"But why?"

"I had the absolute worst addiction there is. I'm a gambler who loses. Then I became a thief."

"Gambling?"

"It started with lotto tickets. Before I knew it, I was back and forth to the casino in Montreal every chance I got and then some, getting deeper and deeper in the hole, until finally . . ." He shrugged. "And then, as so often happens, I picked up another addiction to cover the disgust I felt. I found that there are pills. Legal pills. In the drugstore. All you need is a sympathetic doc. And hey, when you wear the collar, everybody is sympathetic to your screw-ups. Makes them feel better about their own when the clergyman goes down. Especially a doctor. They love fallen priests." He laughed then. "I'm not being bitter about it. It's all my own fault. From the get-go."

"I don't know what to say," I said.

He held up his hand. "Say nothing. It's all behind me now. It's history. No more addiction. Except for the smokes. I tell them all that, but it's like they're waiting for more. Waiting for the big one."

"The big one?"

"The sexual stuff."

I shrugged, hoping he would stop there.

"But when you have my kinds of addictions, celibacy is a snap. Sex couldn't possibly match the ecstasies I've experienced. Sex is for the uninspired as far as I'm concerned."

"I suppose you're lucky," I said. And I realized he was watching, waiting for my disclosure. "I've never had the problem," I said finally.

He stared at me and the look said, You can talk to me, and I believed him.

"I have to admit," he said, and I assumed it was to change the subject, "now that I've given up on the military and the class-room, I can't begin to imagine what your calling could be."

"My father was a soldier once," I said.

"There you go. I wasn't entirely wrong. You were perhaps *ordained* to be a military man."

On my second visit to Dr. Shaw, he asked me: "Have you ever had . . . self-destructive fantasies?"

I hesitated, then I said: "Yes."

"But you've never acted on them."

"Obviously not."

He laughed. "I mean . . . no false starts, or . . ."

"No."

"And do you recall the circumstances that might have inspired these . . . fantasies?"

"Very clearly."

He waited. I cleared my throat.

"I struck my father once," I said.

"You struck . . . ?"

"With my fist. I hit him. And he fell." I know the trembling is obvious.

"Would you like a drink of water?" says Dr. Shaw.

"No, thanks. I'm fine."

"Try to go on."

"I don't think your father was ever out here," Danny said. "He didn't know anything about his connections. Seemed to me to be something else he didn't want to talk about." He laughed.

"So, what did you two manage to talk about to pass the time?"

"Well," said Danny, scratching his chin. "He talked an awful lot about yourself. The sun rose and set on you. Yourself and your sister."

"Yes," I said.

"I think your father only mentioned Effie the once. In a roundabout way. Something about her being away, for a long time, not having much contact. Whatever."

"Yes. Effie. So he didn't talk about her?"

"No. Not that I remember."

When I look back now, it seems that Dr. Shaw and I sat staring at each other for an hour, but it might have only been a minute.

"There was a misunderstanding," I said finally.

He raised an eyebrow, professionally puzzled.

"I know what you're thinking," I said. "We've reached the crux of my problem."

"Why don't you tell me about it?"

"He was fixated on my sister. I misunderstood."

The panic swells until I must struggle to squeeze breath into my lungs. And discover I am sitting on a hard wooden chair at the kitchen table, face drooling on the pages of a book. A philosophy textbook. It is called The General Science of Nature.

A sip of water helps. Dawn is not far off.

"The incident itself was nothing. It was tied into larger matters, many of them mysteries, before my time. Something from the war." I shrugged, hoping I'd deflected him.

I hear a floorboard creak. I just sit. Waiting. The moment has finally arrived. The shadow pauses near her bedroom door. A match flares briefly. I catch a waft of hellfire. His eye sockets appear empty as he leans into the cigarette. He draws deeply, the ember revealing a face I barely recognize. He turns toward the door.

Dr. Shaw was waiting.

"Look," I said. "You have to understand the family situation. There was my father, my sister and me, just the three of us, no mom. Our father was damaged by something that happened during World War Two. In Holland. There was an incident. A girl was killed. The details were never very clear. But it had a lasting impact on my father and a friend who was with him at the time."

The doctor made a note, briefly. "How was she killed, the girl?"

"A knife."

"And your father never explained?"

"Only cryptically. Apparently she shot his friend and was about to kill him. It seems he got her first."

"Did he ever mention why . . . she was . . . ?"

"No."

I move quickly, grab a shoulder, slam it to the wall. Our faces are close. His face, my face. The same face. I choke on the reek of yeast and sulphur and old sweat.

What do you think you're doing?

He is looking past me. Were it not for the cigarette, I could believe that he was sleepwalking.

He seems limp but then makes a sudden squirming move, and I feel a jolt. The anticipation of being struck. That's how it is. I feel the blow before it happens. A gift, they said in town. I could have been a boxer. I have anticipation. I hit the closest part of the face that is his face, our face, on the jawline, and he slumps to his knees. I hear a clatter, then I see the knife near his hand and I step back, shocked in the rush of satisfied awareness. The swiftness of it. A flash.

He is making an odd gasping sound between the coughing and sobbing. I think he is going to gag. Now feeling calm, I squat beside him and carefully move the knife.

I didn't know it was you, he says, breathing hard.

He reaches through the darkness, lays a trembling hand on my temple, fingers searching through my hair.

I see my sister standing in her doorway, hands concealing most of her face.

He sees her and jerks back.

There she is again, he says.

He is on his knees, groping for the knife. I grab it, quickly move away from him, hiding the blade behind my back.

That's her again. Look out!

There is a wildness in his face.

Effie is sobbing. Runs back into her bedroom. Door slams.

"And the friend, who was with him in Holland. Did you know him?"

"Yes. He was a neighbour."

"Ever speak to him?"

"No."

"Where is he now?"

"He . . . died."

There is a very, very long silence. The doctor seems to be expecting more. But I am finished.

"You think your dad was having flashbacks?"

"Obviously. What else could it have been?"

He stares, nodding, unconvinced. "And it was after that . . . you had some issues."

"Yes."

"Maybe that's enough for now. We can always come back to it."

I shake my head. "No. I put all that behind me a long time ago."

"Dunc, Dunc, Dunc," the voice is saying in my ear.

And then Jude is leaning over me, whispering fiercely. Hushing me like a father. I sit up quickly and he steps back.

"That's better," he said. "That was some dream."

"I'm sorry," I said, shaken.

"I'm going to have a smoke. I don't care what they say. Okay?"

"Go ahead," I said.

He eased the window up a few inches and pulled a chair close, stared out at the night, puffing thoughtfully, blowing the smoke out through the crack. My sweat became a chilly second skin.

"You can talk about it," he said. "That is, if you feel like it."

"It's an old dream. About an altercation I once had."

"An altercation?"

"It was with my father. It keeps coming back . . ."

"Ah, well. Altercations with our fathers. An old, old story."

"I guess so."

"You called out . . . your sister's name. That was what woke me up."

"Yes," I said. "She was there. What else did you hear?"

"Nothing intelligible." He bent to the window, puffed and exhaled through the narrow space into the impenetrable night outside.

"You didn't say what kind of pills," I said.

"Pills?"

"The ones you took when everything got to be too much."

There was a long silence. Then he made a list. Dilaudid. Percocet. Even Tylenol. Anything he could lay his hands on. Powdered and snorted. "Some inject, but I'm not into that. Have you ever heard of OxyContin?"

"I think so."

"The answer to everything," he said.

"I didn't realize."

"If heaven will feel that good," he said, shaking his head slowly, "I can hardly wait. I couldn't begin to describe it to you." His voice was sad. "It doesn't seem fair." Then he laughed in the darkness.

"What?"

"Any time you think you've found heaven on earth, some bastard comes along to inform you that, sorry, it's really hell."

Jude finished his cigarette and squeezed the ember between a thumb and a forefinger that were yellowed to the knuckles. Closed the window but remained sitting, staring out.

"Do you say Mass here?" I asked.

"Sometimes."

"Tell me the next time. I might go."

"Tomorrow, after breakfast. Have you ever been an altar boy?"

"Long ago."

"I'll need a server."

"Oh, no," I said quickly. "I couldn't—"

"Come on. Do me a favour."

"Okay," I said, suddenly feeling trapped.

"I'm going to try to grab a couple of more hours before the bloody gym-nuisances start at it again." He was quiet for a moment. "Your sister's name is Effie, right?"

"Yes. Did I tell you that?"

"You called it out just now. A lovely name, that. It makes me think of something solid but still . . . mysterious, wild and beautiful. Like the escarpment in the distance."

"It sounds like you might have known an Effie once."

"My dear man, yes, indeed I did."

I thought he was asleep, but he spoke from the darkness once more. "The once I *should* have gambled . . . I never did."

Dr. Shaw asked: "And did you ever discuss it with your sister? Why he was going to her room? What else might have happened?"

"No. We were kind of distant by then."

"I have to ask you: did you think she was being abused?"

"I don't know. Probably. Depending on how we understand abuse."

"But you never asked? Not even after you became a priest?"

"She moved out before then. And shortly after that, everything became complicated."

"The suicidal impulses. They began after this . . . altercation with your father?"

"Not immediately."

"Do you recall when?"

"Yes. My father's friend, who was involved in the incident. The man who died. He killed himself, actually."

The doctor raised his eyebrows.

"Later, in my own life, I'd find myself thinking a lot about what he did. And one day it came to me, objectively . . . that he'd made a reasonable choice, his way of escaping memories he couldn't live with. It just seemed to me to be a legitimate solution. A final fix. For everything."

"There is nothing reasonable about suicide."

"I know that now."

"And what do you think prevented it . . . when it seemed to make sense to you?"

"I didn't have the balls to do it myself."

"And when did you decide to be a priest?"

"Around that time."

He sat silently, thinking. The silence stretched.

Finally I spoke: "So you're thinking that the priesthood was a substitute for suicide?"

"Actually, no. But is that what *you* think?"

"It never crossed my mind before."

After Mass, I put away the cruets and bottles as Jude was folding his vestments. It had been a small congregation. Three people in the tiny chapel. A small, piney multi-faith room without any of the usual stations and statues out of consideration for the Protestants and Jews who might be inclined to go there for prayer or meditation. Wouldn't want to distract them with our idolatry.

Jude had a thoughtful approach to the liturgy, but I noticed that his hands and arms were shaking during the consecration.

"Thanks for that," he said.

"My pleasure," I said.

He was carefully arranging his chalice in a box with a velvet lining. "This is just about the only thing I didn't pawn."

"It looks expensive."

"My father gave it to me. That was why I couldn't bring myself to let it go. The poor old skipper. Hardly something he could afford."

"You and your father were close."

"Not really." He snapped the case shut then turned to me. "So, how long were you in the business?" he asked with a small smile.

"Business?"

"You know what I mean."

"What makes you think that?"

"Maybe just a guess. You're the first altar boy who knew my part better than his own."

"I didn't realize." I could feel my face burning.

"It was at the consecration. Maybe you didn't notice. I just stopped. You kept going."

I felt a surprising sense of loss. Then guilt. "Another priest in denial," I said. "What does that tell you?"

"Oh, I've done it a hundred times. When I'd be playing the tables at the casino, obviously I dressed and behaved like a layman. I think that was half the addiction. The thrill of becoming somebody else. It feels good. We're natural performers, in a way. Always acting in a role of one kind or another."

† † †

I can still see the intensity in the doctor's face. "These suicidal impulses. Did you ever discuss them with anybody?"

"Yes."

He sat, waiting.

"Years later. With a friend. A woman friend."

And then I asked Jacinta directly: "When will you come back? I have learned that it is the only way to the truth. A straight line. I want to know when you will come back from Aguilares. I want you to tell me honestly."

She studied my face for a long time, the eyes exploring. "I will tell you honestly. I don't know."

"Do you want to come back?"

"I want to be here more than I want anything. But there are other factors. There is work to do."

"I don't want anything to happen to you."

She smiled softly, placed her palm on my cheek. "They sent poor Alfonso *here* so nothing would happen to him."

"If you come back . . . I promise that I will become whatever I must become."

"You must become the man Alfonso saw in you. And that man is, for now, a priest." She placed her hand on my forehead to read my thoughts. The way the blind read Braille. "Your dreams rise to my fingertips. And I am not among them."

"I need you."

She shook her head.

"I'm afraid."

She moved the fingers to my lips. "You have everything you need already. There is nothing to be afraid of." She smiled.

"What are you thinking?" I asked.

"That we will never meet again."

"But we will. I'll make sure you'll always be able to contact me. I promise."

"Okay," she said. "You must stay safe to keep the promise."

"But you've never tried to stay in touch?"

Shaw had been busily taking notes, but at this point he was just listening, watching me intently.

"I heard from her once."

"After that?"

"Nothing."

"And was the death of your friend . . . the priest . . . was that officially resolved?"

"It was."

He studied me, waiting for more, then finally looked back down at the file. "Let's talk some more about your father."

"My father?"

"Don't you see the connection?"

"Connection?"

"Your father and the young woman. Your priesthood. They occupy the same place in your memory."

"Place? What place?"

"Despair neutralized by hope," he said.

Dear Pelirrojo:

I hope this letter finds you well and that you will not be surprised to discover that I am still in El Salvador. I have been here for three weeks and plan to stay. I am writing to reassure you . . . that I am fine, and to remind you of your promise to be strong.

† † †

Effie came to see me unannounced halfway through my third week. I was reading in my room when there was a gentle knock on my door.

"You have a visitor."

She wanted to take a walk, so I led her toward the look-off, where Jude and I would sit and contemplate the impenetrable escarpment.

"My God," she said. "It's almost worth provoking a crisis to be able to enjoy a little bit of this."

We just sat in silence for a while. Then I told her as much as I could remember of what Jude told me about the geology of the massive ridge. And then I told her a little bit about Jude.

Abruptly she said: "I couldn't believe it when I heard you were here."

"Who told you?"

"Sextus."

"How much did he tell you?"

"Just that he thought you were having some kind of break-down."

"He should talk."

"I know," she said. Then slipped back into her thoughtful privacy. Abruptly again: "Where do you think it started?"

"I don't know. There's a shrink here who thinks it originates with our parents."

"Very original."

"A fantasy mother. A tragic father. Archetypes, he calls them."

"I went to a shrink once," she said.

"I didn't know."

"After I broke up with Sextus the first time. I figured it was time to look for some new answers."

"New answers?"

"The old ones weren't working for me anymore. They basi-cally all started with two depressing words: 'Poor me.'"

Without thinking, I put my arm over her shoulders and drew her close to me. She said nothing and we just sat like that, silently watching the sun and the escarpment as they drew closer together.

"What else did Sextus have to say?" I asked after a long pause.

She sighed deeply. "If anybody needs therapy, it's poor Sextus."

After another silence I asked: "So what did you tell your shrink about our father?"

"I told him how guilty I felt. For how I despised him."

Before she left, she held my hand for what seemed like an unusually long time. "I realized in the end what our father's problem really was . . . and I'm not talking about the war. He had a bigger problem than that."

"Oh?"

"Wondering who he was. Something as simple as not know-ing who his grandparents really were. Not knowing who his father and his mother really were. Just having the name, with-out the substance or the history. Abandoned in time. Can't you see that?"

I laughed. "When did you learn all this stuff?"

"I've always known the basics, just like you. I never really put it all together until the day I spoke with old Peggy in Hawthorne, last year. You remember?"

"I remember."

"Did you know that Daddy's mother tried to leave him with her parents in Hawthorne?"

"You told me. Who was it you referred to? Hester something."

She smiled. "It must be hard to handle that kind of rejection."

"Does that explain the anger?"

"Partly, I suppose."

"And it's why you've forgiven him?"

She gave my hand a rough little shake before letting it go. "No. I forgave him long before I knew that."

Danny is contemplating the ceiling, arms folded. He seems relaxed.

"I don't suppose . . . doing away with yourself would ever enter the mind of a priest," he said. And then laughed at the absurdity.

"I'm sure it's happened," I said.

"I doubt that."

"What makes you so confident?"

"It couldn't happen. Not with the Holy Ghost looking after you."

"That's where you're wrong," I said.

On a Saturday morning at gym, Jude whispered excitedly: "I've got a pass! Probably because of what we are. They gave me a pass. We can go out for the afternoon. We'll take my car."

"Where are we going?" I said, feeling the sudden surge of childish anticipation.

"There's a place I want to show you. It's on the escarpment. Rattlesnake Point, it's called."

"Sounds inviting."

"We'll stop somewhere for lunch."

We drove in silence, eastward, for almost an hour. In the distance I could see a pinkish haze hanging over the metropolis.

"Imagine living in Toronto, under that," Jude said, pointing.

"I suppose we could just keep going," I said.

"We could. Just make tracks for the coast, eh? Imagine what it would be like down there now. Snow to your knees still, I'd bet. That's what I don't miss. The long winters."

He turned onto a smaller road that disappeared in trees, up the side of what seemed to be a low mountain.

"We're actually going into the escarpment," Jude said. "You should see this place on a nice fall day. The colours . . . it's like fire in all directions. Then it would be crowded with sightseers. It won't be too crowded this time of year."

There were only a few people there that day, older couples with dogs, a few solitary hikers. Taut ropes, attached to trees, disappeared over the edge of a high cliff.

"Rock climbers," Jude explained. "They practise here." He pointed toward Bronte Creek and described the remnants of an ancient Indian village nearby. "A nice brisk two-hour walk. We'll come back to do that some other time." Two large birds hovered in the pale blue sky. "Turkey buzzards," he said happily.

"They look like hawks or eagles," I said.

"No. Just vultures. Scavengers like the others . . . but not as nicely named." He was smiling. "It's all in the name, isn't it? If you called an eagle something else . . . he wouldn't be an eagle, would he?"

I sat down on a large rock, not far from the precipice.

"You know the eagle's secret?" he said. "He never lets us see him scavenging. You only see him soaring. Or sitting high up, somewhere out of reach. Kind of superior. He's *very* discreet about the mundane, the mortal. Like the priesthood used to be. Out of reach. It's easier to mythologize that way, priesthood and eaglehood both."

We were silent for a moment, watching the floating birds.

He stood and stretched. "Nature calls. I know there's a parking lot with a toilet not far from here."

"I'm just going to stay here for a moment," I said.

There was a long silence then, broken only by the gentle sighing of the breeze. In the distance I could see a fenceline, a large meadow in the foreground, trees following the contours of the land, disappearing over a rise, leaving only the sky.

I wondered if Brendan Bell had ever visited this place. I doubted it. He didn't strike me as the outdoor type. But I now knew that Father Roddie had occupied that landscape. Orangeville was over there somewhere. Did he marvel at that grandeur, and his luck?

I heard a voice, realizing that it was someone on a rope, dangling below me on the face of the cliff. I stood up and walked toward the edge, tried to peer over. But I saw only the jagged rocks below.

I felt a creeping chill. Then heard the voice again. It seemed to be from the rope. The words were indistinct. Birth is only the beginning of the journey. Life is but a passageway. Death is just the end of the beginning. I felt the surge of fear and grief. Don't think, the voice seemed to say. Believe in the Resurrection. Follow your faith. The fear is really only longing. The longing to be truly free. Eternity awaits you. Eternal freedom. There is nothing here. You know that now.

But Jacinta? I promised.

Jacinta was a lie, a fantasy.

There is no future. The future is an illusion. There is only now.

I was no longer conscious of the edge, or of the rocks below. Only of the soft meadow and the endless sky. I was suspended on a current of ecstasy, already airborne. Time fused, past, present, future merged, meadow and horizon—one continuum. I was on the threshold of the absolute.

Act. Don't think. You're almost there. I took a deep breath. Closed my eyes.

Jude's hand was gentle on my shoulder. "It's something I could never do," he said, peering past me. "This rock climbing . . . you'd have to have a death wish. Dopes on ropes, I call them."

The voice was soft, the chuckle a low, insinuating rumble in his throat, his fingers now firm, digging into the cloth of my jacket, drawing me back, away from the ledge, toward him.

"You have to be careful near the edge," he said. "The overhang is treacherous in places."

I turned my head toward his voice and he was staring off dreamily, past me into the distance.

Finally, Danny cleared his throat and slowly said: "But you don't think . . . if your friend hadn't come along?"

"I don't know," I said.

"You'd never expect that somebody in your line of work . . ."

And I heard myself ask: "What is my line of work? What do you think my line of work should be?"

The expression on his face was the look of a child trying to understand abandonment.

So I said: "Danny . . . let me tell you what I think a priest should be. I think a priest should, first of all, be human."

I kept it brief. I had a friend once in a place called Honduras. An exemplary priest, perhaps the only one I've ever known. Danny listened, face solemn, until I finished, then just sat for a long, still moment.

Around the silence there was wind. He coughed briefly, cleared his throat.

"Well, well, well," he said. "That's some story."

The clock ticked.

"I guess a fella never really knows what people have to put up with." He shook his shaggy head then stood. "Excuse me for a minute," he said. And shuffled down the hallway.

When he came back, he asked: "So who do you think killed the poor fellow? The priest. Your friend."

"In a way," I said, "I did."

† † †

They'd been gone, our dead Alfonso and Jacinta, for almost a week. Now the cops were back. Calero and a younger man. They were in uniform, and one of them had a weapon you rarely see in the hands of a policeman. It was a machine gun of some type, short and stubby, with an oversized ammunition clip protruding. He had his finger on the trigger out of habit. The third man was a civilian, a Canadian. From the embassy, he said.

"We have a potentially awkward situation," he said.

"How well did you know this woman, Jacinta?" Calero asked.

"Well enough," I said.

"Do you know where she is now?"

I shrugged. "In El Salvador, I presume. That was where she was going."

"You know where?"

"Aguilares, I think. Wasn't that where Father Alfonso came from?"

"Yes. But wasn't she from Chalatenango? Some village in the mountains?"

"I don't know."

"Might she have gone there?"

"I have no idea, and why does it matter? She had nothing to do with Alfonso's murder."

"Perhaps," Calero said. "But we would like to speak with her."

The Canadian then spoke up. There was some uncertainty about the motive for the killing of Alfonso, he said. "The local authorities made certain assumptions at the time, relating to your friend's political connections, some of his past activities. The motive seemed obvious. Maybe it was too obvious. They're now leaning toward another theory. There are rumours, widespread gossip in the neighbourhood. Jacinta was having a relationship with a priest. It seems the rumours came to the attention of her estranged husband."

Did I know that her husband is an army officer? Did I know that he is a major in the FAES?

I heard she might have had a husband once. But I never discussed it with her.

"I would hate to have him as my enemy, this Major Cienfuegos," the younger policeman said.

And after silently consulting the other two, by way of knowing glances, Calero said: "There has been a significant development in our investigation of the tragic death of Padre Alfonso.

"We have arrested a soldier from her husband's battalion. He was attempting to cross the border near Colomoncagua. Under interrogation, the soldier has suggested that the killing of the priest was motivated more by honour than by politics. He admits to the assassination. But we aren't certain who he meant to kill. It was dark. His mission was to kill 'a Red' who was a priest. After inquiries locally, he assumed the target was Padre Alfonso, a well-known supporter of the Communists.

"But we understand you're known here as Padre Pelirrojo . . . Your hair, I presume?"

"They call me that."

"We have to consider the possibility that he got . . . the wrong Red. Can you be of help in that regard?"

"Hardly," I said stiffly.

"Yes," Calero said, studying his hands. "Of course."

"We don't propose to take a chance," the Canadian diplomat interrupted sourly. "We've made our own inquiries. We've been in touch with your bishop and he agrees. Perceptions can mean life or death in this part of the world."

They had made arrangements. I would leave the country that very day to return to Canada.

They were thorough. I quickly packed my bags. An embassy car was waiting outside the door. We all shook hands.

I realized at the end of it that Danny had reached across and his huge hand was on mine, loosely.

"No fuckin' way that was your fault," he said grimly. "No way, José."

"Thanks," I said.

"You have to start believing that."

I nodded.

"I wish I could offer you a drink," he said.

"That's okay."

On day thirty-nine, Jude and I took our last walk together. Sitting on the little bench soaking in the sunshine, he asked abruptly if I thought I'd got anything out of the experience at Braecrest.

"A good rest," I replied. And I actually believe that now, and that there is value in physical fitness. Thinking of Stella, and that tennis would be starting soon. And yearning for the shore. "Do you have women friends?" I asked.

"Oooh ho ho. There's a trick question."

"Sorry," I said quickly.

"That's okay. I never actually tried to have women friends. Not since ordination. But I spent time in monasteries and teaching. Had a couple of women who were teaching colleagues."

"Monasteries?"

"I'm an Augustinian. We have a parish in Ottawa. Which was my downfall. Too much freedom in a parish. We were too close to Montreal and the casino."

We stared into the distance for a while. Spring birds flitted among the budding branches and there was a warm breeze. I thought of Creignish and the chill northwest wind that bores down the gulf this time of year, throwing the occasional defiant snowstorm against the cowering inhabitants. The rains, still harsh and icy.

"The faith," he said. "What a powerful force when you think about it. Paul. Augustine. Luther. Pascal. My God. This notion that we only have to believe in eternity to become a part of it—I could buy into it myself if only it didn't result in the devaluation of this." He spread his arms as if to gather in the vast spectacle before us.

"Paul to the Romans," I said, smiling. "It's all in there, I guess."

He sat up suddenly and half turned. "Did you know what Luther was doing when he came up with that insight . . . about justification by faith?"

I shrugged.

"He was taking a dump. Sitting on the toilet reading Paul to the Romans. And it hit him like a bolt of lightning. Just like that. An idea that would change the world forever." He settled back. "Don't you think that's just perfect?"

"So how do you deal with faith?"

"Look at that," he replied, gesturing toward the escarpment. "I know it is there. I see it. On my worst days? I just think about the escarpment. Or stare up into the universe. That's usually enough. Then, of course . . . I get greedy. Head for the tables, looking for true immortality."

"What will you do now?"

"No more tables. No more pills." He was nodding his head, absorbing his own certainty. "Flee as a bird to the Mountain," he said.

I looked at him, confused.

"Psalm eleven. I read the Psalms for the poetry." He looked off into the distance. "'For lo the wicked bend their bow, they make ready their arrow upon the string . . . that they may shoot the upright in the heart,' or something like that. I'm thinking of taking five weeks and walking from Queenston to Tobermory. I think I can do it, exploring the escarpment and the faith all the way. Avoiding the wicked and their bows and arrows."

I suddenly felt envious and lonely.

"What about yourself?" he asked brightly.

"I plan to spend a week around Toronto."

"That's nice."

"A bit of unfinished business there."

"And after that?"

"We'll see how things turn out in Toronto."

A lone gull came out of nowhere and fluttered past.

"The first few days on your own are the worst," he said with a sigh.

"You sound like you know."

"Ah, well," he said. "This is my third trip here."

"Here's what I'm going to do," Danny said after a long pause. "I'm going to yank my head out of my own arsehole and start thinking of other people for a change. That's what I'm going to do." Then his hands were on my shoulders, face close, eyes shining, booze fumes almost overwhelming. "Time for me to get on with it. And you know what? I'm starting with you."

"Me?" I laughed.

"Well . . . first I'm going to call the wife."

"Where is she?"

"Up at Stella's. She's been up there for a week. She said she couldn't stand it here anymore with me the way I've been."

"I didn't realize."

"It doesn't matter. Tomorrow I'm going to teach you how to drive that *Jacinta* properly. Okay? I've been noticing the little comments around the shore, about you bumping into things.

They're bad for mockery around here. We're going to fix that."
He sat down. "Starting tomorrow. You're going to learn to drive
that boat."

"Maybe we should wait till the boat is in the water."

He studied my face intently. I smiled.

"Good plan," he said.

Walking back, Jude said: "It's always a mistake to identify too
closely with any institution. That might have been our downfall.
Losing ourselves inside the vastness of the Holy Mother Church,
forgetting who we are as people . . . our personal uniqueness."

I must have seemed surprised.

"Institutions are amoral," he said. "We should never lose
touch with our individuality. Once you lose that, you lose touch
with the basics. The right and the wrong of things. I have to
think we're conditioned to do the right thing, as people. But not
as institutions. There's no morality in an institution. It's just
a thing."

I stopped. "You mentioned once that you might have a Toronto
phone number for Brendan Bell."

"Yes. In fact I do. I'll get it for you. I know you'll use it with
discretion."

"Sure," I said.

"It would probably be best if he didn't know I gave it to you.
Assuming he'd remember who I am."

"Of course. But why the discretion?"

"Ah, well," he said, obviously uncomfortable. "A few years
back I was approached about a rather sensitive matter that
involved young Brendan. I wouldn't want to say too much about
the circumstances. But some of the higher-ups back home
thought it might be a good idea if Brendan spent some time in
Ottawa. At my high school there. It's a Catholic school for

boys. They wanted me to arrange something for him. A temporary teaching job. I'd be looking after him, see."

"I see. Do you remember when that was?"

"Oh, God. Five or six years ago, I'd say. I had to tell them I didn't think it was such a good idea, Brendan teaching at a boys' school. Anyway, they thanked me and said they'd work it out some other way."

"And do you know where they eventually . . . put him?"

"Not a clue."

A crow squawked, abandoning a nearby tree.

"To tell you the truth, I haven't heard a boo about him since. Just the gossip . . . that he left, did well in business. But I still have the phone number they gave me at the time. I think some relative of his."

After another interlude of silent walking, he said: "I should give you my number too. So you can let me know how you make out with him."

"I will," I said. "I'll let you know."

Knowing even then, of course, I never would.

{ 28 }

Effie was waiting in her car in the circular driveway in front of reception. Groundskeepers were planting annuals and clipping winterkill from bushes. Residents wandered in the background. She was reading a thick book and didn't see me as I emerged from the front door. I rapped on her window and she smiled up at me. Nodded toward the passenger side. Once I was settled, she leaned across and offered up her cheek. I brushed it lightly. I felt a momentary panic, suddenly connected again to the reality of my history.

"And how was that?" she asked brightly.

"A worthwhile experience," I said.

"I'd love to have been a fly on the wall when you opened up."

"Your ears must have been burning," I joked.

She reached across and took my hand. "How are you really?"

"Fine. A little bit disoriented. But fine."

"I'm looking forward to some quality time. My God, it's been years since we had any time."

"I'm not sure that we ever did."

"I have a visitor," she said. "But he'll be leaving tomorrow."

Her other guest was at the university. They'd both be back at dinnertime, she said.

"Somebody famous," I guessed.

She laughed. "It's only William from Hawthorne. I brought him up for a conference."

"Willie? What kind of conference is it?"

"William," she corrected. "And just hold off the judgments. You don't know the half of it. You don't know what an asset our William really is."

"Really. I'm in the dark."

"He's an anomaly. We probably knew dozens like him when we were kids. But he's one of the last . . . one of those sheltered people who preserves a pure chunk of our history in his head. Intact. In his case, the old poetry and folklore of the pioneers. Orally transmitted. He's quite amazing."

"Poetry?"

"I don't expect you to understand. But I have some scholars over from Ireland and Scotland and some of them wanted to record him, so I dropped him off with them before I went to pick you up."

"And how does Willie Hawthorne feel about being an . . . anomaly?"

"He loves it," she said.

I laughed. "I suppose he's taken my bed."

"You get the guest room. I put William downstairs, in the rec room."

My sister lives in the kind of house I associate with authority. It is built of granite, with corners and projections that make it appear larger than it turns out to be once you're inside. The driveway is of black asphalt that always looks fresh. The neighbours have garages and, out front, hulking SUVs and solid little cars with numbers for names. Though it was still May, the maples and oaks and even the occasional elm were lush with summer greenery. Lawns had been mowed already. It is a street on which misery is difficult to imagine.

The guest room was sparse and clean, with a dresser and a bookcase full of ancient paperbacks and old school texts. Blurry Impressionist prints on the walls. I noted a crucifix above the bed and realized that it had been weeks since I had felt any inclination to pray. I sat on the bedside, slipped my hand into my jacket pocket and found the comforting beads there. It is Friday, I thought. The sorrowful mysteries. I let my eye travel the bookshelves. Nothing interested me. I lay back on the soft bed, caught again between truth and understanding, remembering the sanctuary of faith. I sat up, suddenly uncomfortable. Looked across the room toward where I almost expected to see Jude's tidy bed, and felt a strange pang of anxiety.

I stood at the bedroom window, longing for something larger and more reassuring than a city neighbourhood, even one that seemed to be constructed of granite, brick and limestone. Across the street a pretty teenaged girl was frowning as she spoke on a cellular telephone, sitting on her doorstep, one arm draped across her knees. A large tree branch wavered in front of me, just outside the window, concealing my presence. I studied the girl, her child's face contorted by grown-up anxieties. *Do they notice me? Do they like me? Am I significant? Am I safe?*

She was dressed to be noticed, a tight little sweater that stopped just above the navel. The way she sat, elbows perched on knees, a roll of baby fat fell over the waistband of low-cut jeans. The door behind her opened slowly. A boy emerged, about twelve years old. The girl continued her conversation. He stood behind her, then tugged her hair. She swatted with a free hand without even turning her head. He laughed, hopped slightly out of reach and went back inside.

I thought of Bell. In a moment identical to this one he is going about his business somewhere.

I went downstairs and found a telephone directory. There must have been a hundred B. Bells. I compared each number with the one Jude had given me. No match. I dialed it anyway.

The whirr sounded half a dozen times before I heard the pickup. A man's voice offered a tentative hello. I asked if Brendan Bell was there.

"No. Who's calling?"

"An old friend," I said.

"Well, he isn't here."

"Do you expect him?"

"No," he said. Then, with a slight edge of hostility, "Brendan doesn't live here anymore."

"Oh. I'm sorry to be a bother."

"If you're a friend, you must have heard . . . he's married now . . ."

"Yes. I heard. Would you happen to—"

"I can't help you," he said. And put the phone down.

I was standing with the silent receiver in my hand when Cassie arrived. I hardly recognized her. At each of our occasional encounters it has come as a surprise that she—who is, after my sister, my nearest relative—is virtually a stranger. A woman now, dark-haired and dark-eyed from her Gillis genealogy.

"Well, lookit," she said, throwing down her purse, jacket and newspaper and sweeping toward me.

Cassie works as a journalist.

"You look fantastic," she said. "All lean and mean and clear-eyed. What a waste." She laughed her mother's laugh. "I know half a dozen women who would try to eat you."

I felt the sudden heat in my face.

"And how was the asylum?"

With the uncautious questions pouring out of her, I felt the gloom dispersing. "A cheap holiday," I said. "I recommend it. I took up walking."

"Can golf be far behind? Anyway, I hope you're going to be around for a while."

"A few days. To readjust."

"I'll have to take you out on the town."

"I have a little bit of business to take care of. Somebody I have to locate while I'm here."

"Oh. Anybody we might know?"

"I doubt it. Just an acquaintance."

"Anything I can do to help."

I remembered then that he'd been mentioned in the news. "Maybe."

Effie and Willie arrived shortly after five, noisily speaking Gaelic as they entered. Cassie and I were in the kitchen.

Effie headed immediately for her liquor cupboard. Cassie left the room.

Willie became silent when we were alone, avoiding eye contact. I inquired in my awkward, neglected Gaelic how the city was agreeing with him. *Ciamar a chordadh am baile mor* . . . Effie handed him a glass with a small pool of amber liquid in the bottom.

"Ah, well," Willie said softly in English. "It's a busy place for sure."

"A big trip for your first," I said.

He reddened. Sipped from the glass. "I don't usually," he said guiltily. "Just now and then. Special occasions."

"I understand. All things in moderation, right?"

"I suppose."

"So, what do you think of Toronto?"

"It'll be good to be home again."

"And how is Aunt Peggy?"

"Good. Good. She's with Stella."

"Stella," I said, surprised by my reaction to her name, a sudden longing to be home.

"Right. You know Stella."

"Yes," I replied.

Effie handed me a glass of orange juice.

Dinner was quiet. Afterwards, Cassie took Willie out to see a movie. "We're going to see *Braveheart*," she said.

"Take it with a grain of salt," said Effie.

"What made you decide," she asked when they were gone, "about Braecrest? You've never been a drinker."

"Maybe you don't know me as well as you think," I said.

She studied me then, face full of questions, so I changed the subject.

"Willie seems to be taking to the city," I said.

"He's a pet."

"How old is he, anyway?"

"He isn't much older than we are. But he grew up in a kind of a bubble. Kind of like us." She smiled. "It wasn't exactly . . . normal, was it? The way we were."

"What's normal? Who knew what normal was back then? Before television."

"That's true," she said.

"*Normal.* What a word." I was longing for a drink.

"Do you think of them often?" she asked suddenly.

"Who?"

"Daddy. Sandy. Poor Jack."

"I find it odd, the way you call him Daddy. When did that start?"

"But isn't that . . . normal? To call your father Daddy?"

"When you're nine."

She turned away and the silence fell in the way it always does. After about a minute she walked slowly to a cupboard and poured some more liquor into her glass.

"Maybe that explains your fascination with Willie," I said.

She frowned.

"He reminds you of . . . 'Daddy.'"

"For the love of God."

"Think about it," I said.

She stared at me for a while, glass in hand, eyes searching. "Christ," she said at last. "I hope this isn't what that Braecrest place does to people."

"I get the sense that he doesn't like me," I said.

She laughed. "Listen to him!"

"I think he's a weirdo."

"I'm going to bed," she said.

Saturday morning, Willie was gone before I was up. Effie drove him to the airport. When she returned, she told me he said he was disappointed not to have spent more time with me but was itching to get back home. I said I was sorry to have missed him; there were things we might have talked about.

"Oh," she said, relieved.

"The MacKay boy. Young Danny. You remember him from the Christmas before last. Willie would have known him well. They'd be related."

She frowned. "I think I heard something. Didn't he die?"

"Yes. Last fall. He killed himself."

"Oh? How awful."

"The last time I saw your William, actually, was at the wake. He was there with his mother. The old lady you've been talking to, Peggy."

"He never mentioned it in all the time that he was here."

†††

Saturday afternoon, I started calling all the B. Bells in the book. By the sixth I realized it was an impossible task. Three were women. One sounded too young in the flippant message on his answering machine. The other two denied any connection with Newfoundland.

That night Effie took Cassie and me to dinner in a dimly lit, noisy restaurant downtown. There was casual chat. Mostly about Cassie's work.

"By the way," she said, "somebody will be calling you."

Effie was surprised. Calling me about what?

"Nothing important," I said. "Somebody I wanted to look up while I was here. Cassie was helping."

"Oh. Somebody I know?"

"I doubt it."

"Now I'm intrigued."

"Just an ex-priest."

"Aha."

The dinner was pleasant and the city lights were intoxicating, but I couldn't absorb much of the stimulation. I was insulated from the pleasure by a dense layer of dread.

We went to Mass together on Sunday, to a large, cathedral-like church with an energetic choir and four boys on the altar for the two priests. Large occasions at the university were like this. And holy days in the larger parishes. Theatrical, I thought.

"How does anybody live here?" I asked her afterwards.

Effie just laughed.

"I'm looking forward to going back," I said. "I think I know how Willie felt."

†††

At about mid-morning on the Monday, I answered a ringing telephone and the man asked if I was Father MacAskill. I said I was and he said he heard that I'd been inquiring about Brendan Bell. He said he was a business reporter who worked with Cassie. I told him I had some dealings with Bell but had lost touch with him.

"You and a lot of people." He explained that Bell spent his winters outside the country. He had a home in the Caribbean, where he also did a lot of business these days.

The Caribbean?

"You're Cassie's uncle?"

"Yes."

"Because you're Cassie's uncle, I'll give you a name and number. Just don't say where you got it, okay?"

"Sure."

"I'd be interested in anything you find out. Call this number and ask for Eddie Sudac. He's one of the top people at HREU."

"Where?"

"HREU. It's a union."

"A union?"

"People who work in hotels and restaurants. Sudac will fill you in." He then gave me a Toronto telephone number.

Eddie Sudac had a friendly face and a firm handshake. We met in a sports bar on Front Street, just west of Union Station.

"I'm a Catholic myself," he explained. "Croatian heritage. But I haven't been too faithful to my obligations for a while."

I shrugged and returned his smile. He ordered a beer. I had Coke.

"I have to say that it's people like Bell who turned a lot of Catholics like me into heathens. This here is a fella that really makes you wonder. How do you know him?"

When he was active in the priesthood, I said, I knew him briefly. Had some dealings of a religious nature. Wanted to follow up on a few loose ends.

He made a face. "I hear you loud and clear."

"I understand you know how to find him."

"Oh, yeah. I could write a book on Brendan."

We talked for an hour. I left the bar in a state of utter confusion, attempting to remember a jumble of detail about politicians and unions, union money and hotels, jurisdictional disputes, raiding, lawsuits, intimidation, accusations about stolen funds and money laundering. Somehow Brendan Bell was in the middle of it all. And it all went back to something sleazy in Newfoundland when he was a priest.

"He was one of the diddlers, I understand," Eddie offered in a quiet voice. "At least according to some of our contacts on the Rock."

I told him that I wasn't at liberty to talk about what I knew and that I was sure he'd understand.

He understood completely, he said.

The way he saw it, Bell was connected with important people in Newfoundland and they helped him disappear when he got in trouble. The reason they helped him was that he was in a position to implicate some of them, union people and politicians, in some fairly heavy sleaze of their own.

"It's all kind of sick if you know the specifics." He had a mildly disgusted look. I told him I didn't need the gory details.

He explained that when Bell decided to get out of the priesthood, he had only to contact some of his old cronies who had become big shots in politics and the international union establishment. They had control over millions in pension funds, and overnight Bell turned into a "businessman."

"Must be nice, eh? Having drag like that?" He almost spat. "A front man would be more accurate, for a bunch of, excuse me, fucking crooks and hypocrites. They buy up hotels, using union money. Then the first thing they do is invent ways to replace our union with a pussy outfit that's nothin' more than a front for scabs. Suddenly the hotels are profitable, at the expense of you-know-who."

"I understand he lives somewhere in the Caribbean," I said eventually.

"In the winter. He slithers back when the weather warms up."

And he told me that Bell owned a condominium apartment just two blocks from where we sat. The reality of my unexpected nearness to Brendan Bell was disturbing. What was I doing?

Effie's house backs onto a ravine, so I walked into the urban wilderness to think about my next move. It had rained the night before and there was a menacing fog hanging close to the damp ground. I must know and I dare not know. The whispering voice in the confessional returns. An unfamiliar voice, distorted by outrage or hatred or both. Utterly certain in its condemnation. *Ask that Brenton Bell.* I must extract from Bell the admission of his guilt. I must hear him acknowledge his responsibility as I acknowledge mine. The MacKays must hear us both. We will go together, in joint contrition. I'm as bad as he is. We will beg for absolution.

Bell's smiling face and relaxed manner hover before me. A man untroubled. And I remember all the troubled men I've known, men slowly being crushed by the burden of their obligations or their guilt.

As usual, Effie understands everything and nothing simultaneously. "You had a minor breakdown. It was way overdue."

Really.

"You need someone," she said. "You've been alone too much. What does Stella think of all this?"

I felt a sudden wave of weariness approaching irritation. Enough. "What about yourself?" I asked.

"What about me?"

"You never called him Daddy, even as a little girl. You wouldn't even go to his funeral."

"Oh, that," she said, and sighed. The frown was replaced by a sad smile. She stood, walked to the kitchen counter and stood there. "People do bad things for complex reasons. But nobody is bad, essentially. Right? Evil is rare. We have to believe that. Otherwise memory becomes a toxic pool."

"Perhaps you should have been the priest."

She laughed and threw her hands up.

"That'll be the day."

The woman's voice sounded pleasant when she told me the apartment number and to turn left when I got out of the elevator. She knew my name, she said. Brendan had mentioned me. He wasn't in, but she invited me to come up anyway.

She was in the hallway waiting. The smile was warm. She had rich brown hair and serious grey eyes, a slender body. She asked me to come in, sit. Offered coffee.

She looks like a pretty boy, I thought.

I explained that I just happened to be in the city, that I'd seen him briefly the summer before and decided to look him up.

"I was expecting you," she said.

"Oh?"

"A friend of his left a message on the machine. A former roommate. Said someone from his past was trying to get in touch. I'm relieved it's you. Brendan told me all about you."

"Well," I said, masking my surprise.

"I gather you helped him through some difficulty once."

"I didn't actually do very much."

"He's very fond of Cape Breton Island. He actually talks about buying property there. Maybe a summer place. Loves the people, the culture, especially the music. I've never been, but it sounds beautiful, the way he tells it."

I demurred, offering something about familiarity obscuring the qualities in a place.

"Well, Brendan has a real thing about his time there. He's in Cape Breton now, as a matter of fact."

"Oh?"

"Yes. He flew down two days ago. Said he had some unfinished business down there."

She had no idea what he meant by "unfinished business." But then, there was a lot about the business side of Brendan's life that was a mystery to her.

Effie's kitchen is white and modern and large enough to accommodate a substantial harvest table. On the last night, she was busy at the stove while Cassie and I sat and talked. There was a rice cooker of some kind puffing on the counter and a casserole generating warm, rich aromas in the oven. Through a large patio door I could see into the lush green yard.

Effie asked if it would be okay to open some wine and I said it would be fine with me. She removed a bottle from a cupboard. "Come on," she said. "Just one. Live dangerously. It'll be another half-hour before we eat."

I shook my head. Not now. Not yet.

Cassie asked me to walk with her in the back garden. She held my hand.

Outside, she said: "I hope I've been helpful."

"You have. I found my guy."

"Ah. Great. And how did it go?"

"He's away," I said, laughing. "But now that I know . . . there'll be another time."

She turned and faced me then. "Tell me what you think of that William."

"I don't know what you mean."

"Don't you find him creepy?"

"It depends."

"I swear that he was lurking outside my bedroom door the last night he was here."

"I hope you're wrong."

"I don't think so. The night we went to the movie, he didn't seem interested at all. And afterwards, there was just something. The things he tried to talk about. I don't know, but I couldn't wait for him to get on that plane."

We walked some more in silence.

"I want to ask you something."

"Sure."

"It bothers me that I don't know anything about our side of the family, the MacAskills. It seems to be such a dark hole. Your mom, your dad. There seems to be so much mystery."

"No big mystery. Our mother was a war bride who died when your mother was only four or five years old. We hardly got to know her. Our father was . . . a very damaged man. It was complicated."

"That's what I want to know about. The damage. How damaged?"

I laughed. How do you measure damage?

"Come on," she said impatiently. "You know what I'm getting at."

"I don't, really."

"Was Mom abused?"

I think I just stared.

"I want to know," she said. "It would explain things."

I felt a sudden wave of impatience. Explain things?

"It's just been the two of us for most of my life. Mom and me. Growing up. I often wondered . . . She's different from other mothers. And she's said things about her own upbringing. And about her father being damaged and no women in the house. It's hard not to wonder."

"Sometimes there are no easy explanations for the way we are," I said. "Sometimes we just are. Products of a million little inputs."

"You're blowing me off," she said, and pulled away, folding her arms.

"Okay. Ask me a simple question and I'll give you a simple answer."

"Was Mom sexually abused by her father?"

"No."

Her face was dark with unasked questions, but she just said, "Okay." And then, "Thank you."

When dinner was finished and the dishes cleared away, and Cassie off to her computer, I asked Effie what had attracted her to Sextus years ago, when she was still married to John.

She sighed and examined her empty teacup. "He was the one person I knew who was happy being exactly who he was."

"The only one? Really?"

"The only one," she said.

"So how come you don't just settle down with Mr. Happy-being-who-he-is?"

"Because I eventually can't stand who-he-is-happy-being."

"You could have fooled me last summer."

"Well, when you get to be my age, the devil you know . . . et cetera."

"There are a lot of old devils out there," I said.

"But some of them are more fun than others."

At the airport, Effie remarked that the visit had been unusual and, in a way, enriching. She was holding my hand again. Maybe, she said, this is a brave new beginning. The start of the best part of our lives. She said she was going to make a point of seeing more of me, and that she wanted Cassie to get to know me better now that things seemed to be coming together for all of us.

"Talking about our father was strange," she said.

"A long time ago," I said, "I thought you hated him."

"A long time ago, I probably did."

"Cassie asked me last night if you had been sexually abused."

"Wow."

"Came right out and asked."

"And you told her what?"

"I told her no."

"Thank you." She stared straight ahead for a while. "You said that you disliked him . . . once upon a time."

"Perhaps."

"Was it because of me?"

"Yes. No. I don't know."

"You can do better than that."

"I hit him once. And he fell down. He left me with a load of guilt and I turned it all back against him. Does that make sense?"

"Not really."

"I overpowered him and it revealed my fundamental impotence. That's the best that I can do by way of explanation."

"You overpowered a lot of people in your time, a ghraidh. Usually because of me."

"Never after that," I said.

"I'm glad to hear it. Something good came out of it."

I was bereft of words. I stared at the crowds of people unloading bags and suitcases from taxis and cars and buses, suddenly aware of all the intimacies of separation. Light kisses, hand holding. An unshaven man and a tall teenaged boy stood talking quietly. Then they hugged. The boy kissed the man swiftly on a cheek, then turned and walked toward the automatic doors. The man stood for a moment, looking stunned. A commissionaire with a fat pad of traffic tickets approached him. They spoke briefly.

I opened the car door and climbed out. Fetched my suitcase from the back seat. The commissionaire moved in our direction.

"This summer," she said, "we'll pick up where we left off."

I nodded even though I knew we wouldn't. The journey toward understanding is finished, imperfectly as always. But done.

The commissionaire motioned impatiently for her to leave. She ignored him.

"I'll be turning fifty soon," she said. "I'll be looking for advice." She handed me a large bottle of mineral water. "Here. One for the road."

"What'll I tell Sextus?" I asked.

"Tell him I'll be turning fifty. See how he reacts. Let me know if he gags." She smiled. She could have passed for thirty.

I waited for more, but she laughed, blew a kiss and drove away.

I watched her go. I walked into the airport feeling anxious. Going home alone again.

29

Bobby O'Brian met me in Halifax. Spring was slower here, as usual, grim grey skies clamped down on the blackened land. People at the airport in Toronto were in their shirt sleeves; in Halifax, the air was harsh and gritty. Bob was saying that there had been snow in the morning in Creignish two days earlier. We drove mostly in silence. People missed you, he said once.

Just past New Glasgow, through the naked trees, I could see the Northumberland Strait. Home was on the far side of the water. I felt unsettled, contemplating the reality before me. Endings and beginnings. Bell is over there somewhere, according to his wife.

In Antigonish I asked if we could stop at the chancery for a moment.

The bishop threw his arms around me, calling out to people in the office to come and say hello. You won't believe who's here.

Even the secretary, Rita, seemed surprised at his show of enthusiasm.

When we were alone, I asked straight out, "What about the MacLeod story?"

"Hah. They blinked. Not a blessed murmur."

"Why? What's your theory?"

"It isn't a theory," he huffed. "It's a fact. They have no case.

Some smart lawyer figured that out. Of course, you heard the sad news."

"Sad news?"

"Father Roddie."

"What about him?"

"He passed away, God rest his soul. You didn't hear?"

"There wasn't much outside news where I was."

"I thought I wrote. It was sudden. Three weeks ago. The stress, I imagine. God forgive them."

I studied his face and his perplexity seemed genuine.

"In any case, that would have been the clincher. Who's going to slander the dead, eh? Especially when the evidence was a crock to start with."

I was nodding, unable to suppress the uneasiness stirring inside.

"Anyway," he said conclusively, slapping my shoulder, "it's great to see you. You've taken years off. Now get down there and back to work."

Bobby said he'd heard from the young fellow in Korea. He liked the place but couldn't escape the homesickness. He was thinking about another stab at the priesthood.

I said I wasn't surprised.

We crossed the causeway. After the battering of more than forty winters, it looked like it had been here forever. As natural in the landscape as Cape Porcupine and the hills of Creignish. Is this what happens? Time and winter work together, creating uniformity, knocking things and people down to size?

"I'm glad to hear it," I said. "I never doubted his vocation."

Bob stared straight ahead. "I often think about poor young MacKay. A fella never knows."

He insisted that I eat with him and his wife when we reached Creignish, and I made a show of sociability. I could see, across the field, that there was a light on at the last house on the mountain road.

"Maybe a couple of hands of Auction before you go," Bobby suggested.

"No, I'd better get home. No telling what's there waiting for me."

There was a note pinned to my door: *I hear you've been trying to get in touch. I'll call. Brendan B.*

The house had been cleaned. Groceries were stocked and there was fresh milk in the refrigerator. Obviously a work party had been there. Fresh flowers in an unfamiliar vase at the centre of the kitchen table. I recognized roses. Something else yellow. Green ferns. A little card said *Welcome Back*. It was signed, simply: *S.*

I heard confessions on Saturday and said Mass on Sunday. Everyone enthused about my appearance, and it was true, according to my mirror. I spoke about the reluctant spring, said that the appearance of indifference in the weather was deceptive. Crafted careful allusions to my own condition and noticed an unusual number of smiles. Afterwards, I sat in the empty house wondering what to do with the rest of the day. I studied old photographs and realized, now that I'd lost some weight, I'd begun to resemble my long-dead father again. Anxiety resurfaced. I stood before the row of journals, pulled one. Tried to read, but slept mostly.

I'd been home a week and then Stella was standing in the doorway, hands jammed deep in her coat pockets, smiling. There was something about her hair that caught my eye.

She said she was keen to hear about my trip, when I was interested in talking. She had a clinical interest, she said.

"For sure," I said. "I'm trying to make a gradual re-entry."

"By the way, Danny's struggling. I wish you'd go to see him."

"Oh," I said. "I saw him yesterday. At the boat."

Her eyes were pleading. "Jessie's awfully worried."

Sextus was guarded on the phone, almost formal in his inquiries about my absence.

"I understand you and Effie did some talking."

"Briefly," I said.

"It's great," he said, brightening. "Putting the past to rest like that, finally."

"I don't think the past is that easy to dispose of."

"There's that. When'll I see you?"

"I don't know. I'm still making some adjustments."

"Maybe I'll drop by."

"I'll be here," I said.

The *Jacinta* stands alone now on the shore. The American has launched what used to be the *Lady Hawthorne* and rechristened her: *Sea Snake*.

I wonder what Danny thinks of that.

"Call me when she's ready to go in," he said as I was leaving him. "I'm serious about the driving lessons. I'm going to make a seaman out of you."

From on top of the *Jacinta*'s shabby cab you can see the islands, Henry and Port Hood. There was once a lighthouse keeper and his family on Henry Island and a living community of frugal fishermen on Port Hood Island. Mostly all moved away now. Lighthouses everywhere are now automated or closed and abandoned, or demolished. Isolation is now an option for the wealthy or the odd. A choice.

† † †

I knew him by the shoes. They appeared to be expensive, with tiny leather tassels, the kind that lawyers wear. Out of place in the sand and the coarse grass. Then he bent down and our eyes met.

I was under the boat with a belt sander, grinding off the loose paint flakes. I didn't hear his arrival because of the whine of the machine. Obviously didn't hear him when he called out. Then I saw the shoes, and then the face.

I rolled out and stood, batting clouds of red paint dust from my coveralls. Removed the safety goggles. I wasn't ready.

I'd been through the conversation a dozen times in my mind. It would be unlike other conversations. Calm. A neutral tone. I am not about to judge. Only to understand. I want to hear you speak about Danny MacKay. I want to hear his name issue from your mouth. And in your voice I want to hear remorse. I will not ask for details of your relationship. It no longer matters. All that matters now is atonement.

His hands were jammed into the pockets of his leather windbreaker. A sign of trust. His face was troubled.

"I heard you were around," I said, removing my gloves, stalling, I suppose.

"Yes. Lucy told me you dropped by to see me at the condo. Sorry I missed you. I didn't know you were in the city."

"Up on some personal business," I said.

"You've been asking questions about me." He had his hands out of his pockets now, fingers laced together and folding, open and shut, as if to crack the knuckles. The face had an expression of wary amusement.

I just stared, waiting.

"I didn't know you were an acquaintance of Eddie Sudac."

"I'm not, really," I said. I folded my arms. I'm not sure why.

"I didn't think so. I wouldn't have thought Eddie was your type."

"I don't know anything about him, in fact."

He laughed, kicked at some sand with the toe of his elegant shoe. "Eddie. He's quite a character. You don't know what he does for a living?"

"Union guy, I understand."

"That's what his card says. His real job is to hurt people. For the union, of course."

"Hurt people."

"Sure. Didn't you know there were people like that in the world?"

He had now crossed into a zone of smug condescension and I felt a quiet anger rising. I said nothing.

"Mostly he specializes in breaking reputations. Relationships. Business ventures. Other unions. But he'll also break bones. And there are rumours of worse. That's Eddie in a nutshell."

"Interesting."

"He could hardly wait to get the word to me . . . Some priest comes to see him, asking questions, *about me*. Says you two had quite the chat about my history. He couldn't recall your name, but I put two and two together when Lucy told me you were at the condo. So I'm curious as hell how you ended up talking about me to a prick like Eddie Sudac." All semblance of irony was gone, replaced by a dark and threatening anger.

"Actually," I said after a long pause, "I only wanted to find out where you were. I couldn't find you in the phone book."

"Oh. And what was so urgent that you'd end up talking to him?"

"Somebody told me to call him."

"What somebody?"

I felt a strange sensation in my hand and creeping tension through my shoulders, into my neck. And a rising column of outrage along my spine.

"It doesn't matter, does it? You don't really care 'what some-body,' do you?" I struggled to smile.

His face had gone pale and he moved closer. "And what was it you wanted to find me for . . . now that you have my attention?" His accent had regressed at least a generation, to somewhere among the rocks of his birthplace.

I hesitated, but just for a moment. "I want to take you some-where."

"Oh?"

"If you'll give me just a moment to clean up . . . there's some-one we should see."

"I'm actually in a bit of a hurry."

"It won't take long."

"Maybe you'll give me just a tiny clue . . ."

"We're going to Hawthorne . . . It's only ten minutes away."

"Oh. And, pray, what for?"

"We're going to visit the MacKays."

"Well," he said, "isn't that a coincidence."

"How is that a coincidence?"

"I just came from there."

30

I could see Stella's car turning up the mountain road, so I continued on past the church, turned up behind her and followed her to the house. Parked there. We stood in silence for a moment, just staring. I walked toward her, uncertainly. She extended her hand.

"I forgot to tell you the other day. You look good," she said softly.

"Thanks. So do you."

She laughed and patted her head. "You'd say that anyway."

"You did something to your hair."

"No," she said, mildly defensive.

Another silence.

"I'd invite you in—"

"No, no," I finished. "Look at me. I'm just back from the boat. I'm desperate for a shower."

"Maybe later. Come by and have a drink. Or a cup of tea or something."

"Maybe I will."

"I understand you and Danny had a talk."

"Yes."

"I'm glad. I don't know what you said . . . but he seems to be coming around."

I shrugged. "I didn't really say anything."

"Sometimes that's all it takes. A bit of listening."

"Maybe."

And we stood there for a while. Listening.

"Is Jessie still with you?" I asked.

"No. She went home yesterday."

Sunday was First Communion for the little ones. Catholic teachers at the school in town had done the work while I was gone, taught them all the basics upon which to build a vague theology. Saturday I examined them. Who made you? God made me. Why did God make you? Innocent questions masking a hard purpose. Simple answers, sufficient for now. I heard their first confessions and noted that a surprising number had already had impure thoughts. Television, I assume. I muttered meaningless absolutions. Assigned nominal penance. Three Hail Marys and say something nice about somebody you don't like much.

Yes, Father.

" . . . I absolve you of your sins in the name of the Father, the Son, and the Holy Spirit."

Thank you, Father.

And now they had come with their parents for the Holy Eucharist. Nine of them. The responses rolled easily from their tongues. In their faces I could see how faith should always be. It fits them loosely now, I thought, leaving room for growth. It will not always feel so comfortable. I wanted to warn them of the stress that comes with progress, that they'll never wear the faith so easily again. The cruel paradox of faith: with each sacrament, there are new questions and fewer answers. Growth and curiosity, the elements of crisis.

Sunday afternoon I drove to the Long Stretch. I unlocked the gate, drove into the yard and sat for a long time, just staring at the old house. A storage place for memories, mostly all bad. Each generation should destroy the habitations of the one before. Purge all evidence of past corruption. The dead flies and bat shit and dust and memories. Purge them all. Allow the imagination to fill in blanks with sentiment. What's wrong with sentiment? What's wrong with mythology? Both are palatable substitutes for reality.

I have reviewed it all in detail, every nuance of expression, every possible interpretation of every word. "Now that I can't blame you, I blame myself," I said at last. "I should have been able to help him."

Brendan's face was sorrowful. "How do you think I feel? I knew the boy. He trusted me. We'd talk in the confessional. He felt safer there. He told me everything. Can you imagine? Me sitting listening to him, suddenly a source of comfort for him? And hope? But I couldn't do a thing, just try to reassure him." He shook his head, studying his tasselled shoes, hands now thrust again into the pockets of his jacket.

"What did you tell his parents?"

"Nothing. One of them already knows what needs to be known. They can share it when they're ready."

"But there was somebody . . . somebody who . . . ?"

"I know what you need to know and what his father needs to know. But I learned it all behind the double seals of trust and the sacrament of Penance."

"That was your only relationship?"

He studied me for a long, long time. "Yes," he said at last. "Of course it was."

"I had to ask."

He nodded.

As he turned to leave, he paused, as if making up his mind about some serious matter. "I don't owe you or anybody else any explanations. The kid and I had more in common than you or anybody else could ever appreciate. He just knew it. Somehow he could see it in my face, my own miserable memories. Damaged people recognize each other. They see the signs of damage where even experts can't. He trusted me because of that."

I watched his eyes and they seemed to search for sympathy.

"I can't get him out of my mind. I thought maybe . . . by visiting his parents. But it didn't help, any of us. It didn't bring him back. Right?"

His face had the haggard, ravaged appearance of someone older. We just stared at each other for a long time. Until I felt the first pang of understanding.

"You?" I asked.

He nodded. "The memory is strange. You suppress, but never forget. That was why I didn't think I was much help to him. Lost in my own self-pity. Try to imagine being a victim and a victimizer, locked up with yourself. You don't have to believe me. Just try to imagine it."

He walked to the car and opened the door. Then he stood with an arm resting on the roof. And he said: "If it's really important . . . if there is such a thing as a culprit in situations like these, then you should start looking closer to home. I shouldn't have to tell you that . . . you could have looked it up yourself. It's in all the literature."

I watched him drive away.

There was but one thought in my mind. It is finished. But there was no feeling of relief.

{ 31 }

Saturday afternoons always brought at least one sinner. Some alarmed adolescent or guilty husband. At the very minimum, one or two old women, remorseful over some small act of malice or uncharitable thought. Always someone for confession on the Saturday. But not this Saturday. Just one would have made the difference.

Bell went away and took the fatal knowledge with him. Look closer to home, he said. And it was as if a door slammed shut. It is finished. Home is always impenetrable. This I know.

I should be relieved. Bell is out of it. Father Roddie is dead, facing the only justice system that matters.

I had one call from MacLeod, but I was barely listening as he spoke. He was angry. I didn't care.

"It's a long way from being over. These things don't stay buried. The story will come out. What happened cannot unhappen. You hear what I'm saying?"

"I hear you," I said. I am learning the new language of indifference. "You have a job to do. I'll be waiting."

"You can count on that," he said, before hanging up.

Whatever.

At five to four I filled a thermal coffee mug and crossed the driveway to the church. I sat in a pew near the confessional, awaiting the sound of vehicles outside, sounds of someone at the

door, the signal to move inside the airless box. Awaiting the rit-
ualistic mumble on the other side, the recitation of their shabby
little privacies. Bless me, Father, for I have sinned.

I used to approach the confessional in dread, knowing it was
where my deficiency as a priest would be exposed. My contempt
for weakness, loathing of failure, unwillingness to grant easy for-
giveness. How long since I have heard a real confession? How
long since I have made one?

The air was still, as it usually is when heavy with moisture.
It had been like this for two days. Spring had finally arrived
behind the last thrust of the North Atlantic winter, and it was
warm and humid. A Saturday in June. Two days ago the fog
rolled in and stayed. You could see it advancing, a great slow,
soft wall moving northward out of the strait. The day before,
I'd launched the *Jacinta*. Today I'd hoped for sunshine. From
the front room in the glebe I could see a patch of flat black
water beyond the road, just below the hanging fog.

Danny Ban had booked the boat carriage. Its owner and a
boy were there early. When I arrived, they were manoeuvring
the long wheeled contraption around and under the *Jacinta*.
When she sat securely on the rig, they carefully backed her
into the harbour. Danny was on board, standing at the wheel,
and he started the engine with a roar just before they set him
free. He backed out into the centre of the harbour, blue smoke
puffing from the stern, oily water gushing from the boat intes-
tines, then gently moved toward the dockside.

"If there's sunshine tomorrow . . . we'll go out," he said.

But the day was dense with fog.

It was four-fifteen. Still nobody.

††† †

I came *that* close to asking Danny Ban straight out. An older, wiser priest, back in the days of our unconstrained authority, would not have hesitated. He would have placed a paternal arm around those massive shoulders and spoken as if to a child.

"We should explore the past for clues . . ."

Maybe tomorrow, I thought. When the sun is shining. When we're on the water, closer to our primal unity.

"Perhaps," I said aloud at four-thirty, "I should go to the harbour. Just to check. Perhaps he's there."

I removed the stole, folded it and placed it in my pocket, and left.

Sextus jokes that the place has a bipolar personality. Sunshine makes it garrulous and sexy and reassuring. Under fog, or the lowering clouds that occupy the sky for long periods of time, it becomes dour and melancholy. As I drove north, the sea was smooth and dark, the leaden, drooping sky almost touching the water.

It was nearly five when I arrived at the harbour, which was deserted except for one battered pickup truck. There didn't appear to be anybody around. The tide was unusually low, *Jacinta*'s cab barely showing above the wharf.

"That's an interesting name, all right."

I turned and with an inexplicable feeling of annoyance saw that it was Willie Hawthorne, leaning against a wall. When he moved toward me, he seemed unsteady. He reeked of stale alcohol.

"Foreign, I would say."

"Spanish," I said. "It's a flower. A hyacinth. In English."

"She survived the winter pretty good."

"I guess we all did."

"I guess the last time I saw you was in the big city. That was something, eh?"

"I hear you're a celebrity up there."

He laughed.

I could think of nothing more to say, so I tugged the bowline to bring the boat closer to the wharf so I could climb down.

"The fella that owns that one had to run to town for something," he said, nodding toward what had been the *Lady Hawthorne*. "You heard the American bought her. Some name he gave her, eh? The *Sea Snake*."

"Different," I said.

"It suits."

Something in his voice made me turn to face him. There was a strange insinuating smile on his lips.

"I don't suppose you'd take a shot," he said, pulling a flask from his pocket, "after going to all the trouble to get dried out."

I waved a refusal, turning again toward the rope.

"He was snaky, for sure, Danny Ban's young fella, and he was sure as hell going to fuck that boat up, pardon my language. The way he used it. Woulda been a shame. A nice boat like that." He examined his bottle. "I keep forgettin' you're a priest. Sorry."

"Don't worry about it."

"No, the young fella was headin' for a bad end anyway. No big surprise to me when he done himself in, the way he was."

I stood then, listening, suddenly a captive.

"No big surprise to me. No way." He was looking past me, off into the distance, as if he could see something important there. Chewing on the inside corner of his mouth. "I know things nobody else knows."

"I don't know what you're talking about," I said, turning back to my boat.

"I heard all about Creignish. Him calling that young fellow from Creignish a fruit. You think. And himself worse."

"Listen, I don't want to—"

But he was now talking to no one in particular and I strained to understand what he was saying. The unsolicited words bubbled out. "He was a misfit from day one, he was. I know first-hand. Then along comes that priest, that Brenton Bell. Another one. Don't think I didn't know. One of those damn perverts from Newfoundland. You can spot them a mile away."

I realized that I had turned to face him, now mute. *You ask that priest, that Brenton Bell they sent down here.*

"From the time he was nine or ten I could see it in him, true as I'm standin' here." He was nodding vigorously.

"Shut your mouth," I said finally. But it was as if he couldn't hear me.

"Sure enough, I know first-hand. The way he was, that little Danny."

"Shut up!"

"First-hand. They come on to you when you're weak. It's how they work. He'd know when I'd be drinkin'. I'm only human."

"Shut your goddamned mouth."

"I'd give him money."

I stepped closer, but he was staring off toward the road. "I'm just waitin' for that American to come back from town. I'm gonna tell him the whole story. He said he was gonna write it up. Maybe put it in a book. About that priest and what he done. That Brenton Bell."

I have, so far unsuccessfully, tried to remember the next moments, to reconstruct the precise sequence of small mental and physical events that followed. I have even considered drugs or hypnotism, for it seems, when I am being overwhelmed by doubts about myself, to be crucial that I know precisely what happened on that wharf. Something always blocks the memory, prevents the clarity. And I wonder: is it fear? Is it the fear of whatever conscience-driven power takes over reason when our faith in Mercy finally deserts us? Is it the fear of our capacity for self-destruction?

In my struggle for objectivity I see myself again, now kneeling there, head hanging, upper body propped on stiffened arms, knuckles hard against the concrete decking. My shoulders are heaving, lungs struggling for air, throat expelling ragged sobs. There are clouds hanging low over the boats lined up along the dock. I am the only living thing. Where is William?

I raise my head and look around me. But there is nobody to be seen.

A lone seagull enters the frame, lands with what I sense to be some kind of urgency at the edge of the dock.

There is a primal sound, a soft moaning, not unlike the wind. Standing near the transfixed seagull, I look down. And now there is unwelcome certainty: images that I try to reconcile with the man I'd always thought I was, the priest, advocate of hope and reconciliation.

William was lying near an open hatch, body contorted. One leg was obviously broken. He was trying to move an arm, trying to speak. Blood oozed on a thigh where the flask had broken in his fall. The mouth struggled, but no words emerged, only a gurgling groan. Then one hand fluttered slightly in an unmistakable gesture. A silent motion, signalling for help.

My bloodied hand seeking comfort in a pocket encountered a soft silken fabric there, the confessional stole, symbol of my power to diminish the finality of death and in doing so expunge the fear of it. William's eyes were fixed on mine, lips struggling to produce a sound until, at last, one faint word escaped.

"Father?"

The wet mouth struggled some more. Again, the single word. *Father.*

And then: "Help me, Father . . ."

I remember staring down at him, a terrible frenzy of revulsion thundering. And then I turned and walked away.

Driving away from the wharf, I thought of Mullins, turned northward. Driving up the long hill near MacDougall's, I met a car I didn't recognize, then saw the American behind the wheel. Terrible words of judgment echoed in the memory . . . *That day, a day of wrath, of wasting, and of misery, a great day, and exceeding bitter. When Thou shalt come to judge the world by fire.*

I had the power to mitigate the wrath and wasting. I had an obligation to expel the misery. I pulled quickly to the shoulder of the road. Started to turn the car. But I knew it was pointless to go back. We can never go back.

Minutes passed like hours. Or were the hours like minutes? Reason rushed back once again when a raucous fire truck roared past, lights flashing. A howling ambulance was close behind.

I turned the car around and followed them toward the shore.

Half a dozen curious spectators were standing at the wharf side, peering down into my boat. There was a kneeling woman, blonde head close to Willie's ashen face, looking for signs of life. Unnoticed in the commotion, I stepped away. Two firemen disappeared over the side. Another dragged what looked like an oversized ironing board with Velcro straps from the truck and handed it down. Two ambulance attendants had a gurney waiting.

Only the American seemed to notice me. "You're the priest, aren't you? MacAskill?"

I just nodded.

"I'm Dave Martin," he said, holding out a hand. The expression on his face seemed to be saying, Shouldn't you be down there too?

But he said nothing more, and he turned away.

A police car arrived just as the paramedics were lifting Willie over the side, transferring his still form to the gurney. The Mountie walked over to the group. There was a discussion that I couldn't hear. Then he turned and stared at me, suddenly remembering. He smiled and walked over.

"That's your boat?"

"Yes."

He brought out a notebook and a pen. "You're looking well," he said.

"Thanks."

"You know this guy?"

"He's from Hawthorne," I said, and spelled it out. "William. Beaton, I think."

He wrote carefully.

"He lives with his mother."

"Any idea how this happened?"

"We were talking—"

"When were you talking?"

"Just before."

"What happened to your hand?"

"I'm not sure. He was drunk. Kind of hysterical. I must have looked away for a moment."

"Wait here." He walked to the ambulance and climbed into the back, re-emerging moments later. "What were you talking about?"

"Personal matters," I said.

The policeman studied me suspiciously. "Personal?"

"I know him. We know people in common. Frankly, it's all a blank right now. What exactly happened."

"Have you been drinking, Father?"

"No," I said, maybe too sharply.

"I had to ask. I'm not implying anything. I hear you've been away."

"Yes."

"It was a good move. Going away. You missed some excitement. Or, maybe, the lack of it. I think you were talking to MacLeod, that reporter." He was smiling.

I nodded.

"Messy," he said, shaking his head.

The ambulance pulled away slowly, the silent coloured lights revolving. Stopped momentarily at the road then turned northward.

"Shouldn't they be moving faster?" I said.

"There isn't any point," the Mountie said.

"We don't know that," I said, fighting desperation.

"There's a doctor here."

"What doctor?"

"Her," he said, pointing to the woman who had been crouched over him, looking for signs of life. "He broke his neck in the fall. Where will I be able to find you?"

"You know where," I replied.

"Okay. I'm going to spend some time here, going over your boat. You have no objection?"

"None," I said.

"Maybe when we talk . . . we can . . . catch up on a few other things."

"Maybe."

Much later, after the policeman came and left, it is important to remember the exact moment when I realized that my life had ended. The sequence of events is vivid now, preserved in the memory with extraordinary accuracy. I was in my study. There was bronze light falling through the doorway, illuminating a patch of wall. I turned and stared toward the large picture window in the living room. The fog had gone. The sky was a rich blue. It was a new day. I turned back to my desk.

Beside the journals I had stacked there near a cardboard box, I had placed the photograph of my father and his friends, Sandy, Jack . . . three young men, their transient optimism preserved by the camera for all time. Two soldiers in fresh army uniforms. Jack in his work clothes. And the dead buck draped over the fender of the truck. Only the face of the deer seems to reflect the gravity of where they are, the knowledge of what lay before them. Hunters and hunted. Indistinguishable, in the long run.

The photos and the journals spoke to me of failure. The tragedies that are the product of our inadequacies. One individual, the son of God who was also God, promised redemption from the consequences of our unavoidable failures. It is now so clear. The promise of redemption is another myth.

A peculiar sensation passed through me. And I wondered: Is this what Sandy Gillis felt? And Danny? Is this what the devil tried to tell me on the Niagara Escarpment? That faith and hope are fantasies? Can this be true? My faith is just another culture?

I knew a man who lived and died for faith and justice. And I believe his sacrifice brought hope to faithful people.

Could I ever be that man?

Then I remembered: It is Sunday.

I took a notepad and a pen. Wrote: *No Mass Today.*

Walked across the driveway and pinned the note to the door of the church. The air was fresh with the first scents of summer, dampness and new growth and the earth stirring from its sleep. The broad blue bay breathing softly.

I returned to my desk, studied the stack of journals for another moment.

Then I placed them in the box. All, that is, but two. The two Honduran years. There is still one secret I cannot share.

Stella called. "I just heard," she said.

"I'm sorry."

"No. You don't have to say it." The voice was firm.

"Could you come by?"

"No. I have to go and see Aunt Peggy."

"Of course."

"Maybe tomorrow."

"I understand."

"Are you okay?"

"I think so."

"Just hang on."

Sunday afternoon, the Mountie came again.

"There was a witness," he said.

"Oh?"

"The witness said she saw him waving his arms around in front of you and kind of staggering. He had a blood alcohol reading of .31. He was bombed. There was some grappling. First she thought it was a fight. You moved so quickly she wasn't sure if you were trying to steady him . . . or what. I guess she's not exactly sure just what she saw." He studied me for reaction.

I just stared back. "Who was the witness?"

"That doctor. She's with the guy who owns the boat behind yours. That writer from New York. She was the blonde, declared the guy dead at the scene."

"And what about her husband . . . the writer? . . . Did he know anything?"

"Not a thing. He wasn't there. But he confirms old Willie was pretty out of it, talking a lot of foolishness earlier on."

As he prepared to leave, the policeman told me I didn't have a thing to worry about.

"Maybe you have time for a coffee," I said.

"All the time in the world." And he walked back into the room and sat.

I studied the nameplate on his jacket. *Cpl. L. Roberts.*

"What does the L stand for?" I asked.

"Leo."

"I'm guessing you're a Catholic."

"Good guess. Though not a very good Catholic."

"I suppose you know your prayers. The act of contrition."

"I know that one," he said, smiling. "What's this all about, anyway?"

"I had a friend once, a priest, who used to say that the act of contrition was just a bunch of words. Good words, of course. But not an act of anything. He was a big believer in action, my friend."

"I suppose saying I'm sorry and meaning it is an act of sorts. Speaking as a lapsed Catholic."

"That's exactly what I would tell him. But he was stubborn. The only real act of contrition is a deed that involves some kind of sacrifice."

"That's pretty extreme," Leo said, lifting his coffee cup.

"My friend would say contrition is supposed to lead to changed behaviour. And nothing changes without action, sometimes violent action."

"Pretty radical," he said, shaking his head sadly. "Where's your friend now? Or maybe I shouldn't ask." He smiled.

"It's a long story," I said, remembering my father's favourite evasion.

The box of journals was between us. I hesitated for just a moment. Then I shoved them toward him.

"I don't think I'll have any further use for these."

† † †

The bishop phoned moments after he received my letter.

"I'm not buying any of this crap. It's all stress related. You need a complete sabbatical. Take a year. Go to the Holy Land. Study. We'll send you to Rome. Or just do nothing for a while."

I thanked him. Said I'd think about it.

"Anyway, just so you know. I'm tearing this letter into little pieces. It never happened. You hear me?"

"I hear you."

"I know the whole story. I have my sources. Blessings sometimes come in strange disguises."

Stella walked across the field, came in the back way.

"This is private," she said. "But you have to know. I'm confident it won't go anywhere from here."

I nodded.

Only she and her sister knew about it. "Danny Ban must never know."

"Willie blamed the boy," I said.

"The boy was nine, for God's sake," she said.

Stella was the first to come to terms with what had happened. She took a professional position, persuaded her sister that it had to be their secret, for Aunt Peggy's sake.

"I'm sure you understand," she said. What would have happened to Aunt Peggy if they'd turned Willie in? Even if he avoided prison, Danny Ban would have killed him. So they agreed on silence, for Peggy's sake. Nobody would ever know, just Stella, Jessie and, of course, young Danny. "This is not uncommon in close families," she said.

I agreed. All families have secrets. But why, so many years later, did the boy do this?

She shrugged. "He became friends with a young priest from Newfoundland. They talked a lot. Then rumours started. Probably related to the scandals over there, where he was from. You know the way that people are. I know the rumours bothered Danny. I think he felt, somehow, threatened by them."

"Where do you think the rumours came from?"

"It's anybody's guess." She was silent then. "I guess that's all there is to say. I thought you should know, for your own peace of mind."

"Thank you," I said. "That's a big secret to carry around . . . you and Jessie."

She smiled. "I'm sure you know all about the burden of big secrets."

"Once, you mentioned a place in the Dominican Republic."

"Yes," she said.

"Maybe I'll take you up on that."

"Just say the word."

I hesitated. "Maybe you'll come too."

"Maybe. And then again."

"Then again what?"

She placed a cool hand on my cheek. "I make a poor substitute. I learned that, long ago, the hard way."

"Substitute for what?" I said weakly.

"I think you know."

I could only nod, silently.

"I'll drop off the keys to Puerto Plata, and the name of the woman who takes care of it for me."

"Okay."

Danny Ban was crossing the parking lot at the mall in town when he spotted me. I hoped he wouldn't. There was too much to explain. Too much to suppress. But he was moving slowly in my direction, using two canes now.

"Hey," he said. "I was half expecting to get a call Sunday morning. Then they prayed for poor Willie at Mass. I figured you'd be too busy for boating."

"One of these days," I said.

"I hear you're going away for a while."

"Yes. I was just picking up a few supplies."

"Okay."

"I'll be gone at least a month." I told him that I had a lot to think about. Maybe it was time for a major change of direction in my life.

"That'd be a shame," he said.

"Nothing is decided."

"You'll be back, though?"

"Yes."

"Don't worry about the boat. I'll look after her for you. I've got good memories with that boat."

I thanked him.

His face was suddenly very sad. "What do you think goes through their minds?" he asked.

"We can never know. We can only assume. That there was a moment at the end . . . some kind of peace."

He nodded. "It's a shame, you going. Priesthood needs more down-to-earth people like yourself."

I laughed.

"I'm serious," he said. "People say that."

"No matter what else I'll be, I'll still be a priest. You know what they say: once a priest, always a priest."

"But you know what I mean. I'm not talking about . . . theoretical."

"You can think of me the same as now. I don't plan to change much."

He nodded.

"Just don't call me Father anymore."

"That'll be hard," he said. "I'm kind of old-fashioned that way." And he suddenly gathered both canes in his large left hand and extended his right for a farewell handshake. "Just in case I don't run into you again."

Impulsively, I stepped forward and put both arms around his sagging shoulders, and my head alongside his where he wouldn't see my eyes.

I remember standing like that for a long time, hanging on to his great weakened frame as he gently patted my back, the way you would a frightened child.

And I remember the people going about their weekend shopping and glancing uneasily at two grown men hugging in a parking lot. Wondering what might be going on.

{ ACKNOWLEDGMENTS }

I'm grateful to many friends and colleagues for feedback and advice as this story evolved. I owe special thanks to my agents, Don Sedgwick and Shaun Bradley, for sticking with the project for several years, and especially to Don, who read the manuscript and offered valuable criticism through many drafts. My wife, Carol Off, gave crucial encouragement and guidance throughout the process, and our friend Scott Sellers of Random House of Canada saw merit in the nearly final project when even I was dubious. My editor and publisher, Anne Collins, brought to the story the tender insights and editorial discipline it needed to transcend my many literary weaknesses.

A NOTE ABOUT THE TYPE

The Bishop's Man is set in Janson, a misnamed typeface designed in or about 1690 by Nicholas Kis, a Hungarian in Amsterdam. In 1919 the original matrices became the property of the Stempel Foundry in Frankfurt, Germany. Janson is an old-style book face of excellent clarity and sharpness, featuring concave and splayed serifs, and a marked contrast between thick and thin strokes.